# THE CURSED LAND

*The Last Battle of Moytura Book 2*

## MOLLY J STANTON

Molly J Stanton

# FREE BOOK

Before the Last Battle of Moytura, the boundary between the Fae and human world had closed. Discover how the Fae invasion of Portland began.

**A missing father. A mind-bending mist. An island where two worlds collide.**

Selina Leanabel survives by staying in the shadows, running a quiet apothecary far from the reach of the Fae. But when teen Charlotte Holloway arrives saying she can't go home...literally, with a story of a father lost behind a wall of unnatural fog, Selina's boundaries begin to crumble.

On Sauvie Island, the air is thick with a warding spell that breaks the mind and hungers for the soul. Entering the mist means risking the very stability Selina has fought so hard to reclaim.

**Click below and claim your copy.**

https://dl.bookfunnel.com/l4xleonwpi

You can also visit MollyJStanton.com/pages/badb.html to download your free book.

Shade and sweet water,
Molly

# CHAPTER 1

A root jabbing into her back roused Harper O'Neill from a deep slumber. Hazy bits and pieces of what had happened floated in her mind like papers scattered over water. Her captors must have glamoured her. She presumed she was on her way to Sauvie Island, but whether one day had passed or many, she couldn't be certain.

With wakefulness returned the hard reality that Nuada was dead. In just a few days, she'd grown attached to him. Although she never imagined her father would have taught her about magic and swords, Nuada had protected her and mentored her in much the same way she had always imagined her dad would have, if the Fae hadn't killed him. Now they'd murdered someone else she cared for.

Her breath caught in her throat. The village. Her mother. Her outburst of sorcery had led the Fae right to the doorstep of the Fir Bolg. Then she remembered her magical battle with Gwyn and the deal she'd struck. *Well, that explains the binds tying me to this tree.*

Why wasn't she already being paraded in front of Badb

Catha? If she couldn't break free, her life now was measured in hours, probably, and she had only herself to blame. At least she could take comfort that her deal with Gwyn gave her mother and the others a fighting chance to escape, though she still didn't trust him not to betray her.

Next item on the agenda was her own escape, then she had to find Emilio, Abraham, Alphine, and as many others as she could rescue. How she would do that, she had no clue. She was short on guides. Why wasn't the Phooka there? He'd know how to find Emilio, without Harper having to be presented to Badb Catha on a silver platter.

From out of nowhere, emotion threatened to overwhelm her. Chest burning and lips trembling, she kept her eyes closed. She could hear the Fae murmuring close by.

The tight cord binding her wrists around a tree behind her back had numbed her hands. She tried to shift her hip a little to the side to avoid the root, and the movement brought the burn of overexerted muscles.

"I know you're awake, girl," Gwyn's deep voice called.

Harper kept still and didn't grace the murderous scum with a reply. The crackle of a campfire popped and hissed next to where his voice came from. A rustle of activity told her he was standing and moving toward her. They'd failed to tie her neck to the tree. If he got close enough, she'd headbutt him just for the satisfaction.

"You should eat something. We have a long journey ahead."

His voice was right next to her ear. The smell of caramelized meat made her stomach growl. Still, she continued her game of possum. His demeanor suggested he wouldn't harm her right now, so she opted to tell this patricidal piece of crap to shove off.

Harper opened her eyes and sneered at the offering. She jerked her head behind her toward her immobilized hands. "Get bent. Humans eat with their hands, genius. Besides, the Phooka warned me about accepting Fae food."

She took a moment to scan her surroundings for an escape path and inhaled sharply at the landscape. The tree they tied her to lacked a single leaf. Even more bizarre, she had never seen bark like that, almost black and smooth. More like skin than bark. A thick mist clung to the earth and stretched all around her. She could barely see her legs. This was not anywhere near Mount Hood. She must be on Sauvie Island already.

In front of her, Gwyn balanced the wooden plate filled with food. She took a few moments to observe the man who had stolen so much from her. His mask was off, as was the breastplate he wore over his brown leather hunting garb. Harper's hazel eyes followed the scars peeking out along his neckline to the blue spiral tattoo beneath his eye. Those warm brown eyes were at odds with the rest of his face. When he spoke, a slight smile tugged at the corner of his mouth. The pig was enjoying himself.

"Then it is good that I am Tuatha, not Fae." He tore off a piece of the meat and held it close to Harper's mouth.

Harper jerked her head to the side and wrinkled her nose. "If you think I'll be eating out of your hand, you're dreaming, monster."

Gwyn dropped the food back on the plate and tilted his head. Harper expected anger from a guy who paraded around in a skull mask with fire for eyes, but he only seemed exasperated. He stood, held a hand out before him, and whispered words Harper couldn't understand. Her muscles suddenly felt like clay, and when she tried to move, she couldn't. That included her voice, so she could only shoot daggers at Gwyn with her eyes.

Gwyn ap Nudd walked behind the tree and untied her wrists. Harper's arms stayed in place when the rope fell. He walked back around and crouched in front of her, gently grasping first one arm, then the next, like she was a doll he could pose to his liking. He tied her wrists firmly in front of her, then used the rest of the rope to add to the bonds at her waist. When he finished, her movement returned.

"Shall we try again?" He sat before her cross-legged and placed a piece of meat in her hands.

Harper didn't want to give him the satisfaction, but once the food was in her hand, her stomach overruled her. She crammed the morsel in her mouth and chewed. It was gamy but well spiced. Her eyes widened as a terrible thought shoved its way forward.

"This better not be Fir Bolg," she said, her cheek bulging with half-chewed meat.

Gwyn dropped back and laughed. The head of every elf, kelpie, and sylph gathered around their own campfire turned his way. As quickly as it had come, his laughter ended, like it was foreign to him.

"No, Harper, it isn't Fir Bolg. I kept my word. Their home remains hidden." He placed another piece of food in Harper's now-greasy fingers.

"I'm sure Badb will just send a bigger force to murder the innocent next time."

"Even if I betrayed our bargain, by the time we could get back, they'd be gone. Safe and hidden in a new location." He paused and drew a spiral in the dirt with his finger. When he continued, his voice dropped to a whisper. "They and anyone with them will be safe."

Knowing brown eyes bored into her. Harper chewed slowly and paused after she swallowed.

He glanced over his shoulder to the campfire, then slid across to Harper without standing and pressed his face so close to her ear she could feel the brush of his soft beard against her neck. "Your mother remains safe," he whispered.

She wasn't sure she could believe him. The Phooka had told her the Fae played games. Gwyn may not be a Fae, but this had to be some kind of game. "And why does a murdering maniac care that my mother is safe?" She matched his volume and resisted the urge to headbutt him.

Gwyn drew away from her. His expression darkened and his voice took on a steel edge. "Do not presume to judge things you know nothing about, girl."

The cavalier way Gwyn disposed of the very thing Harper had most wanted in this world when he cut down her mentor set hatred simmering in her heart. He so easily rid himself of a father. She lurched forward against her bonds as though she could snap all that rope with the force of her rage. Oh, how she hoped her magic would surface, but it remained still.

"I know only demons and monsters murder their own fathers. He was just trying to protect me. He was a good man, like my father would have been. You murdered him too."

Gwyn's eyes flashed, but then his shoulders slumped and he looked at his feet. "Then your experience of my father differed greatly from my own."

"Just because daddy didn't give you the job you wanted doesn't grant you the right to cut him down and leave him in the woods like he was nothing." Hot tears rolled down Harper's face.

Gwyn kept his eyes focused on the earth in front of him. "Unlike you, I don't get to pick and choose what orders to complete."

"What does that mean?" Harper expected the fearsome leader of the Wild Hunt to be ruthless. Cold. Like he was when he killed Nuada. The man before her just looked trapped. Not that the revelation changed anything for her. Her eyes drifted to Nuada's sword—no, her sword now—propped up next to Gwyn's mask. If she could get to that weapon, she'd plunge it through Gwyn ap Nudd's heart. She'd avenge Nuada. He'd shown his weakness and with the coldest of hands, she planned to exploit it.

She scanned her surroundings again, expecting to see the tower Nuada had described looming nearby, but the only visible features were mist, dark trees, and the clouded half moon overhead. "Why bring me to the middle of nowhere? Shouldn't we be on Badb's doorstep by now?"

"I brought us to the ingress closest to the tower. At least it was when we left for the village." Gwyn inhaled and tilted his face to the sky. "The island grows, but not uniformly. Since the Wild Hunt left, it's had a massive growth spurt."

"So how far is it?"

"Hard to tell. Maybe hours. Perhaps days." Gwyn was already meandering over to the fire. He returned with more food and a drink that tasted sweet and melted away some of her aches and pains. "For what it's worth, Badb killed your father, not me."

"I know, but you broke my mother." Well, in part. Grief did a lot of the heavy lifting.

"I spared her."

He was behind her, so she couldn't see his face. Why was he telling her this? It had to be part of his game, but to what end? Why was he trying to ease her worry? Salving his own guilt? Demons didn't feel remorse, so that seemed doubtful.

Wordlessly, Gwyn bound her hands back behind the tree trunk and sauntered away to join his band of hunters. Several of them played music on fiddles and flutes they produced from somewhere. Gwyn sat behind them, absently running his hands through the fur of his Gabriel hounds, glancing over his shoulder at Harper periodically.

Hopelessness and guilt seeped back into Harper's thoughts and alternated with improbable escape plans that she immediately discounted once she realized she had no idea where she was. Anyway, the fog made navigation impossible. She let her head fall back to rest on the trunk of the strange tree. A more comfortable posture to contemplate how well and truly screwed she was.

Movement from the corner of her eye froze her breath. For just a second, she swore a pair of eyes blinked high in the branches.

Harper strained her ears, listening for any sound that would give away whatever predator was stalking her from above, but the music from the Wild Hunt made discerning any noises coming from the woods difficult.

Scrape. Scrape. Scrape. That sound was loud enough to hear over the fiddle music. Like claws on bark. And it was coming closer. Above her, a large branch shook as though something big had dropped onto it from above. It was all Harper could do to hold back a scream. And then a pair of incandescent yellow eyes opened ten feet above her. Only one creature she knew had eyes like that.

"Phooka?"

# CHAPTER 2

The Wild Hunt had been marching Harper through the gnarled forest blanketing the island for almost three days. Harper had visited Sauvie Island once before, as a child. On her previous trip, she rode on her father's shoulders and gobbled enough blueberries to sour her stomach. Quaint houses, farms, and lush green trees had covered the southern half of the island.

Any vestige of that bucolic charm was long gone. Now, trees twisted like coiling snakes and looped to stupefying heights. They creaked and groaned incessantly, like they whispered to each other. And every black trunk radiated malice. Branches scraped in the absence of wind and stretched down to snag her unbound hair. Deep in her bones, she knew they wished her out of the forest. Or dead.

The undergrowth was even less welcoming. Most of the woody plants had grown thorns. Not the tiny ones that dot rose stems, but two-inch spikes sturdy enough to pierce deep. The crisscross patchwork of red scratches along her legs was a constant reminder not to stray too close.

And what had happened to the residents? Harper's eyebrows

drew together. Probably the same thing that had happened to her family. Slain or enslaved. Badb Catha and her minions stole everything from Harper the night they slew Gerald O'Neill. And they just kept taking.

She glared at the back of Gwyn's head. Oh, how she wished her magical power was more like Superman's, because she'd cook his brains with her laser eyes.

He was a few steps ahead of her, brown leather boots making no sound against the carpet of pine needles and fallen leaves. Those broad shoulders always slumped slightly. Harper wondered if he had enough of a soul for the atrocities he committed daily to weigh on him, or maybe he simply had bad posture.

Only the blood-red ears of the ghostly white dogs were visible in the dense fog as they formed a broad circle around their master and slid noiselessly through the trees. Half of the elves and smaller Fae fanned out behind while the other half scouted ahead, leaving no opening for a mad dash to freedom. Every step drew her closer to Badb Catha.

At the thought of Badb, Harper's fists clenched and her mouth pulled into a snarl. The one good thing about Celtic Skeletor dragging her to this place was that it moved her closer to her goal. But she couldn't achieve it if Gwyn ap Nudd delivered her to his master, all tied up with a bow on top.

What she'd do alone against the waiting legion of monsters was a problem yet to be solved. For now, she focused on escape. Those glowing yellow eyes she glimpsed in the blackened tree a couple of nights ago looked like the Phooka's, but she'd started to doubt herself. Several days passed. No rescue attempt.

She wanted to believe it was him, but anything could be lurking in these woods. Her life to date had taught her never to hope. People said fear was the mind killer, and perhaps it was for most, but fear had pressed down on her for so long, it was just background noise.

Hopium was a dangerous drug, lulling you senseless with childish wish-fulfillment only to set you up for a bruising fall. It whispered of relief, promised you if you only lied to yourself everything would be all right, you could rest for a minute. Stop squirreling things away and making contingency plans for the thousand ways life could smile, hand you a crap sandwich, and go completely pear-shaped.

No. Best to get ahead of it, plan for the next catastrophe, steel yourself for oncoming chaos, and be ever vigilant. *Don't hope. Do.* Another of Abraham's mottos distilled to a three-word manifesto for her life.

Harper tilted her head down and strained her eyes to check the elves striding behind her. About fifteen feet back, they laughed and chattered, their red tunics flowing around their knees with every stride. No doubt their distance was an attempt to avoid the human stench they incessantly complained about.

She slipped her bound hands into the folds of the golden gown. Short fingers wormed around a bit of the gossamer fabric and yanked a strip free. Before sidling over to the undergrowth, she rolled her neck, feigning stiffness, and checked the faces of her captors. Just like all the other times, none of them had heard the delicate fabric rip or paid her any mind.

It took a dozen steps to inch over to the pathway's edge and release the strip onto a low branch. The Fae hadn't noticed the other strips, but each time, Harper's jaw clenched, bracing for discovery.

Not this time. The elves and their sylph companion strode past the shimmery yellow scrap, contentedly prattling about the 'old world.' She prayed the Phooka would notice the strips. If he really was on the island. But Plan B was a classic. Get to her sword. Then smash and dash.

Her bound hands stretched toward the Sword of Light buckled around Gwyn's waist. Memories of wielding the weapon quickened her pulse. That delicious surge of power. Hot and bright, it obliterated all fear, leaving only the exhilaration of their righteous battle. Together, she and the Cliamh Solais would prevail. Rescue Emilio and Abraham. Free the stolen.

If Badb Catha or Gwyn or the Sidhe stood in her way? Good. It was high time they paid for what they'd done. Together, Harper and the magical blade would slay them without a second thought and be free. That delicious notion brought a small laugh bubbling to the surface.

"Something amusing?" Gwyn halted, swiveling the antlered skull mask back over his shoulder.

"Just imagining hacking your head off with my sword." Harper's singsong voice matched the saccharine smile that didn't wrinkle the corners of her eyes.

"Charming, as always." Gwyn gave the rope a tug.

"Monster."

The eye sockets of the mask flamed. The leader of the Wild Hunt suddenly loomed over her, inches from her face, hand poised over his blade. Heat radiated from his body through the leather breastplate and long brown coat. Even though her knees had turned to water, Harper drew herself up to her full height and tilted her head up to stare right into the mask's fiery eye holes.

"Little girl, you know nothing." The Gabriel hounds closed their protective circle surrounding Gwyn, hackles up. The Wild Hunt coalesced behind them, grinning, teeth glinting in the fading light.

Harper clenched her fists, but not in anger. He stood taller, spoke harsher when he wore that hideous mask, but damned if she was going to let him see her fingers quivering. She forced another laugh. "Hit a nerve, Skeletor? Your murderous actions make you a monster. You sure dress—"

A ring of stones each the size of her head tore from the soil and blasted up into the sky. With a series of earsplitting cracks and thuds, they snapped branches as they fell back down and smashed deep into the hillside. Even the members of the Wild Hunt leapt back.

Gwyn's chest heaved, sending jets of flame from the mask's sockets lashing the tips of the stag's horns. "You. Know. Nothing." Each word scraped over his throat and was forced through gritted teeth.

Harper's legs tightened, eyes darting for an opening, while a single tear slid down her cheek. Damn. She wasn't very good at the whole 'show no weakness' thing. Jaw clenched against more tears, she shoved her emotions into the watery depths of her subconscious and hoped they'd drown there. Best not speak, because if she did, he'd hear the tremor in her voice.

Gwyn reached a gloved hand toward her cheek, snapped it back, and slumped like a deflating balloon. The fire winked out of the mask's eye sockets. For a moment he lingered, the empty holes of the mask trained on her, before he swiveled away, shoulders hunched.

He jerked the rope and resumed his trudge along the path, although much faster than before. Harper jogged to keep up, but she still managed to tear another strip from her dress and drape it over a leafless branch.

That tree root rose under her slipper. There hadn't been a single bump in the path before. She stumbled and thorns grabbed another hunk of the diaphanous golden gown, saving her the trouble of planting it.

Unaware, Gwyn slogged onward. The rope pulled taut and sent her sprawling, face first into dirt and pine needles.

Gwyn bounded back. Thick tanned fingers gripped her forearm, and he hauled her up. "Keep up. We have a lot more ground to cover before we camp."

"You try hiking in a ball gown." Harper clasped a handful of tulle. "Why don't you call that flying horse you had the night you abducted Emilio? Couldn't we fly to the tower instead of traipsing through this hellscape?"

"Don't be in a rush to arrive at your doom." Gwyn's voice was muffled by the mask. "Badb forbids flight above the trees to avoid prying eyes from above."

A quavering howl rose from behind them, prickling the hairs on the back of Harper's neck. Nothing she knew made a sound like that. Closer to a shriek than a howl, so not canine.

Gwyn paused, lifting his face into the air, almost like he sniffed out the creature. Another call. This time from the side and closer.

The Sidhe elves and sylphs crouched and traded hand signals before scattering into the woods, leaving only Gwyn and a few goblins and redcaps guarding Harper.

"Don't worry. You're safe." Gwyn positioned himself between Harper and the direction of the last unearthly call, his masked face scanning from side to side. "The Sidhe will take care of most of them. I'll slay any that get past my Wild Hunt." His rich voice softened.

Harper forced her features to a neutral expression. His reassurance unnerved her more than whatever stalked them. "What is it?"

"Banshee, maybe." Gwyn tilted his ear toward the direction the cry came from. "But banshee mean..."

"I remember that story. Someone's going to die."

Three wails rose in unison.

"They shouldn't be here. Move. Now. Toward the water."

"Why—"

Gwyn was already sprinting, pulling Harper stumbling behind. Rocks jabbed through the thin soles of footwear meant for dancing. The raw throb of blisters joined in to make every step agony. In the distance, the musical trickle of a stream grew closer. Within moments, they arrived at a small creek.

Gwyn didn't slow but dragged her staggering through the water. Once across, he stopped and shoved Harper behind him, sword drawn, coiled to strike. The other arm formed a barrier between his prisoner and their pursuers.

From the creek's far side, several piercing cries rose in unison. Close. Half occluded by mist, shadowy forms flicked back and forth parallel to the creek.

Harper didn't notice her ragged breathing until a thick hand landed on her shoulder.

"It's all right. They can't cross the water. You're safe."

Harper shrugged off his palm.

"My fucking hero." Harper's mouth hung half open. "What do you mean, I'm safe? I'm a prisoner. That's about as far from safe as you can get."

"There are much worse things than being my prisoner."

"Yeah. Like when you pass me over to your gothy boss lady and she kills me. I'll be super ultra safe then."

Harper closed her eyes for an instant and focused on the ring she wore, the one Lord Ezrynhivar had lent her to prove to his sister she was a friend. Previously, it had channeled her magic. Now, instead of blasting everything in a hundred-foot radius, she chose a target. She wanted so badly to summon that blue fire and direct it at Gwyn. But her power had a mind of its own. Nothing. Not a trickle.

Gwyn inhaled a deep breath and tilted his head back to the sky. His hands clenched and unclenched at his sides. After a moment, he unbuckled a horn from his side, drew it to his lips, and played a long call. From both ahead and behind, the Wild Hunt answered with horns of their own, high-toned and low.

"They won't find a way around the water for a day or more. Come. We need to find a place for the night."

He turned and stomped away from the stream, once more tugging Harper along in his wake. After a few steps, a warm, sticky sensation grew inside her shoe. A glance at her feet revealed blood squelching out the side of the slipper.

*That's great.* A perfect addition to the suckitude of her situation. Her foot throbbed with her pulse. Harper planted her heels and jerked the rope binding her hands with all her might. She regretted it instantly. The move brought stabbing pain to her wrists to equal the sharp ache in her feet.

Gwyn lurched to a halt just as Harper plopped onto a boulder and placed her ankle on her knee.

"Get up. We need to make camp by nightfall. We're likely safe, but I'd rather place some distance between us and the banshee." Two of the dogs snorted their agreement.

Harper slipped off her bloody shoe and tipped the red contents onto the earth. Gwyn pulled the mask off and dropped to a crouch beside her. His forehead creased at the blood soaking into the ground.

"I'm not taking another step. If you want to go any further, you get to carry me, *hero*."

"We're in the open here. You will move." His words were harsh, but his expression had softened and his voice was a ragged whisper.

Harper lifted her chin and met warm brown eyes. If they weren't attached to a murderer, those flecks of copper that glinted like metal would mesmerize. She wrinkled her lips to show her teeth. "Carry me or kill me. I'm done being dragged through the woods in formal wear."

Gwyn rose and scanned her like he was seeing her for the first time. Just then a trio of raven-haired elves leapt the stream while the handful of kelpies and redcaps with them sloshed through on foot. The lavender-skinned sylph with large, deep purple wings glided across toward where Harper and Gwyn sat. A network of black scars covered her forearms and shoulder, but her face was untouched. Her delicate features gave her a gentle look, but Harper knew she was anything but.

The winged Fae bowed. "My lord."

"Zalille."

"We forced those hideous, screeching monstrosities back, and there were succubi with them."

Gwyn scowled and pulled himself up to his feet, sweeping the mask into the crook of his arm. "Sluagh?"

A tall Sidhe warrior with his dark hair bound in a braid nodded. "The disgusting flock of avians my party found confirms it."

Zalille clapped a hand over her breastbone. "Human souls? Donn wouldn't dare bring them here. Badb wouldn't allow it."

The elf's fingers hovered near his blade as a trio of black birds launched themselves soundlessly from the uppermost branches of a dark tree. "Unless their sniveling leader plans to betray us."

"Wouldn't shock me. He used to be human." Zalille pulled her pale blue cloak tighter across her shoulders.

Gwyn's nose wrinkled over his scowl. "Doubtful. Without Badb's barrier capping the gateway, those souls would disappear through the portal and Donn would lose his power. That threat alone keeps him in check."

"They're up to something, I'm sure of it," Zalille said.

"Gildor, Zalille, you have served me well. We make camp here for the night. Double the watch, send every available Fae into the woods." He beckoned to the sylph. "I have a task for you, Zalille. Assemble a team of winged Fae and seek the Sluagh. I want to know what they're planning."

Zalille made a half-bow and fluttered out of the clearing. Only Gwyn and a handful of elves remained.

So the Sluagh and Wild Hunt weren't on the same side. Interesting. Harper bit the inside of her cheek and pondered.

# CHAPTER 3

Gwyn knelt on one knee in front of Harper and lifted the mask from his face with a tanned hand, placing it on a nearby stone. He lowered his gaze to her feet, furrowed his brow, and pursed his lips slightly when he scanned the scarlet-streaked footwear.

The Gabriel hounds rested on their haunches in a wide ring, their master at the center while the rest of the Wild Hunt secured the perimeter, far from sight.

Harper curved her spine over her tattered feet. Breathing in shallow pants, her breath tickled her bottom lip as she braced herself for Gwyn's inevitable anger.

His deep brown hair cascaded over his shoulder, and copper-flecked eyes drawn with concern studied her injuries. One hand rested on the earth, and the other inched tentatively forward until his fingertips hovered an inch from her feet.

With a sharp breath, Harper snapped them into the folds of the gown.

Gwyn clasped his arms across his chest. "I can heal them. Or would you rather sit in agony all night?"

She wasn't certain. Images of the leader of the Wild Hunt warred with each other. The familiar masked horror who slayed his own father rose in stark contrast to the kindness he volunteered and his softened features. It was baffling.

It must be some elaborate trick and she refused to play along, but god, her feet hurt. Allowing him to heal the wounds wouldn't change anything, but it would offer a potential benefit: speed. If there was a chance to escape, she'd need to be fast. She nodded and slid her legs back toward him.

His fingers dropped to her arches as gently as a leaf coming to rest on the earth. One side of his mouth flicked into a half smile for a fleeting instant, crinkling the blue spiral tattoo, as his eyes drifted closed, lips moving silently.

Gwyn's thick hands glowed with a soft yellow light, and a warm sensation flowed around her feet like swirling water. The edges of the tattered skin itched as they pulled together and sealed, leaving no trace of injury. Screaming nerves quieted within moments. He opened his eyes and dropped back to sit opposite her, cross-legged.

"Better?"

Harper scrunched her toes and let the bloody slipper drop next to the first. "Yes. Surprisingly comfortable. Thank—" Heat rose on her cheeks. Gratitude toward an accessory to her father's murder was an emotion so alien it left her reeling.

Gwyn smiled. "Good."

Harper detected no deception in his gentle smile, which only raised her defenses higher. "Why good? Would my injuries slow my march to slaughter?"

He regarded Harper with bewilderment. "Because you were in pain," he said, like she was the one who made no sense.

Harper let out a long breath while she searched for something to say, her mouth opening and closing as she stared at him.

Gwyn inhaled and tilted his head toward the sky. "We never finished our earlier conversation. If it matters, I don't know what Badb will do with you. Before—"

"Oh please. Yes, you do. I'm as good as dead. You're killing me as surely as if you ran me through with a sword yourself." Harper kept her voice soft, despite the jab of anger needling her heart.

Gwyn clenched his jaw and turned aside, shoulders rising. "We didn't know you carried the heritage of Eriu or the power of her sister Macha within you. You're one of us. That has to change things. She has to see." His voice was strained.

"How can you be thousands of years old and still be that naïve?" Gwyn bristled at Harper's mirthless laugh. "Even if I am distantly part Tuatha, I'm human. Badb is a genocidal maniac bent on wiping people out. If you bring me to her, you *are* killing me. You don't get a pass merely because it isn't your hand that takes my life."

He dropped his head into his palms and clutched handfuls of his hair. With a cry, he lurched to his feet and paced.

"When Macha gifted you the last of her magic, it left the gateway between worlds incomplete. Now it operates at a substantial cost. You can assist us and make it permanent, save our people. You can't know the suffering they endure through no fault of their own." He leaned toward her, every word punctuated by tapping fingers in his palm.

"Dream on, Skeletor. I'll die before I help her."

"My father saw something in you. I'm having a difficult time seeing what that is. Maybe Badb is right. All humans are blind to any suffering not their own." Gwyn wheeled around and threw his arms wide. "Fine. If you only care about humanity, you could aid them too. Those crow-like Sluagh are human souls, held prisoner by the real monster. Souls are supposed to travel from earth, across the Underworld, to the Undying Lands where they're reborn in a manner of speaking. They're trapped here now. Unable to rest. Unable to bestow the gifts of their life's experience on the next generation. All because your people fouled the world so horribly, the Veil between the Green World and the Underworld closed. Join us, and by keeping the portal open, end their misery and destroy their master, Donn. If you refuse to recognize our suffering, at least see theirs."

Harper realized why the Sidhe hated the Sluagh. Most of them were human once, and Badb Catha loathed anything human even though she depended on their dead to exterminate the rest of humanity. If trapped souls strayed too close to that gateway, they'd slip through and half her army disappeared. That was why she disallowed them on the island. Part loathing, part power. A chill brought gooseflesh to Harper's skin, and she grimaced at her captor.

"Badb Catha will never allow them through the portal. She'd lose half her army. Don't fool yourself; you're still marching me to my death."

His features softened for just a second, a feeling playing across his face that Harper couldn't identify. Regret? Exhaustion? As quickly as it had come, it faded, replaced by his studied indifference. "I will do what I must. And until then, I'll see that you arrive unharmed as is my duty because of the vow I made to you."

"Whatever." Harper held out her wrists to him, risking a glance up into the tree where no amber-eyed crow perched.

"I don't expect you to understand."

"Because I'm human?"

"Because you are ignorant, rash, and impulsive."

"That's the nicest thing a patricidal douchebag has ever said to me."

He cocked his head. "Douche. Bag?"

Harper laughed. The idea of trying to explain to an ancient demigod what a douchebag was only made her laugh harder. Between chortles, she fussed with the tattered hem of her golden dress and said, "Trust me, it's bad. Real bad."

Gwyn growled and swept his mask from its resting place. In one movement, he dropped it over his face and his fist flew. The impact of his hand against the tree sent shock waves down the trunk that Harper felt ricochet up her spine. Reflex made her wince, and she clamped her jaw shut to stifle a yelp. Now he towered over her, the eye sockets of the grisly mask flaming. She'd pissed him off. Good.

He hissed through gritted teeth. "Can you not see the scars my people bear? That's what humanity did to us. Vengeance is justified. And don't tell me you mewling animals wouldn't do the same in our position."

Gwyn spoke some truth. If the environmental havoc wreaked by humans trapped her in a nightmare land, she'd fight to the death to change it. She craned her neck up at Gwyn. "But the answer isn't the slaughter of an entire race. No matter which side does the slaughtering."

"No? Are we supposed to ask nicely for you to lift the boot off our necks?"

He had a point.

Gwyn spun on his heel and paused. "I suppose it's not entirely your fault you're a failed species. Most of the Tuatha abandoned you so they could wallow in peace in the Undying Lands. Even forsaking those of us who remained in the Green World." He drew himself upright and strode to meet a Sidhe woman who emerged carrying a stack of clothes. Her mane hung in loose curls, artfully arranged to hide the black leathery flesh on her left cheek, but it peeked out anyway, marring her beauty. A flick of his masked head sent a male elf—Gildor, Gwyn had called him—moving to guard

Harper. The elf wore his gleaming hair long, the sides bound at the back to keep it out of his face. Harper guessed he bore the same dark scars, but none showed on his angular face.

Harper watched Gwyn from the corner of her eye while Gildor gripped her leash and fixed her with those glittering black eyes. He didn't even try to mask his distaste; rather he scanned her up and down and wrinkled his nose like she was a pile of refuse he was forced to smell.

Gwyn lifted his fingers to his mouth and whistled, summoning his Gabriel hounds. "This is Lobelia. She will help you change into more appropriate clothing." He nodded to Gildor. "You are in charge while I'm away."

Gildor arched his eyebrows. "Away, master?"

Gwyn nodded. "Banshee and incubi mean the Sluagh are on the island."

Lobelia's nostrils flared. "They may merely be rogues."

"Perhaps. I intend to discover if my ancient nemesis brought his Sluagh here and what he schemes."

Gildor passed the rope to Lobelia. The woman coiled it up and yanked, propelling Harper vertical.

"Follow me, human."

"Got no choice, elf."

Lobelia dragged Harper into a dense copse of pine trees, green and with the fresh scent of fir. She laid the pile of elven clothes on a broad grey stone. Harper lifted her bound hands to eye level.

"How am I going to change with my hands like this?"

The elven woman rolled her eyes, stepped behind Harper, gripped the top of the dress, and tore. In seconds, Harper wore nothing but her undergarments. The chill air raised goosebumps on her flesh.

"Sit." Lobelia slipped skintight black pants, like the ones the elves wore, on to Harper's legs. Though thin, they were quite warm. "Put these on." Lobelia thrust a pair of tall, dark grey boots

at Harper. While she dutifully pulled them on, the elf tied her
waist to a tree and unbound her hands so she could slip on a red,
midthigh tunic.

"Do I get the shiny armor too?" Harper asked dryly.

"If it were up to me you'd march through these woods naked."

Lobelia looped a hunk of rope around Harper's wrists before
loosening the knot that held her tight to the tree and binding her
arms tight to her sides. As the elf stood, two of her companions
strode into the clearing, Gildor and another woman with a
shoulder-length bob, both wearing malicious smiles and narrowed
eyes.

"A shame to waste such fine clothes. We'll have to burn those
once Badb slaughters the animal." The male elf wandered a wide
path to avoid proximity to Harper.

"Our *master* demanded we make it more comfortable. If you
ask me, making it march all the way to the tower with bleeding feet
is fitting punishment for defying us." Lobelia squatted beside her
pack and plunged her ivory hand deep inside before slipping
something she withdrew from its depths into her pocket.

The other woman moved behind the tree, emerging on the
opposite side. Harper followed her progress with narrowed eyes.
She'd spent enough time in a bully-infested schoolyard to know
when the sharks were circling. Whatever they planned would be
humiliating at best. The dark-eyed elf drew her boot back and
slammed it into Harper's ribcage. Hard.

Harper yelped and bared her teeth. Beads of sweat broke out
on her lip.

"Shiora! What are you doing? If Gwyn—"

"Keep your voice down, Gildor. He'll be gone for a couple of
hours and the others are still out, casting wards on the perimeter.
He'll never know unless you keep making all that noise." Shiora
stared down at Harper and ran her tongue along her gleaming
teeth.

Fresh bruises flowered on Harper's shoulders and back. The blows that the trio of elves rained down on her strategically were hidden well beneath her clothing, concealed from their master.

A roundhouse kick from Lobelia sent Harper flopping onto her side where she remained. Not that she had much choice. Her head swam and stars burst inside her eyelids.

# CHAPTER 4

Worries about Harper launched Eileen to her feet, pacing in the cabin. The last time she'd seen her daughter was when she'd fled the council meeting, her hand blazing with blue electricity. The Fir Bolg who'd observed the showdown with the Wild Hunt had described the bright white surge in her magic, and the deal she'd struck to go willingly with Gwyn to save them all.

The malignancy spreading on Sauvie Island wouldn't likely leave Harper alive for long, so that first day Eileen had tried to go find Harper herself. Serotina and Aeld stopped her. She'd be powerless against the Fae on that island. Both of them reminded her of Harper's strength and importance, urging her to wait for Serotina's emissary before acting.

A sonorous, rumbling song swelled, reminiscent of the chanting of monks but deeper and with less structure. Eileen forced herself to slow and listen.

Voices fell away and others rose in a gentle storm of a cappella music devoid of words. Despite the improvised nature of the Fir Bolg song, patterns formed. New each day. A reflection of the ever-shifting natural beauty of the Green World. Eileen hummed along in her much higher voice. In the fallout from the attack just a few days ago, this simple daily ritual of peace grounded them and kindled hope.

Even though the battle had raged just outside, the Fae failed to breach the magically cloaked village, thanks to Harper's growing power. Despite that, Chieftain Aeld insisted that remaining there was too risky. And so the entire community, along with their Fae guests, packed a few cherished possessions and fled for a secondary cluster of tree homes built as a refuge against the steady march of human encroachment.

In the sanctuary, they mourned the disappearance of young Paegrinn in a beautiful ceremony involving the entire village burying their hands in the earth and conversing with the mycelium. Wispy bioluminescent threads crawled from the soil, spiraling around the limbs of the Fir Bolg. For hours they remained, singing the threads to the surface, speaking silently to the world through the network. But the mycelium had no awareness of Paegrinn or Harper.

At one time, before industrial damage, the fungal network extended unbroken throughout the entire continent, like the nervous system of the earth. Today the net was still vast but existed as islands because of dead patches caused by modern agriculture, pollution, and other human damage. Her daughter may simply be unreachable by the fragmented fungal network. Eileen willed herself to believe that as she rubbed the flats of her palms on her thighs, uttered a weak groan, and leapt up.

Eileen's thigh caught on the rustic nightstand with a thud that sent pencils and paper clattering to the floor. Like everything in this new place, Eileen's cabin was more cramped, less cozy. She gripped the last handmade charcoal pencil and restacked the paper, placing the handful of pencils back on top.

Her room might lack electricity or much temperature control, yet she preferred it to the home she and Harper had shared in

Gresham. Too many painful memories there. Life with the Fir Bolg represented a true new beginning for Eileen, and the best way for her to help her daughter. She just needed to convince more Fae or Fir Bolg to accompany her to Sauvie Island and find Harper. Somehow. The plan got sketchy after that.

She plopped onto the edge of a bench that stretched halfway around the circular hut and cradled her head. The terror that her child was already dead blared like a klaxon during every waking hour.

*No. She's capable. The Phooka and probably Paegrinn are out there now. They'll find her.*

The garrulous murmur of passing voices refocused her on their task, and she searched her messy room for her bag. The urgent work of establishing the new village distracted her from constant rumination about Harper.

Eileen buckled the blue nylon holster round her waist and thigh and checked the snubby shotgun was secure inside. Then she slipped the small harvesting knife Glani gifted her into the satchel that dangled above the weapon.

The little bag was a gift from one of the youth, Holl. He'd made it for her himself. Soft tan fabric identical to the bags every Fir Bolg wore, but sized for a human. The embroidery on her primitive-looking satchel was unintentionally hilarious. The words 'Keep calm, and sparkle on' scrolled over the flap, hand-stitched in very plain brown letters, right above the antler buttons.

Holl had decided the tacky shirt Eileen was wearing when Nuada and Harper first brought her to the Fir Bolg was beyond repair, but he figured if someone had elaborately embroidered the phrase across the garment, it must have been very important. He'd also removed a handful of the sequins from the shirt and stitched them into the spiral patterns curving around the letters. The notion he believed the cheesy phrase held a deep meaning made Eileen chuckle despite her anxieties.

The dull thud of hooves on wooden planks broke her from her packing. Eileen adjusted the satchel around her shoulder, emerged from her hut, and waved a greeting to her foraging partner for the day.

"I remain utterly offended that these hairy louts insist on sending me. *Me.* The King of the Dusk Court, searching for food. They're the ones whose culture never progressed past the hunter-gatherer phase. Let them go digging for tubers. I have an empire to run." Lord Ezrynhivar lounged in the doorway, one hip against the edge and an arm draped high over his sweeping horns. Despite the task at hand, he still insisted on dressing like he planned to hold court. His long dark hair hung loose to his chest, cascading over a shining shirt in the deepest blue that contrasted with the pale grey skin beneath. Jet black hooves peeked out from drapes of green and black fabric wrapped around his waist.

"Aeld made it clear. You are free to go, but if you stay you work."

His red eyes sparkled. "I didn't think he meant *me.* That's why I have servants."

"You do know we're not attending a debutante ball, right? Digging tubers and hunting for mushrooms calls for more casual attire."

"This *is* my casual attire."

Eileen swept a hand over her Fir Bolg clothes. Long brown tunic and tan pants to match the satchel. "Just ask. I'm sure they can make you something more suitable."

Ezrynhivar rolled his eyes and stuck out his tongue. "I have a certain image to maintain."

"Why are you still here, anyway? The council is over." Eileen smoothed her bleach-blonde hair into a low ponytail and strode along the high boardwalk toward the twisting stairs that would deposit them beyond the safety of the invisibility spell. She soaked in the towering pine trees and the network of homes nestled in the branches.

"Simple. Serotina remains."

"And?"

"And the attack by the Wild Hunt lent some credence to what Nuada said. And I don't trust her."

Eileen shrugged. "I'm sure she feels the same about you."

"And here we are, both unwilling to give the other the slightest advantage by our absence from the center of events. Both of us sending spies to the island to gain the upper hand."

"Have your spies learned anything about Harper?" She'd made it exactly five minutes without dwelling on her daughter.

"Nothing new. I'll bet—"

"Yeah, they won't kill her immediately. Too valuable. So everyone says, but what makes you so sure?" Eileen pined for reassurance the way she'd yearned for the bottle. Like alcohol, the relief wouldn't last and in moments she'd need it again.

"Her blood. I think Badb Catha might require it more than we know."

The dark Fae's words failed to deliver the shot of comfort Eileen needed, so she turned to her second refuge: making half-baked plans. She'd racked her brain for a way to convince someone here to search for her daughter. Because she remembered the ache of losing a loved one, she refrained from using Paegrinn's disappearance to manipulate Aeld, but she was running out of time. She planned to get Glani on board first. The healer seemed to have Aeld's ear more than anyone. Hopefully, Paegrinn's plight would urge them to at least send out a rescue party.

"After you." Ezrynhivar stretched out a hoof and dipped a low bow to the spiraling stairs coiled around a sturdy fir tree. The murmuring voices below suggested they were the last to arrive. Eileen crept down each step. Their swaying and creaking quickened her pulse.

With a hop, her feet hit the ground, and she joined the party. Above, Ezrynhivar leapt over the side of the walkway. With a *foomph*, leathery black wings unfurled and he glided gracefully down to alight in the midst of the group.

Four Fir Bolg warriors and Serotina's white satyr servant smiled and welcomed their new recruits. The cloven-hooved Fae paced in circles, wringing his hands, all the while glancing up at the safety of the arboreal village.

"Latreus, it'll be okay. We'll be back before you know it." Eileen crouched in front of the little Fae. His golden eyes met hers and he forced a smile.

"You are kind, Eileen."

"Can we just shoot the goat for food?" Ezrynhivar narrowed his eyes at his rival's footman and pointed to the longbows two of their Fir Bolg companions carried.

Latreus scampered past Eileen and stooped, shaking, behind a well-muscled Fir Bolg. The broad-chested man scowled at the Dusk King. "We don't slaughter other beings for sustenance."

"Ez, don't be a douche." Eileen rested her hand on the satyr's shoulder.

Without a word, the leader of their foraging team loped off down the slope to the west and the group followed. Fengre stood almost as tall as her male counterparts and carried her thick spear as added protection. Grey strands streaked the pile of hair she wore bound into a tight bun atop her head. Pictures of various Fir Blog weapons adorned her satchel. Eileen guessed her role in village life was akin to security.

Their hosts kept a steady pace, though much slower than their long limbs were capable of because of the mixed composition of the foraging party. Though Glani and Paegrinn had healed the damage caused by years of deep alcoholism, Eileen wasn't in peak cardiovascular health and her breathing came fast and ragged.

Lungs burning and a sharp stabbing pain in her waist, she soon willed every stride.

Latreus scuttled along between Fengre and the biggest warrior he could find, occasionally casting furtive glances over his shoulder at Ezrynhivar. The King of the Dust Court glided at the rear, effortlessly banking around tall trees and swooping over dense undergrowth, his customary bored expression on his face.

Fengre called a halt in a verdant patch of meadow between rolling hills. Though they'd only jogged twenty minutes, Eileen's body thought she'd sprinted a mile. She dropped her head between her knees to relieve the stitch jabbing at her side.

"There should be plenty of wapato down there." Fengre pointed to a wide stream meandering below them. "Those plants with the big arrow-shape leaves. Pull them up and collect the tubers. When your packs are full, empty them into this one." She placed a pair of thick sacks that could hold several small children in the clearing. Then she showed them samples of edible mushrooms and leafy plants to seek.

"Fan out but maintain visual contact with at least two others at all times. And keep a lookout for black birds or enemy Fae. You see one, or anything out of place, shout." Fengre gestured toward the stream. "The faster we're done, the sooner we're back at the village."

"I trust myself more with the wapato than mushrooms. I'll harvest those," Eileen said.

Fengre nodded, and the group spread out along the forest floor.

Eileen enjoyed the work. The plants lifted from the ground easily, with a rich, earthy scent. She had just begun her second trip to the big bags when a guttural squawk turned her blood to ice. *They can't have found us yet. It's not possible. It has to be just a crow.*

Eileen spun around, scanning for the black avian forms of the

Sluagh. A deep scream arose to her left, inside the ring of underbrush. One of the Fir Bolg.

They'd been discovered.

Adrenaline dulled the stitch in her side and spurred her instinctual dash for cover. A cry burst from her lips when she smacked into Ezrynhivar.

Below them, a pair of Sluagh had dropped from the sky and spasmed into skeletal shapes with skin braced against bone and milky, unfocused eyes staring at their prey.

They'd caught the villagers off guard, and gaunt hands already grasped a Fir Bolg. They were seconds from draining the life from the Sasquatch while he swayed, a dreamy expression on his broad features. *The Sluagh feast on souls, lives lived with depth, the longer and deeper the life, the sweeter the meal.* Nuada's words played unbidden in Eileen's mind. Wise and ancient, a Fir Bolg would be an irresistible feast for the Sluagh.

"No!" Eileen screamed, raced down the hill to help the trapped Fir Bolg, and slammed to a standstill. A pale hand gripped her shoulder like a vise and shoved her back down behind some undergrowth. "Let me go," she hissed. "We have to save him."

"Too late for him. Let's not meet the same fate. Unusual for them to attack the living. Strictly forbidden." Ez pulled her around, narrowly avoiding three more reptilian birds. They shuddered and snapped as tiny bird bones elongated into human shapes. Tattered wing membranes poured over their backs. They advanced on the satyr and the remaining Fir Bolg, who dropped into defensive stances to fight for their lives.

"We can't leave them."

"We're going to draw them off." Ezrynhivar pointed to the right where more Sluagh joined, who looked a lot like Ez.

"What? How—"

"Because you're going to make them really, really angry." The Fae King flicked his head to her hip. "Use your shotgun."

Eileen's quaking hands fumbled over the strap that secured the weapon in the holster. It slid from the nylon, 20-gauge shells already nestled in the barrel. The iron felt reassuring in her grip. Ezrynhivar squinted at it like it would bite and edged away.

The gun had no shoulder stock; instead it sported a pistol-type grip. Eileen did exactly what the guy who sold it to her warned her not to. She lined the weapon up at head level to sight down the barrel at the incubi. The adrenaline gave her tunnel vision as she clicked off the safety and braced her core for the recoil.

"Aim at the ones who look like me."

She pushed out with her left hand, cradling the underside of the barrel while she pulled back on the grip and squeezed the trigger.

# CHAPTER 5

The little shotgun cracked, the recoil slamming into Eileen, but her preparation kept her shot accurate enough and one incubus dropped, writhing on the ground, his shrieking so loud Eileen winced. Within seconds, he fell still. His friends crouched, raised their horned heads, and screamed at her. It worked. All the Sluagh focused their rage on her. The remaining Fir Bolg scattered for the underbrush.

"I hit him in the leg. He... He can't be *dead*." Eileen shook her head. "I aimed low to not—"

"Iron. Run." Ezrynhivar shoved her forward, and she ran.

The king's hooves kicked up clods of dirt as they hammered the ground. Eileen struggled to keep up, but flapping wings and heavy footfalls approaching urged her onward. Every stride left her farther behind Ez. He risked a glance over his shoulder and knitted his thin brows.

"Holster the shotgun," he said.

"What?"

"Just do it. Now."

Eileen obeyed as Ezrynhivar halted and threw his long arms

around her waist. Her face pressed against his silky hair. The scent of exotic spices filled her senses. The Fae took two more running steps and launched himself upward. Eileen tightened her grip around the Dusk King's neck.

A single low chuckle rumbled in his chest, then the anxiety knotting her muscles melted and warmth radiated through her core.

"Did you just glamour me?"

"A little. Can't have you falling apart and getting us killed."

Eileen wasn't sure how she felt about that, but it hardly mattered. The remaining four incubi took flight, red eyes boring into her.

"You can outrun them carrying me?"

"No, but if we reach the chasm ahead, we can make a kill box."

Eileen twisted her head back. Looming pine trees thickened. The incubi, and Ez, would be forced to land, but the smaller Sluagh could glide between the branches with relative ease. Then a ravine filled the horizon, a deep rocky crease cut into the mountain. Eileen thought she knew what he was planning, but it all depended on timing.

Ezrynhivar grunted when his leathery wing slapped on a tree trunk and they ricocheted into a sapling. Wispy limbs whipped Eileen's arms, leaving stinging lines on her back. Their pursuers experienced similar challenges and soared higher. As soon as they were out of sight, Ez banked and glided along the edge of the ravine.

She had little time to plan before they landed at the rim. Craggy stones jutted below in the deep shade. She relaxed her grip on her flying partner, but he didn't release her.

"Not yet, you'll need cover," he whispered into her ear, red eyes surveying the highest crest on the trench's lip.

"But I—"

His wings flared and swept two full strokes perpendicular to the ground, bounding closer to the brush. He deposited her under a thick patch of scrub. "I require some of your hair."

"What?"

"No time." He wound his fingers through a platinum lock and pulled.

"Ouch!" She slapped him away.

"We get one chance at this, so I sincerely hope your first shot wasn't a fluke. When I shout, you fire." He offered her a lopsided grin that looked more like a grimace. "And do try not to shoot me."

"No promises."

Ezrynhivar's eyes widened.

"Kidding. What are you going to do?"

He pointed at the sky. "First kill the little ones. Then become the bait for your trap."

"Great. Leave the puny human to take out the hulking dark Fae."

Ezrynhivar jabbed his chin at the Mossberg in Eileen's hands. "That makes you the most dangerous thing in these woods this afternoon, so you get the hard job."

"I lived at the firing range for years after Fae murdered my husband. I can hit them." Her mind flashed back to the twisted mask of agony the first incubus wore, and her eyes welled. She had to take additional lives if they were to escape and safeguard the Fir Bolg. She gritted her teeth. Feelings could be dealt with later.

Ezrynhivar scanned the network of branches before launching himself at the shadowy bird shapes above. Eileen lost sight of him, but the terrified screeches of avian Sluagh betrayed his position. She popped another shell into the gun and waited.

The Dusk King reappeared, diving to the bottom of the ravine. Wings folded against his back, he tilted his chin at Eileen and nodded. His lips shaped unheard words and he shrank, hair lightening to blonde, clothes morphing to match her light brown outfit. An identical copy of Eileen sprawled over a flat stone, gripping her ankle.

It was more than a little disconcerting to behold a perfect replica of herself, but the wait was short. Four huge shadows flickered across the gap in the canopy above the ravine, banked, and plummeted straight for Ezrynhivar. Eileen inhaled a long breath, lifted the shotgun, and braced her back against a tree trunk.

They landed right next to her Fae companion. The spell that had turned him into a middle-aged human woman evaporated to the shocked expressions of the surrounding incubi.

"Now!" Ez bellowed and hurled himself toward the clouds.

Eileen aimed the gun at the incubus farthest from the king and squeezed the trigger. Ezrynhivar streaked into the sky just as her primary target and another Fae collapsed and writhed before falling still. The other two dashed up the ravine.

Teeth gnashed. Claws flexed. And fiery eyes shot daggers at her. The barrel slipped beneath sweaty palms and quaking fingers. Ez's glamour sedative vanished under the urge to flee. The firing range had never prepared her for this.

"We're going to make this slow, human," one incubus called.

The other laughed. "You'll pray for death before we finish you."

Eileen answered in steel. The shot echoed off the stone walls of the ravine. The closest Sluagh tumbled to the bottom, wailing all the way down. She'd missed the last one because the small shotgun traded accuracy for portability.

With a bellow, the last incubus unfurled massive wings and swept high, wingspan blocking out the late afternoon light. No time to reload. Eileen scrambled forward in a stooped dash, but he was already on top of her.

Long claws shredded her shoulder, and a gush of hot blood coursed down her back. She screamed and spun around, eyes riveted on the twisted face of her attacker. The incubus hovered, teeth bared for the kill. Eileen froze. A high-pitched ringing in her ears blocked all other sound.

She really wanted to see her daughter one last time before she died. A desperate autopilot kicked in and Eileen flicked her hand so the barrel of the gun pressed against the bare skin of the Fae's arm.

His flesh sizzled. The incubus bellowed and reared back, but even injured he was faster than she was. His clawed fist walloped her jaw and the world flickered dark. Eileen floundered and nearly lost her grip on the weapon.

The incubus coiled for another blow. She grasped the gun with both hands and shielded her face with it. The Fae's forearm met it with the hiss of burning skin and he wailed.

The injuries slowed him; she seized the advantage and slammed the grip of the firearm under the creature's chin. Crack. She winced. The Fae tumbled back and caught her shirt with clawed fingers. Eileen fell forward with him and shoved the muzzle against his cheek over and over.

Weakened and gasping for breath, the incubus held up a shaking arm, the fury in his eyes replaced by terror. Tendrils of effervescent magic caressed her body. Suddenly, the incapacitated Fae radiated beauty. The sensation evaporated as fast as it formed. The cool steel barrel of her gun shattered glamour like the grip shattered Fae jawbone. Otherwise, she'd be swooning over the monster while he slew her.

She growled. "You tried to glamour me?"

"Please," he muttered in a low voice.

Eileen hesitated. The shotgun dipped. He lay injured, maybe dying from iron exposure. Was she really so cruel to kill him when she'd won? But if she allowed him to escape, he'd betray the Fir Bolg to Badb.

Her hesitation cost her. The incubus lunged at her, knocking the gun from her hand. But he was still weak, and Eileen recovered more quickly. Scrabbling on her hands and knees to the fallen weapon, she swung the barrel up at the attacking Fae.

"Have it your way." She shoved the gun against his cheek, hard, holding it there while he gagged and thrashed. "I'm sorry," she whispered as he stilled. He sprawled on his back, scarlet eyes staring at the sky, matching red rivulets of blood trickling from the side of his raven-haired head.

Chest heaving, Eileen staggered back several steps. She'd only seen one dead person before. Her husband. The Fae lay crumpled, just like her husband had lain in their living room. Gerald's face projected itself onto the sculpted features of the incubus, and all her walled-up emotions broke free.

*Killer. You're a killer now. You're as bad as Badb Catha.* But the vacant eyes, burned flesh, and misshapen jaw of the Fae marked her as no mere killer. She'd brutalized the man. What would Harper think? Would the Fir Bolg want her back in the village?

A strangled cry bubbled up from the bottom of her lungs. She staggered back, wide green eyes riveted on her handiwork. Her foot caught a branch and she tumbled. Flailing legs propelled her backward, behind a scrubby bush.

When she could no longer see the Fae's body, she rolled to her side, clasped her knees to her chest, and bit back screams so forcefully her tongue bled. She stifled her revulsion, not because she worried more Sluagh would find her, but because if they did, she'd kill them too if it meant keeping Harper and her Fir Bolg family safe.

She whimpered and clutched her own head. *It had to count for something. I had no choice. Keeping the village safe helps Harper. It had to help. It had to. Murderer. Killer.*

The rustle of wings overhead froze her breath. *How many Sluagh attacked us? Did I miss one?* Her fingers coiled around the shotgun, but she didn't move. She hadn't reloaded. Branches snagged her hair when she pushed herself deeper into the undergrowth, firearm clutched before her. She waited, wide eyed, as the steady thud of hooves drew closer.

"Eileen?"

"Ez." Relief collapsed her spine.

"You get in a fistfight?" he asked, eyeing her blood-clumped hair.

Tears welled up and spilled down her cheeks. Impulsively, she raced to the Dusk King, threw her arms around him, and wept.

"Saw your handiwork. Brutal and impressive." Ezrynhivar maneuvered her to arm's length.

The Fae looked fascinated. He shouldn't be. Eileen's stomach flip-flopped again, her throat tightened, and hitching sobs drove a torrent of tears. "I killed them al—" The words choked, ending in a silent sob.

"That was the idea."

"I- I'm not a killer."

"The pile of bodies would seem to disagree."

Blood-streaked hands flew up over her face, and she pivoted away from him. Gulping deep breaths, she attempted to quiet the emotional storm. Heavy footfalls arced in a circle and Ezrynhivar drew up in front of her again. A pale-clawed hand, surprisingly gentle, tilted her chin to his.

"Stop this right now, Eileen O'Neill. You are not this weak."

"Wha—"

"Gun or no gun, the number of mewling humans who could take out five of my kind in a fight is vanishingly small. Tears are beneath you. You did what you had to do. Those incubi would have led the Sluagh to the Fir Bolg and drained us all without a second thought. So you tell me, what other choice did you have?" He punctuated his last sentence with a clenched fist.

"But I'm not a killer."

"Yes, you are. And that is a splendid thing, for you are also a savior today."

"You have an awful way of comforting people."

"I'm not comforting you. I'm making you see reason. If you plan on being any part of helping Harper, the handful you just killed is merely the first. You'd better become accustomed to doing what's necessary, or go back home and do whatever it is the gutless human masses do." He shifted her cheek to the side to get a closer look at her head wound. "The bleeding has stopped. Any dizziness? Can you walk?"

Eileen nodded. "The village is that way, right?"

Ezrynhivar flicked his eyes to the treetops and his expression became studied and impassive. "Yes, but we can't go back there yet. The avian Sluagh may all be dead, but we can't be sure. We should walk awhile. Away from the village." He paused and tilted his head as though searching for the right words. "Make sure none of them are following us."

Her leaden legs made the prospect of shambling through the forest demoralizing. They meandered along deer paths. The king seemed mindful of her state and kept a slow pace while he scanned their surroundings.

"Is it unusual for an incubus to live outside of the Sluagh hive?" She hadn't intended to speak her thought.

Ez's face pinched. "I'd hardly even call the shallow husks you dispatched incubi."

"Do you all, um..." Eileen kicked a pinecone into the brush. "Are all incubi soul-eaters?"

"Thinking of shooting me, Eileen?"

"I'm just trying to figure out who my enemies are." And salve her conscience.

Ez inhaled and his posture relaxed. "It's true we drink of the souls of people."

Eileen recoiled.

The Dusk King halted, clasping her shoulder. "It's not what you think, but it is complicated." He paused and his face glowed.

"We feast on passion. The heat of sexual energy." Ez twined his fingers through Eileen's hair. She drew away and he smiled. "It's true that in the heat of passion, some of us go too far and can kill our partners, but even in the Unseelie Court, most do not anymore."

"Most?"

"Judgy. Your kind have more than their share of serial killers, and do not your business leaders extract all they can from everyone?"

He had a point. "Then why did the incubi join the Sluagh?"

"The same reason your own society's evil do what they do. Power. A great evil leads the Sluagh. Donn. He was human long ago and was charged with safeguarding the human dead when the Fae and Tuatha moved to the Underworld. And like nearly all of your race, he succumbed to the lure of power."

Eileen harrumphed. "Not every human is a power-hungry zealot. There are a lot of good people out there."

Ez's laugh held no mirth. "Then they are few, or weak enough to be useless." They resumed ambling along the path. "Donn learned that if he consumed the souls of the dead instead of shepherding them to the Underworld, his power grew. The avians are human souls, bound to do Donn's bidding, and food for him and the Fae who joined the Sluagh."

"That's horrible."

Ez nodded. "The banshee always were like flies to a corpse. It surprised no one when they joined the host. But as the Green World decayed and Fae power waned, some incubi sought a way to gain dominance. The energy they get from feeding on those trapped souls is exponentially greater. They've become disgusting, irredeemable bottom feeders, and you did us all a favor by killing them."

A sour taste slid down the back of Eileen's throat. A bit of the guilt lightened with Ez's words. "I guess I—"

The croak of a crow and a flash of black wings dropped them both into a low crouch.

They stared at the bird. It looked small for a crow, but the bird was perched high on a pine bough. Eileen squinted and thought she made out leathery wings, not feathers, and a glint of red eyes.

"I'm not sure that's a crow."

Ezrynhivar squinted up at the creature. "It isn't a Sluagh. I'd have sensed it, and it would have attacked."

Another lit on a branch above the first. Those wings definitely looked more batlike than feathered.

"Unless they're following us to the village. Maybe we should keep walking to make sure it isn't a Sluagh, or you should kill it."

"Likely a juvenile, and it's far too high for you to be sure it's Sluagh. But if your bloodlust isn't sufficiently slaked, you could simply shoot them from here."

Eileen quailed and watched the birds. Ez was probably right. She fell in behind him and willed her aching feet to plod along. Besides, the sky had darkened, and she didn't relish the thought of being in the woods after nightfall if the Sluagh were still close by.

The flutter of wings whispered overhead. She strained her senses to determine whether it had been the soft beat of feathers or the sharper snap of leathery Sluagh wings.

# CHAPTER 6

The sound of a lute brought her around. She risked opening one eye ever so slightly to orient herself.

The sky in the east lightened in hues of green and dusty blue. Dawn neared. Shiora's shining black hair feathered across her pale cheek as she bent to check on Harper.

"You awake, human?"

Harper's throat clenched, but she remained as unmoving as a stone.

"It's faking. I can hear its breathing quicken." Shiora punctuated her statement with a kick to Harper's side. The air rushed from her lungs with an *oof*.

Harper levered herself to her elbows and narrowed her eyes.

"Still with the disrespectful attitude," Gildor said.

Lobelia reached into her pocket and pulled out something hidden in her palm. "It needs another lesson to learn its place."

Shiora's ruby lips smiled. "It's a slow learner."

"This would be so much more fun if glamour worked better on it." Gildor's eyebrows flicked up, and he eyed Lobelia.

"I've got an idea." Lobelia opened her fingers to reveal a handful of berries.

Shiora inhaled. "Faerie fruit. If Gwyn finds out…"

Gildor shrugged. "Badb would find it amusing. Gwyn'll whine about it, but she won't let him punish us."

"Time for breakfast, human." Shiora laughed, and Gildor held one of the pink berries between thumb and forefinger.

Harper clamped her mouth shut and whipped her chin over her shoulder. Gildor kneeled beside her, wound long fingers in her hair, and yanked her head back. Harper screeched through her nose. Damned if she was going to eat that berry. She couldn't guess what effect it would have, but it had to be terrible.

At her other shoulder, Shiora knelt and punched her in the ribs again. Harper bit the insides of her cheeks to fight the instinct to scream, gaze focused on the berry dangling over clamped lips. The elven woman's obsidian eyes glittered as she reached up a scarred hand and pinched Harper's nose shut.

Damn. Hands bound, Harper strained impotently. Seconds ticked by. She knew eventually she'd have to open her mouth to inhale, and Gildor would pop that berry into it. Maybe she'd spit it out, that or bite off one of his fingers.

Harper refused to let these pretty monsters see her struggling. She parted her lips, shoved her face forward, and clamped her jaws down on Gildor's hand just as he crammed the berry halfway down her throat. He yelled and jerked his arm away. She was inhaling to launch the berry back at him when Shiora's hand clenched over her mouth and her teeth clacked together.

The berry's silky insides oozed out between her molars. The flavor was like nothing she'd ever tasted. Blueberry, nectarine, and heaven in one perfect orb. The fruit tingled on her tongue and brought waves of ecstasy. If bliss had a flavor, this was it. Her body went limp, and weightlessness buoyed each limb. Everything was splendid. Everything was joy. Love. Peace.

Musical laughter came from both sides of her. She rolled her head to one side, then the other to meet the eyes of Gildor, Shiora, and Lobelia. Why was she so mad at them? They were her best friends.

As soon as the effervescent, loving feeling began, it started to recede. Like bathwater cooling. Joy drained away as the flavor of the berry faded. No. It's too soon. She had to have another one.

"More," Harper said. Her friends scowled at her. "Please. More, please. Please."

"You see, Shiora, it can be taught!"

"Just one more, please."

Lobelia bent at the waist to peer into Harper's face. "And what will you do for another?"

"Whatever you want." The scintillating joy all but gone, Harper could think of nothing but the perfect pink of the little berry. Humiliation and anger stalked the shrinking perimeter of her happiness.

"What should we force it to do, Gildor?" Shiora clapped her hands with a giddy smile.

Gildor ran his hand along his jaw. "We can't harm it in any overt way."

"Make love to the tree, then?" Lobelia said.

Shiora laughed. "Eat dirt or feces?"

"Kiss our feet." Gildor smirked.

Shame joined anger and grief over the lost joy, because somewhere deep in her mind, Harper knew she'd do any of those things for just one more taste. One more moment of perfect happiness. She hated them for it.

The elves continued to debate. Harper's nostrils flared with each breath, but the elves were too busy giggling to notice the glow of blue flame covering her hands bound behind her. There it was. Her magic had a horrible habit of not being there for her when she wanted it, but it arrived, riding the cresting wave of her righteous fury. *That's it. Anger. That must be the spark.*

She fiddled with Ezrynhivar's ring and thought of pushing the surging magic into it, not letting it run wild like it had that night at the Mystic Island festival. No, she wanted to ram every last drop of her power down Sidhe throats. Make them pay. The tingling of her hands intensified. She felt the bonds weakening, rope snapping fiber by fiber.

Harper smiled.

"Oh, I think it actually likes that last one." Gildor smirked.

Shiora mimed a gag. "You'd tolerate its mouth on—"

Harper widened her cold smile, yanked her arms forward, and sent sparkling blue fire blasting at the jeering Sidhe. They sailed backward, smacking into the earth. Just as fast, they snapped to their feet, blades drawn.

Shouts and the thud of footfalls promised she'd be overrun in moments by the rest of the Wild Hunt. Harper swung her hands around, sucked in a breath she envisioned stoking the flames of her magic, and sent a writhing, crackling arc of power into the line of approaching Fae who seized, spasmodically jerking, and fell.

"You'll regret that, human." Gildor rushed her, blade ready to slice Harper to ribbons, Shiora and Lobelia on his heels, whispering words under their breath.

The elven women proved the faster of the trio. Before Harper could refocus her magic for another blast, threads of glamour snaked under her defenses, worming their way to her thoughts. Love bloomed in Harper's chest. She'd never harm these lovely creatures. Dizziness washed over her like a cloudburst.

The blue glow on her hands flickered to embers while the elf woman drove her armored shoulder into Harper's stomach, forcing the air from her chest. Reacting on instinct, Harper brought the faintly glowing fingers of one hand to the back of the woman's head and pushed energy into her skull, while with the other she whipped a tendril of power at Gildor and Lobelia. Shiora screamed and fell to the side, motionless but breathing, while the other two elves lost their footing and slammed into each other, dazed.

Harper doubted her sorcery would keep them unconscious for long. She quickly glanced around, spotting the glint of metal where Gwyn left Nuada's sword. She raced for the weapon, snatched it and her pack from the ground, and sprinted for the trees.

# CHAPTER 7

Eileen stared straight ahead as Glani, the healer, bustled about tending her injuries. The fuzzy white mycelium wound from the plank floor to her shoulder, back, and face, dulling the pain as the fungus healed her physical wounds.

However, the lingering images of her battle refused to recede. Flashes of sprawled hoofed bodies, the sizzle of iron against flesh, and worst of all, the pleading eyes of the last incubus she'd killed.

A plate of warmly spiced food steamed untouched on the cot beside her. She didn't think she'd ever be able to eat again. In place of her appetite, a familiar craving whispered promises of comfort. Some wine, a splash of vodka, and her shame would melt away. For just a little while, she wouldn't see their faces. Or Gerald's.

"Eileen, your tea." Glani gestured to the steaming liquid, causing the shells and decorations in her long braids to tinkle like wind chimes. "It will help, I promise."

Eileen nodded and reached for the brew, quaffing it in one gulp. She stuck out her tongue and gagged. "Ack! That's awful." Bitter and sour all at once.

"You're thinking about the poison again." Glani's rich voice held an abiding softness.

Eileen frowned and took a bite of the spiced grain to wash the wretched tea flavor away.

"I can read it on your face. You want this all to simply disappear without doing the work."

"Well, I didn't ask for what happened today."

"Didn't you?"

Eileen felt her anger like lightning traveling down a metal rod in her spine. "Have you ever killed anyone?" When the Fir Bolg healer didn't reply, she continued. "Then you don't know what you're talking about."

"So you carried a deadly weapon you had no intention of using?"

Glani's calm infuriated her. Or was it because she had no suitable answer? She'd been arming herself to the teeth for years to protect her daughter from whatever killed her husband. Looking back now, the weapon collection was more talisman than anything, a false sense of safety, but she hadn't considered what it would be like to actually shoot to kill.

Eileen sighed. "I didn't want to use it. I never wanted to kill anyone, not even Sluagh."

"Thank you." Glani perched on the edge of the cot and placed her hand on her friend's shoulder. The half-smile she and the other villagers wore radiated compassion, although her eyes hinted at sadness. "If you had not been willing to fire your weapon, more of our people would have been killed."

"But why do I feel like a murderer?" The last word was choked by a sob she strove to hold back. Eileen dropped her head and warm tears splattered her thighs.

"Because you are a loving and kind person. It was because of that love you acted today like one of our own warriors to protect the innocent from harm. The Sluagh couldn't be stopped otherwise, and now you must make room within your soul for a new you. A bigger you. One brave enough to do whatever is necessary to defend others, and one courageous enough to carry the burden of the spiritual work required to contain such power."

Tears coursed down Eileen's cheeks, and she twisted the seam of the blanket in her fingers. "I'm breaking apart."

"Yes, you are. But now you choose how you put the fragments together again. Either way, the old Eileen O'Neill is dead. A new Eileen is born. It happens every day, only some days the shards are smaller, the shattering more complete. The poison you dream of drinking will only prevent you finding the pieces. Keep you broken."

Eileen curled her toes against the silky polished wood of the floorboards. "I think Lord Ezrynhivar tried to tell me the same thing in the forest. He was a lot harsher about it, though."

Glani's face creased. "As Nuada's herald, there is more we must ask of you today."

The mention of Nuada brought an ache to her throat. He lay just a few doors down from her now. Silent. The mycelium had fixed his wounds, but he did not stir and his skin was cold.

Aeld had told her Nuada's head and heart remained intact enough for him to be revived by the Tuatha in the Cauldron of rebirth, owned by a Tuatha called the Dagdha. If Harper took up the quest Nuada laid on her and reached his people in the Undying Lands, he could live again. Until then, the Fir Bolg had named themselves his protectors.

Eileen needed Nuada's wisdom now, but she was certain he'd want her to convince the Fir Bolg and the Green World Courts to join to confront Badb Catha. That was the best way to save Harper, and that was what she planned to do.

Eileen smoothed her hair into a low ponytail and slid to the bed's end. The tea must be working. Strength returned and the weepy feeling receded.

"I'll help you any way I'm able, Glani. I owe your people a debt I can never repay for aiding my family."

Glani smiled. "We offered aid with no expectation of return. Aeld wishes for the council to discuss today's events and decide our next move. They gather now."

"I have little to add."

Glani smoothed away the remaining mycelium from Eileen's face and shoulder and left her to dress for the meeting. She slipped into the supple tan pants and flowing tunic she'd come to prefer over her street clothes.

When Eileen arrived at the dining hall of the arboreal village, the others were already seated and in the midst of a heated debate. Aeld was leaning over the table's end with his thick hands planted several feet apart.

Ezrynhivar lounged to his left, chair teetering on two legs, arms crossed over his chest. His herald was notably absent. That was curious and somewhat out of character, because Ez reveled in the rapt attention of his servants. He'd been kind to her in his way, but Eileen still distrusted him. So many incubi joined the Sluagh, but Ez had not, so she tried to brush that concern aside. But then she remembered the black birds near the village he'd dismissed as crows, and her mistrust kicked up again.

In contrast to Ez, Serotina frowned on the other side of Aeld, her back ramrod straight in the dryad's saddle mushroom chair Paegrinn had made for her. Worry for Paegrinn tightened Eileen's throat. Behind the Queen, Latreus perched at the edge of a simple stool, hooves swinging while he twisted the tip of his coiled horn between quaking fingers. The poor satyr's golden eyes darted about the room, most frequently landing on Lord Ezrynhivar.

Next to the satyr, with her tiny nose in the air, sat a Fae Eileen didn't recognize. She also had the legs of a goat, but dark brown, and were she standing, she'd be much taller than Latreus. The woman had no visible horns. Skin the color of yellowed leaves contrasted with her waist-length cascades of shiny, deep emerald hair. Layered clothing crafted to resemble a dozen species of leaves matched the late autumn trees. Wrappings of pale chartreuse fabric covered her lower arms. The Fae appeared sweet and good-natured, but Eileen, eyeing her clawed fingers, surmised she could be deadly in a fight.

"Ah, Eileen, thank you for joining us. I trust your wounds are sufficiently healed?" Aeld held out a furred hand and motioned her to the spot next to Serotina.

"Yes, thank you." She inclined her head to the others and slid into her seat. Across from her, the ogre Hieronymous smoothed the white lace doublet around his neck and flashed her a broad smile. The lanky goblin, Twitch, scribbled notes behind him.

"We were just pondering how the Sluagh discovered this secret place so quickly," Hieronymous said.

"And we've decided there are only three possibilities," said Serotina. "Chance. We failed to cover our trail. Or we have a traitor in our midst." Her green eyes flashed at the Dusk King while the branches in her long, mossy hair rustled.

"Yeah. So you missed little." Ezrynhivar tipped his chair farther back and waved a dismissive hand.

"A traitor. No..." Eileen shook her head. The Fae may be alien to her, but she refused to believe they'd betray the Fir Bolg or their own kind.

Hieronymous swirled a red liquid in his cup. "Badb has been here longer than we feared, so it is possible she has spies in any of our Courts."

"So much easier among the dark Fae," Queen Serotina said.

From the corner of her eye, Eileen caught Ezrynhivar rolling his eyes.

"The light may look fairer but deal fouler. They—"

"Lord Ezrynhivar, enough. Bickering gets us nowhere. The decision before us is whether this village remains secure, and the safe return of our guests to their respective Courts." Aeld's words were calm and deliberate.

Eileen scooted to the edge of her chair. "Wait, everyone's leaving? Just like that?"

"We have the matter of our promise to this council. Unlike the Dusk Court, the Dawn pledged our assistance." The dryad queen swept a branched hand behind her and the emerald-haired Fae stood. "Eileen, this is Melinoe. She is a glaistig, fleet of foot and powerful in both battle and magic. She will journey to Sauvie Island and find Harper."

Melinoe bowed. "I am honored to stand in service." Viridian lips parted in a wide smile below sparkling yellow-green eyes. "I just know Harper and I will be great friends."

Eileen swallowed and chose her words carefully, running through Nuada's list of do's and don'ts when dealing with Fae. Don't thank them, it triggers a debt. But show gratitude; Fae can become violent when basic manners are violated. "I am fortunate you are helping my daughter."

Melinoe's smile beamed even wider, and she rose to the tops of her hooves. "You honor me with your trust. I'm ever so excited about beginning my journey and am off straightaway. I might be the first Fae in a hundred years to help a human."

Melinoe bowed deeply to her queen, who inclined her leafy head. Then the glaistig hopped to attention and scuttled toward the door.

"Wait!" Eileen called. The Fae paused mid-stride and a shadow flickered over her face. "Please, wait. And tell Harper—"

"Yes?"

Eileen had no idea what message to pass to her daughter. Anything she thought of seemed insufficient and silly. "Just tell her I love her."

Melinoe's hooves clacked along the wooden floor as she sidled to Eileen. Long clawed fingers were surprisingly supple as she clasped Eileen's hand. "Don't be sad. I will find Harper." That dazzling smile broke over her features again. "I can't wait to meet her."

Eileen nodded, fearing her voice would crack.

When she turned back to the table, Ezrynhivar had all four legs of his seat planted firmly back on the floor and his pointed teeth were bared. And then it was gone. He levered himself back in his chair and draped himself in his habitual studied nonchalance. "Well, wasn't that sweet?" he said. "Now can we return to discussing how we're able to safely leave this place? I grow tired of camping."

Eileen chewed her bottom lip. "They attacked us a second time. If that isn't the proof you all need, what would it take to wake you up?"

"We all appreciate what you've been through recently, Eileen," the dryad queen said with a saccharine smile, "but a chance encounter with a pack of Sluagh doesn't imply a plot to start the Third Great War. The Sluagh have become a problem ever since the Veil thickened. Nevertheless, my people are more selfless than the dark. We will remain and render our assistance to the Fir Bolg until our emissary returns."

Ez wrinkled one side of his nose. "Normally, the Sluagh are a plague only in human cities. There is little for them to feed on in the wilderness unless they know precisely where some tasty treats are holed up. Which is why I, for one, believe we've been betrayed." Ez narrowed his eyes at Serotina. "So the Dusk Court will also remain to assist our big, hairy friends." His smile revealed overlarge canine teeth and radiated a malicious chill.

Hieronymous cleared his throat. "Lord Ezrynhivar's point is the most troublesome to me. The Sluagh were a minor threat, but burgeoned since the Industrial Revolution. Though their numbers are great, they never rode with the Wild Hunt or were drawn to natural places in their long history. My contingent will return with me to Fògradh Lodge. If the Sluagh are seeking your people, Aeld, someone must work on the outside to discover both the how and the why."

The Fir Bolg chieftain tapped a hand across his heart and inclined his head to the solitary Fae. "If the Sluagh are joining their human counterparts in their encroachment farther into our homeland, it's more reason for you all to return home. You are safer—"

"Just like that?" Eileen slumped forward, then gestured at both Fae Courts. "Don't we get to decide what level of risk we're comfortable with?"

"I'm sorry—"

"Badb's assassins all but killed Nuada on your doorstep, slaughtered several of your people, possibly your own son, and still you take no action."

"We are a people of peace, we no longer—"

"I killed today. Took five lives to protect this village and everyone in it. Nuada. My daughter. Even the Phooka fought side by side with you, and yet you play Switzerland and stay out of it?"

"Switzerland?" Aeld's forehead wrinkled.

"Glani gave me something to hold on to, and it's the only thing keeping me from shattering under the strain of what I did today. She told me sometimes peace is not the way, and lives must be taken in defense of the defenseless."

Ez smirked. "I seem to recall telling you much the same standing over your pile of Fae corpses."

"Yes, you did, and you were right." Eileen clenched a fist and held it toward the Dusk King. "Chieftain Aeld, the gathering storm of war is overhead. The only choice you have is whether you die hiding from it, or whether you fight to save everything you can. I think Glani sees that, and maybe more of your people do too."

Aeld lowered himself back into his seat and cradled his

forehead in one huge hand. "The Fir Bolg cannot enter another Great War."

"So you'll let the rest of us die while you sit in your treehouses and chant?"

"You know not what you ask. After the first two Battles of Moytura, so few of us remained. Human incursion has destroyed even more than the wars did. If we fight in this war, it will mean the end of our race."

The silence in the dining hall was palpable.

Eileen's chest ached, and she drew in a deep sigh. She'd found herself again among the Fir Bolg. This culture, despite the fact she was surrounded by Sasquatch, felt like home more than anywhere she had ever lived. The idea that it teetered on the brink of fading into nothingness was unthinkable.

"But if none of us stands against this evil, don't we all fall into oblivion?"

# CHAPTER 8

Harper crashed through the thorny underbrush, leaves lashing her legs like hundreds of tiny whips. The early dawn sky offered some light, but not enough to illuminate the writhing roots, ready to catch her feet. A painful jab lanced through her midsection, although she didn't know if it was from the injuries sustained in the camp or just a stitch in her side. Years of being a desk jockey had put a damper on her sprinting skills.

A high quavering wail from the left turned her blood to ice. Banshee. Even the insects stopped their hum, and the trees paused their relentless scraping. She'd focused all her worry on the Wild Hunt, forgetting something darker stalked her.

Bat-winged silhouettes flitted across the remnants of the milky moon, pushing her quaking legs faster, creating eddies in the fog. Coarse avian cries mingled with the screech of the banshee.

She risked an upward glance at the flapping shadows rustling overhead in nearly leafless branches and stumbled to one side, smacking a trunk with her shoulder, but she kept sprinting toward the deeper cover of a thicket ahead.

A line of broad-shouldered shapes with gleaming black hooves, sweeping obsidian horns, and batlike wings leapt from the underbrush. With a yelp, Harper dug her heels to the earth, sliding partway to the incubi before wheeling off to her right.

She'd barely regained her footing when black birds rained down in front of her, jerking and snapping into the wasted forms of the Sluagh. Harper slowed to a stop and whipped around, wildly scanning for an opening, but the ragged banshee closed off any hope of flight. Gaping mouths, rheumy eyes, and claws at the ends of impossibly long fingers, all ready to dissect and devour her. Their flowing white hair and dresses spiraled and writhed even though no breeze stirred.

Harper's stomach lurched. Too many to fight, but she grasped the sheathed Cliamh Solais anyway, ready to draw it.

"I was hoping to steal Gwyn's prize away from him. Never expected it to just blunder into my clutches. It's my lucky, ducky day." A tall, gaunt man in diaphanous grey robes emerged from the circle of Sluagh, lifted a knobby hand, and waved strips of golden fabric. "Leaving me a trail was quite considerate, love." A high-pitched tittering laugh oozed through his smug grin.

Harper's skull pounded at the sight of the shreds of her gown. Any hope the Phooka picked up her trail again extinguished. She really was alone. She bared her teeth at her attackers.

Iridescent black feathers cascaded from the neckline of ash grey robes that swirled around the man like a storm as he pivoted to his minions. "Go. Engage the Wild Hunt and keep them away from my new treasure. Badb Catha will finally embrace the Sluagh when *we* deliver her prize, not that milksop Gwyn ap Nudd."

Wordlessly, half of the banshee and incubi fanned out through the woods, and most of the avians glided through high boughs.

"Well, my pretty, introductions are in order. It is your great honor to cower before Donn, Lord of the Dead." Donn lifted his black staff overhead, dramatically, the crystalline sphere at the top catching the hazy light. "Further cordiality must wait, love, can't have Gwyn stealing back my little prize." His trim mustache and short, cropped black beard ringed a toothy grin.

Clawed fingers snatched the Cliamh Solais and swept Harper's pack down her arms, then bound her wrists in front of her. Being tied up was getting old fast.

*Out of the frying pan and into the fire.* Her grandmother always said that when Harper was about to make a poor choice.

The clarion call of Gwyn's hunting horn and the baying of the Gabriel hounds denied her new captors time to admire their conquest. The Wild Hunt would not relinquish its quarry so easily. Just her luck to be the trophy in a sycophantic war between Badb's minions.

Donn clutched her right arm and shoved her, stumbling, as the Sluagh charged through the bent and foggy woods, half flying, half running between the creaking shadowy trees.

Rough hands gripped Harper's waist and hoisted her up to glide across the low mist for a few hundred feet. Their leader was thin, but he boasted strength well beyond hers. Donn held her sword in his other hand. Not that she could use it with her wrists bound behind her. They touched down again to avoid a thick network of low canopy.

Dammit. She'd been so close. Or had she? She had no actual idea where she was going or what other monsters lurked in the mist in this expanding, changing land. *Face it, Harper. You're lost, outnumbered, and outclassed. Even if you can escape hipster undead guy and his nightmare squad, Gwyn will only catch you again.*

On some level, the situation seemed familiar. Before Nuada and kelpies, she'd been trapped in a crappy life with a pair of dead-end options. Now she was trapped on a crappy island with a couple of factions who both wanted her dead. At least there was symmetry. Or was it cemetery? A laugh tumbled unbidden from her. Days of adrenaline pumping in her veins every moment made her giddy.

The corpse-white hand around her waist gave her a shake, but their pace didn't slow. A copse of bent trees ahead forced the troupe to land again. When Harper scowled over her shoulder at the gaunt figure dragging her through the forest, hysteria flowered. All the stresses and shocks of the past weeks bubbled up.

Were it not for the long, tattered grey robes and the crow wing headdress nestled in scraggly black hair, Donn would blend in with the hipsters of downtown Portland with his pencil-thin moustache and beard complementing his cartoon villain ensemble. Sanity frayed further. This guy should be at a microbrewery somewhere asking the server if the beer was gluten free, not kidnapping women on strange islands.

A chortle bubbled up at the image, and she risked another sideways glance at her captor. He had a single diamond earring. Of course he did. An eruption of pent-up emotion poured out as a torrent of laughter.

"Naughty, naughty girl. Making noise to lead the Wild Hunt to me." He ended his sentence with his own high-pitched titter.

"Love the beard, emo dude. You, your own evil twin?" Harper burst out laughing again. The force of it doubled her over, and she overbalanced her captor. When he listed sideways, her weight teetered on her floppy ankle. She fell sprawling, dragging the Sluagh leader with her. The web of branches overhead scraped and rustled like dry laughter.

Instantly, incubi and banshee surrounded them, ready to defend their fallen master. Harper faced a ring of bared teeth and claws.

"Get up, my lovely."

His British accent matched the attempted aristocratic beard. Harper levered herself up. Her ankle buckled, sending her crashing back down. It didn't feel sprained or broken, but it still had the floppy weakness of an overextended joint.

"What are you playing at, love? I said get up."

"I can't. I think I twisted my ankle."

"This your grand plan then?" He bent from the waist and swiveled his face to be level with Harper's as she sat on a boulder, rubbing her ankle. "Slow us down so Gwyn can catch us?"

"What?" Harper stared at the man, threw her palms up, and shook her head. A din of squawking and flapping wings rose overhead. "Isn't Gwyn your boss? Why—"

"My boss? Oh no, my lovely. I was and will be again his replacement." He swept his hand across his waist and bowed lower. "Thousands of years ago, humanity wrenched Inisfáil from the Tuatha. As Fae and Tuatha alike retreated beneath the hills, Gwyn's power over human souls waned. Because I was the first human to die on Inisfáil, I gained control over the dead. But Badb always favored her own kind and placed her trust in Gwyn, even though it is I who serve her best. Bloody nepotism. But when I present you to my Dark Lady, all that will change."

Harper rested her head on her knees and laughed. "Let me get this straight. You think you're hot shit because you were a bad enough soldier to be killed in battle first? Lord of the Dead sounds like a sarcastic joke, not the high honor you make it out to be."

Donn bristled. "Only because Eriu cursed me when I first arrived at Inisfáil, but she could not have foreseen the power she truly gave me."

"Well, from what I know of my great-great"—Harper waved her hand to indicate a lot more 'greats'—grandmother, you must have already been a weapons-grade dick for her to do that." That got a rise out of him. *Lay down the sword. Just drop my sword so you can tell me off.* "Insolence doesn't become you, my lovely." Spittle flew from his lip as he bit off each word. "I'll show you real power." He flung the hand not gripping her weapon into the air and a single black bird descended. Harper cringed at the crunching sounds of its transformation to its humanesque form. Every bone visible beneath taut skin, empty white spheres for eyes. Harper shuddered.

The Sluagh's knees wobbled while he studied his own shape in utter confusion, then scanned the ring of creatures. Donn walked behind the Sluagh, running his pale hand across the soul's bony shoulders.

"This one has been with me for over three decades. Oh, how I've savored him. He once lived in Germany, composed music of such beauty the heart ached when he played. Until the Nazis came for him." Donn flashed a sly smile at Harper. "He survived the worst of humanity. Warehoused at Auschwitz amidst the direst of circumstances, he uplifted others and never once lost faith that the world was a good place." Donn's face hovered a millimeter from the man's neck. "He survived and the music he wrote after, sublime enough for the heavens. Even as he lay in agony, dying from cancer, he still believed his life was beautiful. He was an old soul. Forged and honed through many mortal walks on this earth. Had the Veil been open, had he the opportunity to add this last lifetime to the mystic Cauldron of Rebirth where souls are dissolved, stirred, and reforged, humanity would have been the better for it for generations.

"Instead, he became mine, like millions of others. Almost spent. He doesn't remember who he was anymore, but I do. I was saving such sweet broth for a more special occasion, but you'll have to do."

Harper inhaled sharply and drew herself up on her wobbly ankle. Her hand reached instinctively to rescue the poor Sluagh. Stabs of icy pain spread across her skin like frost crystals forming on a window when the banshee clutched her wrist and forced her aside.

Shivering from their cold and her own anger, Harper could

only watch as Donn ran knobby fingers over the man's cheek, tilted the Sluagh's chin up, and opened his bearded mouth impossibly wide, jaw unhinged like a snake swallowing his prey.

Donn inhaled a sucking breath, like a vacuum. In and in and in, he inhaled without pause, a breath that threatened to never end. His eyes glowed a faint red as sparkling tendrils of light flowed from the open mouth of the poor soul and into Donn's lungs. The Sluagh's body convulsed while a low moan rose and fell in intensity.

Harper watched, sharp pains jabbing her chest, as she stretched her fingers out to clasp the hem of Donn's robes and pull him from the soul, but they slipped through her grasp. The man's bones snapped as he arched away from his tormentor, face contorted. Harper clamped trembling hands over her ears to block out the crack of bone and howls of pain. Horrified but unable to do anything to stop it, she hunched over her legs.

Mercifully, it was over fast. Within a minute, the poor man slumped, nothing left of him but dust. At least he was finally at peace, and if Donn was right, humanity was the poorer for it. All the composer had been, the bright light he'd shone in deepest darkness, lost forever. And merely to provide a tasty treat to the evil standing before her. A tear slid down Harper's cheek while Donn shuddered, eyes closed, a dreamy smile on his face.

Harper sat, chest heaving, biting the inside of her mouth to hold back more tears. She forced herself to breathe fast and deep, willing rage at Donn so her magic would kindle. But the abomination she witnessed was the cold water of fear and sorrow, dousing any spark of anger.

"That, my lovely, is power." He licked his lips.

"So you and the Sluagh are parasites?"

"More predators." Donn glanced wistfully down at the patch of dust that was all that remained of the composer. "Not too many like this one left. Souls today are mere junk food. Plentiful, tad salty, and lacking in richness." Donn's glittering eyes narrowed, and he ran his tongue across the bottom of his teeth. "You want to know the best part?"

Harper rolled her eyes. "No. But I'm betting you're going to tell me anyway."

"Gwyn swore to serve Badb Catha just to have three days each year to continue the *sacred duty* his father saddled him with shepherding souls to the Cauldron and thus prevent them joining my Sluagh. Oh, he tried to save as many human spirits as he could, but people are inherently self-destructive. They polluted. Extracted. Destroyed the earth so much the Veil thickened and now the dead can't leave, anyway." Donn's grating titter swelled to a cackle. "She gave him his three days, but humans betrayed him too. Trapped themselves, and now I claim them all. He sold himself to Badb for nothing!" Donn bent at the waist and wheezed with laughter. "Gwyn's useless. A slave. While my kingdom and my power grow every year."

Suddenly, a lot about Gwyn made sense. *Some of us don't get to choose which orders to follow.* Unlike the Sidhe, who appeared to serve willingly, Gwyn was indentured. Her throat ached and she swallowed hard. For just a moment, she felt sorry for Gwyn ap Nudd, until she replayed the moments when he slew his own father.

Gwyn wasn't worth her compassion, and conflicting feelings about him was something she couldn't afford. This revelation changed nothing. He'd hand her over to Badb, so he was still her enemy. She refocused on her current adversary.

Harper had met dozens of self-important powermongers exactly like Donn. Status-hungry swaggering fools in business suits, treating their subordinates at the office like they were worthless. She knew exactly how to push their buttons.

"Oh." Harper shrugged and rubbed her ankle. From the corner of her eye, a shadow flickered. She squinted and could barely make out the shape of a black wolf. When the canine swiveled its head toward her, she saw the pinpoint glow of yellow eyes. Her heart leapt. Maybe the Phooka had found enough of her breadcrumb trail and followed the Sluagh as Donn collected her markers. If she could keep this arrogant blowhard talking, she might give the Phooka time to pull off whatever rescue plan he had in mind.

"Oh?" An incubus ducked the scabbard of her sword as his master threw up his hands and stuck his neck toward Harper. "That's it? Oh?"

"Well, it just seems..." Harper bit her lower lip and cast her eyes to the ground.

"Spit it out, love."

"It's just, if you were really that powerful, you'd have taken me from Gwyn face to face. You only captured me because I got myself out of his camp."

Donn tittered and wagged a slow finger in her face. He looked like someone who'd just uncovered a big secret. "Tricky, tricky, love. I see it now. You're in league with Gwyn. Trying to undermine me. Keep me from—"

"Oh yes. That's the logical conclusion. I faked a sprained ankle, so the dude with the antlered mask instead of the dude with the bad evil-twin beard is the one to lead me to my death. Brilliant detective work, goth Sherlock."

From what she could see, very few of the Sluagh host remained with their leader. With the Cliamh Solais in her hands again, they'd be doomed. A delicious warmth radiated from her ribcage with the memory of her prior conquests with the blade. Harper's eyes slid to her sword still gripped in Donn's hand. If he'd just put it down, she could grab it and cut them all down. Maybe not the avian forms above her. They were victims too.

Donn swiveled from her and regarded the ring of his minions like an actor reading his audience. The trees overhead rustled and something dropped from above, clacking against the boulder before rolling next to her knee. Donn was speaking in hushed tones to an incubus or he'd have noticed the projectile.

After several seconds, she worked the fallen object from beneath her leg. A tiny strip of paper was tied to the rock.

As soon as she thought no one would notice, she peeled the note from around the stone and worked it flat. No small task with her fingers clamped together and her hands shaking with the fear of discovery. Small, flowery handwriting proved a challenge to read, so she hunched as close as possible to the note, tilting it slightly to catch the light.

*Rescue. Outnumbered. Be ready. Follow the green light. Eat this message.*

Relief sent the air rushing from her lungs. The Phooka. It had to be. Only he would be as cloak and dagger to suggest she actually eat the note. He really was here to save her. She'd feared those yellow eyes she glimpsed that first night were a mirage.

Relief faded to frustration. Little difficult to be ready for whatever mystery plan her shapeshifting pal had dreamed up to spring her from the Sluagh when she was bound tight. Her ankle was another wild card. It had supported her weight, though it ached during Donn's evil peacocking, but she'd only know for sure when she put weight on it again.

A breeze ruffled her hair and sent the note flipping over to her thigh. She slammed her wrists on it before it blew away. As she wriggled the paper under her palm, she noticed a smaller message on the back corner.

*Use the rock, stupid.*

Harper picked up the little stone between her fingers and felt around the edges. One edge of the rock had been chipped and ground to a sharp edge. Perfect for cutting through rope. A smile broke across her face. *Phooka, you're a genius.*

# CHAPTER 9

Emilio hauled his eyelids, sticky and each weighing a ton, open just to slits, revealing only more darkness. Thoughts refused to congeal in his sluggish mind, but he had the sense it was night. The tiniest movement took herculean effort, like someone had submerged him in water. Cold, smooth metal met his exploring fingertips. Yet moments ago, he'd been in a wooded clearing with Selina, Jerome, and the others. Hadn't they escaped?

No, that wasn't right. Memories of a black-clad woman with flaming red hair standing center stage surfaced. He screamed and bolted upright, head clanging into a bronze ceiling, then crashed to the chill floor. A whimper bubbled in the back of his throat, sounding small and alone in the dark.

Mystic Island. The festival. That's why his thoughts were filled with fairies and trolls. He'd been to a costume festival, and didn't he try that new drug Dust again? The one that made you see such wondrous things? Elves and goblins seemed unreal, a Dust-induced fantasy, though he remembered actual pain. And fear. A beautiful monster had sliced through a guy in a vampire costume who tried to run from... *Them.*

Yes, that was after the party, but before the clearing outside the tower where they'd caught him trying to escape, and some kind of confrontation with that evil red-haired woman. And then.... And then....

So many broken images of a harrowing journey arrayed before him like puzzle pieces scattered on a table. Out of order, they refused to resolve into a complete picture.

Sharp pains radiated from his forehead. Maybe he'd been knocked out in the fight outside the tower. He let his head fall onto the metal floor; the cool of it against his cheek soothed his fevered thoughts. He strove to not think about his situation, tried to force himself to sleep so he could wake up back in his apartment in Portland. But once he started pulling at the threads of recall, memories wove a tapestry of horror. He recalled his clandestine trips through the Erimus Pharmaceutical building. The files and the genetic match to something his abductors called the Abraxas profile.

Then he remembered the green liquid flowing into his veins, the jeering elven faces, and the icy fingers of mist crawling over his body. He screamed, tried to stand, and instantly regretted it. His head ricocheted against the low ceiling with a clang. White-hot spikes of agony in his skull sent him crashing back down to the floor.

They did something to him. He couldn't remember anything after the sensation of his internal organs melting while he hung suspended in the center of a mist ball, but now he languished in a cage inside a pitch-black room. That couldn't be good.

He pulled his knees to his chest and ran shaking hands through his hair.

"Gah! What the—"

His fingers came away sliced to ribbons and sticky wet with what he could only assume was his blood. Emilio screamed again. As fast as he'd been cut, the lacerations healed, the edges of the wounds itching and tugging toward each other like an invisible needle stitched them simultaneously. A tingling sensation ran the length of each closed wound. He squirmed.

Emilio started to hyperventilate. For several seconds, he froze. *What have they done to me?* Emilio pressed his face against the floor and every muscle quaked. He tried to ignore the nerve endings in his body that seemed to suggest an extra set of arms was growing from his shoulders.

Locked between curiosity and terror, he curled into a paralyzed little ball for several minutes. Eventually, the need to know what they'd done to his body won, and a shaky hand crept toward his scalp again. Gingerly, he ran his fingers along his hairline, where they met dozens of thin metal edges, like strips of paper-thin metal sheeting. He whimpered and maneuvered trembling fingers along the long side of one of the strips. Beneath his fingertips, parallel ridges ran like toothpicks at the center of each piece.

"Feathers?" His voice sounded too loud. He traced his forefinger around a single shaft. Oblong with razor-sharp edges that sent fresh blood flowing. It definitely felt like some sort of metallic feather.

He levered himself to a half crouch, legs clamped to his core. A trembling hand ran along his arms and back. Bigger, sharper feathers carpeting his shoulders flayed strips of flesh from his palms. And his fingertips encountered something else. A horror worse than metallic feathers. *Oh please no, I'll do anything. Please don't let it be true.* His nerve endings were right. Something grew where it didn't belong.

Blood gushing from his hands and forearms, Emilio screamed and screamed.

# CHAPTER 10

Harper pressed the sharpened stone between thumb and forefinger and curled her wrist around the back of her other hand. At such an awkward angle, only the tiniest of movements were possible, so she made them quickly.

She kept her face frozen in a cultivated adolescent pout. Whenever Donn turned toward her, she palmed the little stone.

Donn's robes swirled as he pivoted from the incubus. Already that insipid grin cracked his hipster face as he sauntered over to where Harper sawed at her bonds.

Deep in the woods, an ululating horn blast pierced the silence, flattened in tone by the fog. Donn's triumphant smile evaporated, replaced by bared teeth and a taut posture. The incubi pressed themselves against black tree trunks and dragged their swords free with a cacophony of scrapes.

Donn charged at Harper, fist clenched. "Nooooo!" he screeched. "Vile, evil girl. I knew you were in league with him." White strings of spit flew from his trembling bottom lip.

The Lord of the Dead was clearly unhinged, though partly

right. If she was to be served up to Badb Catha on a silver platter, better by the lesser monster.

The hunting horn sounded again, close enough this time to include the baying of the Gabriel hounds from both sides. Relief blossomed in her chest. If she could snap her bonds, she might escape and find her friends while the Sluagh and the Wild Hunt clashed.

Donn barked orders.

Harper's fingers see-sawed across the ropes as fast as the dull ache pulsating in her wrist would allow. She was almost through.

Donn rounded on her. She clamped a hand over the stone just in time and swept her gaze around the encampment for either the green light or glowing amber eyes. Neither were there, but flashes of white bounded past, and she glimpsed the red ears of Gwyn's dogs. Their master was never far behind.

Gwyn sailed over the undergrowth and landed on one knee between Donn and Harper, fingers splayed over the ground. With a grunt, Harper forced her wrists apart, and the ropes snapped, already using the rock to propel herself to the left of Gwyn just as he raised his blade and lunged toward Donn.

Her pack lay between the warring Lords of the Dead. In one fluid movement, she bent and swept it onto her back. With a hop to her right, she cleared the remaining distance to Donn, snatching the Cliamh Solais from his grip on her way past.

"You fool, she's getting away," Donn shrieked, but the clash of metal on metal assured her neither would follow for a moment.

For once, the foreboding trees and mist closing around her were welcome, hiding her from her batshit-crazy soul-sucking captor. Banshee screeches and the clatter of battle raged behind her, enough to cover the noise of her escape. Eventually, either Donn or Gwyn would prevail and pursue. She hoped to put distance between them and find the Phooka before that happened.

Harper dashed through the woods as quickly as she could with her weakened ankle.

A craggy branch tangled in her hair while another lashed her cheek. As she smacked the grasping twigs, a root rose and caught her ankle, sending her smashing into a tree trunk, then hip first onto a stone. As she clawed her way vertical, hostility poured from each trunk, every bit as thick as the fog.

Where was that little green light? She didn't dare call out for the Phooka, so she crept along more quietly now, toward the last place she'd glimpsed the amber glow of the Phooka's eyes.

Inch by silent inch, she slinked away from the battle. But then why suddenly did it sound as though she moved toward the battle, and not away from it?

*You're just spooked and disoriented. Probably got turned around when you stopped to scan for the Phooka.* The sun hovered over her right shoulder. Keeping the hazy orb in her gaze, she swiveled on her heel so that it hung over her left shoulder, one hundred and eighty degrees from the shouts and din of the skirmish. Satisfied she had her bearings, she started forward, groping through the rheumy fog, moving quickly while feeling for obstructions to avoid another tumble.

She'd traveled roughly the length of a football field before swords clanged and Fae yelled in front of her again. Harper's mouth became dry and her gaze darted to the sky. She swore she heard branches scrape and patchy leaves rustle despite the lack of breeze. There hung the sun over her right shoulder, and ahead, shadowy forms lunged and traded blows, backlit by the scattered light.

*Where are you, Phooka?* The moment she finished her thought, a tiny emerald light bobbed a dozen feet away and to her left. *Follow the light.* She didn't know what the glow was; too big to be a firefly, and wisps of green flames flicked all around it. With a glance back toward the battle to confirm her enemies weren't pursuing, she sped off toward the light.

It shot ahead so fast, Harper couldn't keep up. The clash of swords and banshee wailing receded with each stride. Somehow, the flickering orb kept her on the straight path.

She abandoned stealth and pumped her arms and legs to maintain pace with the green glow. For once, the infernal trees lay still. No tripping roots or snagging branches. Blood rushing in her ears, she pushed her sprint to her maximum speed, but it wasn't enough. Far ahead of her now, the light disappeared somewhere deep into the woods.

She stumbled to a halt, palms on her thighs, sucking in breath after breath. Without the little glowing savior, she feared the woods would only lead her back to her captors, so staying in one place seemed like the safest choice.

Out of nowhere, the green light zipped a revolution around her head before streaking forward. She wasted no time loping behind it before it just winked out.

"Wait! Don't go," she whispered, staggering to a stop once more.

Ahead, a pair of glowing yellow eyes blinked.

"Phooka?" Harper whispered.

"Your sprinting skills leave a lot to be desired," a snarky voice answered. The undergrowth shuddered, Paegrinn and the Phooka emerged on one side, and an unknown Fae with brown goat's legs and green hair emerged from the other.

"Paegrinn?"

Harper raced for her friends, her heart bursting with relief and joy. The Phooka's hooves tapped the hard ground as he ran. Phooka and Paegrinn reached for her at the same time and swept her into a tangled hug.

"I can't believe you found me," she said between hitching breaths, equal measure sob and laugh.

"Oh my goodness, I'm just so glad to meet you, but we're not safe." The green-haired Fae clasped her hands beneath her chin and beamed, then scurried toward a deer path. The sounds of the skirmish between the Sluagh and the Wild Hunt resounded in the distance.

Harper relaxed away from her friend's embrace and half-jogged after the mysterious new Fae.

Paegrinn hoisted his spear and loped shoulder to shoulder with Harper, pointing to the glaistig's back and speaking in a hushed tone. "This is Melinoe. Serotina sent her. She helped us track you after you escaped Gwyn."

The Phooka rolled his eyes and drew along Harper's opposite side. "Pffft. It was me who located her today," the Phooka whispered. "Never needed some sycophantic light—"

The Phooka's quiet rant died on his lips when Paegrinn's massive spear shot up, directed at the undergrowth, while Melinoe drew a long, thin blade and bared slightly pointed teeth.

Harper strained her ears for sounds of pursuit. "I don't—"

Icy hands shot out from the bushes and clamped around her waist. Incubi and banshee rose from every direction. The Phooka, already in his wolf form, bounded into the fray, teeth gnashing. She couldn't see Paegrinn or Melinoe, but she heard the thud of Paegrinn's pointed staff slamming into enemy Fae and weapons clanging.

Harper slammed her head backward. Pain lanced as her skull whammed into Donn's jawbone. Crack. His neck popped backward with a snap like a dry branch. Donn screamed a high-pitched sound like someone strangled a goose, but his freezing hands never lost their hold on her waist.

Harper lurched her upper back partway around, wrapped her teeth over his shoulder, and clamped her jaws. Another shriek. This time, his grip loosened enough for Harper to throw her weight forward and break it.

"Cheeky little bitch. You'll pay for that."

She staggered ahead just as Donn regained his composure. The only weapon she had was Nuada's blade. *Drawing this sword has serious consequences and must occur for the purest of reasons.* Nuada's words replayed their warning.

She smiled, remembering how the blade understood her, melted all fear, and whispered of glorious victory. For those few moments when she and the Cliamh Solais vanquished the Wild Hunt in that stairwell in Portland, she'd known both peace and righteous strength.

Donn was the purest evil, and she hated him for ravaging the composer. Seemed to her like a prime reason to draw the Sword of Light, cleanse that corruption from the worlds. Yearning for the weapon's power, its certainty, brought fire to her chest. *This demon doesn't stand a chance against us.* She caressed the scabbard with a lover's touch.

With a cold grin, she wrapped her fingers around the Cliamh Solais' grip, and pulled. His death would be swift.

Harper's arm shot into the chill air. Her palm burned where the textured grip scraped her skin, but the blade clung to its scabbard. *What the hell?* She had an awkward yet solid grasp. The sword should be free.

No time to deliberate. Donn launched himself at her, shrieking. She did the only thing she could do. Rolling aside in a headlong dive, she flipped back to a low stance and swung the weapon, still in its scabbard, at Donn's head. She missed but caught him in the shoulder, sending him staggering away, torso hunched.

"That's just about enough out of you. I'm positive Badb will still reward me with a place at her side if it's your shade I bring to her instead of an insolent little girl."

Harper's eyes widened. She wasn't sure what a shade was, but she assumed it was one of the crow-shape souls. She held the scabbard in one hand and the grip of the Sword of Light in the other and pulled with all her might. Stuck fast, it refused to budge.

The buzz of a thousand wasps filled her head. She'd experienced the symptoms of panic before, and her fear crescendoed when Donn curled his fingers into claws at the ends of wide arms while his mouth yawned. Farther and farther it stretched until his jaw reached nearly to his waist. A sound, half yawn, half dry moan rose and fell as Donn inhaled.

"Phooka! Paegrinn!" She tried to yell, but her voice came out in barely a whisper. Pinpricks covered every inch of her skin, like blood returning to a sleeping limb. Except the prickles flowed in a single direction, to Donn. Glimmering threads emerged from her skin and wound their way toward the gaping mouth. When each left the surface, it felt like peeling off a hundred minuscule band-aids. Her lips contorted into a silent scream.

Banshee cackled, and the Phooka and Paegrinn called her name. Harper forced her legs to move, to run, but every limb weighed a thousand pounds. She was helpless. She was being eaten alive.

Ahead, Melinoe broke through the undergrowth, leathery black wings unfurled above her, claws raised, ready to strike. She turned and thrust her sword through the attacker's chest, but three Sluagh closed on her as Donn continued to devour Harper's spirit.

Something big crashed through a stand of reedy trees at Donn's back. Branched antlers gleamed in the pale light. Gwyn ap Nudd sprinted past Donn, shouldering him to the side.

He leapt between Donn and Harper, landing in a wide stance with his left hand stretched toward the Lord of the Dead. A gleaming lance of white lightning splintered from Gwyn's fingertips and pierced Donn's chest. Harper barely registered Donn's incoherent scream as Gwyn's other arm crushed her in a tight embrace. His silken hair smelled of pine.

"Don't worry. You'll be safe," he whispered, lips brushing her ear.

The dirt beneath her feet writhed, the milky sun reeled overhead, and the trees careened around them. Harper's head swam, and she clasped Gwyn's neck because he was the only thing not whirling.

As suddenly as the disorienting sensation began, it ended with a popping sound like a cork rocketing from a champagne bottle. And then silence, peppered with the hum of insects. No sounds of battle. Harper opened her eyes, not realizing she'd squeezed them shut. A stream wound a looping path down an incline, and the forest here was more like the usual Douglas fir that populated the Pacific Northwest instead of the gnarled black shapes from the woods she'd just been in.

"How—"

Gwyn's arm released her, and she staggered back, eager to avoid recapture.

He hunched at the waist, mask falling at his feet. His bearded face lifted toward her.

"Wasn't sure that would work with two of us," he said. And collapsed.

# CHAPTER 11

Waking up in his cramped cage wasn't any easier the second time. Or the third and fourth. The other few times, he'd not even moved. He lay there, the hard, flat cage bottom gnawing into his bones. He barely registered the pain because gibbering prayers to his grandmother's Catholic god to change him back, fidgeting in his cage, and chewing his fingernails filled his day.

Whatever genes the drugs and mist had switched on, he desperately hoped someone could turn off again and he'd return to his old, flamboyant self. Human. Not some unholy Fae hybrid.

"Selina? Jerome? Alan?" Emilio called out into the dark of the lab. His only answer was the hum of the ventilation system and the rhythmic thud of multiple footsteps in a busy hallway. Levering himself onto his knees, he pressed his face against the bars and squinted to discern the lab's contents. Hard edges of wood and glass cabinets caught in the sliver of light from the door's bottom. A few shelves dotted the rear wall. Other than the sparse furniture, he was alone.

"Oh no. No, no, no," Emilio moaned and rocked himself. He

remembered Breas and Badb Catha grilling that whimpering douche, Jones, about the high death rate.

Sweet Mother Mary, was he the only one who survived? He flopped into the corner of his prison and curled himself back into his little ball. Sharp feathers nicked his flesh and fresh blood flowed. If his friends really were dead, they were the lucky ones.

Emilio imagined his family's faces if they saw him now. Most of them had disowned him when he came out. How would the rest react if he showed up like this? Metallic feathers, and whatever was growing from his back that he refused to explore. Who knows what else was wrong with him.

His hands shook, waves of anxiety racking him. Every thought shoved him nearer to panic. He had to get out of here. Now. The darkness suddenly threatened to press the breath from his lungs. His rational mind knew his cage couldn't shrink, but his animal brain believed otherwise and the walls edged closer to the pen. Heart pounding, he kicked the bars again and again, each impact punctuated by a strangled yell.

Screams of panic slid into shouts of defiance when anger took over from fear. Who were these demons to do this to him? What gave them the right?

"I'll kill you. I'll kill you. I'll kill you all." Rage sent his kicking into a flurry of strikes. Spittle flew from his lips. Fury was powerful, better than shrinking with dread, and he stoked the rage with images of slicing elven faces with his feathers.

*Feathers. I have feathers.* The shock of that simple fact poured cold water on the flames of anger and he crumpled back to the floor. The sudden clenching sensation in his chest forced out a howl. A lament for the life the Fae stole from him. Looking like this, he'd have to live in hiding. No apartment. No career. No more concerts. He'd never be in love. Who could hold him in his arms now and survive it? He laughed amid his tears. Who'd even want to? In every way that mattered, they'd killed him.

"Keep it down, my young intern. You've woken half the wing with your wailing and banging." A smooth, arrogant voice preceded a flood of light as Breas, Dr. Jones, and the elf Callon entered the room.

"What the hell did you do to me?"

"Doctor, could the procedure have resulted in brain damage?" Breas brushed a stray lock of his pale blond hair from his cheek and peered in at Emilio.

"Uh. No. Maybe. I- I don't think so."

"Relax, doctor. It was sarcasm. My intern figured out what we did to him before his final transformation in the mist. He's playing dumb."

"It's slightly less hideous than the last one." Callon leaned against the door with a wrinkled nose.

Breas's smirk widened. "Don't be such a snob, Callon. He's breathtaking. I can't wait to see what he can do." He tilted his head toward his shoulder with an up-ticked eyebrow. "And this 'Harper' you kept hollering about in your sleep wouldn't be the same Harper O'Neill we've been searching for, would it?"

Emilio dropped his chin to hide his reaction. Whatever horrors were forthcoming could only be worsened if they confirmed he knew Harper.

Breas adopted a languid posture. "Your reaction told me all I need to know. This revelation doesn't change anything now, but Badb will be delighted to know we have a proverbial ace up our sleeve where it comes to the heir."

The doctor pushed his glasses back up the bridge of his nose while thin, shaking fingers struggled to line up a silver key in the latch. "Stay away from me!" Emilio kicked the cage door and bellowed a string of obscenities at his captors. The doctor staggered back, dropping the key.

Breas dragged over a wheeled chair and lowered himself into it. He rolled close to the cage and peered at Emilio through the bars. "I'm disappointed in you. Where's your scientific curiosity? Your awe at what we've achieved together? You've even saved the doctor's life today." Breas swiveled his head toward the doctor, who knelt on the floor, fumbling around for both his glasses and the dropped key.

"G- got it." Dr. Jones stood and smoothed his lab coat with a flick of his eyes to Callon before trying the lock again.

"Fuck you!" Emilio pummeled the cage door with his throbbing feet.

"Have it your way." Breas beckoned Callon.

The lights gleamed along his obsidian armor as he strode toward Emilio, flowing red fabric sweeping the floor as he knelt. Emilio's lips drew up, revealing his teeth, and he tracked the crisscross of black scars that marked the Sidhe's time in the dying Underworld. The fading away of gnarled flesh coincided with a warm tingling feeling. Emilio's face softened, and he exhaled in ecstasy, hoping for a kind word from Callon.

"There, Dr. Jones. You see, he can be reasonable."

Dr. Jones didn't seem very certain of that. His trembling fingers turned the key. The door swung open, and the scientist leapt backward in case of attack.

Somewhere in the depths of his consciousness, a voice whispered to Emilio to push back. His life depended on it. The beautiful man before him was dangerous. He shuddered and forced his head to the floor. Visual contact broken, the glamour drained from him fast. He scraped together all the willpower he could muster and shoved at the sweet tendrils of control snaking through his thoughts.

"Stay out of my mind," Emilio bellowed.

"Callon. Quickly." Breas wheeled himself back to a safe distance.

Rough hands grabbed Emilio's feathered hair and jerked his head up. A gasp escaped Callon when he noticed the blood trickling from his gloved hand, but his surprise didn't slow him down. In one fluid move, the elf jammed what felt like a metal collar around Emilio's neck and clicked it shut at the front of his neck.

"Remarkable." Dr. Jones overcame his fear and bent near the prison. "His feathers actually are metal. Will he be strong enough to fly, I wonder?"

*Wait. Fly?* In his shock, Emilio hadn't fully thought through the implication of feathers sprouting through his hair and along parts of his body. Wings. That was what he felt growing beside his arms. Of course, things with feathers had wings. An instinctive hand shot over his shoulder to his back and found exactly what he feared. From where his shoulder blades should be, bleeding hands found a new joint as thick as his arms and covered in more razor-sharp feathers. Emilio had grown wings.

He gulped hard and reached his hands to his neck. Whatever Callon had put on him couldn't be good. Sliding his fingertips between the metal and his skin, he pulled and instantly regretted it. Every nerve in his body caught fire. As soon as he released the band, the pain stopped.

High musical laughter focused his attention on that arrogant jerk, Callon.

"Oh, do try that again. I'll forever cherish the look on your half-breed face," the elf said.

"Enough, Callon. I think it's time to see what skills our intern and his friends possess. Badb awaits us on the training grounds." Breas pushed off the desk and rolled his chair back to the cage, just like an adolescent would. "Emilio, let's take a little walk."

"Bite me. I'm not going anywhere with you."

"Oh, I think you will."

Breas nodded at Callon. A radiant smile spread over the Sidhe's face. Long fingers reached toward Emilio, then twisted into a fist. He didn't want to scream. His enemies enjoyed it too much, but he did. Over and over again. The fire he felt when he'd touched the collar paled compared to this.

Aquamarine cuffs peeked out from charcoal sleeves as Breas held up a hand. Callon unclenched his fist, and the agony subsided like switching off a faucet. Emilio collapsed, sweating, to the white and gold floor.

"Let's try once more, shall we?" Breas drew himself to his feet and stood at his full, imposing height. When he spoke, each word was measured, calm, but with an edge that left no room for negotiation. "Emilio, shall we take a walk?"

Dr. Jones scurried away from the cage door, allowing space for Emilio to crawl out on his hands and knees. In his peripheral vision, he caught the smirk on Callon's face and the way he looked down his nose at him. Could he close the distance between them and take a swipe before white-hot agony seized him? He didn't believe so. The only remaining option was to do as he was told.

Breas walked a slow revolution around his prize. "You are right, Dr. Jones. He really is remarkable."

Emilio pressed his lips together and stared straight ahead, eyes unfocused.

"It's an abomination. Neither Fae nor human." Callon folded his arms across his chest, teeth bared.

Breas shot the Sidhe an exasperated look. "Come, Emilio, see what you've become." Breas's hand hovered at Emilio's elbow. The other gestured toward a cabinet with a mirrored back filled with glassware.

Emilio wasn't certain he wanted to see himself; visual confirmation threatened to make it all too real. So he withdrew a step, preferring his tenuous grasp on sanity.

"Come now, what's done is done. There's no avoiding it."

His former boss had a point. Might as well tear the band-aid off all at once. Hey, if he lost his mind, perhaps none of this would matter to him anymore. He'd spend his days gibbering in the corner, blissfully unaware of the surrounding horror show.

Clenching his fists, arms held stiff at his sides, he willed himself to step to the side and examine the image of himself behind test tubes and flasks.

"Oh God, no." Emilio's hands dragged trails down his cheeks. He turned, shoulders hunched, and choked back more screams.

"At least it knows it's a horror." Callon spat the last word.

"I- I think he's beautiful," Dr. Jones said.

"Oh my God, what am I?" Emilio forced each word out between hitching breaths.

The doctor scurried over to stand next to him. His smile stretched ear to ear. "If I had to guess, I'd say you're now part human and part Alicanto, a metal avian cryptid. Dr. Chan is going to owe me dinner. I hypothesized that the Fae markers in your DNA would contain the same regional differences that make your skin brown and your hair black. He thought it would be random. You are clearly from Latin America somewhere, and so is the magical part of you. The Alicanto is from Chile. The others have shown a similar—"

"Fix this. Change me back." Emilio grabbed Dr. Jones by the lapels, eyes darting about the room. A second of agony forced him to recede. Callon stepped near with his fist clenched. Emilio raised his hands, and the pain stopped.

Breas towered a full foot taller than Emilio. Even behind his experiment, his head showed fully in the reflection. He swept a hand to the mirrored cabinet. "Why would you want to return to being an ordinary human?"

Emilio looked into his own alien eyes from across the room. Instead of dark brown, the eyes looking back were tan, with a bright red ring, and they perched over features which had become slightly elongated and sharper. The blue streak in his hair contrasted with the long gunmetal feathers that now carpeted his scalp. Shorter feathers capped his shoulders, hanging over the white tank top he still wore. A thick carpet of them blanketed the back of his neck and back. But most shocking of all were the wing joints, indicating a massive pair of wings grew from his shoulder blades.

Only part of his reflection showed in the cabinet. He lowered his head to examine the rest. Feathers the length of swords, and every bit as sharp, nearly reached the floor. Next to his wingtips, he noted his toes had become slightly scaled and terminated in serrated toenails.

"Ouch!" He smacked a hand over his neck reflexively.

Breas hovered at his left shoulder, holding a gleaming feather. A bright red line flowered beneath his thumb when he dragged the edge across it.

"Amazing." He passed the feather to Dr. Jones. "We must not keep Badb waiting. Come." Breas strode to the door and held it open for Emilio.

When he failed to follow, Callon approached and leaned in close, nose crinkled. "Give me a reason, freak."

No other choice left to him, Emilio trailed Breas into the hallway, followed by the elf. Every Sidhe, redcap, human, and goblin bustling about the halls stopped and stared when the trio walked past. Slack jaws and whispers chased him through the building. Breas led them out the east exit, and along a path bristling with trees straight out of the Halloween store. In a few minutes, the group emerged into a grassy clearing, and Emilio gaped.

Badb paced in front of a contingent of redcaps and elves who had led their own hybrid guests to the field. Each prisoner was clad in the same white tank top, blue-green medical scrub bottoms, and ornate bronze collars with a sparkling red stone in the middle. Badb smiled as she examined her new recruits, running her hand along the purple, flower-filled hair of Tamika, who hunched, wide-eyed and shaking, looking almost unaware of her surroundings.

Tamika Sani had transformed into something of surpassing beauty. Her deep black skin now gleamed with a midnight blue sheen. Almond-shape, deep purple eyes matched her voluminous curling hair, which had sprouted purple, pink, and blue flowers of many species, blooming and closing incessantly. Tamika had grown wings also, wide butterfly wings blue at the top, fading through orange and settling into a bright pink at the bottom.

Next to her, Emilio guessed it was Alan who cowered, his back turned partway to the ring of Fae. The middle-aged accountant had morphed into some species of tree Fae. Skin like birch bark, grey hair, and a new flowing beard that appeared to be more moss than hair. Short horns of branches grew over each brow. Too-long arms ended in curved claws.

"Selina? Is that you?" Emilio shouted across the clearing.

"Emilio! You survived."

His friend's smile looked alien on her predatory new features. Emilio had always been comforted by Selina's round, matronly face. She reminded him a lot of his grandmother. The countenance that greeted him now showed little hint of softness. Pale blue skin covered her body, still pudgy but emanating a superhuman strength. He waited about ten feet from her, but even at that distance, her pale-yellow eyes, ringed in red, pierced the air. It was the teeth that were the most out of place. Long and sharp, like a mouth full of blades. Large, pointed batlike ears rose above her black curls, the only feature of the old Selina still fully intact. The skin of her arms faded from that pale blue to a deep red and ended in claws.

She tossed her curls and shrugged. "I look better than you, Harvey Birdman."

Emilio laughed in spite of himself. She'd been kidnapped and experimented on the same as them, but she never lost her sarcastic wit. Her warm smile clashed with the predatory shape of her new body.

"Look who's talking, Vampirella."

"Hey! You're close. Looks like my Romanian side is also my Fae side. They made me part strigoi." The corners of her mouth curved down. "Jerome didn't make it."

Tamika's wings flitted, and she turned away.

A lump formed in Emilio's throat. Jerome had been a gentle giant. At least now he was at peace.

"Silence," Badb yelled. "This is not a reunion. We're here to measure your strength and see if all this trouble has been worth it."

Callon shoved Emilio into the center of the circle of Fae beside his friends.

Badb's porcelain features pulled into a smile that failed to touch her eyes. "The best way to discover what you're made of is to see how you fare in battle. Attack!"

In a flash, blades were drawn and a battalion of various Fae rushed the quartet.

CHAPTER 12

Shock froze Harper, and she wavered, staring down at Gwyn's prone form, breath stalled in her throat. Her mind stubbornly refused to catch up. The white gleam of the mask glinted, and she clambered a safe distance from the leader of the Wild Hunt.

"Phooka? Paegrinn?" She stumbled in a circle, scanning for any sign of her friends, but her only companion was Gwyn.

He'd rescued her from a literal fate worse than death. From Donn, who was supposed to be working on the same side, with the same objective: to deliver her to Badb Catha. In a mystifyingly dramatic move, Gwyn had pushed himself past his limits to prevent Donn draining her soul. Probably only because Donn was an out-of-control psycho killing the prize Badb needed alive, at least initially.

Evil always turns against itself. Either a line from the Bible or one of the Phooka's movie quotes.

The Phooka. He, Paegrinn, and their new friend had found her, and thanks to Gwyn's prodigious feats of sorcery, she was lost again. No trail to lead the Phooka to her side, because she was pretty sure whatever magic Gwyn had cast to warp them here left

89

no evidence of passage. Warp was the best word for the sensation that still stirred her head rush. They'd remained stationary and the woods had simply shifted around them, depositing them here.

She revolved slowly in place, relief sagging her shoulders. Mist snaked along the ground, but it was wispy thin. And the trees were towering Douglas fir with their acrid, fresh scent. Beneath thick bristled boughs, verdant undergrowth shed its leaves, littering the earth with yellow and orange debris. None of the dark, gnarled trunks or the spiked bushes smothering the island grew here. Almost like this patch had yet to be swallowed up by the magic transforming Sauvie Island.

Her gaze fell back to Gwyn, and unfamiliar emotions bubbled to the surface. With a soft exhale, her head tilted to the side and she let her eyes trace the contours of his face, recalling the gentleness in his voice before he'd swept them here. At rest and devoid of brooding and malice, he emanated a rugged handsomeness.

If Donn spoke the truth, Gwyn had surrendered his freedom to save as much of humanity as he could. It must have driven him crazy watching their spirits obliterated to slake Donn's bottomless appetite when he'd sacrificed to keep them safe. Lying there in a heap, he just looked alone and vulnerable. She inched toward him, fingertips trailing down her neck while her eyebrows drew together.

She pinched her forehead and squeezed her eyes shut before retreating. Second-guessing the enemy's motives was a dumb move. Letting her guard down could cost everyone she cared about. To banish the warm, uncomfortable emotions toward him that brewed inside her, Harper conjured an image of Gwyn standing over Nuada's lifeless body. *I think they call this Stockholm Syndrome. He's not your friend. He didn't really save you, and he'll hand you over to Badb the first chance he gets.*

*Only because he has to.*

The Wild Hunt's master did not stir. An awful thought formed in Harper's mind. Now was her opportunity to level the playing field. Probably the only one she'd get.

She lunged toward his prone form and snatched up his sword. Since hers refused to leave the scabbard, his would have to do. Harper poised over him, blade clenched in both hands, tip pointed at his heart. With a strangled cry, she plunged the weapon down.

And pulled back an inch from his body. Her eyes traveled the path of the blue spiral tattoo beneath his eye like she walked a labyrinth. The sword trembled in her grip. He was defenseless. All she had to do was drive the blade into his chest and one of her most powerful enemies was dead. Her chances to set Emilio free and keep her mother safe increased with the death of Gwyn ap Nudd.

With a yell, she brought the blade back up to its high start, ready to end his life. No one deserved it more than he did.

*He was a good man, once.* The Phooka's words echoed through her thoughts along with memories of Gwyn reassuring her about the Fir Bolg and her mother's safety. Nuada had believed there was good still in his heart, but he had little choice. This monster was his son.

She squinted at his face, the sword still hovering over his ribcage. His masked presence was the monster that invaded her dreams, but now he seemed small and profoundly alone, like Harper had been for so long. The deepest irony was the shared understanding she'd yearned for that she'd glimpsed in her enemy's wistful, copper-flecked eyes.

She couldn't force herself to do it. If she skewered him while he was defenseless, she'd be no better than he was.

Her gaze fell on the grisly antlered mask lying next to him. With a choked yell, she swung the sword and smashed it into the mask. It broke into three large pieces. Gwyn still did not stir.

With the flat of the sword she bashed at the mask, pulverizing it. Then she went to work on the horns. Her booted foot stomped them. Over and over, she smashed her feet into them until only fragments remained. It might still haunt her nightmares, but she'd denied Gwyn his hiding place.

The Phooka's voice played in her mind, telling her how deeply she'd regret leaving him alive. "I'm nothing like them." She said it aloud.

Gwyn shifted, and Harper's spine shot ramrod straight, heart racing. She swung his sword to face its former master, who still slumbered. But for how much longer?

Time to put some distance between them. Eventually, the rest of the Wild Hunt would come for him, or the Sluagh would. She needed to be far from this clearing when that happened, and she needed to find her friends.

She took a moment to work the Sword of Light through a strap on the outside of her pack and clipped it in place with a carabiner. She kept Gwyn's weapon in hand as she absently bent down and pulled his coat more fully over him, like she always did when she discovered her mom passed out on the couch. Then she loped into the woods toward the sun still climbing in the east.

As soon as Gwyn was out of sight, she leaned on a tree, the chill autumn air burning the back of her throat. She was utterly screwed. Lost. No clue where to go next or what to do when she miraculously found Badb's tower.

For her to save Emilio, a string of events needed to happen, each less probable than the last. Get herself unlost, rally her friends, find Emilio, then pray either her sword would decide to obey or she'd become angry enough to go nuclear with her sorcery. More likely, she'd bumble around in these twisted woods for weeks, starving or stumbling upon some new breed of Fae that would eat her brains or something.

She ambled through the mix of pines and dark trees, warming herself with visions of her eventual triumph and revenge against

Badb Catha, until a familiar sight sucked the wind from her proverbial sails.

Gwyn ap Nudd lay on his side twenty feet ahead, the remnants of his shattered mask shining in the light. Not again. She cursed and kicked a fir tree.

A series of high, clear howls rose in the distance. She recognized their mournful sound. Gwyn's hounds. Leave it to those spectral demons to be one of the few creatures who could navigate this island without being led in circles.

Harper slid Gwyn's sword free and inched away until undergrowth hid him. Ascending a low rise afforded as much high ground as was available. Any moment she'd be fighting a pack of wild ghost dogs alone.

Another string of howls came from the west. Very close.

A hand clamped over her mouth and stifled her scream.

"Shut up unless you want to be a Scooby snack," whispered a voice with a thick Jamaican accent.

Harper pulled her head around and strained her eyes behind her. Paegrinn and Melinoe crouched behind a pair of wide tree trunks. She relaxed and the deep brown hand came away from her mouth.

"Phooka, you found me. How..." Harper shook her head.

Melinoe tapped her nose. "The Cwn Anwyn, Gabriel hounds you call them, always find their master, and we pursued them. I'm about the best tracker in the three worlds." She tapped her upturned nose again and beamed.

Paegrinn grunted. "We better go. Those dogs are close."

# CHAPTER 13

A tornado of teeth, claws, and swords lashed them from every direction. Emilio's new body shifted into autopilot. He squatted, kicked against the earth with his shining gunmetal wings unfurled, and flapped, ascending a dozen feet. A cluster of dripping human form kelpies squelched toward Tamika, baring sharp canines. She screamed and staggered, cowering.

"Tamika!" Emilio shouted to her and pointed at her colorful butterfly wings.

Her body must have taken over just like Emilio's did. Gossamer wings beat so fast they became a bright blur, and Tamika glided, weaving side to side like she fought to control her new talent.

"Higher," Emilio said once Tamika's zig-zagging flight leveled off. She wobbled a bit, fingers grasping at thin air, and nodded. The pair cut a wavering line through the sky as they strove higher. In seconds, he smashed into an invisible barrier.

"Ow!" Emilio barked while Tamika dipped low, avoiding a similar crash.

"What the hell?" Tamika's purple eyes flicked up.

"Must be some kind of barrier." Emilio lifted a hand overhead and pushed on something smooth like glass. Solid.

"Guess we're not flying out of here, then."

Emilio shook his head. "Not without them, anyway." Alan had tried loping away, and a gaggle of redcaps swarmed in his wake.

Tamika pointed at his neck. "You got one too."

Emilio nodded. "We all did. You try to tear it off?"

"Yeah." She shuddered.

Beneath them, their earthbound companions were having a harder time evading their Fae attackers. Alan whimpered when he careened into a trio of elves, and Selina maintained a broad stance, using her claws to swipe at advancing redcaps. Several of the little Fae clutched bleeding gashes, yet they still attacked because Badb priced failure high. Selina was tough; Emilio trusted she could hold her own.

Alan bellowed, and Emilio tore his attention away from Selina. One elf had sliced his shoulder open while another dove for his legs. In seconds, his rough, bark-like skin was covered in cuts. Not deep enough for damage, but deep enough to hurt. Emilio doubted Badb would allow the Fae to harm them, but Alan might not have connected those dots. The poor guy was an accountant from the suburbs and had been in a state of shock since their arrival. He'd only been at Mystic Island to watch over his daughter and her friends. He lacked Selina's history with the Fae, or Tamika and his own exposure to the toughening battles that came with poverty. Emilio had to help.

"We're about to have unwanted guests." Tamika's eyes were saucers, and she fluttered away from a line of sylphs with swords drawn, launching themselves into the sky.

"I'm coming, Alan," he called, then turned to Tamika, who hovered, airborne, in a state of shock. "Still probably safest in the air. From the looks of them, you're faster. Stay up as long as you can."

He recalled from watching videos on *Animal Planet* that when birds wanted to dive fast, they pointed their heads down and folded their wings tight along their bodies. So he did that. And instantly regretted it. The ground rushed up at his face at lightning speed. He panicked and spread his wings again. The sudden halt to his descent popped his back.

His initial trajectory would have landed too far from Alan to be much help, so he changed his approach, soaring above his friend. He pointed his feet down, half folded his wings, then unfurled them to land between Alan and the elves. *How can I even know how to do this?*

Badb, Breas, Callon, and Dr. Jones observed a few feet away, attended by a handful of shabby, blissed-out humans.

The tallest of the elves, a young man with a short sword in each hand, stalked Emilio, a fierce smile on his face. His friends, two women, advanced behind him, blades drawn, black hair trailing in the breeze.

"Emilio, what's happening?" Alan pulled at strands of green beard to examine them. The man was quaking.

"They're testing us, I think."

Alan wasn't focused on their attackers. He held his branchlike hands up to his face. "They changed—"

Emilio flinched. He had no weapon. The tall elf lunged and swept his blade toward him. Emilio whipped his wing across his body like a shield. Sparks flew when the sword slammed into the longest feathers and slid down harmlessly. Emilio laughed out loud. He wasn't weaponless, after all. Dozens of swords bristled from his wings.

Alan cringed behind him while Emilio curved a wing over his friend and faced off against two women.

"I must admit, they are more than I'd hoped." The silky tones of Badb's voice was its own edged weapon as she and her retinue ambled a slow path through the fight.

Emilio was close enough to hear the smile in Breas's voice. "Emilio, the feathered one, is the strongest of all. He'll become a formidable weapon."

"He flies like turtles don't." Callon's voice was dry.

The elves rushed them, but Emilio dropped low, pulling his wings tight. As they neared, he pushed off and flung his wings wide. Flats of feathers smacked against elvish armor with a jangle, knocking them end-over-end.

While their attackers shook off their daze, Emilio focused back on the conversation, wings poised around the gibbering Alan.

"He needs flight training, that's all. Perhaps Zalille can give him some lessons," Breas said.

Badb scowled at the doctor. "But will they be able to glamour and control the human chattel we've collected?"

"Um. Well. I- I- I don't know. This is just their first test." All the color drained from Dr. Jones's face at the flash of Badb's rage. Wind gusts blasted the field with damp, chill air and Badb drew her long black cape tight, refocusing on her experiments.

The pair of elven women recovered, separated, and dove for Alan, joined this time by a kelpie.

The accountant screamed. Emilio leapt backward, bent over him, and swept his wings around the terrified man in a metallic embrace. Thin blades clanged and scraped down his feathers.

Alan curled up in a ball beneath Emilio, in the shelter of his friend's wingspan, and wept. Tears left trails on his birch-bark skin.

Emilio laid a hand on the man's shoulder. "I'm here, Alan."

"Can they change me back? I want to go home." The last word descended into a wailing moan.

"Get the spriggan thing up and make him fight." Badb jabbed a hand at Callon. "I want to see if he's useful."

Callon tossed his long straight hair over his shoulder and advanced on Alan and Emilio. Oh, how Emilio wanted to punch the haughty smile off the elf's face. Emilio's old bullies had tormented him because being gay made him different. His new bully hated him because of what Breas and Dr. Jones had turned him into. Both things were out of his control.

"Watch out, Emilio," Selina called, digging her claws into a pair of redcaps who'd strayed from their cluster. They'd be soaking their caps in their own blood tonight.

"I see him." He glanced up to mark Tamika's location. As close to the invisible barrier as possible, she led the sylphs on a chase.

This was wrong. What they had done to them was wrong. Ambushing them and forcing them to fight was wrong. Emilio's jaw clenched and unclenched in time with his fists. He wanted to slice Breas and Badb with his razor-sharp wings, but he doubted the choker would let him get that far. Impotent rage simmered beneath his skin. He moved to cover Alan, wings spread wide, ready to slice Callon to ribbons if necessary.

But isn't that what they wanted? They'd forged them to add to the comparatively small size of their army relative to the human population. The very last thing he desired was to give any of these evil monsters a single thing they desired.

Time to be Ghandi.

"Everyone!" Emilio shouted. "They want us to fight, but they're not harming us. If we give them what they want, this will never end."

Every sword, claw, and fireball-filled hand paused as they all turned to see the man—well, creature—who shouted.

"They'll kill us, Emilio," Alan moaned through his tears.

"They won't harm us. Look at the lengths they went to make us. We're more valuable than even him." Emilio pointed right at Callon. Then he crossed his wings at his back and squatted.

"He's right," Selina called up to Tamika and sat beside Emilio, her arms resting on her rotund stomach.

Tamika snapped out of her daze and sank from the sky to sit on her shins next to Selina. Even Alan pushed himself from his side to sit cross-legged and cross-armed in line with his friends.

Breas edged a few steps from Badb, who paced, fuming, beside him.

"Bad move, my young intern. If you won't fight, they'll just kill you." The button on his shiny grey suit jacket fell open as he swept a hand over the Fae surrounding the four friends.

Emilio noticed Alan's resolve falter, and Tamika twisted her hands in her lap. He thrust his chin out. "No, you won't. No way you'd risk damaging us. I'm betting there's a lot riding on Project Abraxas being a success. Besides, you'll hurt us either way, through fighting or through torture. And I, for one, don't want to become a killer like you. So piss off."

The Fae gnashed their teeth and brandished their swords, just waiting for a signal from their masters. Emilio filled with pride when his friends lifted their heads and straightened their backs. Even Alan.

Badb held up a pale hand, and silence descended. The Tuatha marched through her ranks to tower over Emilio. Her red hair swirled like a crackling fire. Emilio's heart pounded even harder at her approach. The woman radiated power.

She dropped to a knee and grabbed his neck. Sharp nails dug into his skin and drew blood. "Oh, how you're going to regret this." As she stood, she opened her palm and the scarlet gems in the center of their chokers blazed with light. She snapped her fingers closed, and the agony began.

The quartet screamed and writhed, clawing at their necks, arching their backs. Badb opened her hand, and the misery ceased. A shiny black boot rested against Emilio's neck. Reflex sent his hands to tear at her foot.

Badb's hair brushed across his face when she bent to peer at him. "Fight. Now." Blood-red lips pressed into a thin line. She lifted her foot so he could speak.

"Fuck. You." Pressure intensified on his trachea so he couldn't finish his sentence. But he finished it in his mind. *Bitch.*

She scanned the faces of the other three. "The rest of you. Get up and fight."

"Or what? More pain? Seems that comes either way. So I second Emilio's fuck you." Selina turned her head and spat. Tamika nodded, wide-eyed.

The collars flared bright, and the quartet seized again, limbs flailing while they howled and clawed at their throats. It felt like lava and needles and electricity all at once. His body took on a life of its own, jerking and spasming, feathers slicing into his flesh, mending as quickly as they sprang. That bought a reprieve.

Badb flipped her palm back over, and the pain stopped. She bent over Emilio again and jammed her boot on his neck, creating a cracking sound in his trachea. "Breas, this one has accelerated healing. Even faster than the Sidhe. Interesting." Reaching a hand to his shoulder, she plucked a metal feather, and then drew it across his bare shoulder. She smiled when the skin sealed before her eyes.

"Yes, I imagine that's good, or he'd bleed to death walking down the street," Breas said over her shoulder. He clasped his hands behind his back and tilted forward slightly, examining Emilio like the experiment he was.

Badb lifted her foot. Emilio rubbed his aching throat, but the throbbing persisted, suggesting internal damage healed more slowly.

Badb clapped and pointed to the cluster of starry-eyed human servants. Callon nodded, grabbed a woman by the elbow, and dragged her toward his mistress. The middle-aged woman didn't struggle, just plodded along behind Callon, the same blissful expression on her face as before.

Emilio thought she couldn't be more than about forty, but the evidence of a hard life had etched itself on her features. Stringy brown hair hung over her cheeks, and she wore the same tank top and green scrubs combo they all did.

The instant the poor woman reached them, Badb clutched her by the throat. The glamour faded from the woman, and her eyes rolled. Gurgling half yells squeezed from her open mouth.

Emilio tried to stand, but Breas kicked his legs from under him. "Such a disappointment, my young intern. I thought you'd learn faster than this."

A piercing laugh rang from parted red lips. "Well, Emilio." Badb flexed the hand around her prey's throat, eliciting another string of choked moans. "You seem to enjoy playing the savior. Since you won't fight on threat to your own well-being, perhaps saving these wretched souls will inspire you to explore your new talents."

Emilio gathered his knees beneath him, eyes flashing. He pushed himself to his feet, but the gloved hand of Callon forced him back to his knees and pushed him low.

"Kneel before your queen."

Badb pulled the woman inches from where Emilio knelt. From beneath her cloak, she pulled out a long dagger and plunged it into the screaming woman's midsection, drawing a jagged line from one side to the other. Emilio's stomach clenched. The metallic scent of blood mixed with the putrid stench of intestines. The screaming was unbearable. He slapped his hands over his ears, his own blood seeping between his fingers when feather met flesh.

Badb released her grip on the poor woman's throat and she collapsed with a thud, bleeding out in front of Emilio. Callon's pushed Emilio's face inches from the dying woman and held him there.

"I'm so sorry," he whispered, tears streaming from his eyes. "I'm so, so, sorry." He reached a hand out to cup her face, the only small comfort he could offer her as she died. A tortured yell tore from his throat. He might as well have killed her himself. What was he thinking to stand against these demons?

Badb kicked the dead woman aside and gripped Emilio's chin. Wrenching his face up to hers, she shouted so that the others could hear. "This is the cost of disobedience. For every hour you refuse to fight, another dies."

# CHAPTER 14

Emilio's thoughts slowed to a crawl and narrowed to a single notion. *My fault. My fault.* The woman's brown eyes stared into the sky, empty. Her hair spilled around her in looping coils while her blood spread along the ground, soaking into Emilio's pants. He wondered if she had children, people who missed her. That thought wrenched another tortured grunt from his burning throat. Callon gripped his shoulder like a vise, forcing him to remain close to the body. *I caused this. All my fault.*

"This is not your fault," Selina whispered to his right.

Badb sneered. "Oh, but it is."

"You murdered this poor soul yourself. Emilio did nothing." Selina's fiery response earned her a backhand from her guard, a muscular elven woman, her shining hair in a high bun.

Emilio barely registered the exchange. The fallen vagrant captivated his attention while the ringing and rushing in his ears muddled all other sounds.

From his left, Alan nudged him with his shoulder. The half-tree man hovered at the end of a dark tunnel. Alan widened his eyes, glanced at Badb, then shrugged his shoulders like he was waiting for direction from Emilio. For his part, Emilio thought his leadership served pretty much to just get people killed. Alan misplaced his trust. Despite his failures, his friends all looked at him, foreheads creased with concern. He'd never understand why, but they waited for his direction. Refusal to fight had been his idea. If he didn't shake off his paralysis, what came next could be worse.

At a slow nod to them, their bearings uncoiled and their eyes narrowed. Except Alan. He hunched over his knees, eyes roving around the clearing, panting. He wouldn't be much help unless Emilio could steel his nerves. Hell, calming his own was taking everything he had.

"I trust they're ready to fight now. Get them up."

Elves hauled the quartet up and shoved them toward the middle of the training grounds. The feel of his feet rolling over the springy grass grounded Emilio back in the present. With each staggering footfall, his vision brightened. On either side of him, his friends marched, fear on their faces. Each of them risked furtive glances at him, but it was Selina who broke the silence.

She moved to adjust the drawstring on her pants, whispering in Emilio's ear. "The only power we have now is keeping as much secret as possible."

They arrived at the broad, treeless clearing. Every elf except Callon settled into attack positions a few yards out in a ring around them. Badb, Breas, and their retinue clustered at the edge of the training grounds. The remaining six human servants stood next to Badb, all wearing identical dreamy smiles, while the dark lady poised with her blade, ready to strike them down.

"You will fight or we'll slay them one by one." Callon's grip on Emilio's arm tightened, forcing a grimace. "Personally, I hope you don't because more stinking humans will die, and perhaps my lady would let me exterminate whatever you are. You..." He searched for a word. "You... *Netherfae*." Callon gave Emilio a hard shove before strutting back to his Sidhe entourage.

Netherfae. Callon might have meant it as an insult, but it was as good a name as any for what they'd become. Not human anymore, not quite Fae either.

"What do we do, Emilio?" Tamika asked in her newly musical voice, like flutes and harps all at once.

His companions' expectant faces brought a cold sweat to his body. Selina's suggestion was wise. They had to fight the elves to keep more human prisoners from a grisly death. But if the Fae underestimated their creations, that might benefit their next escape plan, or yield a way to break the control the Fae had over their captives. Just like his grandmother taught him in their flight from the cartels in El Salvador, you looked after each other, all escaped together.

And the Buddha said to live in the present. The power to help his new family was in the here and now. Whether Emilio's transformation was permanent or if they'd ever escape from their tormentors were questions for another day.

Suddenly, Badb Catha and this entire island of monsters seemed less frightening. They might look terrifying and have formidable powers, but at the core they didn't differ from the gun-toting cartels that tore apart his home country. Warring factions fighting for dominance, and they didn't care who they hurt to do it. Badb's tactics weren't really that different. She was just a thug with a horned headdress and shiny black leather clothing.

"Okay. Selina is right. Our power lies in keeping any magic or enhanced abilities secret." He spoke in hushed tones. "Avoid their attacks if you can. Fight them only defensively. If magic surges up in you, or you think you can move super fast like the Flash, reel it in. When we get out of here for real, surprising them with just how strong we are may be our only shot."

The other three nodded, eagerness lifting their shoulders.

"Time grows short," Badb shouted, another human victim already kneeling before her drawn weapon.

"Don't hurt them. We'll fight." Beside him, Selina flexed her clawed hands. Alan and Tamika pressed as near as possible to Emilio without being sliced by razor-sharp feathers. Alan looked bad, like a shellshocked civilian in a war zone. Emilio leaned into him. "Stay close to me, I'll protect you." The poor man's saucer eyes had become a startling shade of green with no pupil, but he nodded and managed a half smile, more grimace than grin.

"What if they kill us?" Alan's voice cracked.

Selina's voice was almost a growl. "They won't. Remember, we're too valuable. More valuable than those elves. Those malicious assholes will try to hurt us though."

Alan swallowed hard. The ring of elves burst toward the Netherfae, weapons drawn as though they'd failed to read the memo about not killing the experiments.

Tamika responded first. She sprang into the air, bright wings humming. Emilio desperately wanted to join her, but he'd promised Alan he'd look after him. He spread his arms and wings wide, Selina at his back and Alan safely between them. Their attackers focused on Selina, while Emilio kept Alan safe by flicking a metal wing at any elf who came near.

Selina gnashed her pointed teeth and charged one of the approaching Sidhe, the woman with the high bun wielding a short staff with a blade at each end. The elf leapt, the staff sweeping an arc aimed at Selina's chest. At the last second, Selina dove under the weapon like she was sliding into first. Then she changed momentum, flipped into a low crouch facing the elf's back, and walloped her hard between the shoulder blades. The elf fell forward, face hitting the ground with a thud, and she sprawled motionless, out cold.

Two men rushed Emilio, a short sword in each hand. He pulled Alan toward his chest and swept his wings around them again and let the blades clatter harmlessly against his feathers. Sparks showered the elves.

Foolishly, the arrogant bastards pressed close. Emilio smiled at Alan. "Watch this, my friend, it worked great before." With a yell, he launched himself to his feet while he hurled his wings outward with as much force as he could muster. Elves flew, whamming into the earth flat on their backs.

"Hah! Nice one!" Tamika shouted above him.

An elven woman, long braids swinging over each shoulder, glared up at Tamika. Glowing hands sent fireballs slicing toward the winged Netherfae. Tamika shrieked and dodged the first two. The third caught her leg, leaving a blistering burn. Howling, she lost altitude. The elf leapt straight up. A gloved fist coiled around Tamika's shimmering ankle and yanked her from the sky. The Sidhe loomed over Tamika, another fireball simmering in her upturned palm.

Alan bellowed and extended a hand toward his fallen friend. Eyes widened. Jaws dropped. The accountant's branchlike arm stretched and kept stretching. Fingers became whiplike appendages that lashed the spellcaster's face, leaving trails of red. Other vines smacked weapons out of the grip of anyone near Tamika.

Tamika smiled at him and picked up a thin blade knocked from the Sidhe's hands.

Emilio shot him his most reassuring smile. "Great work, Alan."

Elves already advanced on Alan, since he'd proven to be a bigger threat than Tamika. Emilio curled his wings close to his friend. "Come on, get yourself a taste, monsters." He rattled his wings.

The battle continued like this for several minutes. They avoided as many attacks as possible and defended where they could. Selina had been correct. The Fae inflicted a scratch here, a bruise there, enough to hurt but no lasting damage.

Badb drew a finger across her throat. The elves halted their assault and stepped back from the Netherfae.

Breas swaggered onto the field and approached Emilio.

"You know, my young intern, I feel like none of you are really trying."

"We're not warriors." Selina pointed at Alan. "He's an accountant."

"But the parlor tricks you've shown suggest you are powerful. Or at least you'd better hope you are. The warrior part will come with training."

"I hated Phys. Ed. I'll skip that," Tamika said.

In answer, the gems at the center of their collars flared to life and gave each of them a jolt of pain. Alan gibbered. Emilio placed a hand on the man's tree bark shoulder as Badb moved to join Breas.

"I think these four require more incentive to take their first training session more seriously."

"What do you have in mind?"

A finger tapped the bottom of full ruby lips. "Time is short. I need our army ready to wage war in weeks, not months or years. Placing our cattle in harm's way motivated them to fight. I wonder if they'd engage more fully in defense of them."

A wolfish smile briefly bloomed on Breas's face. Then he sighed and shook his head. "Motivating the workforce is the perennial problem of a CEO. We tried the stick. Perhaps the carrot will inspire a more vigorous display."

Badb waved to Callon. He nodded and herded the remaining human servants to the middle of the field. At a nod from him, the elves drew their weapons and aimed them at the people.

"My warriors, you may kill as many as you'd like, on my signal." A mirthless laugh punctuated Badb's command.

Emilio's jaw dropped along with his heart. There must be a dozen elves and only four of them, well, three. Paralysis had a vice grip on poor Alan. The blissed-out cluster of six humans didn't stand a chance.

"We have to defend them, but remember the second part of our plan," Emilio whispered, hoping his friends would catch his drift but that his enemies would not.

"And what plan is that?" Badb asked.

"To kick your ass if we get the chance."

Badb laughed. "Impudent little fool." The Tuatha merely pointed at the collar at his neck. She looked past him to her warriors. "Now." Her tone was matter of fact.

The Sidhe rushed for the humans. Tamika and Emilio threw themselves at the sky and raced to intervene. Even Alan shook off his stupor and loped to stand between the elves and the prisoners, all eerily still and smiling at their attackers.

Emilio folded his wings and plummeted, landing in front of two younger prisoners. His wings cut a low arc, biting into the legs of two approaching elves where their armor did not protect them. Both of them fell, screaming and grasping their bleeding calves. It felt good to strike back.

Ahead, Selina shielded a trio of people, weaving herself around every jab and thrust of the elves' black swords. She ducked a high thrust and swung her open clawed hand up under the arm of the elf with the topknot. Blood coursed down the elf's side and her sword arm dangled limp at her side, but what Selina did next disturbed Emilio.

Selina looked like a starving man before a grand buffet. She brought the elf's arm up to her lips and licked the blood from her wrist and fingers. Her yellow eyes glowed red, then she lunged for the Sidhe's companion who was making a run at one of the people. Emilio thought she was fast before; after the grisly snack, she moved with the speed of elves.

Alan threw his head back and bellowed, his shaggy moss beard whipping around him. Emilio followed his pained stare to see

Tamika fall from the sky, surrounded by Sidhe. An elven man lunged for one of the smiling people behind her while Tamika snatched a dropped sword. Tamika flicked the blade up, but the Fae knocked it from her grip.

The accountant roared again. Green shoots and vines exploded from the ground around the elves. As Alan flung his hand to the side, the vines followed and whipped across elven faces and tangled elven legs.

"Enough!" Badb called. "Doctor Jones, your results are most impressive. Breas will procure as many healthy candidates as you require from the local prison."

"T- t- thank you, Majesty." The scientist's glasses dropped off his face when he bowed low.

Breas tilted his head. "I hate to rain on the parade, but unless our creations prove more resilient to the weaknesses of the Fae, they will be of little value. And we have yet to see if they possess the universal Fae skills of glamour. Creating an army of Netherfae —charming name, Callon—is both too costly and too time-consuming for a full-scale assault in human cities. We still need as many regular humans as we can find, and the Netherfae need to have the skills to use them like puppets, like Fae could."

"Well then, Doctor, prepare to test them against known Fae liabilities."

# CHAPTER 15

"I'm glad to see you." Harper stood on tiptoes and threw her arms around the Phooka's neck.

After a moment, she felt long fingers rest on her back.

"Well, with Nuada gone, you're the new Chris Tucker to my Jackie Chan. So I'm glad to see you too."

It was as close to tenderness as the Phooka got.

"Except I'm the one with the martial arts training, and you're the wisecracking loudmouth." Harper drew back and smiled. "When Gwyn did his warping trick, I thought you'd never find me."

The shapeshifter shrank, and the Phooka's natural form replaced the tall black man. "Actually, those wretched dogs found you. We just trailed them." His long ears twitched this way and that, and he stood on the tips of his hooves.

Melinoe exhaled and narrowed her eyes at the Phooka while tapping her nose. "I'm the best tracker in the three worlds, so *I* traced the dogs. You two followed me, technically. Harper, sweetheart, are you okay?"

Harper licked her lips and nodded. "Yeah. Glad you had that trick up your sleeve."

Melinoe's broad grin revealed slightly elongated canine teeth. "The hounds are bound to Gwyn so they always find their master. It was simple, really."

"We better go. Those dogs were close," Paegrinn said quietly.

The Phooka positioned himself between Harper and the glaistig with a frown. "Sasquatch is right. Further reunions can wait until we put more distance between us and those infernal lapdogs. They'll stay with their master, but the rest of the Wild Hunt will follow."

He and the Fir Bolg youth pivoted and strode ahead. Paegrinn, his spear at the ready, constantly scanned the path while the Phooka, dagger in hand, checked the periphery.

Melinoe capered to Harper's side, a beatific smile lighting her features. "Harper, sweetheart, I hope it eases your mind to know everyone at the Fir Bolg village was safe when I left. Your mother's safe and they found Nuada."

"Nuada?" Harper's heart soared. Maybe the Fir Bolg healed him. "He lives?"

"Oh no, sweetie. If the Cauldron of Rebirth is ever located, he could be reborn. He's between—"

The Phooka scampered back to Harper with narrowed eyes directed at the glaistig. "No time for Millennial lallygagging."

Harper nodded at him and rested a palm on Melinoe's shoulder. "That is good news. Perhaps you can share details when we're safe." But Harper already knew her mother and Paegrinn's people had been spared, because Gwyn had done her the kindness of telling her. One of a growing list of contradictions the Tuatha displayed at every turn.

Paegrinn paused near a rise. The Phooka let his hands slap against his thighs with an exaggerated head roll. "This is why you two would be the first to die in a chainsaw massacre. Standing in the open, yakking away while the psycho stalks you and the audience gives a collective facepalm."

"What's going to lead the Wild Hunt to us is your prattling, dark Fae." Melinoe closed her eyes, tilted her chin, and raised both palms toward the cloudy sky.

The Fae's hands glowed with a clear light, and every footprint, each snapped branch that marked their passing, lit up as though marked by a spotlight. One by one, she singled them out, their trail extending beyond sight.

One palm flipped parallel to the earth, and with a sweep the footprints vanished. Blades of grass stretched taller, branches healed, and a scintillating wave like bubbles in soda burned away what Harper presumed were any less-tangible traces of their passage.

The fingertips of Melinoe's other hand twitched and wove. Footprints sank into the dry earth, twigs snapped, and that bubbly trail arced into the forest to Harper's left before returning to its master. "There. Our trail leads in another direction." She minced a snaking path to the Phooka, the magic trailing behind, wiping any trace of their movements. "And we'll leave no evidence of our passage."

The Phooka flapped a dismissive hand. "Light Fae parlor tricks. I feel safe." He scuttled to catch up with Paegrinn.

Harper squinted at the trail. Not a hint that anything had disturbed even a single fallen pine needle. "That's pretty cool."

Melinoe's tawny eyes lit up while she smoothed a long fabric leaf back into place over her leg. "I'll walk behind, keep our passing hidden."

All Harper wanted to do was lie down and sleep for a decade, but she forced herself to trudge after her friends. Listlessness had seeped into every muscle since Donn's attempt to consume her. Only the dull aches and sharper jabs from her injuries kept her alert enough to function now the immediate danger had passed.

It seemed as though they walked for an hour, but Harper guessed it was more likely a few minutes. Screeches and howls echoed from all sides, similar to the banshee's keening but too distant for certainty.

A breeze with barely the strength to disturb a blade of grass caused the trees to overreact. Branches whipped Harper's forearms hard enough to bring long welts, although they failed to touch Paegrinn or the two Fae.

"I hate this place."

The Phooka nodded. "It doesn't seem to like you either."

Harper brushed her sleeves back down over her wrists and resumed lumbering behind the Phooka. The ankle she'd twisted spasmed, and she tumbled down with a yelp. "Shit." Levering herself to her other side, she dragged her leg under her weight to stand, but her thigh muscle quaked and she toppled over.

"Harper!" All three of her companions dropped to their knees beside her.

"I'm fine, guys—"

The Phooka narrowed his golden eyes. "Liar. You're favoring your left foot, and you look ten years older."

"I overextended my ankle trying to escape, and Donn..." How could she explain what the Lord of the Dead had done? "Well, he drained me like he does the Sluagh, but Gwyn sort of saved me, which is why I couldn't kill him back there."

Melinoe's eyebrows shot up. "You left him alive?"

The Phooka smacked his palm on his forehead. "Just great. You know what happens when you leave the minion alive and he escapes, don't you?" When Harper didn't answer, the Phooka wagged a finger in her face. "The big baddie comes and kills us all. I hope you're happy."

Melinoe cocked her ear up toward the trees and eased her sword from its scabbard. "I'll watch the perimeter."

Paegrinn peeled up one of Harper's eyelids while the shapeshifter prodded her ankle.

"Ouch. That's really unnecessary. I'm fine."

"You had part of your soul drained." Paegrinn's hands hovered an inch from her body and he ran them along her core and limbs. "And you've got a cracked rib. We need to get you to a safe place to rest. It'll take time for you to recover."

A dark shape flickered in the corner of Harper's eye, flitting between high branches. "What was that?" she whispered.

Paegrinn and the Phooka rested fingertips on their weapons and scanned the sky. Paegrinn relaxed and pulled his bag across his lap. "I didn't see anything."

"Me either." The Phooka patted Harper's shoulder and stood. "But I trust Princess Sparklehooves as much as I trust politicians and for the same reason. I've got your backs." His shape dissolved and when it reformed, he growled in his favored wolf shape and joined Melinoe's patrol.

Twenty feet away, Melinoe continued her slow revolution around them, dagger drawn, sniffing the air. The glaistig was on alert but not alarmed, so Harper relaxed slightly. Probably just a normal bird. Definitely not Sluagh. Her heart skipped a beat at the image of the ragged avians.

"Eat this," Paegrinn's rumbling, gentle voice commanded as he placed a slice of dried mushroom in her palm. "It will relieve the pain. The mycelium can give you back some of your strength." He pulled off her boot. His eyelids closed and a multitonal drone emanated from his throat.

Harper nodded and popped the medicine into her mouth. Bitter. She stuck out her tongue after she swallowed it.

Filaments thinner than a single hair snaked from the ground, caressing her ankle and pushing between the threads of her clothing to find her injured rib. The bone crackled as the mycelium did its work. Her body sagged and Harper rested her weight on her elbows.

More fuzzy wisps wound around her ribcage. Paegrinn's song shifted to higher tones and rainbow shards of light lifted through the mycelium and tingled as they crossed her skin and brought a pleasant warmth in her chest, chasing away the weariness like light chases shadows. This was the same forest magic that had healed her fractured mother. Harper thought her heart would burst with gratitude to Paegrinn and his people, who'd done so much for her.

Sharp caws and a tornado of wings shattered the moment of peace. *Sluagh. They found us.* Harper shot to her feet with renewed vigor, the delicate mycelium tearing away. She wavered before finding stable footing, still not at full strength but able to fight. Those were definitely crows. Red-eyed crows.

"Badb Catha's personal pets," Melinoe shouted as a black corvid dive-bombed her, meeting the tip of her blade and dying with a croak. A dozen more followed, and she ducked into the underbrush, jabbing at the flurry of wings.

The Phooka shot Harper a concerned look. "Stay back. We'll take care of them." The shapeshifter coiled and sprang into the air, morphing into a small black dragon.

The dragon wasted no time. With a high-pitched shriek, he rocketed above the swarming crows and sent a spurt of fire arcing from his mouth into the midst of the flock. A dozen burning birds pelted the forest floor.

A single crow lit on a branch ahead of Harper, extending its neck. It tilted its glittering red eyes as though assessing her and parted its beak. If a bird could grin, that was the expression on the crow's face. With another squawk, it shook its iridescent feathers and spread its wings.

"Kill it, Harper! Badb sees what they see," the Phooka-dragon shouted as his broad wings slapped two more from the sky.

Harper lunged for the bird, but it had already taken flight, a series of short squawks like laughter pouring from its beak. Her failed pursuit opened her to attack from behind, where Paegrinn swung his spear in a wide arc, too slow to catch the birds.

"Duck," the Fir Bolg shouted and curled his open hand. In a ring around Harper, six thick cords of mycelium flew from the soil and knocked the attacking corvids down, where they were immediately covered in writhing tendrils of fungus.

Melinoe skewered another flapping crow while the Phooka incinerated three more. Paegrinn's fungal whips lashed, whistling in every direction, knocking aside any bird that came close to Harper.

The single crow, the largest one who'd studied her, lifted its head and cawed over the din. Every black bird broke off its attack and spiraled in a cyclone. A second guttural call and the storm of birds lanced for the dragon Phooka.

The corvids descended on the shapeshifter like piranha, so thick the dragon disappeared in their midst and lost altitude. Harper and the others sprinted to the swirling mass, weapons pummeling any crow straying within range.

Beaks jabbed, claws tore, and the cacophony of their cawing was deafening. The Phooka screeched and fiery plasma poured from his jaws even as they shredded his flesh. He flew a tight circle and feathered forms burst into flame, raining down amidst his blood.

"Phooka! No!" Fear for the Phooka seized Harper's throat as she sliced more black shapes off her friend.

Melinoe lobbed a watery ball of sorcery at the fray that exploded, leaving the Phooka unharmed but flinging the crows from him just long enough for him to bring his clawed feet together and blow a jet of flame into a large ball.

Harper and Melinoe slashed with their blades while Paegrinn guided the fungal whips to their targets. With a bellow, the Phooka released his fire spell and the ball exploded, catching the flock in a fiery sphere.

Smoldering crow corpses rained down amidst the bitter scent of burning feathers.

The Phooka landed with a thud and faded to his true form. The wounds peppering his furred body appeared superficial, but he swayed, clasping at a branch to remain standing. With a lopsided grin, he pointed at the charred avian carcasses. "Colonel's secret recipe. Finger lickin' good." Then he collapsed.

# CHAPTER 16

Eileen yawned and stretched her legs underneath the cotton sheets, the fabric supple beneath her skin. She rolled on her side and pulled the memory foam pillow from the other side of the bed to her chest. But the Fir Bolg possessed nothing as modern as memory foam.

The pillow tumbled over the side of her queen bed when she shot upright. Green mini blinds, broken for as long as she could recall, hung at a rakish angle, only half blocking the dreary rain shower outside. Her hands did a better job blocking the daylight. Rubbing her eyes failed to dispel the hideous brown shag carpet.

Home. In Gresham? How?

Another gathering, at which she failed to persuade Aeld and the Fae gentry to take a stand and help her daughter defeat the evil growing on Sauvie Island was the last thing she recalled. The meeting had broken up shortly afterward. Ezrynhivar walked her back to her room.

But what had happened next? Did she dress for bed, or was her brain writing in that daily ritual to cover for the gaps in her recall? She thought she remembered Glani leaving her some herbal tea that tasted like flowers and mint. Yes, there was tea, to soothe lingering regret from killing Sluagh, and her new frustration at the fracturing of the council.

And after that... Sedation. That was it. As soon as she finished the tea, her eyelids drooped and exhaustion plunged her into the oblivion of sleep. She hadn't even changed clothes before falling onto her cot.

They'd drugged her and dumped her back in Gresham. Throat constricting, Eileeen threw off the covers and raced for the living room. Someone from the village must be there. They wouldn't just abandon her. Unless her killing the Fae meant she now brought darkness to the village and they wanted rid of her. But Glani hadn't thought so.

Overturned chairs, broken glass, and deep scratches in the walls greeted her at the end of the hallway. She spared the devastation only a passing glance, flung open the front door, and raced halfway along the walkway.

Frigid pavement and even colder rain slowed her charge. A few pedestrians bustled along the sidewalk, umbrellas spread over business suits. Eyebrows lifted and paces increased. A short woman in a fitted coat swept a manicured hand along her auburn hair and crossed the street to avoid contact. Eileen looked down. She still wore the Fir Bolg clothing, and with bare feet, the ensemble was definitely out of place in the suburbs.

Across the street, a tall man in grubby jeans loitered. The hem of his grey coat dusted his knees and matched the well-worn boots. Shoulder-length black hair hung in studied wild disarray. He scanned her outfit up and down, shrugged, and lifted the lid of a trashcan. At least the indigent gentleman approved of Fir Bolg fashion.

She wasn't sure what she expected to find outside. The urge to move had overridden all other motives and driven her to do something. Anything. Cold rain soaked through her clothes and kissed her skin with icy droplets. The disheveled man watched her flick the water from her fingers and slouch back toward the doorstep. No doubt he was wondering why her trash wasn't out for inspection.

Shivering, she turned the thermostat to eighty and headed for the shower. A pot of coffee promised to focus her thoughts, but first a change of clothes.

Eileen worked a blue fabric band through her locks to form a messy bun. She'd missed her hair appointment while in the arboreal village, and a thick line of grey-streaked brown made a harsh edge where the pale blonde ended. She doubted she'd bother to color it again. Her time in the forest had completely realigned her priorities. And right now, the only important thing was helping Harper. Only she didn't know where to begin.

In such a short time, the Fir Bolg had healed her, soul-deep, and now they'd abandoned her. Hot steam pouring through the shower curtain promised relief. After that, coffee. Coffee was always salvation.

Slipping back into the pink fuzzy slippers she'd previously worn every morning at breakfast felt alien, but her feet were cold, so she tolerated them. In her rush to escape the house earlier, she'd missed the scroll on the living room coffee table, perched atop the pouch Holl had made her. She lifted the tube from the soft fabric bag.

"Keep calm and sparkle on." She laughed and traced the embroidered letters.

Collapsing onto the 1970s rust-colored couch, she slipped off the strand of fiber tying the scroll. Shaking fingers unrolled the fibrous paper. Lines of flowery script suggested one of the Fae had translated for the Fir Bolg. She clutched the letter in her hand and read aloud.

"Eileen, returning you to your previous home became necessary. Please understand our decision considered only your safety; we welcome your presence among us. The Sluagh draw ever nearer. When the emissaries from the Green World Courts leave, we move again, deeper into hiding in our most protected of sacred spaces. Because we cannot be certain how the Sluagh discovered the village, you are not safe among us. Please know this is a burdensome choice for Aeld. In your short time in our community, you have become a part of us. We won't be whole without you. Never did we dream of a harmonious relationship with one of your kind.

"We know it will be difficult for you to be still and wait for your daughter's return. The role of the witness can be the hardest of all, especially for the short-lived races. We urge you to not seek her. Doing so will only place you in peril. She has all she needs to complete her task. Trust in her.

"Perhaps one day we will send for you again. It is our deepest hope that you reside with us once more. Partly because you protected us by sacrificing that which is most precious: your self-image. And you challenged us to reconsider our place in this world. For those things, we are grateful. But for now, live your life. Create a new harmony for yourself among your people, and above all, be happy. I've included some gifts in your satchel. Your friend, Glani."

Eileen's face constricted with quiet sobs. Despite Glani's words, she still felt cast off. A long, aching breath brought waves of tears and blurred her vision. Her one chance to keep her daughter safe had been convincing the Fir Bolg and the Green World Fae to enter the conflict. Now she was beached in suburban Portland. Powerless. Useless. While Harper fought monsters miles from here. She might as well be a thousand miles away because there was nothing Eileen could do to help her now.

She slipped the tan satchel around her neck, pulled her knees under her chin, and wept. She was failing Harper all over again.

# CHAPTER 17

"Phooka!" Harper dropped the sword and raced to his side, crashing to her shins.

Paegrinn already knelt beside the Fae.

Her friend's wounds were many, but they seemed skin deep. "What happened?" Harper laid her hand against his soft fur, face pinched with concern. He lifted his head slightly. His half-lidded golden eyes were devoid of their usual mischievous glint.

Melinoe snarled. "The largest survived. If he returns to Badb, she'll follow him back here." The raucous caw of a distant crow cackled as if in answer. With a flick of her thin blade, Melinoe hopped in pursuit, then paused. "There's an abandoned house due east of here. Wait for me there. I'll kill the beast and make sure you're not followed." Melinoe smiled again with her eyebrows high, brought her palm up beside her face, flapped a quick wave, and shot into the undergrowth so fast it looked like she simply vanished.

Harper stroked the Phooka's long neck ruff with one hand and rubbed her jaw with the other. Meanwhile, Paegrinn hunched over his fallen friend, examining the wounds and pulling the Phooka's eyelid open. So close that the whiskers on his face brushed against the Phooka, the Fir Bolg peered into his eye.

Paegrinn unslung his tan satchel from his shoulder. "Hmm." He stuck a finger into the largest wound and brought it to his mouth. The Phooka yelped and weakly swatted at the Sasquatch's hand. Paegrinn stuck out his tongue, gagged, and spat.

"Monkshood. Deadly stuff." Paegrinn spread fingertips to the earth and uttered an ululating drone. Mycelium leapt to life, closing the gashes and tears on the shapeshifter's frame.

"Those winged bastards," the Phooka whispered. His head flopped back to the ground with a whole-body spasm.

"Poisoned? How?" Dread made Harper feel heavy.

The Phooka sighed. "In ancient times, Badb's pets dipped their beaks in it before battle."

"Can you help him?"

Paegrinn was already rustling around in his bag. "I think so. But he'll need some time to fully heal."

Harper let out a breath and twined her hair with her hands. She shifted the Phooka's head onto her leg and grasped his long black fingers in her own.

Paegrinn ground desiccated mushrooms on a stone and drew out some packets of different powders and dried herbs. "This will help his system fight off the poison, but he has to drink it. We need water. There's a pond below the next rise." He motioned with his chin, his hands busy with his work.

"I've got just the thing." Harper slid the Phooka's head off her lap and stood.

With a shrug, her backpack slid down her arms. She unclipped the aluminum water bottle that hung tucked in the outside pocket of her bag and headed toward the pond, pausing to look at her friends, suddenly anxious about leaving their sight. "Won't the forest lead me in circles?"

The Phooka shook his head. "My influence should extend that far. Keep you on the straight path."

Harper retrieved Gwyn's weapon and jogged up the gentle slope. Her heart pounded against her ribcage like it wanted to escape. She didn't know what she'd do if the Phooka died. The depth of her affection surprised her. Much of the time she spent being annoyed by his antics, but he'd fought as hard as Nuada had to safeguard her. The warnings from Selina, Ezrynhivar, and others seemed unwarranted; other than Emilio and her mother, the Phooka had proved himself her closest friend.

She arrived at the pond and crouched by the water's edge. Foamy algae floated on the surface in thick clumps. She imagined a slick, glistening horse's head rising out of the bracken and shuddered. This place had become something dark and strange, and the weight of its malice pressed from all sides.

She dipped the bottle in the water's edge and held it under. The gurgling and bubbling as liquid flooded in sounded too loud in the darkening wood. She wrinkled her nose, wishing for the Phooka's sake that she knelt by a stream and not this foul little pond.

On the far shore, a gentle ripple formed. It widened out in slow circles, then a v-shape wave pointed right where Harper crouched. She gasped and plunged the bottle deeper, trying desperately to get enough for the medicine before whatever darted beneath the surface could reach her.

Satisfied she had enough, Harper tore her hand out of the water and scrambled back on her hands and feet like a crab. The v-shape sped toward the bank like an arrow loosed from a bow, halting with a slosh mere inches from where the bottle had been.

A low hissing laugh emanated from the direction of the pond. Harper swallowed hard as a pair of pale eyes rested barely above the surface. Long wisps of hair fanned out from the top of a rounded head and wound their way through the clumps of algae and pond plants. Thin membranes flicked across the eyes, and with a *sploosh*, the creature was gone.

Harper held Gwyn's long silver blade in front of her as she rose to her feet and wove between the trees more slowly than she'd like. The mist drifted and dragged behind her, making it difficult to see the ground. She couldn't afford to lose the bottle of brackish water to forest and fog, so she felt her way inch by inch through the woods back to her companions.

She arrived with the water just as Paegrinn maneuvered the Phooka to a seated position with his rear to a tree.

"How is he?" Harper's voice wavered. She passed the bottle to Paegrinn and crouched on the other side of the Phooka.

"His wounds have mostly closed. That's a good sign. But the effects of the poison will be harder to treat." Paegrinn was feeding the mixture he'd ground up through the small opening in the water bottle. The Phooka's eyes opened halfway. Harper tried to smile at him reassuringly.

"Your bedside manner sucks," he muttered. "I can clearly see how worried you are. It's stressing me out." He managed a small smile.

Harper cupped his chin. "Of course I'm worried."

"It's only a flesh wound. I've had worse," the Phooka said in his best British accent.

"He's definitely feeling better. Already back to quoting movies." Harper's smile flickered and disappeared.

The way Paegrinn shook the herbs and water inside the bottle looked like the healer was attempting to craft his first martini. After the vigorous shake, he held it to the Phooka's lips. "Drink all of it."

The Phooka took a sip. His face wrinkled and he stuck out his tongue.

"Is that troll urine? Because it tastes like troll urine. Blech."

Paegrinn rolled his eyes and held the bottle back up to the

Fae's mouth. "How much troll urine have you swallowed? Now keep drinking."

The Phooka inclined his head. "Fair question. You could have at least put some sugar in it." Between every gulp, the Fae clasped his throat, bugged his eyes, and was generally melodramatic.

Paegrinn rubbed his forehead. "Just finish it. We need to keep moving." With a deep sigh, the healer wiped the last of the mycelium from the Fae's black fur and ran a palm where the injuries had been the thickest.

"Don't give up your day job," the Phooka said. "Yeouch! Oof! You're more of a torturer than a doctor."

Paegrinn sighed and continued his ministrations.

Scowling, the Phooka pushed himself up onto doddering legs and promptly collapsed in a furry heap.

Paegrinn was already jamming herbs and the bottle into their packs. "Hopefully, the house isn't far. We shouldn't be moving him this much," he whispered to Harper and scooped the Phooka into his arms.

"Did you slip a mickey into my troll urine?"

Harper sighed, watching the Phooka drift to sleep in Paegrinn's arms. She didn't think it possible for a black-furred Fae to look pale, but he did. "Is he going to be all right?"

"As long as we get to a resting place, probably. You need to rest too, and it's getting dark." Paegrinn hugged the Phooka closer.

"We can't afford to rest with both the Sluagh and the Wild Hunt on our trail." But Harper's aching body pleaded with her to agree.

Paegrinn shrugged and they plodded toward their rendezvous with Melinoe. Harper wished the elven clothing she still wore had a hood, as a slow rain began to fall.

They'd only walked another hour before Paegrinn insisted they make camp. He quickly wove branches into a small lattice and Harper gathered moss to press into the gaps between the sticks and vines.

They didn't risk a fire. Instead, she huddled beside Paegrinn and the Phooka and dreamed of the warmth of the campfires in Gwyn's encampments.

She doubted she'd sleep, but exhaustion claimed her quickly.

# CHAPTER 18

When Harper woke, surprisingly refreshed, she and Paegrinn shouldered their bags. The Fir Bolg picked up the still-slumbering Phooka and they set off through the forest.

A howl in the distance quickened their pace.

Only concern for the Phooka and dread of discovery by Sluagh or Gwyn sharpened Harper's focus on making steady progress and away from the quivering in her gut. Despite her best efforts, anxiety painted scenes of the worst outcomes onto the blank canvas of mist and cloud. Prime among them, the fear that Emilio was already dead, or that Gwyn would go back on his word and the Wild Hunt would find the Fir Bolg village and her mother hiding within it.

After an hour of trudging, the Phooka yawned and stretched. "Are we there yet?"

Paegrinn peered down at his patient. "I don't know what a human house looks like, but we haven't seen anything but forest and mist."

The Phooka shifted in the Fir Bolg's arms. "Surprised Gwyn

hasn't caught us yet after someone who shall remain nameless left him alive."

Paegrinn gave Harper a peaceful grin. "You made the right choice, Harper. My people don't kill unless absolutely necessary, and certainly not a defenseless enemy."

"Your people never encounter a single moral grey area, hiding from the world in treehouses," the Phooka mumbled.

Unbidden, visions of Gwyn's chiseled jaw and warm eyes brought a momentary flush to Harper's cheeks. She shuddered. "Phooka, you said he was a good man once."

"Ancient history. He killed his own father. That's all you need to know about who he is now."

"Is there a way to kill a Tuatha where they can't be resurrected in the Cauldron?"

The Phooka's golden eyes narrowed. "Yes, by severing the head or cutting out and destroying the heart. Your point?"

Another contradiction joined the stack of confounding and utterly perplexing examples of Gwyn ap Nudd's recent behavior. Harper pursed her lips, a palm absently rubbing between her shoulder blades. "He had plenty of time to do either of those things to Nuada. I couldn't have stopped him."

Paegrinn blinked rapidly, his head tilted. "Gwyn's a Tuatha, so perhaps he still shares their moral code."

"Pffft. That monster joined Badb in the early days, and resentment at daddy hollowed him out long before even that."

"I think he saved my life." Harper recounted the story of her time with Gwyn and Donn, carefully leaving out how it seemed he defended her and the kindness he showed healing her feet.

Paegrinn spoke first. "See. There is still honor in him."

"Honor?" The Phooka laughed and slumped deeper into Paegrinn's arms with a wheeze. When he continued, his voice was hoarse. "He's merely following Badb's orders. Any heroics against that psychopath Donn were in service of that."

Harper studied the swirl of the clouds over the disc of sun. "He traded his freedom to counterbalance Donn's predations."

"Irrelevant. He—" The Phooka coughed, flailing his hooves in Paegrinn's embrace. "You get another chance at ending him, you take your shot. Even if deep in his cold stone of a heart he's conflicted, it won't stop him from serving his master. He swore an oath. He's bound to Badb Catha above all others. Never forget that."

Harper nodded. The Phooka had a point, though she'd sensed Gwyn's anguish. *I will do what I must.* Well, so would she.

Paegrinn leaned down and paused, meeting Harper's hazel eyes. "You saved my people with your magic. Thank you."

Harper smiled up at her giant friend, lifted a hand, and squeezed his shoulder. "Any time."

The Phooka weakly waggled his fingers between them. "That's not the important part. You used your magic again. How did you summon it?"

"Anger."

The Phooka's jaw dropped. "Bloody awesome, you're just like the Incredible Hulk."

Harper gave a joyless, silent laugh. "And about as controllable. You two have any Fae or Fir Bolg tricks for summoning it when I need it?"

"No," both her friends said at once.

The Phooka hacked and rubbed his sternum, Paegrinn eyeing him closely. "Fae magic doesn't work like that, and these hairy hippies use mushrooms for theirs. You're on your own there. But if it's emotions for you, maybe you can learn to control those."

Unlikely. Even the experts in Harper's life had driven home the point that feelings could not be controlled. Not long after her dad's death, Harper had been in a fight at school after a classmate remarked that she had to wear tattered, secondhand clothes because she didn't have a father to buy her nicer things. She'd exploded on the girl, slapping, kicking, and pulling her hair. That incident led her to the principal's office, then to a visit with her caseworker, and finally an emergency session with her therapist. She'd fully expected the woman to tell her she shouldn't have been angry at the other student, but the counselor agreed what the girl said was pretty nasty and that anger was normal in that situation, but that Harper had been wrong to lash out.

None of that made a shred of sense to ten-year-old Harper O'Neill. "I beat her up because she made me mad, but you just said it was normal to be mad."

"Feelings make us wish to do something to change them. It wasn't your anger that was wrong, Harper. It was what you did with it."

Young Harper didn't want to harm anyone and regretted hurting the other girl. "Teach me how to make the feelings go away. Or how to keep just the good ones." A tiny glimmer of hope had lit in that moment. Maybe, with this woman's help, she could stop feeling terrified and alone all the time.

What the psychologist said next stomped out that hope, just like recalling it did in the present. "Feelings can't be controlled. They're different from the part of you that thinks. We can only make better choices about acting on them."

That was the last time she engaged in her therapy. She'd found other ways to not feel the things that made her small and weak. She'd hunted down every last spark of hope and stamped it out because it hurt worse when none of the hopes came true. Still, somewhere in the emotional desert she created for herself, where repressed rage burned, desiccating every good thing, some seed planted by her parents in better times grew spindly and pale in the dark.

With sagging shoulders, she regarded the Phooka. "Not so easy."

Paegrinn bobbled his head to their left as they reached the

high point in their winding path up a hillside. Visible through gaps in the fog was the edge of a small pond. "The Phooka could use another dose of tea."

The little Fae stretched tall in Paegrinn's arms and forced his ears upright. "Actually, I feel like taking a walk, might pull through without it." His bravado didn't last, and he collapsed back into the crook of Paegrinn's arm.

Harper dropped her backpack on a fallen log and unclipped the bottle. "I'll get some." She navigated the hill to the pond, anxiety prickling her skin, recalling the creature lurking in the last pond.

Creeping to the shore, she lowered the bottle toward a break in the bracken, eyes scanning the surface for any disturbance in the stillness. Across the small pond, footprints led away from the opposite bank. Her breath stalled in her chest.

She yanked the empty bottle back, stood, and leaned over the water, squinting. A curving furrow angled deeper into the wood and her heart plummeted. They were her own footprints.

# CHAPTER 19

Emilio should have guessed by now that a 'different sort of testing' simply meant torture.

Part of him wanted to make a break for it. Let the Fae slaughter him, and he'd never have to face the creature they'd forced him to become. But the others depended on him. If Harper really was embroiled in this nightmare, she needed him too. Once the people he cared for were safe, he could turn his attention to undoing the magical genetic procedure and go home.

What the quartet endured presently made Emilio yearn for the swords and claws on the training field. All four of them were dragged from bed early and now lined the back wall of a vast room with an overhead surgery theater complete with stadium seating jutting far to the center. Badb, Callon, and their usual retinue of Fae species packed the seats, safe from the vapors, iron, and magical blasts bombarding Emilio's group. Only Breas and Dr. Jones remained with their experiments, safe inside bright yellow hazmat suits.

Jones and Breas hunched over a table at the far side of the lab, preparing whatever hell they'd dreamed up next. Because Badb had leaned forward, face pressed against the glass, Emilio guessed the first test had been pivotal. Iron. If Fae touched it, the metal weakened and even killed them. Cities were full of iron, so Badb's Underworld forces could never strike a serious blow to humanity there.

Dr. Jones had forced the four to grasp bars of iron, even hold pieces of steel on their tongues, both to no effect. Emilio suspected the final test was for the pure sadistic glee of it, although the rationale had been to test for healing powers. To press red-hot iron bits against the skin of a living thing revealed the Fae as not merely cruel, but sociopathic. But they'd discovered all Netherfae except Alan possessed accelerated healing, although the accountant's woody skin proved more resistant to injury. Blackened streaks still covered his skin where they'd tested their grisly hypotheses.

Emilio stood strapped to an upright operating table. They hadn't bothered to secure his wings away from his flesh, so with every scream and jerk, his razor feathers sliced long lines in his skin. He couldn't tell whether the weakness in his limbs and the simultaneous brain fog were from exhaustion or blood loss. He didn't enjoy the predatory longing on Selina's face when she looked at the red puddles beneath him. Images of the way she'd licked the elf blood off her hands refused to recede.

On his other side, Alan gibbered. If the other Netherfae were on the banks of insanity, poor Alan had been swept into the whitewater. Tamika called to him from the opposite end of their line.

"Alan, listen to me. You can make it. It'll be over soon and you can rest, hon." Her voice sounded more like musical instruments than a human voice, multitonal, layered, and stunning.

The accountant moaned and lashed his head.

"Look at me, Alan. Look at me."

Alan strained against the strap across his shoulders. He craned his neck just enough to meet Tamika's purple eyes.

"You can do this." Her voice took on deeper undertones, like it mixed with a cello. She focused on him from the tops of her eyes. "Hear me, Alan. You are strong. You can endure this."

Alan slumped and the tension drained from his face. "Yes. I can do it." He nodded and dropped his head back against the metal.

"You're the most kick-ass accountant I've ever seen. You took out a bunch of those douchebag elves with one strike," Emilio said.

"Yeah, but I just want to go home. Maybe look for my daughter." Alan refused to acknowledge that the daughter he'd chaperoned to the Mystic Island Festival might also be one of Badb's prisoners.

*Poor man. He doesn't realize none of us can ever really go home. Not like this.* At least Tamika's vocal hypnotism had calmed him. Emilio hoped their enemies hadn't noticed her performance. That talent might come in handy, especially if it also worked on Fae.

"Guys, they're heading back." Selina jerked her head toward Breas and Dr. Jones.

Their plastic suits creaked and rustled like vinyl furniture. Behind Breas, the doctor dragged a canister shaped like the propane containers Emilio's family hooked up to the barbecue back in Portland. Emilio's stomach flip-flopped.

Breas pushed his shielded face toward Emilio. His voice sounded crackly, like it emanated from a tin can, exactly like a badly tuned AM radio. "None of you inherited the Fae's unfortunate weakness to steel. Fae share another weakness, making them unsuitable for city combat, because human pollutants sap their strength. Your last trial of the day will test how well your systems resist the toxins found everywhere humans gather."

Dr. Jones swung the canister close to Emilio and opened the valve. Breas lifted a second one effortlessly with a single arm and plopped it beside Tamika. Foul gas poured from the canisters, reeking of petrochemicals and the cloying sweetness of decay.

"What is this stuff?" Selina coughed. Her head jerked instinctively away from the grey jet of nastiness spewing into the room.

"Pollutants from cars, factory smoke, sewer gas. The usual air humans create." Breas hovered next to Emilio. "This will take a few minutes."

Breas clasped the doctor by the elbow and ushered him into the hallway ahead of him. A minute later, the pair reappeared in the theater above, beside the Fae spectators.

Tamika retched. The sparkling midnight blue sheen on her deep chocolate skin dulled. Even her eyes paled, turning almost clear. "I feel dizzy."

Emilio opened his mouth to respond, but a long line of coughs rushed out instead. Above them, Badb eyed Tamika with a frown.

"Tamika, pull yourself up straight and act like you're okay. They're watching."

"Badb wants us to battle in cities. They'll probably cull the ones who can't," Selina said. Not a single cough escaped her lips. The noxious fumes seemed to have little effect on her.

"You can do it, Tamika." Alan's quivering voice ended in wheezing coughs. His craggy skin had blackened all over, just like tree bark did near smokestacks. The man must have felt dreadful, but he stared straight ahead and attempted to muffle every cough.

Emilio stared daggers up at the seats. They'd taken everything from him. Murdered innocents in front of him. Even as his family fled their country, he hadn't hated the gangs and cartels. The hopelessness of mass poverty drove people to do things they normally wouldn't do. He didn't despise them for seeking the protection of gangs or the relative prosperity they brought.

When they'd arrived in the States, even the derision others cast on him by terms like 'wetback' didn't make him loathe those people, because his grandmother taught him that, too, was merely a symptom of fear.

But now, for the first time in his life, Emilio hated. He despised every last person responsible for what happened to him, Fae and human alike. Alongside the molten vitriol of his loathing slithered an oily coating of guilt, bringing with it a burning, sour taste in the back of his throat. Good people weren't filled with hate. Then again, he was no longer people, and it was all their fault. They had to be stopped.

When he glared up at Badb and her assembly, his heart bristled with scorn the same way his body bristled with sharp feathers. Delicious fantasies of slicing every one of them to ribbons with his wings brought a warm flush along his limbs. An unkind smile spread over his features and his muscles twitched, anticipating the sensation of slashing Badb and her minions to pieces. At least as a monster, he had the means to strike back and perhaps shepherd the innocent to safety. Still, they had to play it smart.

"Show no weakness and remember to hide what you can," Emilio said through gritted teeth.

"We need another escape plan." Tamika's voice was barely above a whisper.

"They'll be watching us after the last time. Plus, we're even more valuable to them now," Selina said.

"Escape and go back to what?" Emilio said before a torrent of gags and coughs. "Will your family recognize you? Or will they scream and run from you? No. They made us into weapons, and we can turn ourselves against our creators. End this." Reality descended like the severing blow of an axe. He'd feared that revelation the moment he'd awakened in his monster form. Speaking it aloud was like crossing a Rubicon. Coughs mingled with moans came from the others, and he knew they sensed it too.

"We might as well be dead," Tamika whispered.

Selina growled. "With every death is a rebirth. We may be in a better position than anyone to strike a blow against Badb and keep our families, everyone's families, from meeting the same fate as the human captives. Eventually, they'll take us to the city, to test us there. If we escape, I know a place we'll be welcome." The Romani woman barked a guttural laugh. "Ironically, its name means Exile's Lodge. My ex-husband created Fògradh Lodge as a place where Fae and magical beings from all magical realms could be at home."

"I don't want to be near any more Fae," Alan said. Emilio's face pinched in concern at the rattling cough punctuating his words.

"Not all Fae are like these. Most want little to do with humans. A few may actually help us," Selina said.

Emilio glanced at her. "We can't leave the people here behind. We have to get them to safety."

"I don't think that's possible. There's only four of us. We'll be lucky to free ourselves." Tamika's head lolled forward, but she forced her face to lift toward their audience.

"We're not leaving them. We're not like these demons. We leave no one behind." Since he woke a stranger in his body, despair was all Emilio felt, but now he felt hope and a sense of purpose.

Further planning would have to wait. Above them, Breas, Dr. Jones, and a contingent of Sidhe rose and started back toward their experiments.

Selina dipped her head at her friends. "I think it's over, Tamika. You made it, Alan."

Tamika only nodded. Her butterfly wings had lost nearly all their color.

The Sidhe hovered across the hall, sleeves pressed across their mouths and noses. Breas and the doctor entered in their bright yellow suits and one by one wheeled the four into the hall where the elves unbound them.

Emilio slumped against the wall. He never thought he'd be so thankful for fresh air. The fuzzy cloud over his thoughts lifted a little with each deep breath. Emilio and Selina gripped Tamika's hands on either side of her, to hold her upright surreptitiously. The woman looked pale and listless. The bright flowers in her hair had withered to dry husks. Alan's skin lightened a few shades. It would likely take time for its birch bark tone to return.

Breas sauntered around the quartet and lifted the helmet from his suit. "Amazing. Each of you withstood substances that would have killed even the Sidhe."

Callon narrowed his eyes and sneered right at Emilio.

Emilio sneered right back. "Fan-fucking-tastic."

Breas chuckled. "For now, you have earned yourselves a rest. Tomorrow you learn to take control of others, so I hope you recover quickly."

They were all too exhausted for a snappy rejoinder. The Netherfae shuffled along between clusters of the Sidhe in their shiny black armor. To Emilio's dismay, the elves herded each of them into a separate room.

Callon leaned into Emilio's line of sight. "Oh, you thought we'd allow you time together to plot your escape?"

Emilio shrugged. "Kind of. You seem pretty dim."

The elf's beautiful features twisted. "I'll knock that chip off your shoulder in training, human."

Emilio's wing feathers made a pleasant tinkling sound, like a hundred swords ringing from their sheaths. He shook them for effect. "Perhaps you'll get close enough to try. And I'm not human anymore."

"You're an abomination."

"Right back at you, Scarface."

"Insolent little—" Callon lunged at him, blade sliding from its narrow sheath.

"Enough." Breas shoved the elf aside. "Let them rest."

Breas pulled the door to another small room open and ushered

Emilio inside. The tiny room was spartan, a chair, a small table, and a bed the only things inside. All the same, Emilio hadn't seen a bed since the day they abducted him from Mystic Island. He looked forward to drifting to sleep in softness rather than on the floor of a cramped cage or strapped to a gurney.

"Word of advice, my young apprentice," Breas said. "Don't antagonize Callon. He hates your kind more than most. And don't attempt to escape." He pointed to the collar Emilio wore. "It would be very painful if you tried."

Emilio nodded. When Breas exited his room, Emilio dropped over onto the bed, lying on his stomach with his dangerous wings draped across either side. In moments, a trio of goblins bustled in with a tray of food. He wolfed it down like a starving animal, surprised that it was actually quite good. Being Netherfae rather than fully human afforded him nicer snacks, at least.

When he completed his meal, weariness took him back to bed. Mercifully, sleep drew him down, down toward the bliss of unconsciousness. Idly, he worried about Tamika, concerned at her reaction to the toxins.

And then she was there, sitting cross-legged on a pink Barbie comforter, with Selina beside her. The sounds of traffic ratcheted his head to the open window. A steady stream of cars hummed far below. The trio were in a child's bedroom. Tan carpet. Black-skinned Barbie dolls on the shelf above the twin bed.

"Tamika? Selina?"

They turned toward him. "Emilio! You're here too." The blossoms had re-bloomed in Tamika's purple curls and the midnight shimmer returned to her skin.

"What..." Emilio's mouth gaped open. "Is this place?"

"Where is this place?" Selina asked.

"My bedroom when I was seven. The only time and place I ever felt safe. Before my mom left us and we moved every few months." Tamika smiled, hopped off her bed, and walked a small circle around the room.

"Where's Alan?"

Tamika closed her eyes. Full magenta lips pursed. "I think he might be asleep. He's not coming when I think about him."

"I- I was just drifting off. This has to be a dream," Emilio said.

Selina shook her head. "It's not a dream."

"I was thinking about whether all of you were all right," Tamika said. "How much I wanted to talk to you, and then I was here. If I didn't really want to see you, I'd be freaking out right now."

"I was worrying about you because you looked pretty green back there. I wonder if we have to be thinking of each other simultaneously," Selina said. The half-strigoi marveled at Tamika. "The Fae can create illusions like this with their glamour."

"Yeah, but we're not all blissed out and dopey," Emilio said.

Tamika shrugged. "This feels different from when the elves glamoured me. Like our minds are connected, or a piece of you is here with me in a memory."

Emilio leaned forward. "This could be useful."

Tamika's eyebrows shot up. "I feel it fading, like it's breaking apart."

Suddenly both rooms overlapped in time and space, quite disorienting. Barbie dolls rippled and faded while the simple wooden chair in Emilio's prison snapped into focus. He called out to his friends, but he was alone.

# CHAPTER 20

She buried her face in her arms and choked back a frustrated scream. Against the grey sky, the trees creaked and scraped. Harper knew in her heart they mocked her.

"This goddamn forest! We've walked a circle." Harper threw out her hands, palms up, then let them slap against her thighs.

Paegrinn arrived at the bank, broad forehead creased. "Impossible. The Phooka is with us. We should be able to push through the looping paths. It's still early evening. I tracked our bearing with the sun and now the rising moon."

Harper waved a listless hand across the pond. "I can see where I scrambled away from whatever lives in the water."

Paegrinn squatted, maneuvered the Phooka out of his arms, and meandered along the water's edge. "I don't understand."

Beside her, the Phooka lifted his head halfway and peeled his eyes most of the way open. Harper chewed her lip to prevent her frustration from boiling over and making some mistake that would bring bloodthirsty Fae right to them.

"It's just like Nuada said. This place has become just like the

Underworld. The transformation is further advanced than either of us feared. I'm too weak now to keep the magic at bay, so it leads you where it wants you to go," the Phooka said.

Paegrinn's eyebrows arched as his jaw dropped. "My dad said the Underworld has no straight lines, therefore, to get anywhere you must make them."

Despair, every bit as chill as the damp air seeping through their clothes, snaked tendrils into Harper's heart. "How are we ever going to locate Emilio?"

Paegrinn handed them each a handful of dried grains and berries from his bag. Grasping the bottle, he shambled closer to the pond. "I better fetch the water. The being guarding it might object less to a Fir Bolg than a human."

Harper curled her fingers around her food and assessed the Phooka. The tea must be working. His demeanor and color had improved. He gulped down his snack and licked every crumb from his fingers.

"In answer to your question, the Underworld is... let's say for ease of understanding, more fluid. Malleable. It'll make finding Badb's fortress more difficult but not impossible."

Harper hicupped and wrinkled her forehead. "Malleable?"

"Humans." The Phooka dragged a palm down his cheek. "You've experienced the phenomenon for days and still don't get it." He tilted his face to the sky. "The land itself can expand or contract. Sometimes, the journey between one place and another is short. Others longer."

"How can distance change every day? Space can't vary like that." Though her recent experience suggested otherwise.

The Phooka sighed and shifted onto his side. "Not here in the Green World, it can't. At least not normally."

Harper's brain refused to make sense of it. She shook her head and rolled a dried berry around the edge of her palm. Hunger won out, and she popped it in her mouth. It was sweet and earthy at the same time.

The Phooka tilted his chin, face pensive, then he thrust his finger in the air and smiled. "The Underworld, and now this island, are like the TARDIS. Please tell me you've watched *Dr. Who*. I'm aware your tastes in most things is rubbish, but you have to at least know about the TARDIS."

Emilio was a hardcore fan, so she'd seen her fair share of episodes. She nodded. "I'm not a fan, but yeah. It's bigger on the inside."

The Phooka's eyes rolled up and his furry hand flew to his chest then flipped to his forehead before he flopped over onto his back in a mock faint. "Not. A. Fan? I'm stuck on this shambolic misadventure with someone who has absolutely no taste for great works of fiction." He levered himself onto his side, propped on an elbow. "Regardless of your poor taste, yes. It's bigger on the inside."

Paegrinn turned from the pond with a new batch of the Phooka's medicine. The gentle giant cradled the Phooka's head with a huge palm and brought the bottle to his lips. The Phooka flapped at him.

"Get your hands off me, you damn dirty ape!"

"Ape?" Paegrinn nudged the Phooka's arm aside and pressed the tea closer.

"If you think I'm choking down more of that vile glop, Dr. Zaius, you are sadly mistaken."

Harper rolled her eyes and sighed. "Just drink the medicine, Phooka."

The little shapeshifter gagged and sputtered, claimed Paegrinn was the one poisoning him, but drank. The Fir Bolg scooped out more of the berry and grain mix and distributed it.

"Okay, so the island's larger than it was, but how did that end up putting us back here?" Paegrinn tilted his head and closed his bag.

"Because"—the Phooka held up his index finger and traced loops in the mist—"when something is bigger on the inside than outside, the way you get all that extra space into the same footprint is to fold it, crinkle it up. It can get infinitely bigger, but also more convoluted, and the creases can move around. A rare few are able to force changes in troughs and crests, warp them to create passages, transport objects, or hide treasures. Most of us can't do that, but we can keep the land from messing with us and stay on the straight path."

*That's how Gwyn transported us away from the Sluagh. Manipulated the crumpled paper effect.* Harper shuddered. That must require massive power.

Dismay swelled inside her. The journey to Badb's fortress could take days. Or weeks. While she stumbled in circles with a sword that refused to draw, horrible things were probably happening to Emilio and Abraham.

Paegrinn shook his head. "I still don't understand it."

"Doesn't matter. I have a way to help us navigate better." The leather satchel appeared again at the Phooka's side. He flipped it open and rummaged inside it.

"Is your bag also bigger on the inside?" Paegrinn asked.

The Phooka only smiled in response. "Aha!" he cried, drawing out a glass lantern with a bright light bobbing inside. Harper studied it. It was the same color and size as the little light that guided her away from Gwyn and Donn. He held the lantern up to his face. The little greenish light about the size of a golf ball bashed itself against the glass like it wanted to fly down the Phooka's throat. He shook the lamp gently and the orb hovered in the center of its cylindrical prison. "Knock that off, Alina. I have another job for you. Complete your task successfully and your debt is absolved."

A squeaky chirp came from the jar.

"Yes, Alina, you'll be free."

The Phooka opened the lantern and the green light zipped out. She zoomed around their heads twice before coming to hover inches from the Phooka's face. Gossamer wings much like a dragonfly's buzzed behind the creature, a blur like hummingbird wings. A tiny face was visible along the top of the orb, her eyes narrowed at the Phooka. The little creature was beautiful. Harper suddenly felt like she didn't know the Phooka at all. She'd believed him a friend.

"Were you seriously keeping a captive in your bag? What the hell is wrong with you?"

The Phooka tore his attention from the orb and raised his eyebrows. His tone was flat and lacked any of its usual levity. "Alina is not exactly a prisoner. She owes me a debt, which I am calling in now to help you save your friend. After she completes her task, she will be free to do as she pleases."

"How horrible." Harper folded her arms across her chest and stared at the swirling, low mist. Beside her, Paegrinn drew back.

The Phooka raised his head, level with Harper's gaze. "There is a lot about us you don't understand, and where we're going, you had best pay attention and learn quickly. We take debts deadly seriously. It is the way of things. Trust me, Alina is getting the better part of our bargain."

"You've saved my life more than once. Was that just to extort some debt from me?" Harper scooted a safe distance from the Phooka, suddenly mulling over Melinoe's words about dark Fae.

"No." The Phooka's voice was flat. "You did not ask for my assistance. I offered it freely. You can relax. You owe me nothing. Alina, however, knew very well what she was getting into. Will o' wisps are much too hasty for their own good." He grinned and returned his attention to the green glow in front of him.

Just when Harper thought she'd figured the situation out, her friend and guide turned out to be perhaps more sinister than he appeared.

"Now then, little Alina. Your task is to guide us to a farmhouse to the east, and afterward to a big stone citadel on this island. Once we are at the front door of that fortress, your debt to me is paid and you are free to go." The tiny light bobbed up and down and chirped. Alina rocketed up to the tallest tree's tip, a green glow against the cloudy sky. She paused before zooming back down, gliding inches from Harper's head as she darted ahead and hovered in place.

The Phooka swept his arm toward the will o' wisp. "Alina will guide us along the straight path; even if the island purposely attempts to thwart us. It's a talent of her kind." He attempted to stand on quaking legs but collapsed. When Paegrinn didn't move to assist him, he threw up his hands and plopped back down. "What?"

Paegrinn's eyes were on the tiny Fae. His expression was one of concern.

Harper swallowed hard. "Phooka, how can I ever trust you again?"

"I think your answer lies in my deeds so far. You must understand my people are very different from yours. We are capricious and mercurial, yes. But there are rules. Unlike humans or Fir Bolg, we must follow them, whether or not we like it. Fae can no more change these aspects of ourselves than you could suspend the law of gravity. What lies ahead will be treacherous in countless ways, because of Fae encounters. And the intricacy of those situations will require my expertise. I suggest we follow Alina before our many pursuers find us again."

Paegrinn reached down and swept the Phooka up. "Does this mean you are indebted to me now?"

The Phooka smiled. "I suppose it does. Name your price."

Paegrinn did not return the smile. "No price. What I give, I give freely."

Harper ran through the past couple of weeks in her mind. She dusted herself off and slung her backpack back across her shoulders. She had to admit, the Phooka had been unwavering in his presence and in her defense. But in light of what she'd just learned, she wondered what debt the Phooka owed. And to whom.

# CHAPTER 21

Eileen O'Neill bustled around her small house in an old navy blue sweatsuit, hair bound in a high, messy ponytail. Either the shock at her abandonment or the stress on her body and soul over the past few weeks had pushed her to sleep even before the daylight drained from the overcast sky.

Early to bed, early to rise. For the first time in a decade, she'd risen with the sun instead of clawing herself from bed in a hungover haze. Hunched over her white porcelain sink, she raised her chin and searched her own eyes in the mirror.

On their own, her fingers strayed to her cheeks and explored the contours of her face to confirm their reality. The woman staring back at her resembled the pharmaceutical marketing director she'd been when Gerald was alive. Gone were the etched lines of anguish and the puffiness of alcohol use.

Eileen leaned closer to the sink so her face hovered just a couple of inches from the smooth mirror. She studied herself, half expecting to meet the steely eyes of a killer, but only a concerned parent stared back.

Tears pooled. This time, tears of relief. Gratitude to her daughter and the Fir Bolg threatened to bring her to her knees. The first tear brought a tsunami. To the northwest, her daughter fought her way through God knows what to save her friend, and to the east, Eileen's new family fought for their lives. And none of them needed her.

"Well, guess what, Eileen, that's entirely your own fault. When you climbed into the bottle, you retreated from the world, from Harper. You left a ten-year-old girl to raise herself because you were weak. And broken. No wonder no one needs you."

*You know what, Mom, the wrong fucking parent died.*

A choked croak and a sharp inhale that was almost a scream bookended a long series of silent sobs. Eileen staggered back, slid down the wall to the floor, and clutched the bathmat to her chest. There it was again, that sensation of her ribcage splitting open by the torrent of agony she feared would never stop if she let it out. She thirsted for vodka like she'd crawled across the desert on her stomach.

Who would know if she drank for just one night? Anyone she cared about was miles from here.

"No!" She balled up her fist and pounded the checkered tile floor. The sharp bite of pain made her instantly regret it.

She'd attended a handful of Alcoholics Anonymous meetings when Harper was still young. Child Protective Services had required it. She'd gone to just enough to fill up the book of sheets they'd given her, then stopped once the heat was off. Stinking thinking. She remembered that one. The slippery slope of rationalization, denial, self-pity, all fell under the broad umbrella of stinking thinking. She'd rolled her eyes like a lippy teenager at that one, but they might be on to something.

She recalled two prescriptions for stinking thinking: call your sponsor and healthy distraction. Eileen had no sponsor. She eyed the house. It was a mess. She'd clean that. That would qualify as healthy distraction. Then she'd either feel better or fall asleep from exhaustion.

Several pairs of bright yellow rubber gloves marked the first casualties in Eileen's war on entropy. She swept, scrubbed, and decluttered for a few hours before a wave of dizziness sent her collapsing on the couch, feet propped next to the Fir Bolg satchel, head dropped back to stare at the stuccoed ceiling. She'd avoided opening the bag and retrieving the gifts Glani left inside, certain doing so would push her to the bottle.

Her stomach made a sound like a feral beast. That's right, she realized, she hadn't eaten since she got back home. Over a day. She pulled her head off the back of the couch and scanned the part of her handiwork she could see.

She had no idea how the sliding doors were back in one piece. The Fae had shattered it. Broken glass shards still littering the dining room carpet confirmed her memory. Nuada must have mended things and disposed of the bodies while she and Harper packed. He'd left the deep gouges in the walls, tears in the carpeting, and the missing cabinet doors.

Another rumble from her stomach motivated her to get up. She instantly regretted swinging the refrigerator door open. The smell of soured milk hit her like a solid object. It paired well with the browning head of lettuce and green, fuzzy... What was that? Cheese. Perhaps the food in the freezer had fared better.

Eileen stood on her tiptoes to root around through the bags of frozen vegetables, ice cube trays, and the little blue ice packs Harper used to keep her lunch cool. Her spelunking revealed nothing that she could make quickly or that she trusted not to poison her.

The cupboards contained stale bread, canned vegetables, and pop tarts. Looked like it was suddenly shopping day. Icy dread seeped into her bones and she shuffled to the sink where she leaned, head dangling beside the faucet. She'd barely left the house before all this, and doing so now would drive home the fact that she really was back in Gresham. Glani would tell her avoiding difficulty wouldn't help.

*You battled the damn undead. The Safeway doesn't stand a chance.*

In the stillness, guilt whispered terrible thoughts. Rationally, she understood her actions had been the right ones, but a stubborn voice insisted on chastising her for it. The same self-inflicted punishment for allowing Gerald to be killed in front of her joined forces and battered her. The craving for vodka promised to send it all away.

Eileen didn't give those feelings time to take root. She shoved off from the sink and scurried down the hall to the shower.

Hot water melted a lot of the tension. The heat and droplets kissing her skin were delicious. She pulled on a pair of boot leg jeans, a green shirt, and a white Portland State hoodie. The sky threatened rain, although when did it not? She tied a rain jacket around her waist.

The difficult part involved searching for her bank card and the rest of her wallet. She found her oversize brown purse, with ten dollars inside, but none of her cards.

"Think, Eileen, what did you do with them? Oh no. You packed them when you fled the house." *Shit.*

It would likely be futile, but she checked the pockets in her Fir Bolg clothing. Not like there were ATMs in the arboreal village, but hope springs eternal. Not there.

She stood beside the coffee table in the living room. The last chance lay inside the satchel. She didn't want to unpack that just yet. Leaving the contents a mystery felt like a connection to her friends. Once it was opened, their parting seemed truly final.

She perched on the edge of her seat and, with shaking hands, pushed open the flap. She slid her fingers inside the soft fabric and drew out a sizable packet. They'd tied a handwritten note, in the same writing as the letter, to the outside.

*This is the medicinal tea we used to heal your body when you arrived.*

Eileen smiled. Somehow, they knew she'd be struggling right now.

She reached her hand back into the bag and withdrew a smooth wooden pendant. Turning over the little piece in her hands, a tear trickled down her face. She'd noticed the symbol carved in Glani's quarters, the mark of her family. Three delicate mushrooms, stems weaving together and ending in a spiral. In the center of the spiral, a little blue opal rested. Another bit of medicine Paegrinn and Glani had used in her healing.

The tiny note tied around the cord said simply, *You are one of us.*

Eileen swept the tear from her cheek and pulled the necklace over her head.

Her next foray into the pouch found her ID and bank card. That must be how they'd found her house. Some of the more worldly Fae likely helped them. There were more items inside, but she'd had enough for now. She nestled the cards into her tan bag and stepped out into the crisp fall air.

A sea of brown grass coated in decaying leaves greeted her. This time, passersby didn't avoid her. An unconscious hand, piloted by anxiety, drifted up to clutch the necklace before Eileen left her home sober for the first time in more than ten years. Thankfully, the sidewalk outside her house stretched empty, the buses having already taken children to their classrooms and workers to their offices a few hours ago. Neither she nor Harper had bothered to buy a car because Harper took the bus to work and Eileen walked the few blocks to the liquor store when she needed to.

The Safeway was about half a mile from the house. She

hopped down the steps and took off at a brisk pace, admiring the carved pumpkins and lawns full of fake gravestones along the way.

She rounded the last corner to the strip mall. An unkempt person sprawled on the sidewalk, lurching to his feet at her approach. Long grey coat, beard stubble, and studiously messy hair marked him as the same guy she'd seen the day before. She braced herself for the wave of body odor that usually accompanied someone who'd clearly spent the night drinking.

"Hey, help a guy out? Got any booze or money for booze?" He spoke with the faintest of Irish accents. The man lacked the ripe tang she dreaded. In fact, his studiously wild locks gleamed, and he smelled of Old Spice. He stood, swaying on his feet, a lopsided smile wrinkling his right eye.

Eileen met deep brown eyes. "No, I don't drink anymore."

"Very aderble, admirbull. Um, admirable of you."

She awaited the waft of stale alcohol breath, but it didn't come. Eileen reached into the handbag. She never went anywhere without provisions. Her hand brushed the cold steel of the little Walther .22 she kept inside. Provisions always included protection. In a few seconds she found them—a handful of fruit and nut bars. With a warm smile, she pushed the snacks into the man's palm.

"Here, take these, it's all I have right now."

"Thank you, you are too *kind*." He flicked one of the bars between his fingers so she could see the world 'Kind' on the label.

Eileen smiled. "There's a shelter on Burnside. It gets pretty cold at night these days."

The man grinned and nodded, raising a finger to point at the pendant. "That's an unusual necklace." His speech was a mix of his accent and an intoxicated slur.

Her hand clasped the piece at her chest. "A gift from a good friend." She smiled and pivoted to continue her journey to the Safeway.

"Maith thú, my friend," the man called after her.

It sounded like he said *maw hoo*. After a few steps, she cast a glance back over her shoulder. The tall man was moving away from her, hands in his pockets, no hint of drunken stagger to his stride.

# CHAPTER 22

Afternoon light failed to puncture the thick grey clouds that threatened another dousing of rain. The trio had trudged along behind the zig-zagging will o' wisp for hours, mostly in silence. The glowing Fae zipped in and out of the woods but always remained in sight. They made a much better pace with her in the lead, but the Phooka's condition worsened with every step, and Harper's exhaustion returned.

Ahead, thick trees parted and the paved remains of a road stretched into the distance, like a dotted line on a map visible through a clearing in the low mist. Power lines hung slack between utility poles snapped by the warping and buckling of the island. Some poles listed to the side at steep angles and a few were strewn, broken beside a patch of pavement.

Harper sighed and crossed her arms. "I hope this farmhouse isn't much farther, it's getting late." Part of her wanted to press on to find Emilio as soon as they could, but none of them were in any shape for that. The reality was, she and the Phooka needed another day or two to fully heal.

Paegrinn nodded, most of his head hidden behind hunched

shoulders. "Me too. I need to reassess the Phooka and it's time for more medicine." The shapeshifter stirred and mimed a dramatic gag.

Alina spiraled out of the fog, bobbed up and down, and guided them toward the left. Harper followed her waggling dance, and laughed, pointing ahead. A two-story farmhouse and an old red barn peeked from the mist like islands. Around the buildings, the roofs of several pickup trucks hovered just above the white blanket.

Beside the home, the neat line separating forest from cultivated fields had already morphed into a jagged edge where new trees and patchy undergrowth invaded, like the wilderness hungered to overtake the precise rows of corn.

"What is this place?" Paegrinn scanned the compound with an expression of wonder.

"It's a farm. A place where we grow food."

Paegrinn pointed at the rows of cornstalks. "All the same kind? You must really like whatever that is."

"Corn. Other farms grow other things." Harper wandered close to a red pickup and screamed.

A man dangled half out the door, cloudy eyes and open mouth gaping at the sky. He'd been torn to shreds some time ago, judging by the decomposition. She retched and covered her nose with her sleeve. "Maybe staying here isn't such a great idea. What if the Fae who did this is still here?"

"No Fae did that," the Phooka said. "The iron in that truck would have protected him from my people. Something else did it."

"I was about to go back and search for you. I thought you'd gotten lost."

Harper screamed and drew Gwyn's blade from her belt. Beside her, Paegrinn brandished his pointed staff at their green-haired friend.

"Demon! Kill it!" the Phooka yelled.

"Melinoe." The air rushed from Harper's lungs. "Don't sneak up on us like that. I almost skewered you."

The glaistig broke out into a wide smile. "Oh my goodness, I'm relieved you're still safe, Harper. I'm so excited to finally have time to get to know you."

The Phooka narrowed his eyes at Melinoe. "Laying it on thick, light Fae."

The glaistig turned her chin up and swiveled her back to the Phooka so she only faced Harper. "You're so amazing. If half the stories I've heard are true—"

"Stories?" Harper wrinkled her nose.

"Goodness, yes." The Fae's eyes had the same fanatic glint Harper associated with TV preachers. "You're part Tuatha. You and Nuada fought the entire Wild Hunt alone. And won. You're so strong."

"I fought too! And the Hunt wasn't alone. Dozens, no, hundreds of—" The Phooka levered himself higher, but Paegrinn's hand pushed him back down.

Harper's brow furrowed. "I killed a lot of your people that day."

"Oh sweet Mother Danu, not *my* people, silly." Melinoe's smile widened and she swished a hand across her face, batting her eyes. "My people are the Dawn Court. You haven't killed a single one of us yet." Then her features darkened and her fist clenched by her side. "Have you?" she asked through gritted teeth.

Harper took a step back and steeled herself. "Not that I know of."

Melinoe burst out laughing. "You should see your face!" The Fae sidled up to Harper and elbowed her playfully in the side. "I'm joking. But really, not any human I've ever met could sway My Highness Queen Serotina. You are as eloquent as you are fierce. We're going to have so much fun together." The glaistig hopped up and down on her tiny hooves, clapping her hands like a fangirl at a boy band concert.

Her chipper demeanor felt like nails on a chalkboard, but Harper supposed she should be thankful Queen Serotina kept her word.

Melinoe narrowed her eyes at the Phooka, clasped Harper's elbow, and swiveled their backs to the others. "I know you're super nice, but we should leave the dark Fae right here and find your friend on our own."

"He's helped me from the start and rescued me from Gwyn. Well, you all did."

"Did he? Or was it me showing up that forced his hand?"

Harper glanced over her shoulder at the Phooka. "What do you mean?"

"Why did it take him days to find you? He's Fae, like me. He should be able to stay on the straight path, not be led in circles. It only took me hours to pick up your trail. The little green light he sent—"

A wavering screech rose from deep in the wild woods to the west. The hair on the back of Harper's neck stood on end, and the same terrified expression mirrored on both her Fae and Fir Bolg friends.

The Phooka fixed Melinoe with a suspicious frown. "I thought you used your super speed and tracking magic to lead all the baddies away from us."

"I did, but in case you haven't noticed, this island is essentially like the old country. Banshee. Elves. Fae are everywhere." The glaistig refused to even look at the Phooka, but she pointed up at the tiny green glow of the will o' wisp. "I'm wondering why you didn't use the will o' wisp to find Harper when you arrived instead of blundering around for days." She sniffed and positioned herself between Paegrinn and Harper.

The Phooka's flailed in Paegrinn's arms and he sputtered. "I was saving her last service to me until we found Gwyn and needed to escape!" He scrambled around to fix the glaistig with flashing yellow eyes. "And why were Paegrinn and I never pursued by Badb's minions until you showed up? Makes me wonder—"

Harper glanced sidelong at her ailing friend and pulled her lips into a thin line. "Stop arguing. We need to get inside, away from whatever's out here."

Alina zoomed back to them and flew a couple of circles around the group before streaking off toward the farmhouse.

Melinoe stared at the retreating green light. "How'd you capture a will o' wisp anyway? I didn't think there were many of those left."

"Probably because they are prone to making poor deals." The Phooka waved a long black hand in the air. "Of course, I was quite generous with her."

"Typical dark Fae. We light Fae don't enslave others." Melinoe shook her head in disapproval.

"Tell that to all the changelings you enchant. Light Fae are all the same, sanctimonious—"

"Enough. Both of you. It's getting dark and we'd better go inside." Harper picked her way step by step after Alina. Mist clung to the ground, low and thick. She took a last glance at the truck, silently apologizing for the man's death.

"I already looked inside. It's old, mostly wood, so safe for Fae. And no more corpses." Melinoe fell into step behind Harper.

Harper's throat ached, choking back tears when she saw a young woman, younger than she was, sprawled across a half-rotted picnic table in the yard. Harper crept up the creaking steps, opened the front door, and hesitated. "Hello? Anyone here?"

"There's no one. I made sure." Melinoe clip clopped into the living room.

The home sported some high ceilings. Even so, Paegrinn's head brushed against the rafters. He had to duck for every light fixture or doorway. His bushy eyebrows raised and his jaw dropped. The Fir Bolg's shaggy head rotated all around, soaking in the sights of his first human house.

Two long couches in a hideous woodland deer print took up much of the room's space. Little porcelain statues of children with sappy smiles cluttered every horizontal surface and made an odd contrast with the hunting lodge vibe of the rest of the decor.

"Melinoe, can you please close the shutters and drapes?" Harper showed her how to handle the knob to secure them.

The glaistig nodded furiously. "And I'll put up some warding spells so nothing gets in." She scurried into the next room to begin her work.

Paegrinn laid the Phooka on a tacky couch while Alina fluttered up and roosted in the rough-hewn rafters, adding her green glow to the den. The shapeshifter's head drooped instantly onto one of the tan throw pillows.

"I'm going to need some water for more of the healing brew," Paegrinn said.

The Phooka stuck out his tongue. "Gah. I'll take my chances with the grim reaper."

"I'll see what I can find in the kitchen." Harper walked into the next room, a dining room. She ran her hand along the thick table, the scratches and dents beneath her fingers telling the history of decades of shared family meals.

As she rounded the corner to the kitchen, she flicked on the light switch. Nothing. A hulking white electric stove sat useless, taunting her with the unrequited promise of a hot meal, but a narrow wooden door promised either a closet or the basement steps. She sucked in a breath, mentally preparing for the scurrying of bugs once she flung it open.

"Hah! Jackpot!" She stepped into a large, very well-stocked pantry. A propane camping stove, at least ten cases of bottled water, and a plastic bear jar of honey. Maybe the Phooka would dial down the melodramatics if she could sweeten his medicine.

When Harper returned to her friends, the shapeshifter's protestations were already underway.

"Ooooh! Yeoch! You'd make a better coroner, Nurse Ratched." The Fae smacked at Paegrinn's brown, furry hands.

The gentle giant merely sighed, rolled his eyes, and continued to treat his patient. "This would be over much faster if you'd sit still."

"I found plenty of water in the pantry." Harper passed each of her friends their own bottle.

Paegrinn slid a crystal ashtray of dried mushrooms and herbs to Harper. "Just like last time, mix them with the water."

"At least the humans make their medicine taste like cherries and bubblegum, not like green death." The Phooka clasped his throat and gagged.

Harper wiggled the bottle of honey. "My mom always said a little sweet gets the medicine down."

"Your mother put scotch in her medicine."

Melinoe leaned over the table toward Harper and licked her lips. "Is that honey?" Harper passed her the bottle, and she squeezed about a quarter of it into the brew, shook it like a cocktail, and slid it across the table to Paegrinn like a seasoned bartender. "May I have some too?" she said, eyes riveted on the plastic bear.

Harper shrugged. "Sure. It's not mine."

The glaistig squeezed another quarter of the bottle into her mouth and let out a shuddery breath. Across from her the Phooka did the same with his medicine, and his face settled into a half-lidded, satisfied smile.

Harper smiled with raised eyebrows. "You two look like Homer Simpson with a doughnut." Melinoe and Paegrinn cocked their heads, and Harper giggled. "It's a human cartoon."

"The good stuff always gives me the munchies." The Phooka

grinned, ripped open a bag of Cheetos, and popped two orange treats in his mouth at once.

"Car tune?" Paegrinn asked.

The Phooka gulped down his snack. "Yeah, like a video but with paintings and lots of watered-down show tunes." Orange dust sprayed from his mouth.

Harper laid a hand on her friend's shoulder. "I found a camp stove back there. I'll make us some dinner." She dusted her hands on her pants and ducked into the kitchen where she busied herself making pasta with marinara sauce, guessing the vegan Fir Bolg could eat some of that.

To her surprise, Paegrinn loved the spaghetti. His laughter boomed throughout the house when Harper showed him the trick of sucking a single noodle through pursed lips. He consumed nearly his whole plate that way. Soon his fur was clumped with red sauce. The Phooka ate his food with lidded eyes and dropping ears, although he perked up watching Paegrinn slurp noodles.

"You look like the first Fir Bolg vampire."

"World's first vegan vampire. That's got to be a movie someday," Harper said. The Phooka met her gaze, and they cracked up. Paegrinn and even Melinoe joined in.

Harper's eyes rose to Alina's roost up in the rafters. She held out a piece of bread. The little Fae turned her back on the offering. "It's okay," Harper said. "No strings attached. I'll just leave it here and if a mouse or a will o' wisp should happen to want it..." She got up and laid the bread on a nearby rolltop desk, adding a dollop of honey to entice the tiny Fae. There was a twitter and Alina darted down, smiling after she took a bite.

The Phooka flipped on his side after he ate and fell asleep. Paegrinn pulled a colorful crocheted blanket over his patient and peppered Melinoe and Harper with questions about what nearly everything in the home was for.

Melinoe shot to her hooves. "Oh my! I'm the worst. How could I forget?" She wound a hand through her green locks and tugged.

"Forget what?"

"I promised your mother I'd tell you she loves you and is proud of you."

"You met my mom?"

"She's the bravest, most amazing human I've met." She lifted her spine and a radiant smile revealed her long canine teeth. "Except for you. She saved the entire village from the Sluagh, you know." Melinoe's wide eyes made her look like a zealot.

"My mom?"

"Gosh yes, she's fierce." Melinoe told Harper about the Sluagh attack and how Eileen and the Dusk King had fended them off. The glaistig mimed what she imagined the fight looked like. She shot at a rocking chair with her finger and even nailed Ez's snooty vocal inflections. Paegrinn asked about Glani and his father.

"You performed your task well, and it makes me happy to hear your story about my mom." Harper chose her words carefully to avoid thanking the Fae and triggering a debt.

Over Melinoe's shoulder, something white flickered in the gap between shutters and Harper's heart skipped a beat.

"Paegrinn, Melinoe, blow out the candles. Now," she whispered. The two bustled around the room and extinguished the light before joining her at the window.

Keening emanated from the forest, raising the hair along Harper's arms. Immediately after, a stocky blonde woman staggered out of the twilight woods and lurched for the house.

Harper gulped. "We have to help her." The last word died on her lips. A spectral white figure emerged between the dark tree trunks, white locks snaking over her head. Banshee. How did they find them so soon?

With a howl, a banshee swarm broke from the trees straight for the fleeing woman, but the cloud of dark avian forms arrived first, covering their victim in a mass of undulating wings. The woman's dying scream pierced the dusk air.

# CHAPTER 23

Though the flapping, squawking flock pulled away from the poor woman, the body had disappeared beneath the milky fog.

Donn strode from the forest, fingers steepled in front of his chest, and reached out a black gloved hand, palm upturned. Beckoned to her new master, the woman's tattered corpse levitated skyward, head lolling.

The Phooka stirred behind her. "What are you looking at?" His voice was too loud.

Melinoe rounded on him with flashing eyes, a finger to her lips. "Sluagh," she whispered.

The shapeshifter rolled off the couch and stood leaning on the armrest. His form shimmered at the edges and started to stretch and pull into the shape of a wolf before collapsing back to his natural state. He hunched, braced against the sofa, panting.

The Fae Sluagh and Donn surrounded the remains of the woman, mouths wide, the sparkling blue essence of her soul disappearing down their gullets as her flesh melted away, leaving the gaunt spectral frame of a Sluagh behind. The woman dropped her head forward, arms wide, scanning her new body before collapsing into an avian shape and joining her new siblings roosting in a fir tree, her physical remains mercifully hidden by the mist.

Harper's eyes refused to pull away or stop their rapid blinking, and her breath paused. They'd just witnessed the birth of a Sluagh.

"What was—" Paegrinn spoke first.

"That's the fate of all humans now. Trapped until Donn or his Fae Sluagh finds them, brings them to their master, and they feed. Not one soul has made the Underworld journey to be stirred in Cauldron of Rebirth for over fifty years. There's almost nothing left of the brew," Melinoe said in an uncharacteristically somber tone.

The Phooka's ears drooped. "Like a soup that's become merely watery broth that doesn't nourish."

Melinoe nodded her agreement with the Phooka. First time for everything. The click clack of her hooves was muffled by the braided rug as she circled the room, meeting Harper's unspoken question with pinched eyebrows. "When you die, your soul is supposed to cross the Underworld, where the hag Cerridwen takes the sum of that spirit's journey and adds it to her bubbling cauldron. All the memories, insights, creativity, added and mixed with thousands of others."

Harper crinkled her nose. "A witch cooks us? How horrid."

"Believe me, it isn't." The Phooka clambered back up onto the tacky couch. "It is how your life contributes to the growth of your race, for Cerridwen stirs them until they reduce to their essence and combine with all the others in a rich brew. She feeds one ladle to each new life to start their journey in the Green World. Contained within it are all your talents, traits, innate skills, and intuitive knowledge, the foundations of your story. What you construct on top is part choice, part circumstance, but with no foundation, you can build only illusions."

"So I might have a little piece of Ghandi or Mozart in me?" Harper said.

Melinoe nodded. "And generations of others, good and bad."

Harper had thought of Badb and Gwyn as monsters, and they were. But the true evil stood just outside. A bottomless pit of mindless consumption, draining the spiritual truths, transcendent songs, transformational experiences of countless lives, impoverishing generations to come. The sublime and the profane of human existence, less meaningful because it was simply gone. For all time.

Donn faced the farmhouse and sniffed the air. Instinctively, Harper drew back from the window, her heart racing. It remained lighter outside than in the house, so he couldn't possibly have seen them through the windows.

"I thought Ms. I-Can-Run-Like-the-Wind here had covered our escape and led the Sluagh and the Wild Hunt away from us."

Melinoe scowled at the Phooka. "I did, but they could have stumbled on the actual trail, now hush."

"You were here before us. How do we know you didn't just bring them here?" The Phooka bared his teeth.

Melinoe balled her fists at her side and stepped toward him. "That's something a dark Fae like you would do."

"Uh, guys, we have a big problem." Paegrinn pointed outside. "They're coming."

A cloud of leathery wings arced straight for the house, the broad hooves of the incubi kicking up clumps of sod while the banshee soared in front. The souls dropped onto the porch and scattered across the lawn in human shapes, shambling toward the doors and windows.

The Phooka tried to shapeshift again, to no avail. "Harper, I'm too weak to be much use."

"Just get your sword and be ready to fight if they break through," she said, her blade already poised to strike. The Sword of

Light rested on the dining room table. Now would be the perfect time for it to decide to leave its sheath, but she didn't bother to try.

Paegrinn took up a position at the front door with his staff at the ready, while Melinoe clopped to the back of the house, a long dagger in each hand. Her full lips moved, and strange symbols glowed all along the walls and windows.

"Will that keep them out?" Harper called.

Despite the dire circumstances, the glaistig beamed at her. "No one's broken them yet."

Harper's shoulders sagged with relief.

"Then again"—Melinoe shrugged—"never tried to block this many of anything before."

"Great."

Paegrinn dropped to one knee and placed his hands on the floor. A deep rumbling formed in his chest. The sound grew louder, and white filaments snaked between the floorboards and sprang through his fingers. They spread out to the exit and along the windowsills, weaving into thick cords, reinforcing the glaistig's magic. When they covered the entire door, they turned brown. The Fir Bolg thumped the network with his spear. Satisfied it sounded solid, he resumed his defensive stance at the doorway.

The Sluagh rushed the house from every direction. An incubus slammed into the door. Without Paegrinn's fungal reinforcements, he'd have broken through.

The first group of human Sluagh was close behind. Outstretched arms met window glass, and a flash of green light sent them scattering, careening into the night air. A ring of bodies tumbled down all around the house. The second wave endured the same fate. So far, so good.

Paegrinn built another layer of mycelial cords across the entrance for good measure. The Phooka stood next to him, propped against the doorframe, sword dangling from his hand.

Wave after wave flung themselves at the house, but none broke through. Just when Harper thought they might survive the night, Donn's black boots echoed on the front steps.

His pale bearded face appeared in the window, shit-eating grin still attached.

"I know you're in there, love. I can smell your life force. Open the door so we can chat."

Harper scanned the faces of her companions. The Phooka shook his head slowly. For the second time, he and Melinoe agreed on something. From across the house, she mouthed no.

Paegrinn moved to stand directly behind her.

"Come, come now, love. It's over. Nothing is served by playing this silly game of hide and seek."

Harper nudged the right side of the shutter open just enough to frame Donn's face. Of course, the Sluagh knew they hunkered inside, but Harper believed it was far from over. If she opened the shutter, at least she could tell him to piss off face to face.

"There. See, you can be reasonable. Now why don't you and your little friends come out, and we'll get you to Badb straight away."

"Hard pass." Harper gripped the blade tighter to avoid showing him how badly her hands shook.

"I've got you surrounded, love. You can't stay in there forever. It's over." Donn held a hand next to his face and beckoned her with his index finger.

"I don't know. The place has a hip hunting lodge vibe. We like it here. What do you say, Paegrinn?"

The Fir Bolg pointed the sharp end of his staff straight at Donn's throat. "I always wanted to live in a human house. We should definitely stay."

"Most of us are dead, love. We can wait an eternity. Can your little friend Emilio?"

Mention of Emilio drove the air from her lungs. Harper braced herself on a wooden chair. This had to be another trick. "How do you know about him?"

"Know about him? I've seen him. Though the last time he wasn't looking too good. Tell you what, come with me now and I'll ask Badb to let him go."

Emilio, please no. He has to be okay. She wanted to ask more, but she'd never get a straight answer. They had to find a way out of the farmhouse and past the Sluagh. Emilio depended on her. She shook the feeling back into her arms and legs and drew herself tall. "We'll escape just fine on our own. We'll rescue him ourselves."

Donn giggled through lips pressed into a tight line. "I can't wait to hear how you propose to do that, love."

"Easy, *love*. Eventually, the Wild Hunt will find us too. We'll just wait for them to kill you right there on the lawn. I've already escaped from Gwyn twice, so I figure my odds are much better with him than with you." Harper closed the shutter again and took a shaky step back from the window.

Donn giggled. "We'll see, love. We'll see."

"Harper." Paegrinn pointed to the line of banshee sweeping for the upstairs windows. If their assault continued, the magic holding them back would eventually weaken.

The idea hit her like a freight train. Guns. The Fae in their small group may not be able to touch them, but she and Paegrinn could.

"Paegrinn, I have an idea. Follow me." Footfalls hammered the floor, clattering the china in the cabinets.

Harper flung open the doors to a tall wooden cabinet. Inside were a half dozen shotguns and some assorted handguns. One by one she tore the drawers open, hoping for at least one box of steel bird shot. She wasn't sure about the Sluagh who were human souls, but she was certain the iron in the shot could take out an incubus, probably the banshee too. If they wanted to knock on the door, she intended to pump them full of iron.

"What are you searching for?" Paegrinn's whiskers tickled her neck as he bent over her shoulder.

Lead shot, .22 rounds, .38 rounds. Everything but what she needed. "Something with iron in it. Ever fired a gun before, Paegrinn?"

"I don't know what a gun is."

Harper yanked a long shotgun from its rack and thrust it out to Paegrinn. "This is a gun." She tapped the barrel. "You always act like it's loaded and keep that end pointed at the ground and not at anything you don't intend to kill right now."

"I don't want to kill anything right now or ever." Paegrinn held the stock between his thumb and index finger, the barrel definitely aimed at the floor.

"Well, keep that barrel pointed down." After a pause, she turned to her friend and stretched her arms up to lay her hands on his shoulders. "Life seemed simple back in your village. It's not like that out here. More often than I'd like, choices narrow down to kill or be killed, or kill to save another from a senseless death. Right now, it all comes down to who dies. Them. Or us."

The corners of Paegrinn's mouth turned down and he slumped a full foot shorter, but he nodded once slowly.

With a sad smile meant to be reassuring, she resumed her search for steel ammunition. She tossed box after box of ammo onto the floor beside her. She'd all but decided to just try the lead shot when she pulled out a carton of bird shot shells. "Bingo."

Harper grabbed the other shotgun, laid the shells on an end table, and stepped beside Paegrinn. The sounds of shrieks and hooves battering their defenses caused her hands to shake. "Do exactly what I do." Harper showed him step by step, through cracking the gun open in the middle, sliding in the shells, and preparing it to fire. Despite having never seen a gun, he proved a quick study.

"Locked and loaded." Harper smiled up at her friend. "Follow me."

Harper brought Paegrinn over to one of the side windows. "Melinoe, will iron cross your magical barrier?"

Melinoe wrinkled her nose. "Should cut through any Fae magic."

"Good." That gave them a distinct advantage, at least until they ran out of steel shot. "Watch me first, Paegrinn, and keep your gun pointed at those floorboards."

The Fir Bolg nodded and kept his weapon safely pointed away while he parted the mycelium from the window's edge.

Harper slid the window down just enough and braced herself with the stock resting on her shoulder. "When I pull the trigger, this thing is going to be very loud. When you try, it's going to feel like a horse kicked you in the shoulder. You point the barrel toward the nearest Fae and do this."

She took a breath. "Fire in the hole!" she bellowed and squeezed the trigger. Melinoe and the Phooka screamed and Paegrinn let out something more like a howl. The stock slammed into Harper's shoulder and she staggered back half a step.

"For fuck's sake, what the hell was that?" the Phooka called.

"Shotgun," Melinoe said.

"I did say fire in the hole."

The effect on the Sluagh was immediate. Two incubi who waited ten feet from the house fell to the porch and didn't move. A handful of banshee screeched and clawed at their bodies where they'd been hit, and the black birds scattered.

"Think you can do that, Paegrinn?" He nodded. "You get two shots, then you have to reload like I showed you. Shoot only when they get close, because we don't have too many of these." Harper deposited half a dozen more shells on the windowsill next to him. "You take the west and south side. I'll handle the east and north." Paegrinn nodded.

Before Harper reached her station, Paegrinn hollered, "Fire in the hole!" followed by a loud crack. "Oh no, I think I got one."

"I think you got them all," the Phooka yelled from upstairs. "They're retreating on his side."

"Great!" Harper pointed her gun out the eastern window. Paegrinn seemed to enjoy yelling 'fire in the hole,' so she continued their impromptu tradition. "Fire in the hole!" she bellowed and sent the Sluagh fleeing on her side of the building.

The horde retreated to a safe distance.

The Fir Bolg gathered his friends into his arms and crushed them in an embrace, but their moment of peace evaporated when Donn pressed his face against the window.

"Ho, ho, ho, love." There was another high-pitched laugh.

Melinoe scratched her head. "What a strange thing to say."

Harper's face melted into panic. She caught the Phooka's eyes where she saw the same realization dawn.

"They're pulling a Santa." The Phooka hobbled toward the fireplace in the living room.

"Paegrinn. Fungus, up the chimney! Melinoe, warding spell!" Harper barked as they raced for the fireplace. Harper and the Phooka crouched, swords poised over the hearth.

Within moments, the wail of the banshees came from above. The flue was pretty narrow, so they'd have a hard time getting two floors down to the companions. Melinoe chanted next to the rumbling Paegrinn. Wisps of mycelium lashed together and snaked into the chimney.

Melinoe panted and fell back. "Too much iron. Can't."

Iron tools, pokers, dustpans, littered either side. Harper thrust them aside while Alina squeaked beside her.

"It's up to you, Paegrinn."

The healer was too focused on his work to hear her. The mycelial cords swelled inside the flue. But the enemy Fae were already on their way down. The dry sounds of claw on brick rocketed closer at an alarming speed.

White hair dangled just above the hearth when Paegrinn's chant rose to a bellow. The banshee shrieked as a wall of mushroom closed around her, crushing her within the chimney.

That was close. Anger and fear made an adrenaline cocktail that left Harper sweating and shaking. But she gritted her teeth and stamped to the door.

"Bah, humbug, asshole." She flashed Donn her middle finger.

# CHAPTER 24

The regimented rhythm of captivity and the autopilot forced by exhaustion made each day bleed into the next in the Erimus Pharmaceutical tower. Emilio estimated four, maybe five, days had passed since their gruesome tests.

The bustle of life in the citadel never ceased. Bands of Fae hustled through the tree-ringed portal and returned with new Underworld refugees. Others, armed to the teeth, disappeared off the island to return with more humans or enemy Fae who either became fodder for genetic extraction or living batteries for the gate.

First thing every morning, the Sidhe taught the Netherfae to battle with swords, staffs, and improvised weapons. After a meal break, their magical lessons began.

The collars they wore weren't merely the glamorous flair that so perfectly accessorized surgical scrubs and punished them with blinding agony for the slightest transgression. They had a darker purpose. That purpose revealed the Netherfae's role in Badb's imminent war. Emilio and his friends were conscripted generals, forced through the sorcery of their abilities and amplified by the torques to puppet groups of Dust-addicted people.

Netherfae could go where Fae could not, but Badb's true genius was using humans to battle their own kind. An elegant solution in a perverse sort of way, because each soldier killed by the opposition was also a win for Badb.

The situation felt hopeless, but Emilio's mind worked overtime, devising tests and plans. A systematic approach solved almost every problem. That's exactly what he hoped for the experiment he was about to try.

A side effect from his metal plumage was that his wardrobe became disposable. When covered in sharp gunmetal feathers, garments were single use; he tore at least five a day. The Fae tired of bringing him fresh ones, so they stacked dozens in a corner and retrieved the shredded castoffs when they brought his meals. That would be soon, so he had only minutes to conduct his clandestine test.

His hypothesis about his sadistic jewelry was that the collar worked like electricity, through contact. That's how it felt when the pain lanced into his body. It always started first where the collar touched his neck. If he could insulate his skin, perhaps the misery would end and he could neutralize this obstacle to escape.

He tore another two strips from a tattered tank top. The pile of them at the corner of his bed looked like fabric spaghetti, complete with splotches of red. This was going to hurt.

Emilio took a heavy breath, rolled his head across his shoulders, and mentally steeled himself for the white-hot misery he was about to inflict on his own body. He hoped the chokers didn't signal the Fae when they activated, or he'd be in deep guano.

Before he changed his mind, he grasped the end of a long strip, brought his fingers to the collar, and thrust the piece between the

metal and his neck. He didn't notice the bruising when his knees
hit the marble floor because of the searing agony everywhere else.

Teeth clacked together as muscles seized. He traced the lip of
the choker, shoving the fabric down as he went. With a last jittery
shove, the first piece was in, his hands fell away, and the choker
quieted. For a moment, he paused while his muscles uncoiled. If
he let himself pause too long, gasping on his hands and knees, he'd
never work up the will to complete the experiment. With a
whimper, he willed his quaking fingers to clasp a second fabric
shred.

*Come on. You can do it. One down. About two to go.* He
jammed another strip in. Just a single inch of his tan skin met
silvery metal. One more push and he'd discover if his theory was
correct.

A moan escaped through clenched teeth, but he snatched up
the smallest piece of fabric and shoved it into place. The chokers
hadn't been activated this long before, and every muscle stiffened
in protest, but the torture stopped as he yanked his hand back.

For a moment he rested, seated on his shins, chest heaving.
Droplets of sweat dripped from the ends of his black and blue hair.
Slapping feet and guttural goblin speech meant time grew short.
Now or never. He drew in a long breath and held it. His trembling
fingers reached for the collar's lip. He squeezed his eyes shut and
let the tip brush the metal.

Searing pain was his reward.

"No," he whispered. It hadn't worked. Either the collars
operated on a purely magical principle, requiring no contact, or
fabric conducted whatever power made them work. He didn't
relish the prospect of experimenting with more materials, if he
could even get any, but he was fresh out of other ideas.

The sounds of the Fae making their rounds grew close. His
heart dropped. He hadn't thought this experiment all the way
through. He'd borne the pain of inserting the makeshift insulation.

Now he had to rip it out before some surly goblins caught him up to no good.

It turned out to be much easier than lining the collar. He barely needed to touch the device, but it still throbbed. With a grunt, he flung the shirt bits back on the pile and flopped stomach first on the bed.

Physical aches faded eventually, but becoming an evil monster was forever. The fact they forced him to slide into the minds of Dusted people and hurt them didn't stop the actions from being his actions, his mistakes that harmed them. Every nick and blow his puppets endured were intense ghost pain, Emilio sharing in their suffering. But even that was easier than sharing their terror. *How many Hail Marys absolve that, abuela?*

He must have dozed off. A vicious banging jolted him fully awake. Callon. Pounding on the bedframe with the flat of his sword. The haughty Sidhe kicked the leg for good measure, shoving the bed a foot along the floor.

Emilio levered himself up on his elbow and dragged a palm across his cheek. "Morning, sweetheart." He gave Callon his most romantic smile, then puckered his lips.

A bent old man shuffled behind the warrior with a plastic tray of food. His wrinkled face wore the vapid euphoria of the Dusted. Callon snatched the food from the man, held it in his outstretched hand, and let it fall to the floor.

"Eat. Pig."

Anger darted across Emilio's eyes. He knew better than to show it. His throat still burned from the last time Callon decided to 'teach him some manners.'

"How thoughtful of you. I hate getting crumbs on my bed. Care to join me?" Emilio flashed a grin more sneer than smile and plopped down cross-legged in front of the ruined meal.

Callon wrinkled his nose. "Be in the hallway in five minutes." The elf turned on his heel to leave.

"Pendejo." Emilio whispered.

"What did you call me?"

"Pendejo. Spanish for light of my life."

"Five minutes."

Emilio had no intention of eating from the floor. He wasn't sure if it was the food, or if his transformation hadn't been the success they believed, but ever since he emerged from the mist cocoon, food failed to satisfy and he grew weaker every day. A craving for something else he couldn't fully discern hollowed a ravenous emptiness in his core.

Mealtime complete, he followed Callon to his lesson. One downside to being covered in metal feathers, aside from the obvious, was that they efficiently conducted the chill autumn air. Walking outside jabbed his skin with a hundred tiny ice picks. The shiver passing through him created a sort of tinkling music, like wind chimes.

Callon and Emilio were the last to arrive. Emilio's friends were already lined up in the center of the field, each with their Sidhe escort. Behind them, a couple dozen people milled. Their slack faces meant Fae had dosed them with Dust. Guess they'd canceled weapons training for the day.

A separate group of less robust humans sat ringed by redcaps and goblins. They were insurance against any further insurrection or any refusal to pilot their respective batches of soldiers to battle one another. Refuse to play by the rules meant someone died. The cold beast of hatred rattled its chains inside Emilio's heart, waiting for the opportunity to strike back at their oppressors, but today was not the day.

Callon deposited his charge next to the others. All the Sidhe and the omnipresent Dr. Jones moved to wrap the Dusted people in coats and hung long daggers at their sides, leaving the friends a couple of minutes to chat in inaudible whispers.

"Why are we starting with mind control today?"

"I don't like it."

"I bet they're planning an attack. Probably something small."

"Makes sense. Conditions here in a well-controlled setting don't always shake out in the real world," Emilio said. "A field trip might be our opportunity to escape."

Tamika pointed to her collar. "Not with these."

"And go where?" Alan shrugged.

"To the Lodge. Like I said before, we'll be safe there." Selina glanced around to make sure the elves weren't returning yet.

Emilio gestured with his eyes. "We can't leave these people behind."

"We must until we can come back with more than just the four of us."

"Harper is on her way. She has to be. We'd know if they'd caught her. This whole place would buzz about nothing else. She always has a plan."

"Emilio, even if she brings half the Green World Fae with her, they'd be hopelessly outnumbered." Selina flapped her hand. "They're coming. Hopefully Tamika's mindspace trick lasts even longer tonight. We need our own plan."

"The more I do it, the better I'm getting at sustaining it, I think —" She dropped her eyes.

Callon strode back and forth across the line of Netherfae. "Today you will practice controlling small battalions against each other, armed."

Emilio's chest tightened. The last thing he wanted was to hurt or kill the Dusted victims. This exercise marked a sudden escalation to their maneuvers, from piloting a maximum of two to a simulated combat situation. Selina might be right. This seemed like a logical ramping up to a test run somewhere.

"You two are up first." Callon jabbed his finger at Emilio and Alan, who let out a shaky breath.

Callon assigned each of them six people to control, and they took up positions at opposite ends of the clearing.

A Sidhe woman stood between both sides of mock combatants. Her voice, magically amplified, carried over the entire area. "Your goal is to take down the opposition controller. You will accomplish this by being the first to tag the enemy leader. Remember, should you hold back, one of them dies." She raised a graceful hand to the hostages at the field's distant edge.

"Begin!" Callon shouted.

Emilio focused his thoughts on the choker's crimson gem. As he'd been taught, he imagined his will reaching through the gem and into the heads of his six subordinates. A glistening red filament of light snaked from the stone at Emilio's throat and ended at the foreheads of his pawns. The tendrils flared bright white, then faded to invisible, though Emilio still sensed each one, an ephemeral cord conducting his commands.

Callon said the goal was fifty soldiers per Netherfae, which seemed impossible to Emilio. Puppeting these six would leave him listless and disoriented. He shuddered to think about the cost of fifty.

He sensed the limbs of his troop, like slipping on gloves. He made them all roll their necks and shake out their legs in perfect robotic unison. Their vapid grins never slipped, but from distant corners of their consciousness, fear and rage roared.

*I'm sorry. We have no choice. We've all been forced into this nightmare.* Emilio couldn't tell if his puppets understood him, but the far-off roar of despair quieted.

"What are you waiting for? Attack." Callon waved at the goblins and redcaps off to the side. A pair of goblins, skin like pea soup, clasped a young woman in their long, clawed fingers and held a knife to her throat.

Emilio pushed a series of commands into the hazy minds of his pawns. All six broke into a low run straight for Alan's forces, short daggers braced across their chests. The euphoric smiles never left their faces.

Alan split his contingent into two groups, each sprinting in opposite directions, which forced Emilio into a tough choice. Hold his line and potentially get outflanked, or risk losing control of his fighters because the farther they spread out, the harder it became to control them.

Sweat already beaded Emilio's forehead. If he kept the battle in the realm of pursuit, there'd be less possibility of injury. So he split his forces into three groups. Two, he directed at Alan's from different angles, and a single fighter would break off at the last moment to charge the accountant, tag him, and end the exercise quickly.

The two teams clashed, the snicks of blade on blade filling the arena. A hand smacked the nape of Emilio's neck, breaking his concentration. Alan disabled two of his troops as his attention wavered. The half-dozen jabs of pain piercing through his connections refocused him fast.

"Idiot," Callon snarled. "Never let the enemy divide your line unless you want to die. You left yourself wide open. I have a wager riding on this. If you fail me, I'll make you sorry."

"He's exposed, too," Emilio said and took flight, heading straight for Alan. Behind him, his lone fighter pivoted and fell in line.

Both their lines floundered as their leaders focused their attack on each other. Emilio thought this was the better approach, anyway. He wouldn't harm Alan, and if they battled each other, the humans would not get hurt.

Gleaming wings wide, Emilio dropped toward his bark-covered friend, arm outstretched to tag him from above. Leafy vines shot out of the earth straight at him, causing him to overcorrect and spiral down, head over heels, tumbling over damp grass and coming to rest at Alan's feet.

The accountant reached a branched hand to tag him, but Emilio had already rolled away. He dodged and weaved in and out of the vines leaping beneath his feet.

A boot smacked his ribcage. Callon again stood over him, his fine features a mask of rage. "You're a disgrace."

"Really? I thought I was doing pretty well." Emilio sliced a vine with his wing. "Haven't been tagged yet."

"But you're about to be."

The elf was right. In his battle with Alan, his control over his pawns had slipped. Only four of them fought, while the other two wandered around with slack jaws. Meanwhile, a pair of Alan's fighters barreled down on him, weapons held high over their heads.

Emilio's choker blazed again. He pushed directions to his two lost sheep.

"Nice try, Alan. But not today." Emilio leapt into the sky. "Props for the strategy, though."

"I just want this over fast." Alan's voice sounded strained.

"Me too, buddy."

While Alan had been talking, Emilio sent his last man slinking around the edge of the battlefield while the remaining people from each side fought at the fringes. Emilio flapped high enough to make evading Alan's two attackers easy, but close enough to draw them out and keep the focus from his lone wolf.

Emilio's man found an opening and lunged at Alan. The accountant's dodge came in a flash, while Emilio hovered above, attention riveted on his single attacker, who had strayed too close to another skirmish. Alan bobbed and wove, easily evading the lone wolf.

Emilio didn't notice Alan's team had maneuvered their brawl directly beneath him. With their habitual eerie smile, the tallest dropped his weapon, reached a hand overhead, and tapped Emilio's dangling foot. The accountant won the day, and the exercise had resulted in only minor injury to their human charges.

"Damn, Alan. I never saw that coming. Good work."

Emilio's next breath came out in a scream. The choker flared to life, sending jolts of agony through every muscle and deep into his bones. Six identical screams rose around him. *Oh God, they're still connected to me.* Emilio clenched his jaw through the pain but failed to break the connection. *I'm sorry, I'm so sorry.* He hoped somehow they heard him.

Callon loomed over him, hand stretched toward the choker, and a look of malicious glee on his face. Oh, how he enjoyed the anguish he caused.

"Callon, that's enough. If we damage them—" Alan's elven tutor curved her fingers over Callon's shoulder.

He shrugged it off. "This one still thinks he can best us. I see it in his eyes every time he looks at me." The muscles in his jawline clenched.

"Callon. Stop."

With a snarl, Callon stopped. Emilio went limp and rolled to his side. His Netherfae friends clustered, faces drawn with concern. His little troop lay scattered, crying and groaning. The agony must have shattered what remained of their Dust-induced euphoria because they were clearly in pain. The match was over. What Callon did had no excuse other than his own psychotic cruelty.

Emilio hauled himself up on shaking legs. Fists clenched, he stepped toward Callon.

"See, even now it looks at me as though it wants to harm me. Like it could." Callon tipped his torso to the side and kicked Emilio in the chest.

Damn the consequences. Emilio had enough of this smarmy, self-important douchebag. He regained his footing, lashed one of his wings at the Sidhe, and instantly regretted it. The choker activated with a scarlet glow, worse than before, and dropped him where he stood.

"You know, Amala, I've always hated that we have to drain our own kind to keep the gateway open. Even those Fae siding with human scum deserve better."

Emilio's legs flailed against the dirt, hands clenched fistfuls of grass, and gagging wails bubbled in the back of his throat. The entirety of his existence narrowed to just one thing: torture.

"Callon, Badb will never let you—"

"She definitely will. This is the little revolutionary who led the escape attempt a couple weeks ago."

The pain stopped, and the haughty elf bent over him. "As punishment for your attitude problem, you will receive the honor of powering the gateway tonight."

# CHAPTER 25

Harper peered through an upstairs window. Days had passed with no assault on the farmhouse, yet the siege continued. The Sluagh surrounded the building; the incubi camped in the driveway, complete with a cooking fire and occasional music; and the avians perched in the treetops.

It was the banshee who drove them all mad. The ghostly women drifted about in the low mist, never still, like spectral sharks. If they'd just mill about quietly, they'd merely appear ominous. Instead, they uttered their bloodcurdling shrieks a dozen times an hour. All day and all night. They hovered and shrieked. Then shrieked and hovered some more. The damn things never slept.

Harper's sanity hung by a thread. She had scoured most of the rooms for weapons or supplies to take if they ever escaped. She dragged herself up the stairs to the room she'd claimed, planning to change clothes and check out the attic, but her attention snagged on something else.

On the first night she'd discovered that the wall leading to the second floor was studded with photos. Happy family life and all the normal rituals that accompanied it documented a timeline ascending the stairs.

A formal sitting portrait held a scowling red-haired boy in the front. A brother would have been nice to have, Harper thought. Younger, like this kid. They'd fight over the bathroom all the time and she'd roll her eyes at the way he always wanted to tag along everywhere she went, and he'd make the exact same face this boy made in the picture when she sent him home.

Her favorite photo was snapped right here in the backyard. In it, picnic tables littered the lawn along with barbecue grills. A cluster of people played musical instruments while others danced, but mostly a few dozen friends and neighbors packed the picnic tables, plates piled high with what looked like chicken and corn and potato salad. Her parents used to dance a lot; Harper remembered that. Her parents would definitely be whirling around in front of the little band. Harper would have the biggest plate of food, and she'd not stray far from the grill.

Harper had run her fingertips along the edges of the frames. The higher she climbed, the older the children in them became. A wedding photo crowned the top. Not a dress she'd have chosen. Too puffy. But the groom was handsome. She could envision herself marrying someone like that. The father of the bride beamed with pride, but a twinge of sadness tugged the corners of his eyes. Harper would never see that look on her father's face.

She stared at the gallery, weight squeezing her chest. She'd give anything for even one of the family milestones on this wall. It wasn't fair. *I didn't ask for any of this. I'm getting Emilio, finding my mom, and then we're getting far away from this place.*

Her self-pity stopped dead when she crested the top of the stairs, where a young man smiled, arm tossed over a new truck, probably his first. The red-haired boy all grown up. The same vehicle, a decade older, was currently parked at a rakish angle on the lawn, its owner dangling from the window. The lovely bride and her father had littered the path to the porch, torn to shreds by Fae claws.

Harper's hand clamped over her mouth, a wave of sorrow threatening an emotional storm. She dropped and sat on the top stair with her head in her hands.

This was the fate awaiting Emilio's family, her mom, all families.

Harper's body shook, and she flopped over against the bannister while hot tears coursed down her face. She might be the only thing standing between countless families and ancient, supernatural evil. The weight of it was suffocating. They were so screwed.

The sounds of laughter from the den formed a counterpoint to the shrieking horrors outside and her heavy heart. The back of her hand swept the tears away, then she smiled and rose to join her friends.

Paegrinn's ability to inhabit the present and experience his joy at being in a real-life human house created a peaceful oasis in Harper's heart. Being a mere 117 placed Paegrinn squarely in the late adolescent stage of development for his people. He was the only Fir Bolg youth Harper had met, so she remained unsure if his fascination with everything human was the norm. He was like a nine-foot-tall kid, flitting through every room, examining each trinket and asking what it was for. The wonder in his eyes when Melinoe explained how the television worked or the function of the refrigerator eased some of the tension.

On the morning of their second day, Paegrinn had discovered a shelf of board games in an upstairs room. The Phooka sat up on the couch and taught him to play Risk, checkers, and Sorry—that one really upset Paegrinn. But the game that captured his affection was Monopoly, which was odd, Harper thought, because it represented the antithesis of Fir Bolg culture.

Interspecies game time became the tradition after every meal.

It gave them something to focus on other than the churning anxiety she saw reflected in all their eyes.

Melinoe and the Phooka's weakness to iron made them worry about the metal pieces. Instead of the usual Scottie dog and old shoe, they used the plastic cap of a soda bottle, a porcelain Siamese cat, an arrowhead pencil eraser, and a Lego Batman figure. Batman had become Paegrinn's constant companion ever since he rescued him from a dust bunny behind the bookshelf.

Lego Batman was languishing in jail when Harper plopped down on the overstuffed recliner to continue their game. The Phooka was extorting Melinoe with his hotels on Boardwalk and Park Place.

"I don't understand this game. No one owns the land," Melinoe said as she counted out currency to pay for her overpriced lodgings.

"But humans think they do, and they spend a lot of time amassing it and keeping others out of it. Unless they pay up. Light Fae always have champagne tastes on a beer budget." The Phooka wiggled his long black fingers and Melinoe placed the majority of her meager savings into his hand.

"At least your cat isn't a prisoner like Batman." Paegrinn's elbow propped up his crestfallen face.

"A little luck, and Batman can pay for a ride on one of my prestigious railroads." Harper smiled and rolled the dice, surprised she was able to have a little fun while the Sluagh stalked them outside.

The game ended as always with the Phooka amassing a giant pile of pastel cash and most of the board's properties.

"Interesting, as ever." Melinoe smiled and shook her head. "I better go bolster our protections."

"I'll assist you, again." The Phooka shoved the colorful afghan blanket aside and hopped off his place on the couch. Her shapeshifting friend had more energy every morning. Paegrinn thought he'd be good as new in another day.

"I didn't need your help yesterday, and I don't need it today." Melinoe turned her back on the Phooka, her delicate nose high in the air.

"It was you who overlooked the chimney and nearly got us killed. Or was that your plan?"

"Oh, you were a huge help. I guess where dark Fae are concerned, better to have them lying on the couch than mucking things up with selfish ineptitude."

"Why, you— I was poisoned defending—"

The high-pitched scream of a banshee hushed them, followed by another and another from all sides of the house. The sound resembled a million nails dragging down a chalkboard and froze everyone in place for a moment.

Harper shuddered. "God, I hate that sound." She whisked to the window to peer through the small opening in the shutters. Every once in a while, the Sluagh would test their defenses. Each time, the prelude included an increase in banshee wailing. And every time, Melinoe grew more exhausted, holding the line with her glowing protective sigils. Harper had thought her constant bickering with the Phooka was behind the loss of her usual chipper demeanor; however, watching the glaistig weave her magic along the walls, she realized that the poor Fae was dead tired.

Black shapes dotted the trees, and Donn paced, observed by a large gathering of his Fae. Nothing signaled an imminent attack. Harper drifted over to where Melinoe stood, arms wide, eyes closed, a spell on her lips. More shimmering sigils looped and bloomed over the wall, and the glaistig slumped.

"I wish I could help you with that. You seem more exhausted each day," Harper said.

"You're so sweet. I'm fine."

The wailing of the banshee crescendoed, and the house shook

when the Sluagh battered it from every direction. Donn must have grown tired of waiting.

Banshee and their incubus friends pummeled the magical barrier with clawed strikes and spheres of magic, while avians flung themselves at the upstairs windows again and again. They'd attacked before, the same way, but never for this long. This time, it looked like they meant business.

Within moments, Melinoe slumped, using the bannister to hold herself upright. The whispered words of her spell on an endless loop, Alina joined her, adding her own tiny magic to their defenses. Upstairs, the nearly healed Phooka did the same.

"Melinoe, how are you holding up?" he called.

The glaistig clenched her jaw. "Can't do this forever."

"Oh really? I figure I've got at least half an eternity left in me. Typical light Fae sloth."

"Because you lay on the sofa for two days doing nothing," Melinoe shouted over her shoulder.

Harper and Paegrinn stationed themselves at opposite ends of the house, shotgun barrels poised for a barrage of steel shot. Their reserves of shells had dwindled.

"Fire in the hole," Harper bellowed, and the Fae beat a hasty retreat before the inevitable thunder of her gun. But Harper hit four, a mix of banshee and incubus.

"They're fleeing," Paegrinn shouted.

The Sluagh on all sides fled outside the range of the birdshot while the avians flapped squawking to their roosts. Only Donn remained, his pale face hovering over his billowing robes, fingers steepled before his lips. Instead of retreating, the King of the Sluagh ascended the porch steps one slow step at a time.

Harper moved through the living room and stationed herself on the right side of the front door. Paegrinn moved to the left side. Melinoe, Alina, and the Phooka gathered at the base of the central stairs, prepared to fight.

Donn wagged a finger. "Naughty, naughty, love. Steel shot is a bit below the belt."

Harper pulled her window up and slid the shotgun barrel through. "Damn, my aim was off. I was aiming for their heads."

"This only ends one way."

"You're right, it ends with every miserable Fae dead on my lawn."

That got a reaction. The insipid smile slid from Donn's face. "Soon you'll run out of ammo. And water. Or your Fae friends will exhaust themselves, and then we'll come for you."

"Or Gwyn shows up again and wrings your pencil neck." Strange, the sense of relief that thought brought. "Besides, we have plenty of ammo and we'll pick you off one by one from the windows."

"I'm afraid neither of us has that kind of time, love." Donn swept his hand toward the treetops. A single black bird sailed toward his outstretched arm. "You see, Badb is almost ready to make her first move. That means she needs you out of the way. Fast. And you need to save your little friend before that happens. Come with me now and I'll spare your friends inside. Even put in a good word about your pal Emilio, and I get to secure my place at Badb's side when I present you to her. Everybody wins, love."

"Don't listen, Harper. He's a very bad man," Melinoe said.

"Don't do it, Harper," the Phooka said at the same time. He and Melinoe were on the same page.

Alina squeaked and bobbed up and down.

"Hard pass," Harper said with a grim smile.

"I thought you'd say that, love. I've recently learned you've always had a bit of a stubborn streak, even as a small child." Donn tittered, the smarmy smile breaking over his bearded face. He flicked his outstretched arm, and the bird hopped down to the floorboards.

The Sluagh grew and stretched into a stooped figure clothed in the usual tattered rags of his kind. Head down, he shuffled forward to rest inches from the window. When he lifted his face, Harper's features twisted and a strangled wail fell from her lips. Her stomach felt like she'd taken a point-blank shot from her weapon.

Harper screamed, dropped the gun, and slid down the wall, keening.

# CHAPTER 26

The holes in the wall patched, walls painted, the kitchen floor completely retiled, a new ceiling fan hung, and every single inch of the place, steamed, scrubbed, polished, and organized. The little house gleamed with an order it hadn't seen since they'd moved in, but Eileen was fresh out of projects. She'd treated post-Fae invasion cleanup the way she'd treated the bottle, and for the same reasons: avoidance.

Guilt about Harper's childhood, fears about her friends in the forest, and the surreal reality of knowing monsters existed, mixed to form a catchy little earworm that chased itself around and around through her thoughts. She spit out a fingernail she hadn't realized she'd been gnawing, and started tapping her foot. She had to move. If she sat still for another second, she'd burst.

She paced the hallway for a few minutes, drumming a finger to her temple and muttering under her breath a list of things she had to do, but images of the Wild Hunt tearing Harper limb from limb danced with waking nightmares of the Fir Bolg village burning while the Sluagh herded the survivors to servitude or death.

And just as she'd done while her daughter raised herself,

Eileen only watched helplessly. Paralyzed by her own grief and terror.

Who was she kidding? Even if she found Harper, what skill did she have to fight off a goddess, or wage war on the Wild Hunt? Hell, she'd struggled after neutralizing the incubi even the Dusk King referred to as bottom feeders.

She pushed her fists into her temples and screamed.

"Go away! Stop haunting me. Please, just go away." The last sentence trailed to a whisper choked by ragged panting.

*That's the real reason they dumped you here, you know,* the darkest part of herself whispered. *Because you're useless. A leech. Leeches don't deserve to live with them. It makes sense, really. You'd already crushed your daughter's soul and let your husband die right in front of you. They're sure you'd make all the wrong choices. It's who you are. Harper. Glani. Nuada. Gerald. They're all better off without you.*

She let her head fall forward. "No. No, that's not who I am. She needs me. I love her and she needs me." Her voice was barely audible. Her hand found the mushroom carving Glani had given her, and she gripped it so tight the edge bit into her palm.

*You're thinking about the poison again.* She could almost believe Glani was beside her. She clutched the necklace tighter and squeezed her eyes shut.

*Because you are a loving and kind person. It was because of that love you acted today as a warrior. The Sluagh couldn't be stopped any other way, and now you must make room within your soul for a new you. A bigger you. One brave enough to do whatever is necessary to defend others, and one courageous enough to carry the burden of the spiritual work to contain such power.*

It seemed the necklace replayed those moments with Glani like a recording, because the image of that moment was as vivid as the day it happened. Glani's assessment couldn't be true because strong people don't spend a decade and a half in the bottle, but it was the best defense Eileen had against that dark internal voice insisting she was worthless.

The Fir Bolg believed in her, and Eileen's actions were key to keeping them safe from Sluagh attack. Eileen pushed herself upright, back propped against the hallway wall. Her face pressed into the crook of her elbow, clearing away her tears. Then it hit her. The laundry area. She'd organize that.

Eileen bustled about the tiny basement room next to Harper's suite. Lint littered the floor, so she got to work sweeping it up and depositing it into the dustpan. She felt better already.

The next victim of her cleaning jag would be the cabinet above the washer. She didn't think anyone had bothered to open that in five years. She pulled the white plastic doors open and began to empty the contents onto the dryer. The usual mix of cleaning products, a box of old incandescent lightbulbs. The top shelf looked to be full of stuff even older. Made sense; neither of them were tall enough to reach up and clean it without a step stool.

Eileen rummaged through the room, searching for one. Nothing. So she hopped up on top of the dryer and started dragging junk down from the cupboard. Almost to the rear, her hand closed around a glass bottle. She hauled it across the plastic shelf and pulled it in front of her face.

Smirnoff vodka. A wave of anticipatory euphoria skittered up her spine and her mouth watered. She hadn't even felt her fingers unscrewing the lid or bringing the bottle to her lips, but the chill of the glass made her focus.

She removed the bottle from her mouth and stared at it. *Just a few pulls and you'll be able to relax again. You deserve that.* Her other fingers strayed to the mushroom at her neck and Glani's voice rang in her ears.

*What I know is the poison you dream of drinking now will only prevent you finding the pieces. Keep you broken.* The vodka hovered inches from her lips, bottle wobbling.

A sharp knock at the door jolted her from her internal debate. The bottle jerked from her lips and she scrambled down from the dryer.

A single truth cut through the yearning for chemical relief. Her efforts for Harper may yet meet with disaster, but if she gave in to the drink, ruin was certain.

Before she rationalized further, she hopped to the wash sink and poured the contents down. Then she hurled the bottle toward the trash can, where it shattered against the concrete wall. For a few seconds she crouched, braced against the dryer, panting.

The door. Someone was here. Eileen ran a quaking hand over her hair and straightened her oversize blue sweatshirt over the black leggings before ascending the stairs.

With a deep breath to steady her nerves, she rested a palm on the doorknob and swung it open. Only damp fall air and drizzle greeted her.

Glancing left and right up the street revealed only crunchy leaves tumbling along the sidewalk and a blue sedan rumbling past. *Probably just a noise outside. Who'd be visiting you here?*

With a shiver, she started to swing the door closed when something shiny caught her eye. A silver box about as wide as a dollar bill perched on the Jack-o'-lantern mat. Eileen bent down, snatched the filigree box in her cold fingers, and retreated inside.

Plopping down on the plaid 1970s couch, she cradled the treasure in her lap. It couldn't be from the Fir Bolg because they favored a more rustic aesthetic. The gift had to be from a Fae. Might it be dangerous? But no. If one of them wanted to harm her, they'd just break in.

She slid a finger under the latch and it snicked open. Cradled on rich purple velvet rested an ornate silver necklace. Eileen twined the long chain around her fingers and brought the crystal vial to her face. More filigree wound around the cap, and along the bottom, inside, a pearlescent liquid swirled under its own power.

A protective talisman, maybe? From whom? Ezrynhivar or Serotina? Curiosity drove her to pick up the box. Just the corner of a bit of paper protruded from the plush pad.

Plucking the cushion out revealed a note in an elegant, rolling hand:

*Macleay Trail, Witch's Castle. Tonight, 8 p.m. Release a single drop onto the stone beneath the fallen tree. No weapons.*

Eileen flipped the letter over and inspected the box. It had to be Fae that left it on her step. Her part might not be over just yet.

# CHAPTER 27

"It can't be. Oh my God, this can't be happening." Harper shook her head in her hands.

"Oh my goodness, sweetie, what is it?" Melinoe lowered herself onto the bottom stair and peeked beneath Harper's fingers.

The Phooka and Paegrinn pressed close, each with a hand on her shoulder. "It's just one Sluagh." The Phooka's voice was uncharacteristically soft. "They've stopped for now."

Harper lifted her tear-streaked face. Her throat ached so badly she could barely force the words out. Pointing up at the window where the gaunt face of the Sluagh man still hovered, she said, "That's my father."

"Your father?" Paegrinn stretched his spine up to stare at the poor soul outside.

Harper nodded. "He doesn't look like he recognizes me and he's a prisoner and he's stuck here. Donn's *consuming* him. He's *eating* my dad. Slowly, like the man from the woods." Once she started, an avalanche of barely coherent words rushed out, followed by a strangled scream and a clenched fist slamming onto the carpeted floor.

"Harper O'Neill." A brittle sound, more moan than speech, called through the glass. "Come outside. My Lord Donn offers a truce and guarantees your safety until our talk has ended." Her father spoke like a robotic zombie. No hint of his warm humor or compassion; nothing of him remained other than a haggard facsimile.

Harper pushed herself to her feet and leaned against the wall. With a clenched jaw, she reached for the door.

"Oh no, no, no. You can't go out there. He'll snatch you right up and take you to Badb." Melinoe crept forward on her knees, stopping inches from Harper.

"As much as I hate agreeing with Princess Sparklehooves, she's not wrong. This is a manipulation. A trick," the Phooka said, Paegrinn nodding beside him.

"It's my dad," she whispered.

"Was your dad." The Phooka's ears drooped. "He isn't anymore."

"You don't know that." Harper's eyes pleaded with the Phooka. "Melinoe, how fast can you whip up that protective barrier?"

"A couple seconds, if I prepare."

"Start preparing." She turned to Paegrinn. "Can you move your fungus aside, then cover me with your shotgun?"

"Harper, I agree with the Fae. This isn't a good idea. From everything my people know about the Sluagh, your dad's been too long with them. He's just a shade now, nothing of the man you loved remains."

"I have to find out for myself. If there's any chance at all he's in there..." Harper stood and searched her father's pallid face. Empty, clouded eyes stared back.

Especially as a child, she'd imagined seeing him again hundreds of times, and running into his arms with some minor bump or bruise. He'd sweep her up and spin her in a circle while her feet flailed the air. Then that soft smile would spread over his face and dry her tears like the sun dried the rain. He'd ask, "What's got you down, Rabbit?" Those words always set the world right.

Well, her wish had been granted. Gerald O'Neill waited on the porch, but this time, she'd be the one trying to salve his pain.

She nodded to Paegrinn.

The Fir Bolg crouched to the floorboards and rested his fingertips below the fibrous barrier. It parted, creasing in on itself like a curtain to reveal the door. Harper opened it and stepped through, face to face with the emaciated form of her father.

"Dad, is—"

"If you come with us now, the rest of your friends are free to go."

"Yeah, yeah, we heard that deal before. Next," the Phooka called from the doorway in his wolf shape, bristling hackles raised and ivory teeth bared. Beside him, Paegrinn leveled his gun right at the Sluagh's chest.

"Harper O'Neill, come with us now and the rest of your friends are free to go," Gerald O'Neill repeated in his robotic monotone.

Harper stepped tentatively toward her dad, eyes squinted. Gasps from her friends rang out behind her, and Alina darted out to hover just over her shoulder.

"Dad, it's me. Harper. Don't you remember me?"

She reached out and took his hand.

"No!" Paegrinn shouted.

"Harper don't!" The Phooka bounded up beside her, snarling and gnashing his teeth at the Sluagh.

"Wait, Phooka." The ghostly hand felt colder than the chill air. Like holding frozen metal. It lanced through her arm and down her spine and brought with it a sensation that her insides were crystallizing like ice on a cold window and she'd never be warm again. She shivered. Instantly, a flush of color rose in her father's gaunt face and the empty stare evaporated from his eyes. They even regained clarity and some of their original light brown hue.

Gerald stared at her hand clasping his own, drawing it up to his face. He shook his head and took a wavering step closer. "I know you. How do I know you?"

"Dad, look at me. Think. The last time you saw me, I was ten years old, but I'm grown up now. Harper. It's me, Harper."

"Harper... Harper." His hand strayed to his lips, then crawled across his features like a blind man searching for recognition. "But I died."

Harper bit her lips together and nodded while a tear slid slowly down her cheek. "Yeah, you did. Some demented Celtic goddess murdered you. Fifteen years ago."

He nodded slowly. Harper could almost see the wheels turn in his mind. "Eileen. Your mother—my wife—was called Eileen."

Harper smiled through her tears, nodding vigorously. "That's right. She's alive too."

"Nothing in life is to be feared, only understood." Gerald O'Neill smiled and held his finger in the air. "I told you that once."

"Way more than once. That's what you used to tell me when I wouldn't turn off the light for fear of monsters in the dark. You also said it when I was afraid to go to school on my first day. What a crock." Harper laughed and her dad joined in. For just a moment, they were a normal father and daughter.

"Then I made you talk to the monster under the bed, try to learn what it wanted."

"Yeah, most dads hunted them. You made me negotiate with them. Lame."

"We had so little time before..." The shade's eyes misted. "You did okay after I died?"

"No, Dad." The smile slid from her face, her voice almost a whisper. "It was really hard. Mom started drinking. We were homeless for a while, but I began working and we held things together. We're okay now, she's sober and living with Paegrinn's people." She tipped her head back. Behind her, Paegrinn released his grip on the shotgun and waved.

"I'm sorry I wasn't there for you, Rabbit." He dropped her hand. Bony shoulders slumping, he wept.

Harper threw her arms around him, and a thousand needles of ice sped through her veins. Her teeth chattered, but she wouldn't let go. Her father clasped her in a weak embrace.

"Dad, it's not your fault. You were stolen from us. I miss you every d- d- day."

"Rabbit, what in the name of God are you doing here?" Gerald released her and looked around like it had just dawned on him that his daughter was in the middle of nowhere, mixed up with Fae and ancient gods.

Harper told him about their Tuatha and royal blood, about Badb Catha, Nuada, and the Wild Hunt. She told him about Emilio's kidnapping at Mystic Island. "So I'm trying to rescue Emilio and, I guess, try to stop a war. And now rescue my father."

His face fell. "You can't save me, Harper. I fade a little more every day. There isn't much left about me I remember. Just bits and pieces."

"Yes, I can save you, Dad." She suddenly wanted to tell him everything she knew about him and his life with their family, so he could keep it all with him in his hellish limbo. "I remember all your corny jokes. And Mom told me you met her at a silent Buddhist retreat even though you hated spiritual mumbo jumbo and never could stay quiet for a hot minute. When I was terrified on my first day of school, you got on the bus with me and acted just like the other kids until I laughed my head off and all the fear went away. You were kind, smart, and fun. You were the best dad in the world. Please remember that." She wanted to take away all her father's pain, the years of suffering.

She'd take it all on herself if she had to, if that act would offer relief.

He smiled again at her, his face soft with wonder. "You grew up just how I imagined. Strong and kind. I love you, Rabbit."

"I love you too." Harper pulled him into a fierce embrace, ignoring the icy pain. Then she moved back and gripped his shoulders. "Dad, this is important. Remember what I'm about to tell you. Hang on to it, no matter what. There's a gateway to the Underworld somewhere on this island, in a tower. I'm going to try and close it, but before that happens, you can go through it and pass to the other side like you're meant to. All of you."

He smiled a sad smile. "We're bound to the King. He'd never let us stray that far from him. It's too late for me. But I can shield you now."

"Dad, promise me you'll try to get away. Please."

A shadow passed over his features. "I feel him pulling at me. We're almost out of time, Rabbit. We, Sluagh, I think you call us, share a hive mind. Like the human part of us sleeps, and we're aware of only what Donn wants us to know. You woke me, but it won't stay that way forever, a week or two at most. While I'm awake, I can exert a pull on the others while the King isn't focused on my thoughts. There are so many of us, he can't attend to a single one for long. Tonight, I'll create an opening along the north side of their line. And a distraction. Watch for it and be ready." The warm brown started to fade from his eyes.

"Dad! Dad, don't go. There's so much I want to say." Harper reached her hand out to grasp his once more.

"You've said enough, Harper. Always remember how much I love you. And when you see her, tell your mother I love her too." Gerald O'Neill contracted into his bird shape, then leathery wings beat the air as he winged to where his master waited, arms crossed, at the end of the driveway.

# CHAPTER 28

Once they'd moved him into his own spartan room, Emilio had mistakenly believed his days of sitting in a cramped cage to be over. Yet here he was, jammed into a four-foot cube. Before the wings, the fit had been tight. Now the agony of cuts and contortion competed with the sensation of his insides being vacuumed from his body through his pores every time something came through the gate between worlds. And that happened more often than the last time he'd skulked inside this plaza in his lab tech disguise.

"What in all creation are you?"

A haughty woman's voice drawled behind him, sounding every bit like a Southern debutante. Emilio inched halfway around, careful to minimize damage to himself from his plumage. "I'm Emilio."

"Didn't ask your name. I asked what you were. I've never seen anything like you before. Not in the Underworld and not here in the Green World."

With his wings safely stretched the other direction, Emilio lowered himself to his elbows and swiveled his head to regard the Fae caged next door. The first thing he noticed was striking jet black ram's horns coiling around the sides of her head. Royal blue hair tumbled beneath them all the way to the floor and harmonized with aquamarine eyes and pale lavender skin. "The mad scientist that created me called me part Alicanto."

The Fae wrinkled her nose and ruffled black leathery wings; the tips caressed glossy black hooves. "And the other part human, judging by the odor." A brown hobgoblin whimpered in another cell. "I don't know what an Alicanto is."

Emilio shrugged. "Me either. Clearly some kind of magical bird with metal feathers."

"How horrid."

"Hey, I didn't ask for this. They did it to me." Despair crept in first, followed by anger. "They had no right." He curled up in the bottom of the tiny prison.

"Your human half is showing."

"What—"

"Fairness. Rightness. Sappy fantasies for human children. They did you a favor."

"A favor? A favor! They kidnapped me. Tortured me. Destroyed my life. Turned me into a monster like... like—"

"One of us?" Her expression suggested she'd caught a whiff of something rotten.

Emilio nodded. How he wished Harper was here. Or his grandmother. His brown hand moved along the smooth wooden bars of his cage. He was isolated, cut off from his friends. Memories of starting school after his family's arrival in the United States arose.

He barely spoke English, and no one seemed interested in offering the scrawny, nerdy new kid so much as an anemic welcome. The long benches at the lunch table, meant for a dozen students, sat empty on each side of him. He ate his baloney sandwich surrounded by kids noshing on sushi. He could've disappeared right there, faded out and winked away, and not a soul would've noticed.

Until Harper. She'd been the only kid in school who came to sit with him. They bonded over matching baloney sandwiches and a shared invisibility.

By high school, all he wanted was to be that invisible fifth grader again. His eyes lingered too long on the toned bodies of the football team, and it didn't go unnoticed by the vicious teenagers steeped in the herd mentality of late adolescence. Harper and his grandmother had loved him anyway, been his refuge, and Harper had defended him with words and fists. She'd made his life tolerable when the names and the cruel, twisted faces spewing them out still hurt.

*Faggot.*

*Queer.*

*Fairy.*

"Half-breed. Not exactly one of us."

A breathy laugh escaped Emilio's mouth. "Netherfae." He shook his head. Not exactly one of anything anymore and doomed to never fit in anywhere.

Laughter, sharp and caustic, slithered from the Fae's cage. "Fitting moniker." She pointed at his collar and frowned. "Back in the Underworld, the Seelie Queen used one of those on my mother."

"What did she do to deserve that?"

"Fell in love with an Unseelie. The King. My father."

"They tortured her for that?"

She nodded. "She was too powerful to lose to the Unseelie Court, but my father freed her, allowed—"

The lavender-skinned Fae dropped her head and stared at the floor of her cage, fingers reaching back to clasp her hooves. Before Emilio could inquire about the sudden change in body language, the clatter of footfalls and a voice like a sharp winter wind approached.

"Focus your search on the Rachis Draconis mountain range. King Eveling believes some of the Unseelie gentry may be trapped near the peaks."

"It shall be done, Highness." A Sidhe warrior clutched his hand to a fist and crossed it over his heart.

"Turn to the east first. Spies inform me the hag Bheara is on the move and I don't need to tell you an encounter with her could prove disastrous for your rescue party." Badb Catha swept into the plaza, a dozen elves and countless kelpies, redcaps, and other Fae trailing in her wake. The Tuatha's shiny black boots and breastplate reflected the shifting glow of the gateway to the Underworld.

"Highness, they're ready on the other side." A bent goblin hunched in front of the long lever and panel of dials. Emilio's cage offered him a poor sidelong view of the shimmering center of the circular tree that formed the portal. Gears ground, filling the room with the clanking and screech of metal on metal. The thin, transparent cap across the gateway slid aside like the eye membrane of a snake.

From the slumped backs and fetal rocking the other residents adopted, what came next would, no doubt, be painful. He'd seen it before when he sneaked through this very spot during his previous escape attempt. Images of dead Fae being dragged from their cages replayed in his mind.

"You better brace yourself, Netherfae. This is going to hurt. One team returning, another leaving. Double drain."

The gossamer filaments terminating all over the skin of his shoulders and chest leapt to life. The pull of the life force tearing from his body felt like a giant vacuum sucking energy from every one of the thin leads. Brilliant light pulsed along each one, flowing down to where they lay bound at the base of the cage. Then his life force mixed with the others, flowing through a cord, wrist thick, that split and wound up to each branch of the massive circular tree trunk.

The bark shuddered to life along with the gleaming surface. Emilio felt dizzy. All around him, Fae of every shape and size moaned and wailed, some beating their bodies against their wooden cages. He joined them.

# CHAPTER 29

Harper withdrew to the relative safety of the farmhouse. Her friends gathered around her, but she barely registered them as she slid down the wall, hands gripping fistfuls of hair. To curl up in a ball, fall asleep, and discover this had all been a dream became her deepest wish.

Well, that wasn't quite true. Some bright spots were worth holding tight. The Fir Bolg people saved her mom, body and soul, and Nuada had seemed like family. But everything else that had happened since the Fae entered her life left her feeling hollowed out. The parts of her that misery hadn't drowned, the fires of anger burned to ashes.

Her friends pressed closer. Paegrinn patted her back gently while he knelt behind her, refortifying the door. Alina bobbed over his shoulder like a tiny spotlight, her soft glow illuminating the matching expressions of concern Melinoe and the Phooka wore.

"Oh my goodness, Harper, that had to be—"

Harper raised a hand to cut Melinoe off, then clenched it into a fist and rubbed it along her sternum. It hurt, but that was the idea. Momentary discomfort forced the horror to recede slightly, but air refused to fill her lungs. With a strangled cry, she clambered to her feet.

"Not now, guys. I need to be alone." She gestured at the pair to step aside. With long faces, the Fae moved from the landing, and she raced up the stairs, biting the inside of her cheek.

The clip-clop of the Phooka's hooves echoed in the vestibule. "You heard her father's ghost. We have to be ready to get out of here pronto. Melinoe, you—"

"I don't take orders from dark Fae. Someone should follow Harper."

"She said she wanted to be alone. Typical light Fae interference. Just my luck to—"

"You probably don't want us to prepare because you're in league with the Sluagh. Look at all those dark Fae—"

"Both of you, be quiet. We'll never see her dad's signal if you stand around arguing." Paegrinn's voice held a rare edge of irritation.

Listening to Melinoe and the Phooka bicker wasn't something Harper could presently tolerate. She closed the door to her adopted room and flopped onto the bed. Her throat ached while a list of all the terrible events ticked themselves off in her mind. She felt like a sapling trying to hold back an avalanche. *I don't know what to do, someone please tell me what to do.*

She pulled Nuada's sword across her lap and fished the glowing Lia Fail shard from her backpack. In such a short time, Nuada had become more than a mentor; he was family, and like the rest of her family, he'd been torn from her far too soon. Tears spattered the leather scabbard, leaving dark splotches.

Why wouldn't it draw for her now? Together, she and the Sword of Light had been victorious over the Wild Hunt. The blade sang in her blood, bolstered her heart, and even Gwyn ap Nudd had feared them. Nuada bequeathed it to her with his dying breath, yet the weapon had let her down her when she needed it.

With the Cliamh Solais drawn, she could make Badb pay for slaughtering innocents. This war would end before it began, and the world would be preserved. The stupid shiny rock was dead wrong. Harper let the sword slip from her grasp, pulled her knees to her chest, and allowed the misery to flow.

The weeping eventually stopped, and sooner than she guessed. Only to be replaced by restlessness. She hadn't explored this room much. It must have belonged to the family's youngest girl, the one with the spiky hair. Every wall held Gothic and punk band posters, and a shiny red vanity pressed beneath the window, filled with makeup in dramatic purples and blacks.

The room's prior resident had two closets stuffed full of clothes. If they were fleeing tonight, Harper wanted more practical attire.

She stripped her clothing off and put on what she felt would be the best traveling clothes, choosing multiple layers to keep out the cold. A new pair of deep blue stretch jeans promised the same freedom of movement the elven garb provided. It was bonus that they bristled with metal zippers. She selected a dark purple hoodie with black roses embroidered on it that clung against her curves.

A glint of metal from a pair of spiked boots brought a smile. Steel. Fairies hated iron. Harper swept her hair from in front of her eyes, stooped down, and dragged them from their hiding place. *Emilio would love these.* Gleaming plates covered the heel and arced over the toes. Tiny studs dotted the sides all the way to the tops. Luck smiled on her and they fit perfectly, rising to the middle of her calves. She imagined kicking some redcaps and watching them flee in fear of her footwear.

A wide smile crept across her face when she noticed the matching spiked jacket. She slipped it on. It fit like it was made for her. The sleeves held several rows of studs, and half-inch spikes dotted the shoulders. Let one of the Fae try to grab her in this.

*My armor.*

She swung the closet door closed to reveal the full-length mirror and stopped cold at the stranger she saw reflected there. Where there had been a quiet receptionist slumping under the weight of her world, a determined woman now stood tall. Harper might have no clue what to do next, but right now, she was all that opposed Babd Catha. She had no choice but to prevail. Somehow.

Muffled bickering between the Phooka and Melinoe rose beneath the floorboards. No doubt they were arguing about who was the turncoat. Recent days had given Harper reason to second-guess both Fae. The Phooka had imprisoned Alina, and was it truly chance that their enemies were never far from Melinoe?

Packed, changed, and slightly more pulled together, she clumped down the stairs. Paegrinn had dragged a recliner in front of the door, where he sat with the shotgun across his knees. He opened his mouth to say something, but Harper spoke first.

"I'm okay, Paegrinn."

The Phooka saw her before Melinoe, and the shapeshifter's jaw hung open. "Hey, if we end up at the Thunderdome, you'll fit right in."

The steady clop of hoofbeats from a distant room announced Melinoe. "You look. Um.... interesting." The glaistig cocked her head.

Harper offered a weak smile. "Steel should make the Fae think twice about attacking me."

"Harper, meeting your dad like that must have hurt so much."

Harper brushed aside her friend's concern. "Nuada said at the council that we needed to close the gateway between the worlds. And we will, but not before we give those poor, trapped souls a chance to escape. I owe that to my father."

Alina fluttered down from her perch and zipped several revolutions around Harper's head.

"How are the five of us going to accomplish that?" Paegrinn asked.

Harper perched on the back of the couch covered with forest scenes and shrugged. "No idea. What I do know is we can't help anyone while we're stuck in here. We'll watch. And wait for my dad's move. Then we run. We'll solve the next problem when it crops up."

The Phooka rolled his eyes. "That's a rubbish plan."

"I think it's a perfect plan."

"You would." The Phooka stuck his tongue out at Melinoe. "Suck up."

"You have a better idea, Phooka? Anyone?" No one answered.

"This is so exciting! We're so close. I hope the Underworld is visible from the gateway. I've always wanted to see the homeland of my people." Melinoe clasped her hands beneath her chin and hopped once.

"We should double check the packs, keep them by the door, and take turns watching the Sluagh. No clue what my dad has planned, but we won't have long to act. I've got some lights, matches, and some other things in here." She propped her backpack next to the front door.

"I'll look for more of these." Paegrinn held up a shotgun shell. "Though I don't like how much death this weapon deals." He lifted the gun close to his face.

The Phooka nodded. "My gentle Sasquatch friend, humans are famous for overkill."

"Melinoe, Paegrinn, and you too, Alina, keep a watch out for anything that looks like our chance to get out. The Phooka and I will gather some food."

The Phooka's pink tongue traveled over his lips and he clapped his hands, rubbing them vigorously together while following Harper into the kitchen.

Harper figured they'd pack anything light and not in a steel can. The Phooka rifled through the cabinet adjacent to the stove.

"Aha!" His grin widened as he pulled out a bear-shape

squeeze bottle of honey. He tossed two more next to several bags of chocolate chips atop the provision pile he'd started on the Formica-topped table. The Phooka packed for survival like a child would.

"The last thing we need is sugar and candy if we're going on a long trek."

"The honey and chocolate don't have to be for us. Among the Fae, this stuff fetches a high price, especially when the Veil thickened. Never know who we'll need to bribe."

"How much can that magical bag of yours hold?"

"How many angels can dance on the head of a pin?"

"Well, I found these and there's three more just like them." Harper hefted a full case of snack-size cheese curls and waggled them at her friend.

"Bless you, my child."

Harper deposited all four cases on the table next to honey, bread, and every box of cereal the Phooka could find. She pushed to the pantry's rear shelf, adding anything she thought might store well, including some nuts and dried fruit, granola bars, and jerky. Poking her head out of the door, she called, "You got any cookware in your fancy bag?"

"An aluminum cook pot and a couple of bowls. Why?"

Harper emerged with an armload of mac and cheese and some spiced dry rice meals. "I think that's about all there is that isn't canned."

The Phooka had already crammed half their stash into the grey satchel that appeared across his shoulder precisely when the Fae needed it. Her thoughts strayed to Alina, and she worried about what else might lurk in there. An idea hit her.

"If the Wild Hunt attacked, could we hide inside that thing?"

"I like the way you think, but sadly, no. Living things don't do so well in here."

"You kept Alina in there."

"Alina is very small, and the lantern provided her protection and her own habitat."

"Do you have any other little debtors in there?"

He cast her a sidelong glance and narrowed his eyes. "I told you our world is—"

"Different. Yeah, I know. But it's wrong. You and I can't be friends if you're forcing other beings to be your slaves. Do you have any other living things inside that bag?"

The shapeshifter slid off the chair he'd perched on. With slow, measured steps, he came to stand at Harper's feet and looked up at her. "No. I do not. And I think you might want to step down off your pedestal."

"Really?"

"You seem fine using my debtor to reach your friend. If you were so deeply concerned about her *human* rights, you should have demanded I free her the moment you saw her, and not merely after she led us across this island. You are just as conniving and opportunistic as we are, and that, my dear, is why I think you've got a bug up your butt about what other treasures I might have in my fantastical bag."

Harper reared back like she'd been slapped. His words stung.

"You're right. We should free her now."

"No. In fact, we should not." The Phooka's face softened. "Hers is my debt to collect, not yours. Truth is, she's insurance and we may need her many talents if we hope to find your friend."

Paegrinn's voice boomed from the living room. "Harper, you'd better come in here."

The Phooka shoved the last of the food into the bag and bolted for the den, Harper on his heels. As they slid to a stop behind Paegrinn, the baying of hunting dogs pierced the early evening silence.

"Oh sweet Mother Danu, it's the Wild Hunt." The glaistig's

hands hung in the air, already tracing glowing sigils along the walls. Alina bobbed by her side.

Five red-eared dogs galloped through the mist, eyes glowing like hot coals. Elves and other Fae were close behind.

Donn gathered his forces on the far side of the driveway, and Fae already formed a line across the yard. Donn's hand contorted into a claw as he beckoned the avian Sluagh from the treetops. On all sides of the house, black birds fell like rain, and gaunt human forms congealed from the mist.

A tall figure dressed in shades of brown emerged from the dense forest. A maskless Gwyn ap Nudd strode around the red barn. The wind whipped his shoulder-length hair across his bearded face.

"Well, you sure called that one," the Phooka said.

Gwyn marched straight for Donn, sword in hand, ghostly dogs spread out at his sides. In moments, he'd be in Donn's line of sight, past the edge of the building. Low mist caressed them with each step. The Wild Hunt loped into defensive positions around the perimeter, though the Sluagh outnumbered them ten to one.

"Get ready. The instant there's an opening, we run for it." Harper slung her backpack over her shoulder, secured the Sword of Light to the pack, and slid the blade she stole from Gwyn through a leather belt.

Then she saw him. Her father shambled straight for Gwyn and they paused beside the barn wall, barely hidden from Donn. What was he doing? He was going to get himself killed. Well, struck down at least. Harper didn't know what happened to Sluagh felled in battle since they were dead already.

"Dad, no." Harper pushed past the parted mushroom barrier and reached for the doorknob.

A large hairy hand held her back. "Harper, wait. This may be his plan."

"Gwyn will hurt him."

"Maybe not. Look." Melinoe pressed behind them and pointed toward where the two now stood face to face. Gerald O'Neill leaned close to Gwyn for several seconds, then paused.

Gwyn reached a hand up and patted her dad's shoulder. Harper tilted her head to the side and squinted. That was odd. Why weren't they fighting? The scene was far away, but the gesture looked tender. Meant to comfort, not the grip of an enemy.

With a chorus of shouts, the Wild Hunt rushed Donn from the home's southern side and engaged the Sluagh around the building on a second front. The battle was the only thing keeping Donn from discovering Gwyn conversing with the shade of Harper's father.

# CHAPTER 30

The sky had fully darkened by the time the bus delivered Eileen near the Macleay trail. Behind her, the sodium lights of Portland glowed against the drizzly skies like a bed of embers. Before her lay a narrow path through a dark forest. It looked foreboding, even though it was in a major city.

She dragged her sweaty hands across her boot-cut jeans and checked the laces on her blue hiking boots before digging the flashlight out of the backpack. With nerves on high alert, she loped up the trail toward the Witch's Castle.

All this time in Portland and she'd never visited it. Her husband told stories of sneaking into the abandoned structure after hours. He and his friends would smoke and sit around, debating how they'd change the world.

The last glow from the streetlights winked out when she dropped below a small hill. Eileen slowed her stride and waited for her night vision to sharpen. *It's so dark in there.* She felt naked without weapons. Her hand fished out the mushroom necklace from the black Portland State University hoodie and clasped it. She shook out her limbs, stretched her arms overhead, and pulled her hood forward to block out the light rain. No turning back. Harper needed her. She set a brisk pace up the trail.

A loud *thunk* to her right sent her sprinting with a stifled yelp. With a nervous chortle, she kicked at the acorn that had tumbled into the path. Every creak, crunch, and squeak startled her. Even the rustling of windswept leaves painted mental pictures of long claws and jagged teeth.

The darkness slowed her progress, but she arrived at the Witch's Castle in just over an hour of walking. The flashlight flicking over the stone sent a raccoon scuttling through the underbrush. Eileen wasn't sure which of them was more freaked out.

The structure appeared unremarkable. Colorful graffiti covered many of the walls, but bushy moss reclaimed some of the surface from the spray paint. The fallen tree lay astride the steps, just as the note suggested.

Drawing a deep breath, she ascended the stairs, crawling under the tree rather than climbing over it, and emerged beside a thick rock wall. Moonlight through soaring pine trees looked like lace covering the arched doorway. Rough stone rasped her dry skin when she rested a palm near the arch. *Why did they want to meet here? It's abandoned.* With a last check behind her, she fished the crystal vial out from inside the sweatshirt.

One drop, the note said. What was that going to do? With a shrug, she pulled the stopper out, tilted the tiny vessel, and let a single silvery drop fall to the stone landing.

Eileen staggered back and whacked the back of her head on the dead tree when a blinding light flared to life inside the arch, coalescing into a gleaming pale blue door with a golden doorknob.

"Sweet merciful crap."

Only one thing to do. She shook her head, smoothed her hair, and knocked. She lengthened her spine like a ballerina to make a good impression and eliminate the trembling.

The bright door swung open, and she squawked again. Two creatures loomed over her, even bigger than the Fir Bolg. Greenish wrinkled skin covered corded muscles. Both of them had pointed noses, long ears, and greasy black hair hanging in clumps about their neck and shoulders.

"Um... Uh... Hi. I'm Eileen."

"Welcome to Fògradh Lodge. Me Glawd. Must give weapons." The creature held out a hand that had to be a foot across.

"Nice to meet you, Glawd. I don't have any weapons. I followed the instructions. Did you send the note?"

The other hulking Fae snorted and threw his head back. A sound like gears stripping and geese honking, but much deeper, blasted from his grinning face. He smacked his massive palm on the wrinkly knee that peeked out beneath his filthy loincloth. "Little Fae funny. Glawd no write. No read either." The beast leaned down and pushed thick lips next to her ear. "He slow."

Eileen choked down a retch. The hot, fetid breath rolling from his mouth smelled like rotting fish and something burnt. Her ear rang, because the creature didn't know how to whisper even though he'd obviously meant to.

"You no read either, Brax. You slow." Glawd kicked his friend in the shins.

"You right. Reading for court Fae like this one." In his best approximation of a falsetto, Glawd repeated Eileen's greeting. "Nice to meet you, Glawd." He fluttered his heavy eyelids.

"Welcome to Fògradh Lodge. Me Brax. Must give weapons." The troll bowed to Eileen.

His friend's elbow slammed into his side, eliciting a loud *oof*. "Already did that part. You slow."

Eileen smiled. "It's a relief you are so thorough in your jobs. Like I told Glawd, I have no weapons."

"Pfft." Brax rolled his eyes and slapped a palm to his forehead. "Why no weapons? You slow?"

"No, I—" A puff of wind slid her hood off her head, and suddenly both guards shrank back against the sides of the doorway. The pair wrapped their arms about each other's waist and their knees shook so hard they clacked together. Eileen glanced behind her to see who'd freaked out so much muscle, but she was the only other soul there.

"We sorry. My brother slow. You no hurt Glawd."

As if she could.

"Brax not know you royalty. Royalty strong. No need weapon. You no hurt Brax? No tell boss?"

Eileen looked down at her worn jeans and sweatshirt. No one in their right mind would ever mistake her for royalty.

"Glawd, Brax, when I find your boss I do plan to tell them—"

"Please, please no!" The pair wailed in unison, globby tears spattering the stones. A long string of Brax's green snot stretched within an inch of the landing.

Eileen held out her hands. "Oh, please don't cry." *It's so gross.* "I was saying I'll tell your boss what a thorough and great job you're doing."

Brax sniffed. The snot string whipped back up inside his nose with a wet splat. He dragged a filthy hand across his eyes. "You think I do good?"

"Absolutely." Eileen smiled.

Brax smacked his brother right on the top of his head. Glawd blinked and rubbed his scalp. "See. Me do good. Fancy pants high Fae say so. You get us magic zapped cause you slow."

"Both of you did equally well at your duties."

The trolls' identical smiles revealed quite a few missing teeth. Whether from fights or the lack of a toothbrush, she couldn't tell.

"We make hoity-toity Fae happy?"

Eileen nodded. "Very. And we don't call people slow anymore. It's mean. You just have different strengths. May I go in now?"

The pair flanked the door, gave an awkward bow, and swept their hands toward a set of stairs inside.

The rock steps spiraled below ground, bordered by more rock walls. Beautiful stained-glass sconces lit the way. With a steadying breath, Eileen began her descent. The guttural voices of the trolls faded, each still arguing the reasons the other was slow.

The moment she cleared the first curve in the stairway, lively fiddle music bubbled up from below. And the warm scent of cooking wafted through the air. She doubted this place took Visa. Pity. Something hearty would ease her tiredness after the walk.

As she rounded the final bend of her long descent, her jaw hung slack. Thick trunks of live trees grew where support beams would be. A canopy of golden ginkgo leaves blanketed the vast ceiling. She couldn't wrap her mind around the impossibility of a pub with growing trees underground. Delicate lanterns clustered in the top branches provided a warm light.

Fae of every shape and size packed the carved mahogany bar and each matching table. More hulking beings like the guards played a dice game along the back wall beneath filigree silver shelves packed with curiosities. A band of elves played lively music from a side room. The dance floor teemed with whirling satyrs, fluttering pixies, and many other creatures Eileen had never seen.

*How on earth is the note writer going to find me in here?* The skin on the back of her neck prickled. She turned around and gaped at the reflection in an ornate mirror. On instinct, her fingers traced the tips of her ears. They felt rounded, but they appeared long and pointed in the mirror, jutting up out of an elaborate network of golden braids piled high atop her head. Her PSU hoodie looked like a fitted, floor-length hooded cloak, purple fading to black at the hem and covered with silver embroidered leaves and gemstones. Otherwise, she appeared as her usual self. The necklace was more than an entry key; it was a glamour.

From the back corner of the magical pub, a man in a black leather coat raised his glass at her. She squinted. The guy seemed familiar. Between the distance and the dim light, she couldn't see much of him, and she somehow doubted she knew anyone here, except the mysterious letter writer.

Butterflies flapped in her stomach. Although the Fir Bolg village was alien, they'd welcomed and guided her. This vast subterranean Fae bar threatened her with its strangeness, and she worried the field trip would not end well. The yeasty scent of beer and the acrid odor of spirits watered her mouth. A shot would smooth the jitters.

"Read your future, my lady?" A short, stooped old woman with blue skin peered up at her through a single eye.

"No, thank you." Eileen recognized her mistake as soon as the words left her lips. She cursed herself for pondering a drink because the distraction cost her. Nuada's primer on Fae etiquette told her never to thank them. Thanks were either quite rude or triggered a debt.

The stooped woman spat on the floor at Eileen's feet. In a voice far too loud to come from such a diminutive body, she bellowed. "Thanks to me? Thank me? You dismiss me like a common cur? Do you even know who I am?"

"No, I—"

"Black Annis. And I always take my pound of flesh, every sinew owed to me." The raggedy creature pinched Eileen's arm like she was sizing up livestock. "High Court Fae. Tender, tender." She licked her lips.

Eileen jerked away. "Leave me be." She turned to race out of the room but discovered she couldn't move. Her feet were rooted to the spot.

"I'll leave you be. Soon as I get my snack."

# CHAPTER 31

A small group of Underworld Fae limped, slouched, and staggered through the circular golden tree, flanked by Sidhe escorts. Emilio peered through the opening to glimpse the wasteland on the other side. How anything lived there was both miracle and curse.

Despite the black scars marring their complexions, the Underworld Fae shared an eerie beauty. The smallest looked like an ambulatory flower with a tiny face. She huddled beside a dwarf with blue skin.

But the impossibly tall white woman in the center drew slack-jawed stares. Dressed in heavily embroidered white silk to match her skin and her long hair, she towered seven feet tall or more, like someone had stretched an already thin woman another two feet. The only color anywhere on her wispy form were her startling orange eyes and the scars on her arms and face.

The pale woman spoke with the sighing voice of the wind. "Even when your Sidhe warriors found us, we didn't believe the tales held truth." A smile tugged at the corners of her mouth. Lips parted like she wished to say more, the woman instead dropped to her knees and placed her head on Badb Catha's feet. "I pledge my service to you."

Behind her, every new arrival did the same. From his cage, Emilio shuddered when a grin warmed Badb's face. The same reassuring expression his grandmother wore when the world was unkind to him. That warm smile on the Tuatha's face made his skin crawl.

"Welcome, my friends." Badb wrapped her hands around the white Fae and pulled her to her feet. "Our people will gladly accept your service. For we have a righteous cause and our enemies are legion."

The flower Fae threw her arms around the nearest Sidhe. He drew back at first, but relaxed and returned her embrace. She tilted her petal-rimmed face to his. "You escaped, yet you returned for us..."

Badb gestured to goblins waiting with trays laden with food and drink. They scurried forward to the new arrivals. "It is our devotion. Our commitment to each other and preserving the wild that sets us apart from our enemies. Humanity utterly lacks these qualities and it will be their downfall. Freed from your dying land, you may do as you please on this island. Simply heed the call to arms when the time comes. Together we rescue flora and fauna from annihilation and make a new home for our people. Though we are few, with you fighting alongside us, we will cleanse this world of the human stain. Serve me in the coming war and—"

Boisterous cheering drowned out the rest of her speech. The next troupe of a dozen departing Sidhe stepped up beside the portal while the shouting continued and the Sidhe rescue party smiled and waved to their adoring masses.

"This is going to be bad," the Fae beside him whispered. "Brace yourself."

Emilio had no time to respond before the leads roared to life, worse than before. He'd never had all his blood drained through his pores, but this was what he imagined it felt like. Small crimson pools formed at his side when his body clenched against his feathers. Through gritted teeth, he breathed a low growl.

Two more elves, a sylph, and a kelpie joined the search and rescue party at the tree. "We won't fail you, Highness," the sylph said.

"Make haste. Our first strike draws near. We need more recruits." The jet-black twisting antlers on the sides of Babd's headdress glimmered in the reflected light of the portal.

The Fae nodded, turned, and disappeared through the gateway. The drain ceased at once, and Emilio fell back with a deep groan. Swirling opalescent magic in shades of blue spiraled across the opening, covering the surface again so unwanted guests could neither leave nor sneak into the Green World without Badb's awareness.

Badb reached out a hand and beckoned. A black crow landed on her wrist and ambled up her arm, coming to rest on her shoulder. Badb ran her fingers through the corvid's feathers. "Fiach, my pet, please tell me Donn has finally flushed out our little heir or captured the Fir Bolg."

The bird mumbled and clacked its beak as Badb stared into its dark eyes. Nostrils flared and lips pulled back, revealing ivory teeth. "I knew we should have never let him and his insufferable kind onto this island. Useless." The bird ran a piece of her red hair through his beak while she strode from the room.

*Harper.* A moment of relief flooded Emilio. The first glimmer of hope. She was alive, at least. He wondered what she would think when she saw him like this, if she would even recognize him.

The lavender-skinned succubus lay crumpled at the bottom of her cage. Emilio reached a hand to rouse her. "Are you all right?"

She snapped her arm out of the way. "Don't touch me, *Netherfae.*" She spat the word, just like the elves did.

"Okay, you got it, creepy bat-goat thing."

She narrowed her oversize eyes at him. "I'm a succubus, not a goat-thing."

"And I'm Emilio, not Netherfae, and sue me for trying to comfort you."

"Alphine." Some of the snobbish annoyance melted from her face. "And there is no comfort here. Only death."

"Why does she torture her own people?"

"I'm not one of her people."

"You came from over there?" Emilio gestured at the portal. "Refuse to serve her or something?"

"I used to live in the Underworld, right in the middle of the mountain range Badb mentioned, the Rachis Draconis. Dragon's spine, and when my father made his pact with Badb Catha, my mother smuggled us to this world. We were only children."

"I'm sad to hear that."

"Don't be." Alphine rested her head back and her arms on the tops of her knees. "Badb betrayed our mother, and yet Father still sided with her. We were better off far away from him." Her Southern accent blunted the tragedy of her tale.

"But how did you get *here* here?" Emilio swept his hand around his cage. "Enjoying these luxury accommodations?" It felt good to talk to someone, even a Fae that hated him. Kept his mind from everything else for a while.

"You saw that rescue party head back into the Underworld?"

Emilio nodded.

"Well, she sends death squads just like them anywhere Fae live on earth, rooting out any solitaries, Dawn, or Dusk Court Fae. You either join her fight or end up as a battery for that." She waved a hand at the golden tree.

"Dusk Court?"

Alphine told him about the Green World Courts, and Emilio described their botched escape plan, complete with Ashley's betrayal. She laughed at his failure.

"Hey, at least I tried. From what I see, the fight's left the Fae in these cages."

She glowered at him. "You don't know what you're talking about, half-breed."

"Look, goat-bat thing, all I'm saying is we should all strive for escape."

Her laugh showed no mirth. "How do you propose we do that? Wasn't one failure enough for you? Behold the costs of it." She swept a hand down Emilio's fabulous feathers.

Emilio let out a long sigh and shifted to avoid cutting himself on his razor-sharp plumage. He slid a hand along the smooth wooden bars and bolted upright. The idea hit him like a brick.

"What are—"

Emilio reached over his shoulder and plucked a four-inch feather from the top of his wing. He scanned the room for watching eyes.

"Warn me if anyone's coming," he whispered.

He dropped low to the floor of the cage, bringing the feather to the base of the wood. He drew the edge across the wooden bar, then bent to check for marks. Nothing.

"This is ironwood from the other side. You think you're going to cut through it with a feather?"

"Metal feather, and hope springs eternal, goat-bat thing."

"Alphine."

"Emilio."

"Fine. Point taken, Emilio."

"Fantastic, Alphine." He whipped the feather across the wood for several seconds and checked again. Squinting revealed the smallest of scratches. It was nearly invisible, but it proved that with enough time and effort, his plumage could slice through the bars. Perhaps with several bars damaged, they could kick their way out.

Helping one of the Fae was not high on his list of priorities, but if he'd learned one thing from his last escape attempt, it was that strength lay in numbers. If some of these imprisoned Fae broke free, perhaps he could encourage them to fight Badb's people while his friends and the humans fled.

A silent chuckle rolled through his chest at the similarities of his scheme to Badb's. She planned to use humans to kill humans. He hoped to help some of these Fae break free and use them as cannon fodder to cover his own escape.

"I scratched it. It'll take a long time, but my feathers damage the wood." Emilio plucked a few more from himself and passed them to Alphine.

"Here, pass them down. This is your prison break."

Alphine held a shining feather up to her face and beamed at Emilio. Long canine teeth glinted in the dim light of the plaza.

The Fae looked genuinely happy, and he'd betray her if it came down to it. *God, what have they turned me into?*

# CHAPTER 32

Harper leaned close to the gap in the leathery fungus covering the window by the door. Arms clasped across her chest, she traced lines up and down above her elbows. At first, Gwyn's appearance brought an odd combination of relief and dread. Somehow, she knew he wouldn't let Donn attack the farmhouse, but he would still present her to his mistress and perhaps kill her friends.

He towered beside her father but curled his torso over the Sluagh in the same way a parent might shield a child. Harper squinted and the tip of her nose met the chill glass. They were still too far to pick out more detail, but she swore her dad and Gwyn both nodded before they parted.

Gerald O'Neill's body quaked and shuddered into avian form, then he flapped into the treetops. When the other Sluagh hopped around him in the last slivers of evening light, she lost track of which spectral bird was her father. Her eyes lingered where he'd conversed with Gwyn. For all she knew, she'd just seen her father's ghost for the last time.

"Look. Over there." Paegrinn pointed to a break in the ring of winged dark shapes mobbing the treetops. The black cloud of birds undulated, then half of them landed on either side of a thin trail, crowding the Sluagh already perched in those trees. They remained for a second before the birds split again, farther from the path. Within a minute, not a single avian remained along the entire north side of the home.

"Your father is as brave and true as you are. That has to be our opening." Melinoe snatched her brown cloth bag from the couch and galloped toward the back door.

"My dad said they have a hive mind. He can influence it because he's more awake now, but he probably doesn't have long until they discover his ruse."

"If he's the one doing that," the Phooka said. "Besides, it's a long sprint to the forest's cover. We'll never make it all the way without being seen."

"Phooka, can you glamour us, or use some trick in your bag to make us all invisible?"

He frowned. "Nothing that could cover you and Sasquatch, and Fae would sense it if we glamoured you."

Melinoe waggled her fingers at the back corner of the house. "I think we just got our distraction."

Harper leaned back to glance out the window. A cluster of elves and smaller Fae from the Wild Hunt slunk across the lawn, weapons drawn. Her heart skipped a beat. Gwyn's forces loped straight for the biggest contingent of Donn's Fae Sluagh nearer the home's corner farthest from the narrow escape path.

The Phooka's jaw dropped. "What fresh hell is this?"

"My dad, working with Gwyn?" It sounded ludicrous, but the situation outside the farmhouse was shaping up into a perfect escape plan.

Melinoe nodded while she crept up beside Harper. "No way Gwyn would help us."

Paegrinn was already shouldering his satchel and he clasped Melinoe's pack. "Don't be so sure. He just attacked Donn."

Blades clashed, then blinding flashes of magic collided between them. Gwyn fell back repeatedly and Donn followed until the pair had orbited almost to the far reaches of the driveway, far from the opening in the flock and partially hidden by the barn.

Harper hopped back from the window and snatched her bag, shrugging it into place. Gwyn's actions confused the hell out of her, and she feared it was a trap to draw them out, but it was their only chance. "I think it's more an enemy of my enemy sort of thing. Gwyn's sure he can catch us himself and bring us in. We may not get another opportunity. I say—"

Before she could finish her sentence, shouts, the piercing shrieks of the banshee, and the clang of weapons rang from the southeast. Harper scampered to the door and pressed her face against the cool glass, searching for her father. He wasn't anywhere she could see, but no Sluagh remained on the home's northern edge.

Melinoe beckoned frantically from the rear exit. "Harper, we have to go. Now!"

"She might be right. The Wild Hunt is driving the Fae Sluagh farther from the opening your dad created. The house will block their view for a while." By the time the Phooka had finished speaking, he was a black wolf, hackles raised like a razor blade down his spine.

Harper's earliest memory flashed in front of her eyes. Four-year-old Harper shrieked as her dad tossed her high into the air and caught her. *I'll never let you fall, Rabbit.* And they both laughed.

"Okay. Let's go." Harper shimmied to reposition her backpack between her shoulder blades, heaved a rifle to Paegrinn, and scurried behind the Phooka out the back door. Melinoe and the Phooka already loped through the mist, Alina's green glow lighting the way.

The Phooka galloped ahead much slower than he was capable

of, swinging his long snout over his flank a few times at Harper. At least for now, neither the Wild Hunt nor the Fae Sluagh could see the fleeing companions, and the avians perched in high branches didn't seem to notice them. *That has to be Dad.*

Feet pummeled the hard ground and kicked up eddies of mist. Only the screeching and clanging of the skirmish masked the thunder of their flight. The closer they raced to the relative safety of the forest edge, the less the bulk of the farmhouse and barn could protect them from being noticed.

She hunched low and kept a firm grip on the rifle. They'd only been running for half a minute, but it seemed like an eternity. Harper felt exposed, but for once, the milky mist was on their side.

Her mouth ran dry. The last sliver of protection the building's bulk offered disappeared. The battle between the Wild Hunt and Sluagh was in full view, and that meant so were they, but in seconds, the forest canopy would swallow them.

Alina darted for the trees. Melinoe's pounding hooves carried her nearly as fast as the little will o' wisp. Only his long legs kept Paegrinn anywhere near them. The two Fae were moments away from breaking into the woods when a chorus of high-pitched screeches turned Harper's blood to ice.

A half-dozen banshee had noticed their escape, because they were barreling right for them. White hair undulating in the still evening air, red mouths snarling and screaming.

Melinoe, Alina, and Paegrinn paused at the edge of cover. The banshee swept a low arc toward Harper and the Phooka, long clawed fingers stretched in front of them, pointed teeth ready to tear flesh.

"I really hate those things," the Phooka yelled as he wheeled around, still sprinting but positioning himself between Harper and the banshee. "They remind me of that time I got trapped at a Bieber concert. All the screaming and grabby hands."

"I'm more worried about those teeth." Harper pushed her legs to pump to their limits, but the Fae were gaining on them. In seconds, Gwyn and Donn would see them. She hoped Paegrinn and her Fae friends would save themselves, just keep running. Better to have them free and plotting a jailbreak.

"You got any of that blue fire nastiness in you?" the Phooka called. "Because now would be a good time to go all Emperor Palpatine and fry these things with finger lightning."

Harper searched for the spark of that elusive power, the electric surge of raw energy that saved and cursed her in equal measure, but nothing stirred. She was more terrified than angry. "Nothing."

"Keep going." The Phooka jammed his feet down, careening to a sudden stop. His shape stretched and twisted into a jet-black wyvern slightly larger than the banshee. His yellow eyes glowed with ferocity.

"No way. We fight together." She slid Gwyn's sword free and halted.

Feathery wings pushed the Phooka as far aloft as the island seemed to allow, about as high as the farmhouse roof. He'd just started to fold his wings, diving at the banshee, when a squawking flock of tattered wings and gravely voices blanketed the sky between him and the attacking banshee.

The cloud of avian Sluagh swarmed the shrieking banshee and shoved them out of the sky.

"You doing that?"

"It's my dad. Has to be."

"Run. Stay low." The Phooka dropped beneath the fog in the shape of a slinky black cat, just his tail poking up from the mist.

Harper spared one last second, a quiet goodbye to her father on her lips. Then she saw him. Several of the Sluagh landed and took their human shapes, clawing at the banshee, preventing their escape. Gerald O'Neill lifted his face at his daughter and nodded.

Harper mouthed "I love you." Then she hunched low and

sprinted after the Phooka into the cover of the undergrowth. The rest of the group were waiting behind a wall of thick scrub. Harper dropped behind Paegrinn. The spire of black birds swirled past the now-dead banshee and careened around the house toward Gwyn and Donn.

"He did it. He saved us." Harper rested her palms on her thighs and let her head hang, trying to catch her breath.

Melinoe beamed. "He was so amazing. I hope the rest don't discover what he did for us."

"We need to keep moving," Paegrinn said.

"Anyone know where Badb's tower is?"

"That's a downstream sort of problem." The Phooka pointed back toward the farmhouse. "The current issue is putting distance between us and all of that."

So they ran.

More than an hour of brisk jogging, and the sky grew dark. None of them noticed any signs of pursuit, and the forest was more treacherous at night, even for her Fae companions, so they risked making a meager camp.

"I'll cover our trail." Melinoe cracked her knuckles and rolled her neck.

"Oh, like last time? Is that code for I'll lead our enemies right to our doorstep?" The Phooka crossed his arms and turned away from the glaistig.

"No one's ever tracked me. We keep being discovered because Harper is too nice to think badly of you and kick you out of our company. She's inexperienced with dark Fae treachery!" Melinoe's nose pointed straight up in the air.

Paegrinn rolled his eyes. "Ugh, again?"

"He's right. You two bicker like an old married couple," Harper said.

"I'd never—"

"Technicolor yawn." The Phooka clutched his stomach and

lurched. He jabbed an outstretched finger at Ezrynhivar's filigree ring. "More likely that thing is acting like a homing beacon, bringing every Unseelie Fae right to us."

Melinoe gave a curt nod. "For once the shapeshifter's correct. If you only heard half the stories about Lord Ezrynhivar I have—"

Harper shook her head and slashed the air with her arm. "Trust me, you're all safer if I wear this thing. If I actually manage to summon my magic, you'll be glad I have it." She forced her shoulders to drop. "Melinoe, go ahead. I'm sure they won't find us because of your help." Harper turned to the Phooka. "And I have no choice but to trust you, Phooka."

The Phooka's rabbit ears drooped ever so slightly. Beside him, Melinoe smiled, waved, and disappeared into the hedge with a flurry of leaves and vegetation.

The spot they'd picked was ringed by dense trees and undergrowth; it would be difficult to see anything from far away. The Phooka assured them he could keep an invisibility glamour over a small campfire, so Harper volunteered to gather some firewood while Paegrinn started a meal.

Harper grabbed one of the tiny LED lights and ventured past the underbrush in search of kindling and wood. Alina flitted from branch to branch near the treetops, to ensure the woods couldn't lead Harper astray.

Harper had gone camping as a child because her dad had loved it. In one of his last lessons before Badb killed him, he'd shown her how to choose the right size pieces for kindling and the best wood for creating a hot bed of coals for cooking. Harper gathered bits with wispy dry moss that would catch fire quickly.

Crack.

Harper froze, ears straining to pick up the smallest sound. Another crack, and the crunch of footsteps on bramble and dried leaves. She didn't dare call out because she'd strayed too far to be heard, anyway. Inch by inch, she squatted to the ground and gently placed her firewood next to a rock. She drew upright and slid the thin blade from its home in her belt.

The thing came at her like the Tasmanian devil in cartoons. Limbs flailing, snarling, and spit flying. Wiry hair sprouted along its forearms, ending in formidable claws. Harper ducked, pulse surging, feet rooted to the spot.

The creature paused, cocking its head. Pointed ears pierced through long blonde hair matted with leaves and dirt. The ears marked her as Fae, but the white tank top and green surgical scrubs suggested she was human. Or had been. The thing's tongue traced an eager path around her lips. "Thought you were one of *them*. Not many real humans left on this island since they're either dead or look like me now."

# CHAPTER 33

"Stop." Harper unfroze and poised her weapon for a quick strike. She wished she'd carried the shotgun. "I don't want to hurt you."

The semi-human paused, squatting on all fours a few strides from Harper. "You seem familiar." The creature tilted her face sideways and sniffed the air. "Do you know my dad?"

The blonde put her palms on the ground and hopped her back feet forward with a half-swivel. Blue eyes narrowed, and her tongue made another revolution around her lips. "What's a human woman doing all alone in the woods?"

Harper gulped. "My friends and I are going rescue my friend Emilio from a tower."

Wild eyes and a broad smile painted the wild girl's features. Squatting on her haunches, she sniffed the air, narrowed eyes glittering. "You must be Harper."

"How—" Relief buckled Harper's knees. The sword dropped from her hands when she plopped down hard on the rock next to her scattered firewood. "You know Emilio? Can you take me to him?"

"He talked about you a lot. We were in the tower together."

She crept toward Harper, head weaving from side to side. "He led an escape, that's how I got out."

"So he's okay?"

"Do I look okay?" she said, voice pitched with a high note of hysteria.

"You... You seem..." Harper's stomach churned, fearing Emilio and Abraham were now like this girl.

"Kidding! Last time I saw him, he looked like his old self. I'm Ashley, by the way." Her smile didn't reach her eyes. "But he's in grave danger if we don't get off the island. He needs you right now." She bounded toward the underbrush for a couple of hops. When Harper didn't follow, she paused and beckoned.

Harper shuffled her feet and glanced back. "We need to get my friends. They're just below the rise behind me." Her eyes roved the perimeter, seeking a fast escape route. Something was off about the girl. Besides, if Emilio and the other escapees were fleeing, some reinforcements would help.

Ashley's eyes glittered. "No time. If we can't catch up to them, the woods might twist up and put miles between us and you'll miss your chance. Come." She jerked her head. "Once we're all together, we can go back for your other friends. He's not far away yet."

"But why would they leave you?"

Ashley's face pinched, and a tremor came to her voice. "Look at me. I'm not like them anymore. I'm stronger, so they make me scout behind, to ensure we're not followed. Hurry if you want to catch them." Ashley skittered halfway into the brush.

Harper hesitated. She didn't want to leave Paegrinn and the Phooka, or even Melinoe behind. But this was Emilio. She couldn't come this close to finding him, only to lose him again. Her heart lightened as she pondered rescuing him. Then Alina could guide her friends to the safety of the Fir Bolg village while Harper freed the Sluagh. Afterwards, they could all flee.

*But what about Abraham and all the countless others?* The fates of innumerable people weighed on her like concrete. "You said he led an escape. Did he get everyone out?"

"Only six of us. The Dark Lady has so many more. We were lucky."

Ashley hopped back the way she'd come and motioned for Harper to follow. "Come now."

Emilio was on the move and the Phooka and the others weren't far. Ashley looked like she could handle herself in a fight if something attacked. Harper took a last look toward their camp.

"Just a moment, I'm going to leave a message for the others." She was sure Melinoe would find her trail when she didn't return with her firewood.

Harper grabbed a pen she'd stashed inside the jacket and rooted through the other pockets. In the breast pocket she discovered an old receipt and scrawled a note for the Phooka, telling him what direction they headed and that she may have found Emilio. "Alina, go back and guide the others to my note. Melinoe should be able to pick up our trail."

The tiny Fae squeaked and zoomed back the way they'd come.

With a nod to Ashley, Harper tucked the note between some sticks of her wood pile and followed the poor girl.

Ashley kept a brisk pace, diving under the brush, hopping around roots. She seemed able to keep them on the straight path. Farther and farther, they traveled through the thick, coiling trees. Harper scanned her surroundings for the hundredth time and pulled her jacket tight around her.

Without her friends, she felt vulnerable. The creeping dread that she'd made a mistake left a sour taste coating her throat. She'd never met this strange girl and wasn't certain she could be trusted.

She inhaled deeply while her fingers traced the spiral patterns on the Cliamh Solais's scabbard. Ashley clearly knew Emilio. She'd escaped. *Relax, she's taking you to your friend. If she wanted to kill you, she'd have tried already.* And yet the nagging sense of wrong refused to leave.

"You said they were close? We've been walking for a while."

Ashley sidled next to her and drew herself up to stare into Harper's hazel eyes, cocking her filthy head to the side. "You'll have your reunion. We're very close. It's very dark, they'd have stopped by now. Just a couple more minutes. Then we can all find your other friends and leave together." She smiled and dropped back onto all fours.

The wild girl sounded sincere enough. Harper supposed it wasn't the poor thing's fault she seemed strange, given what they'd done to her. "Lead the way."

Ashley was true to her word. Less than five minutes later, the woods changed, the mist thinned, the trees didn't loom. Instead of black, leafless trunks, they were evergreen and covered with looping vines, like the lush green battled back the ominous woods. An orange, flickering glow ahead cast the bushy undergrowth into silhouette.

"See. They made a campfire. Come." Ashley crouched beside a tiny opening in the underbrush.

*Emilio.* Harper's heart sang. Hope threw caution to the wind, and she crossed her arms over her face and raced through the brush. A few steps and she burst into a scene from a dark fairy tale. A fire danced in a stone ring beneath a dome of woven vines. The grass was low and thick, a lush carpet of green.

Emilio wasn't there. Next to the campfire stood a Fae man, well over six feet tall. He looked as out of place in the forest as Paegrinn would at a desk job. A smartly tailored dark brown suit hugged his muscular form, the orange paisley vest underneath intensified by the firelight. He drew a slender smoking pipe to his lips and inhaled.

Harper slipped her blade free and poised it across her body. The Sword of Light would probably come in handy right about now, but she left it hanging at her hip, fearing it would again refuse to draw. "Where's my friend?" She lunged for the man, but her feet refused to move.

Never ungluing her eyes from Ashley and her Fae companion, Harper shifted her weight to one leg and strained to lift the other one. Nothing. Stuck fast by Fae magic.

Ashley scurried across the clearing to squat next to Harper. "Still in the tower," she sing-songed in a nasal voice and laughed.

"But how—" Harper strained to pick up her feet, but they still refused to budge. "Paegrinn! Phook—" The grubby clawed hand suddenly clamping her throat silenced her call for help.

"He was never going to take me with him! I had to tell her. I had to find my own way out. Emilio is no good. My daddy wouldn't like him. Not one bit." Her face contorted and spittle flew from her lips.

Harper shook her head. "You little liar."

Ashley released Harper's neck and hopped back to the Fae man. "Emilio is the liar. But I got revenge on him. He's still with *her*. But I got away. Santaigh keeps me safe."

The Fae man placed a tanned finger under Ashley's chin, and long, sharp fingernails that curved from his brown hands drew her to a standing position. He blew a billow of smoke from his mouth. Pale blue eyes glowed from underneath a brimmed brown top hat. "And she keeps me fed." His voice was like quicksilver.

"You filthy little liar." Harper opened herself to the bitterness kindling in her heart. She kept her attention on the pair, but a familiar blue gleam bloomed across her hands.

Santiagh brought a languid hand with the smoking pipe to stifle a yawn while the other stretched toward her. A warm wave coursed over her head and ran down her body like a hot shower. She'd felt the tingling heat of glamour before. She probably had seconds before she floated on a blissed-out cloud, completely at the mercy of these two.

The fuzzy sensation peaked only for a second before it ebbed. *Of course, the iron in the jacket weakens Fae magic.* She yanked at her stuck feet, hoping to break that spell and flee, but immobility spread to her arms and her thudding heart extinguished magic's flame.

Santaigh let out a sigh and flicked a hand at Ashley.

"I did good?" Ashley asked while she peeled off Harper's jacket.

"You did very well. Very well, indeed."

"Now you have something else to eat. You don't need me anymore, right?" Ashley's voice took on the nasal edge of a whine. The studded belt joined the jacket draped across Ashley's arm and soon all trace of protective iron was gone.

Harper's breath came in pants. She willed her arm to move, swipe back some of her iron protection, but it hung limp at her side as the immobility spell intensified with the loss of each protective item.

The Fae gentleman flashed the wild girl a grin. "Oh no. That wasn't our bargain."

Ashley slipped off Harper's boots, and the last of her protection against the sweet oblivion of glamour melted away. "But you said you needed me to feed. I brought you another. This isn't fair!" Ashley's voice raised an octave with each sentence.

"Since your mist-changes turned you into a half-beast, you taste quite foul. Not that you had much to offer in the first place. Your desires are all about your status in those light-up boxes humans carry and what clothing you wrap yourself in. As though that could ever make you more appealing. A gancanagh would starve if you were all they had to eat."

"Nooooo! You said you'd free me once you had enough to feed on."

The gancanagh's smile glittered in the firelight. "Oh, my

malodorous beastie, I'm always hungry." He drew in another draft from the pipe and blew the smoke up into the night air.

"No. Please no." Ashley lay in a heap at her master's feet beside Harper's iron-laced clothes.

"Never bargain with Fae. That was your first mistake." Harper's admonition came out slurred.

"Don't weep. Who else will protect you from the hunters the Dark Lady sends for you?" Santaigh beckoned Harper with a single finger, sapphire eyes glowing beneath the top hat.

She tensed her entire body against the magical pull of the gancanagh. She might as well have tried to hold back the tide. The last wisp of magic blinked out from her palms and her feet made twin furrows in the soil as he dragged her to him.

"Ashley, make yourself useful and prepare a comfortable bed for my meal."

The wild girl rubbed her forearm across her eyes to clear away the tears and shambled over to Harper.

"You don't have to do this," Harper whispered to her as the girl draped tattered fabric across a spongy bed of moss.

"Yes, I do. And it's all Emilio's fault." Ashley laid out several bowls of smoking tobacco on a flat rock beside the makeshift bed. When she was finished, she slumped back to sit beside her master.

"Much better." Santaigh dug his hands into his jacket pockets and ambled a slow circle around Harper. He came to rest in front of her again. Honey brown hair coiled beneath the hat. A thin line of beard ran from his lower lip and down his chiseled jaw. He'd be gorgeous if it weren't for the thick horns arcing up from the brim of his hat or the long, pointed ears jutting from its sides.

"If you're going to eat me, I should tell you I taste pretty bad. I eat a lot of fast food. And I'll not make an easy meal," Harper said with a bravado she didn't feel.

Santaigh laughed and drew a toke from the pipe. Leaning inches from her face, he blew the smoke right into her eyes. It smelled of eastern spices and sweet fruits, but Harper coughed. Her captor leaned even closer and inhaled the second-hand smoke swirling over her skin. "I'm nothing as base as a vampire. It's not your flesh I'm interested in. It's your desire." He purred, the smoke snaking from his lips with every word.

"You're not my type."

His face hovered along her neck, wisps of his hair caressing her collarbone. She struggled against the invisible bonds and the fuzzy sensation expanding in her mind. Santaigh dragged his face over her hair, and his hot breath tickled her ear. "No, it isn't romance you desire. Oh, this is a sweetness I haven't tasted in so long."

He pressed so close, she could feel the shudder ripple through his body.

"This is going to be so good. So delicious, my sweet Harper." His voice was barely a breath, those glowing blue eyes half closed, lips parted.

"How do you know my name?" But she knew the answer already. Smoky tendrils wove through her thoughts, probing the parts of her she kept hidden and prying them open for him to see.

"Your desire is so much more primal. More needful." The backs of his fingers ran the entire length of her arm. "Family. The profound longing of the orphan." His other hand cupped her chin, a gentle claw tracing a slow line across her lips. "The yawning maw of the abandoned. The sweetest milk."

Harper couldn't speak. Her entire body hung suspended by the gancanagh's magic, gripped like a spider in a web. Santaigh's warm hand rested on the back of her neck and she drowned in those blazing azure eyes. The Fae didn't break eye contact as he turned his head slightly, took a deep toke of his pipe, and exhaled the smoke over her upturned face.

She felt the smoke filling her thoughts, effervescent and pleasant. The woven roof of the gancanagh's lair receded while the smoke coalesced into familiar shapes. A dresser here, a bed there.

For a few moments, they sat against the backdrop of the changed woodland around her.

Santaigh leaned in once more, like he bent to kiss her. The Fae opened his mouth so wide his jaw unhinged. The sensual lips were replaced by a blood red circle filled with concentric rings of jagged teeth like the mouth of a leech. With the last of her own willpower, Harper screamed.

"My sweetest Harper, I'm about to give you everything you've ever desired."

# CHAPTER 34

"I- I'm sure you don't want my flesh. There has to be something else I can—" Eileen snapped her arm back from the blue-skinned hag.

Black Annis tossed her greasy head back and cackled at the rafters.

Someone or some creature pressed into Eileen's back and every muscle tensed. "Are you trying to end up as her slave, or worse?" A man's voice whispered into her ear, thick with an Irish accent. "You shouldn't be here if you don't understand the rules."

"Now my pretty, as a kindness, I'll let you choose where I take my boon from. Pick those thighs. They look extra tasty." The hag wiped drool off her chin and ran her filthy hands over Eileen's leg.

"You gunna share, Black Annis?" A short, wiry Fae with a blood-red cap called from the growing audience the spectacle had drawn.

"Not with treacherous redcaps!" The hag cackled, grabbing the folds of her tattered grey dress between her fingers.

Eileen felt the Irish man move away, then he knelt before the foul hag, an expression of awe lighting his face.

"Black Annis. I never thought I'd meet you on this side of the Atlantic."

"Bah. Not giving you any either, Irish mongrel." Black Annis rubbed her sharp fingernails back and forth across each other, sharpening them with a sound like metal on metal, her eyes never leaving Eileen's legs.

"Wasn't asking. I'm just excited to greet a sorcerer of your renown. My family has followed your exploits for a very long time." His accent made each word musical.

"Flattery won't get you a taste either."

"It's not this woman's flesh that interests me, though a night or two with someone that lovely…"

"I beg your pardon?!" Eileen glared down at the man. This hag was about to literally eat off one of her legs and he was thinking of sex. Fae clearly weren't much different from human men.

"You can do what you want with her after I get my flesh." Black Annis stared up at Eileen. "Well, what'll it be, my dear? I'm ready for my treat."

The stranger chuckled. "As appealing as that sounds, it is her debt I'm after. Not the payout."

"I'm not a piece of meat to be bargained for," Eileen said, indignant despite her sweating palms and racing pulse. Whoever had invited her here must be close by, needed her for something; surely they'd intervene.

"Yes, you are," Black Annis and the man said in unison.

"I have something far rarer than the flesh of this woman, and exceedingly tastier. I'll trade her debt for what I have stashed in my pocket."

"Bah." The hag studied her sharp claws and pulled her face into a lopsided grin.

The stranger slid forward, dropping himself even lower, so his warm, brown eyes met hers. He drew out his hand from the pocket of his midthigh leather coat and held up a handful of dark chocolate granola bars.

"You!" Eileen said. The stranger tilted his face up to hers and a lock of shiny dark brown hair slipped across his nose. He was less disheveled than the last time she saw him. But in the lantern light, she recognized the indigent man from her street.

"Is that... chocolate?" Black Annis licked her lips, her eyes laser-focused on the man's upturned hand, long nose quivering.

He grabbed one, flipped it over, and rustled the seam away from the ingredients list. "Organic. Says it has honey in it too. And I've got three."

"How many for the leg." The hag jabbed a sharp nail into Eileen's thigh.

"All three for just one leg. The deal of the century."

Black Annis hopped up and down and clapped her grubby hands. "Deal. Her debt is yours." She raised herself up on tip-toes, shielded her lips with a palm, and lifted her chin toward the man's face. "Trust me. Go for the thigh, mongrel."

"Sage advice, but I swore off cannibalism long ago."

The hag's wart-covered jaw dropped, and a wave of gasps and muttering traveled through the gathered Fae. "Fool."

The man dropped the granola bars into the Fae's hand. She already had one crammed into her mouth when Eileen retreated to a safe distance. The hag rolled her eyes and moaned while a collection of other Fae dangled objects, luxurious jewelry, or bones with the hopeful stares of beggars. But Black Annis refused them all.

Eileen crept away from the throng toward the music room, intent on finding a sparsely crowded location where she'd have less likelihood of making another life-threatening faux pas.

"Just a minute, lass. I'm your new creditor. I paid for your freedom with food from my very own pockets."

Eileen froze for a second, her back straightening. She revolved to face the man. He wore what her mother always described as a shit-eating grin. "Food I gave you."

"Aye, that's what makes it so funny." He brought a hand to stroke his cropped beard and covered his smile.

"Who are you and what are you doing here, in this place?"

"Tell you what. Let me call in that debt I just bought. Allow me to buy you a drink, and we'll declare it even."

Eileen glanced back at the bar, at the colorful bottles lining packed shelves. She bet some of their contents would counteract the adrenaline hangover already darkening her emotions. She wished Ez were here; a little boost of his glamour and her tangled mind would smooth out. Then she'd be better equipped to navigate this beautiful and dangerous place.

"You can ask me anything you'd like if that'll sweeten the pot." He gestured toward the dark table in the back where he'd been sitting when she initially noticed him.

"All right. One drink."

"Phelan." He stuck out his hand. "Only give me your first name, never both. Names have power among the Fae."

"Eileen." She grasped his hand, which was surprisingly smooth for a homeless guy.

He brought her knuckles to his lips and pressed a gentle kiss onto the back. "Pleased to be your knight in shining armor, Eileen."

"Most knights don't wear T-shirts with tentacle monsters on them." Eileen smiled in spite of herself and nodded at his Portland Lovecraft Film Festival shirt.

"Fair enough. What would you prefer? The Fae have plenty of nonalcoholic beverages to delight."

Surrounded by powerful magical beings, in an alien culture that nearly cost her a heaping serving of flesh, the stakes were high. One wrong move and she'd not be helping Harper but possibly harming her. Her insides quaked like Jell-O. "Tea? A hot cup of tea would be nice." *But a shot would be more effective, take the edge off, make me more useful.*

"Coming right up, milady." Phelan bowed from the waist and motioned to his table.

The eyes of every Fae in the room darted to her. None of them continued to stare like they had when she'd stumbled into the debt with Black Annis, but they all eyed her, then whispered to each other behind glasses or into pointed ears. The necklace must be magic allowing her to see them, either that or, in this place, they felt safe enough to drop their invisibility glamour.

An impossibly thin woman with gossamer wings and skin of the palest blue bent to whisper in the ear of a satyr. He giggled when butterfly antenna tickled his face. Next to her benefactor, wiry looking fellows with those blood-red caps laughed and punched each other on the arm and in the gut. Over it all lilted the fiddle music from the neighboring room, so she focused on its cheery melody to center herself.

Phelan glanced at her over his shoulder. By the time he turned back to the goblin barkeep, their drinks were ready. He slid a pair of silver coins across the bar, bringing a smile to the goblin's face, then wove his way back through the crowd. He'd removed the metal ring from the brown snub-nosed cycle boots he wore, she supposed because the iron would offend the patrons. She noted a peppering of grey in his short mustache and stubbly beard, yet hardly any in his gleaming hair.

"Hot herb and citrus tea for the lady, extra honey, because I'm the barkeep's supply." He placed a steaming mug on the pitted table and slid to the other side of the elaborate, paisley, curved couch that wrapped around the table. He plopped a beer down in front of himself. "Sweet Mother Mary, I'm a moron." He smacked his hand over his glass and pulled it close to his body.

The cool guy facade totally shattered as he awkwardly attempted to put distance between his guest and the offending beverage. Eileen smiled. "It's fine. I'm in a bar, someone else drinking won't fling me from the wagon." She sipped her tea. The flavor was bright and sweet, with an earthy undertone. Quite delicious. A deep breath through her nose filled her lungs; the nutty aroma of the beer watered her mouth.

She marveled at how their conversation was as clear as if they chatted in a library, despite the deafening roar of the pub. The noisy guests and music sounded faint. *Must be noise cancelling magic at the tables. That's brilliant.*

"You're a gracious guest." He relaxed and dropped back into his loose, devil-may-care posture. He could be the one who left the necklace, but the question was how did he know her, or know anything about her present circumstances with Fae and Fir Bolg.

"Whoever cast your glamour really knew what they were doing." He tipped his beer toward her and nodded once. "If I hadn't met you on the street in Gresham, I'd think for sure you were one of the high elves. And none of the locals have picked up on your identity either. Not even Black Annis."

"The hag? Is she a powerful Fae?"

His eyebrows shot up, and he flopped back against the chair. "You mean you don't know? Black Annis has wreaked havoc all over the British Isles. There're dozens of stories written about her, and still more whispered in the dark. She was old before humans wandered up to Europe out of Africa."

"England? What's she doing here?"

"Fae from all over the northern hemisphere have been drawn to Portland over the past several years. My sources tell me similar gatherings are cropping up in a few other places in the world, too. Australia. Brazil. China. Something big is happening."

"Really?" She focused on her tea, twisting the mug in a slow revolution.

"Let's cut right to the chase. I'll bet you know much more than you're letting on. Maybe even more than me."

Eileen traced a lazy circle on the surface of the table and eyed the least crowded wing of the room, calculating an escape path. Phelan may have helped her, and he seemed nice enough, but what was he doing here, openly human at a Fae bar? Or perhaps not human—glamoured, or a shapeshifter like the Phooka. She'd blundered into a trap with the hag, and the same mistake might be unfolding now.

"I could sense the residual Fae energy inside your house. Something big happened there with powerful forces."

"You were in my house?" Eileen hissed through clenched teeth.

He leaned back, hands wide, palms facing her. "It's not like that. I had to be sure. I snuck in when you went to the hardware store and I touched nothing."

"You had no right."

"I'm sorry, but I'm looking for someone. Someone important. We thought they were all lost."

Eileen's breathing came shallow, and she shifted her grip on the tea mug, ready to swing it at Phelan's head if it became necessary. She didn't like where this conversation was headed.

"Who were all lost?"

"I'm searching for an heir—"

"What in the hell are you doing here?" The rumbling, deep voice bellowed from the direction of the bar.

Both Eileen and Phelan leapt to their feet when the hulking ogre lumbered toward them. A blue velvet jacket with tails hugged the white lace shirt beneath his furry form.

"Hieronymous!" Eileen shouted, relieved and delighted to see her Fae friend. "This man's after my daughter."

# CHAPTER 35

God, she hated that alarm. The thing blared like an ambulance. Harper flopped her palm to the nightstand, seeking the snooze bar, missed, and knocked a book to the floor. Her hand flipped the other direction, smacking the bar, giving her nine more minutes of blissful slumber. Emilio always told her to just use her phone, but she'd grown up with the little digital clock and old habits die hard.

She nestled her face more deeply into her downy pillow to block out the first fingers of dawn sunlight. Try as she may, sleep refused to come a second time.

A creaky groan escaped her lips, and she rolled onto her elbow. Her head swam with the smallest movement, as though she was hungover. *Was I too drunk to remember being drunk last night?*

She peeled one eyelid open and the morning light stabbed through her eye to the top of her brain and lodged there, throbbing. *Yep. Definitely drunk. Must have been a hell of a party to leave a total blank.* The silver lining was that Emilio would fill her in on the details and she could relive the shenanigans. His flamboyant storytelling always made everything sound more exciting than it was the first time.

She rolled her head in a circle and winced. Why was it so bright in the basement? She forced herself up to slouch over her extended legs, assaulted by the sour flavor of unbrushed teeth.

The bedroom held her things, the pink beanbag chair, the wooden desk and bureau. It also sported the sunny bay window and pale blue carpeting of the Victorian-style home she'd grown up in. It was familiar, like an old photo in an album, more memory than present reality.

She flung her legs off the side of the bed and concentrated on the fading images of a basement room in a tiny house decorated with the vomitous colors of the seventies. It felt so real. Like she lived there, and that something terrible happened there...

No. The tiny house was merely a phantasm spun by exhaustion and too much alcohol. Like all dreams, the more she focused on it, the more it receded. Whatever she drank last night sure packed a wallop.

*This is not my life.* That thought seemed more accurate, more real than this sun-drenched bedroom, or the dream with the basement room.

Her mom must be burning some new candle or incense, because the scent of exotic spices and apple wafted from somewhere. She yawned. Gravity carried her too-heavy torso back down in her bed. Her whole body buzzed, beginning with a warmth at the top of her head, like sunlight shining on her hair in summer. A pleasant sensation, and she relaxed into it.

Outside, the sun sank below the horizon on fast forward, and darkness drew over the sky like a cloak. *Wait. My alarm just went off. It can't be night. Something's wrong.* Harper willed her drooping lids open, to no avail. A second before they slipped closed, she thought she noticed tendrils of smoke snaking down from the ceiling.

*What a long day.* She pulled the downy covers up to her chin and let sleep float her away.

God, she hated that alarm. The thing blared like an ambulance. Harper flopped her palm to the nightstand, seeking the snooze bar, missed, knocking a book to the floor. Her hand flipped the other direction, smacking the bar, giving her nine more minutes of blissful slumber.

Harper may have looked forward to those extra nine minutes of sleep, but the bright sun streaming in the bay window cut through the drowsiness and brought a surge of energy.

She swung her legs over the bed and groaned. Every muscle in her body ached like she'd run a triathlon. What had she done yesterday? A party?

She shook her head to clear the cobwebs and tried to force the last night into focus. Wait. I wasn't at a party. I was in a forest somewhere. Camping maybe? Emilio got lost, and I was searching for him.

*Oh, no! He's still missing.*

The blankets tangled around her legs, sending her lurching to one side. Her arm shot out to snatch her phone off the nightstand. It vibrated in her hand as a text from Emilio blinked on the screen.

"You were off the hook last night. See what's left of you on campus later for your first day!"

She flopped on her chest over the bed's edge, face slumping into her pillow. It muffled the laugh at her own expense. "How much did I drink?"

Spotty images of a party with Emilio's friends at Portland State battled with scenes of a dark wood and a sense of dread. Strange beings stalked those woods, but some of them were friends, including a Sasquatch.

*You're cracking up, Harper. Sasquatch isn't real.* She chuckled. She always had the most vivid dreams.

Harper flung her legs over the bed and pressed the balls of her feet deep into the thick carpet padding. The sky-blue fibers squished between her wriggling toes. She lifted her face to a large bulletin board dotted with pictures of her life.

Her favorite was a photo of a cookout at a farm they'd visited on Sauvie Island. Various extended family members crowded the benches beside a smoking grill. Across the lawn, her mother and father danced in front of an impromptu band while she hunched over a plate piled high with potato salad and barbecue chicken. Never far from the food, like always. She smiled, love for her parents warming her heart.

She raced to her closet and flung open the doors. A wall of unfamiliar garments greeted her. Where was her studded jacket? Hangers scraped along the bar as she whipped through stacks of clothing, her anxiety rising with each passing outfit. She'd been wearing it for protection from... What?

The sensation of warmth crawling down her head and spine brought with it a heady euphoria, like bright bubbles, cleansing all the fear and stress from her mind. The scent of spiced apples permeated the air. She suddenly felt very heavy and staggered over to her desk chair, sinking into it with her forehead cradled in her hands.

She wasn't certain how long she sat there, at least a minute. A yawn gripped her, and she pushed the chair back so it teetered on two legs, arms stretched out behind. Boy, she sure must have drunk a lot at Emilio's campus party last night, so much she had strange Alice in Wonderland dreams about a dark forest filled with elves and dragons. *I bet one of his artist friends slipped a little something into my drink.* She laughed.

A gentle knock rapped at the door. "Harper, honey, you up?"

"Yeah Mom, what's up?"

Eileen O'Neill bustled into the room carrying a huge tray laden with chocolate chip pancakes, bacon, and eggs. But none of that was what caused Harper's mouth to hang slack. Her mother laid the tray on her bed and motioned Harper over.

"You look like you've just seen a ghost."

In a way, she had. Her mom looked positively radiant. Golden hair cascaded in loose curls. It wasn't the supermodel makeup that made her appear fifteen years younger either. Even this early, she was already dressed in a tasteful bright pink yoga outfit, and her body was fit, like she actually did yoga. But wasn't her mother sick, like mentally ill?

Another wave of that slithering warmth wormed its way bone-deep and expanded into every corner of her mind, bubbling away all those heavy thoughts. Harper limped to the bed and slid down to lie on her side, legs still dangling off the edge. She squeezed her eyes shut while the heaviness passed.

"Harper, what's wrong?" Her mother appeared beside her, a hand stroking her shoulder.

"I don't know. I keep getting this odd sensation. Dizzy, and my head gets fuzzy."

"Aw, honey, are you nervous?"

"Nervous?" She supposed that was an appropriate description for the sense of not-quite-right blaring like a distant alarm. "Maybe. I guess."

"You were nervous about your first day of kindergarten too. And your first day of high school. But you always excel, and it's always far better than you imagined. Your first day of college will be no different. You got this, sweetie."

Harper remembered her first day in kindergarten. She'd been terrified to get on the bus, so her dad had ridden with her. He sat next to her, played with her toys along the edge of the seat, faked fart noises behind the bus driver, and picked his nose, just like a five-year-old would. She smiled.

"Too bad Dad won't be there on the bus with me acting like some chucklehead frat boy."

"I won't? But I cleared my whole schedule. I was planning to pretend I was on the football team or something." Gerald O'Neill strode through her bedroom door wearing a wide grin and a Portland State sweatshirt, miming a long pass. "Go long, Harper!" he said, and tossed a balled-up shirt her way.

# CHAPTER 36

"Yes, I suppose he would seek Harper." The ogre flicked a thick furred hand, and two of his long-nosed goblin bodyguards flanked their table. "Phelan Kane, I'm flabbergasted that you darken my doorstep once more."

Eileen recognized Twitch from Hieronymous's entourage in the Fir Bolg village. His friend bore a heavy resemblance. Both skinny, green-skinned Fae, their lips were drawn back, and elongated fingers rested on short axes holstered at their hips.

Phelan tensed and slid to the edge of his seat. "Food's still as oversweet as always." The goblins growled and pressed forward as he sidled out of the booth and drew himself up to his full height.

Hieronymous bellowed and sent a shoulder careening for Phelan. Eileen squealed and scurried out of the way, her chair clattering to the floor with a series of sharp thuds.

"You old hound dog, I didn't guess any of you fools had survived the O'Neill Purge, much less still believed in this Quixotic quest of yours." Hieronymous threw arms like tree trunks around Phelan and squeezed. The man's boots dangled like a child's in an adult's embrace, but he clapped a hand on the ogre's back enthusiastically.

"Not so foolish, after all. You're aware of the heir too or you wouldn't have invited the girl's mother to your lair. Erm... fine establishment."

"Would one of you please tell me what's going on?" Eileen said as she bent to right her chair and ended up smashed into her own ogre embrace. Hopefully, that cracking sound wasn't a rib. "I'm glad to see you again, Hieronymous. You too, Twitch."

The goblin scratched the end of his long nose with the back of his hand. "Wouldn't happen to have any of that Dust on you? Need it for more... research."

Eileen shook her head. "Sadly no."

"Rats. Need anything?" He tapped a crinkled fabric pouch strung on his hip opposite the axe.

Eileen mouthed a no, but her insides gave a little leap at the sight of the bag and the potential relief it contained. Surely the goblin had something to ease her churning guts and eliminate the certainty that she belonged cowering in Gresham, not throwing herself into a situation she lacked the skill for.

"Please. Sit. There is much to deliberate." Hieronymous nodded, and his pair of goblin escorts scurried off through the bustling crowd. He lifted a giant hand and motioned the barkeep. In seconds, tall mugs of mead for himself and Phelan appeared, and another steaming mug of tea for Eileen. Then he placed an intricate egg-shape device on a stand in the center of the table and exhaled over it. Tiny gears spun, rings covered in symbols rotated, and a shimmering bubble formed around their table. It showered from the top of the device and oozed down like thick syrup.

"There," Hieronymous said. "It would require a Tuatha's sorcery to eavesdrop on us presently."

"That's amazing. What is it?" Outside the glittery sphere, Fae laughed, feet and hooves pounded the floorboards in a lively jig. Inside, silence reigned as though the pub were a scene in a fantasy movie she watched with the sound turned off.

"Sphaera Indicens. The gnome artisans who made them are all extinct." Phelan laid his face against the table to soak in every detail of the device.

"Indeed. Victims of the Fae Wars that ravaged the Underworld as the Veil was thickening. I possess the last three. But, returning to Eileen's query, I suggest you enlighten us, Phelan. We may be fighting the same battles."

"You can start by telling me who you are and what you want with my daughter." Eileen's knee tapped out a quick staccato against the underside of the table.

"I am a member of the Fianna, one of nine remaining of the Clan Baiscne, bound to serve as the protectors of the High King of Inisfáil and the royal bloodline since before the days of Finn MacCool."

Eileen scrunched up the right side of her face. "Finn MacCool. Like the pub?"

"Named after, but missing the spirit of the man. Finn was the greatest of us. Magician. Warrior. Poet." Phelan tipped his glass.

Eileen fiddled with the handle of her mug. "The only part of that I understood was the protecting the bloodline bit, but it looks like you failed. Badb Catha slaughtered my husband over fifteen years ago."

The ogre twisted the tip of his horn with a long face. "Did you say merely nine remain?"

A profound sadness tugged the corners of Phelan's deep brown eyes. He nodded, his gaze never leaving Eileen. "Before Badb's purge, the Fianna numbered over a thousand across the world. Your husband wasn't her only victim. All but nine of us were killed trying to protect the bloodline."

"I'm sorry. I didn't know." Eileen stretched her hand to clasp his.

"My wife and daughter died defending a family in Milwaukee from Badb and her Unseelie Sidhe. I wish we could've saved your husband, but by the time Badb came for him, only about twenty of us remained. It became impossible to be everywhere." His voice tightened.

"That is why the Fianna search for Harper. To execute their sworn duty. Even if it results in their extinction," Hieronymous said.

"We had no hope anyone had survived Badb's purge, but one night a few weeks ago, we felt the Lia Fail spring back to life and call out to us."

Eileen envisioned the glowing stone Nuada revealed when he'd announced to the gathered Green World Fae who Harper was.

Phelan shook his head and took a long pull of his mead. "What I can't understand is how she escaped and went unnoticed all this time."

"Nuada enlightened us about that." Hieronymous took a few minutes to catch Phelan up on Harper's two branches of Tuatha blood, a granddaughter of Eriu and the recipient of both the power and protection of Macha.

"This is more than I could have ever dreamed. Not just an heir, but of the Tuatha line as well. We might yet win. You must have her tucked away safe somewhere. Where is she?"

"Sauvie Island. Hopefully the Phooka freed her and they're close to rescuing her friend Emilio and the Dusk King's sister," Eileen said.

Phelan spat his mouthful of mead across the table. The pair of goblins scowled and wiped their faces. "She's where?" His jaw hung slack and his head swiveled back and forth between Hieronymous and Eileen. "For feck's sake, who let her waltz right into the lair of the enemy? And with that traitorous Phooka? She needs protection. Training."

"The Phooka fought alongside the village when Harper struck a deal with the Wild Hunt to save the Fir Bolg." Eileen said, insides squirming, unconsciously sliding fingers toward Phelan's mead.

"The Hunt's got her?" Phelan smacked his hands on the table and stood hunched over his drink, stroking his beard. "You're her mother! How can you be so calm? We've got to go. *Now.*"

Eileen's eyes flashed. "For the record, I'm not exactly calm. I'm seconds away from crawling back into a bottle or ending up in a mental institution. Again. I came here because I want to find her too. And if you'd ever met my daughter, you'd know nothing would have kept her from going to that island to rescue Emilio. Is that why you brought me here, Hieronymous? Are we going to find her?"

Hieronymous waved Phelan into his seat. "My spies encountered her collecting water from a pond after she escaped Gwyn, then her trail went cold. If they happen upon her once more, they'll alert me, aid her if they can."

Eileen slumped. News that Harper had slipped Gwyn's noose relieved the continual tightness across her chest, at least until she pondered the other horrors waiting for her.

Phelan rested his head on his arms for a moment, then lifted it. "I'll muster the Fianna. Go to that infernal island and—"

The ogre's voice silenced all protest. "No. Harper chose this path. Badb's gateway requires her alive, and we have the longer game to consider. She proved herself more than we imagined at the council, thus we must trust she is precisely where she needs to be at present. The hour grows late. It is probably best we discuss the particulars in the morning, but I summoned you here, Eileen, because a more immediate and pressing dilemma awaits."

Phelan quirked an eyebrow. "What could be bigger than losing the last heir of Niall to the psychotic Tuatha bent on murdering all humans?"

"There is a mole in the Fir Bolg village."

# CHAPTER 37

The scratch-scratch of Alphine sawing away at one bar of her cage kept Emilio alert enough to keep his eyes open. The imprisoned Fae had fallen into a rotation where a few would work their metal feathers against their wooden prisons for several minutes, while others rested, roles switching when a group tired. Emilio knew he'd be freed at dawn, so he served as lookout.

The first few hours had been easy. Badb retired to wherever it was she slept, and the nightly music and dancing began. None of the revelers paid the caged Fae any mind between groups of new arrivals. Mercifully, only one more rescue party returned that night with a bedraggled batch of Underworld refugees. Their faces wore the same hardened mask of repressed anguish Emilio had seen a thousand times before he'd ever met the Fae.

That expression and the cruelty behind it were the reason his family and so many others had fled his native El Salvador. Gang members had swaggered with derisory grins, their languid, laid-back posture telegraphing the power in their privilege to be comfortable amid the poverty and unrest surrounding them. Anger simmered beneath those steely faces, ready to lash out, kill with the same casualness someone might order a cup of coffee.

Emilio had been a small child the last time he'd seen his native land. Childhood afforded him a single advantage: He wasn't worth noticing, like he hadn't been worth noticing in the Erimus tower. He'd used invisibility the same way he did in El Salvador: to study his oppressors.

Looking a gang leader in the eyes was a dangerous thing, likely to escalate to violence quickly. Most people kept their heads down and shuffled past. But Emilio stared them right in the face and realized their need to lash out at anyone brave enough to meet their gaze. The eyes reveal all, and what Emilio perceived underneath the cruelty and hardness was despair. The despair of a beaten-down people with little hope of anything getting better, of a society forced to resort to a pack mentality merely to survive another day. But more than that, when their guard was down, when the sidewalks were nearly empty, he recognized their longing.

What might the thugs have become had the streets offered them any other option? Teachers? Musicians? They were as trapped as their victims. In those moments, young Emilio had felt sympathy for them.

That same ghost flickered deep in the eyes of Badb's Sidhe militia. Late at night, when the music they played salved their souls, empty stares and listless bodies told the true story. Oppressors and the oppressed in equal measure. A people from a dying world making a pilgrimage across a magical border into a land that would never welcome them. A land that had once been their home.

Those feelings made strange bedfellows with the hatred Emilio felt after his transformation. Compassion and loathing each spoke their closing arguments while he focused on his evolving escape plan.

He guessed only two hours had passed since the music ended. That suggested the time crept close to five in the morning. Callon would come for him soon and another day of grueling training would begin.

"What do we do once we've weakened these enough to break out?" Alphine's huge, deep aqua eyes focused on him as though he had the answers. Just like Selena and the rest had when he led them blundering into a trap. Alphine had been right to rub his face in his failure.

Emilio shrugged. "Up to you. Run away?"

"We wouldn't make it to the door. Why are we trying to cut our way through these bars if there's no escape plan?"

"Only idea I have is to wait for Harper to smash in here and raise holy hell, then run for it. And, as you so delicately pointed out, my last attempt was a colossal flop."

"But you got farther than anyone else. You were only a puny human then. Now you're a..." Alphine looked down at the gunmetal feather she twisted in her hands.

Emilio sighed. "A half-breed?"

"Powerful. A Netherfae."

"I can't promise anything. They move us all over the place. There have to be times when there are fewer of Badb's loyalists in this plaza. Watch for patterns in those moments."

The clatter of footfalls approaching the bank of cages ended any chance of further discussion and Emilio and Alphine quickly lay down and feigned sleep.

Emilio's cage shook when a shiny black loafer slammed repeatedly against the door. "Wakey, wakey, my young intern."

Emilio rolled to his other side and came face to face with Breas bent at the waist, his face inches from the bars. Emilio tilted his head back to find a single redcap accompanying the owner of Erimus Pharmaceutical.

"Where's Callon?"

Breas laughed while motioning for the redcap to unlock the cage door. "You'd rather spend quality time with the Sidhe? I fear Badb has broken you, after all."

Emilio slid his knees in front of his chest. "Scarface is a real peach, coin toss who's the worst of you two. Why are you here? Come to soak in all this fabulous?" Emilio jingled his wings. Beside him, Alphine snickered into her palm.

"Truth is, I need your opinion on something, but if you like spending your nights in there, who am I to judge another man's kink?"

Emilio licked his lips and scanned Breas's outfit like he was a contestant on *Queer Eye*. "Well, brown shoes should never be worn with dark grey. I'd go with black. And thin ties haven't been cool since nineteen eighty-six." Alphine stifled another chortle.

"Cute. It's your scientific opinion I'm after. But if you'd rather stay here with your new purple friend..."

Emilio crawled to the tiny prison's edge, and with a glance at the jeering redcap, slid out into a crouch. "Won't Callon be mad I'm not at training?"

"Callon works for me. Come." Breas turned and strode for the sweeping double staircase. He waved a dismissive hand at the redcap. "I can handle our little lab rat from here."

Emilio twisted his head over his shoulder and nodded to Alphine. She smiled, pointed two fingers at her eyes, then swept them about the plaza.

Emilio thought he'd explored almost every corner of the building during his clandestine night outings before his transformation. Breas showed him how wrong he was.

His Fomorian guide didn't ascend the broad marble stairs leading to the upper floors but instead led him toward the rear of the ground floor, and to the right. He placed a hand over one of the gilded sconces that dotted all the hallways. Emilio took a step back when the wall rippled and disappeared.

Breas shoved his hands in his back pockets and stared at Emilio. "I'm placing a lot of trust in you, my young intern. No one knows about this laboratory except for me."

"You have a secret lab inside your secret lab?" Emilio stood on tiptoes to see around Breas and into the room beyond. The only thing visible looked like a massive aluminum tank with steam roiling off it and a fiery light emanating from its center. "That's a whole new level of paranoia."

"More like a secret passage, and let's just say I have a little side project I don't want Badb to know about yet."

Emilio's shoulders shook in a stifled, ironic laugh. "That's so cliche. Backstabbing your own partner-in-douchebaggery."

"Oh, I'm quite loyal to our cause. But I also know how high her hopes can sail, and how unpleasant it would be for every single being in this building to dash them."

"Let me see if I fully grasp your stupefying idiocy by showing me this. You're putting your faith in a victim of your magical mad science show. One who loathes you with every ounce of his existence. This is the guy you trust to not tell Badb Catha you're working behind her back."

Breas nodded.

"And why wouldn't I tell Badb in exchange for something?"

"Because if Badb finds out what I'm working on before I'm ready, your friends will meet with an unfortunate training accident." Breas smiled like they were the best of friends.

"You have a building full of scientists and things that can do magic. Why do you need an intern with a bachelor's degree?"

"Don't sell yourself short. I choose only the best and the brightest for the Erimus internship program. You impressed me when you pieced together the Abraxas Project, and I'm confident you can assist me with my side hustle."

"What if I refuse? Kill my friends?"

Breas loomed over Emilio now, a hand resting on the wall

behind him. "No. But isn't spending your nights here, in a lab, better than being Callon's plaything or being drained?"

The smarmy jerk had a point. "On one condition."

"Name it."

"I want to be back with the other three Netherfae. Not in a room by myself."

Breas wagged a finger. "Oh no, I remember what happened last time you five... Well, four now, spent too much time together."

"Oh, okay." Emilio slouched against the wall and used the edge of his shirt to polish a wing feather. "Best of luck with"—he swept his hand in a circle—"all that."

If they could be closer again, the four of them might be better able to explore the mindspace Tamika could draw them all into. Even if Breas didn't agree to allow him in the same room with the others, just being nearer would benefit them, since Tamika's power seemed to depend somewhat on distance. Then they could figure out how they were going to get out of there. His new succubus friend might help, if she survived long enough to weaken her jail.

Breas's features darkened and he clamped his lips between his teeth. The Fomorian paced back and forth up the hallway for a few seconds, hands behind his back, one tapping the palm of the other. He came to rest and leaned over Emilio once more.

"Fine. With extra guards. You may share meals together and some free time, but I insist on separate rooms in the same wing. Do we have a deal?"

"Deal."

"Splendid!" Breas clapped his hands and moved over to the secret doorway. Emilio stood on his tiptoes to glimpse what lurked in the tank, but the wall was already disappearing.

"We aren't going inside?"

"Not yet. You're due at mealtime and then at the fields. I'll leave some information under the mattress of your new room.

Study it closely. When my side project is, shall we say, more formed, I'll come for you."

# CHAPTER 38

The late summer weather in Portland took pity on Harper for her first day of college, with merely a few wispy clouds in the skies. Even if they banded together, they'd fail to wring out enough precipitation to moisten an envelope, much less rain out the afternoon. The wind from the open window whispered through her brown wavy hair. She slipped her hand outside and cut an undulating wave motion through the rushing air, smiling at the way the wind first pressed her palm up, and with the slightest bend in her finger, urged it back down.

She glanced over at her father, his hands on the wheel at ten and two, precisely like they taught her in driver's education class. Gerald O'Neill was tall and thin, yet muscular from years as an avid runner. His sandy brown hair was cut short but still retained hints of the free spirit beneath. A swirl here, a spike there. Corporate life never tamed him completely.

"Do I have something on my face?"

"What? No." Harper smiled and shook her head, dropping her eyes to study her backpack.

"You keep staring at me like I have a huge booger hanging out of my nose or a big ol' glob of egg on my chin."

"If you had something that gross stuck to your face, I'd stare at you like this." Harper brought the flats of her hands to her cheeks, gave him a wide-eyed frown, and feigned vomiting.

"Well, if you had snot running down your lip, I'd stare at you like this." Her dad reared back and pulled the most ridiculous face possible while keeping one eye glued to the road.

They both laughed as the car sped along the highway. They fell into a well-worn rhythm of light banter that was like a warm blanket on a chilly day. She and her dad must have had hundreds of similar lighthearted exchanges, but she recalled few and not any specific moment of banter from the past.

Harper peered at him again before swiveling her head to count the mile markers whizzing by the window. *He shouldn't be here with me.*

"Harper! Harper, the mycelium is—"

"What did you say?" The voice didn't sound like her father, but what else could it be?

Gerald's forehead creased. "I didn't say anything. Why?"

Harper rubbed her cheeks, the weird voice already fading. "My mind must have wandered."

"Seriously, Rabbit, something's bothering you. You're not yourself today. What's got you by the tail?"

How to tell him when she couldn't put her finger on it herself? She had the perfect life. Her future ahead of her, everything she ever desired, but somewhere deep down a voice whispered none of it was hers. Ridiculous. Who's life would this be? This was her family. Her city. Their house. All of it familiar. And yet...

"It's a workday. You seriously took the morning off just to drive me to my first day of college?"

"It's tradition! I've taken you to every single new school since kindergarten. I expect to drive you to graduate school in a few years too."

The image of her dad on the bus when she was five brought a smile to her face. But that was the only time she could specifically recall him on the first day of school. Surely there'd been others. Fourth grade, middle school, high school. She squinted her eyes and tried to force those times to surface, but they remained blank. She could only remember that he'd accompanied her, like she'd read it in a book somewhere, not lived the experience.

And that was the problem, the rock in her shoe. The vast expanse of details she couldn't recall between the age of ten and right now. The muscles in her shoulders and legs tensed. Almost immediately, her scalp started to tingle and warmth poured down her face, trickling down her neck. All tension melted, leaving well-being, completeness, and the faint scent of apple.

"I don't know, Dad. This morning I got this crazy idea my life was fake. It overwhelmed me. It's silly."

The car rounded the corner and a big sign announced their arrival at PSU.

"Rabbit, I was confused and anxious when I started college too. I knew who I was in high school, where I fit in. But at the university, all that was gone. I felt like a stranger to everything, like I didn't know who I was anymore. I guess what I'm trying to say, is what you're experiencing is normal."

"Thanks, Dad." A lump formed in her throat. If the fear in her mind's dark corners was correct and this wasn't her life, she desperately wanted to keep it.

"Remember, when you're standing at the threshold between your old life and the new, there's always fear. But that's simply energy. Focus it on action. Use it to propel you forward and there's nothing you can't do."

"Jesus, Dad. Now you sound like Mom. You get into her esoteric books library again?"

Her father wiggled into a parking space a block up from the bookstore. The sidewalks bustled with new students and their parents, and moving vans still littered the dorm area. Harper and her dad emerged from either side of his white Mercedes and soaked in the scenery.

"Too bad your mom had that board meeting this morning. Let's give her something to enjoy between budget reports and proposals." Gerald stepped around the vehicle and slung an arm across her shoulders. With his long arm extended above, he snapped a selfie with the campus as a backdrop.

"Send it to me too." Harper bent back to the floor of the car and fetched her backpack. It was featherlight, but her trip to the bookstore would change that. She planned to grab the books for the two classes she had this afternoon and return tomorrow for the rest.

Harper slung the bag over her shoulder. Her dad stood there, a sappy smile on his face.

"Well, Rabbit, this is the end of the road for me. Work awaits. I'm so proud of you." He opened his arms and Harper stepped close, throwing her arms around his neck.

"Means a lot you came, Dad." She burrowed her face against his shoulder. His yellow polo shirt smelled of laundry detergent and woodsy aftershave.

He clapped her on the back of her shoulder and drew away. "See you at home. I can't wait to hear about your first day."

"I'm sure it'll be riveting. An epic tale of syllabi and lugging heavy books all over campus."

Gerald O'Neill raised his arm in a farewell wave and started toward his car. Seeing him turning to leave, Harper's heart tightened, and the thought that she'd never see him again bubbled up from some place deep inside.

"Dad!" She raced the few steps to him and gripped him a fierce embrace. "I love you."

"Love you too, Rabbit." He drew back and gazed into her face. His hand tucked a stray bit of hair behind her ear like he'd done when she was little. "What's all this about?"

Harper sniffled and swallowed the lump in her throat. "I know it's stupid, but it just seems like ages since I last saw you is all."

"Well, we don't spend as much time together as I'd like. Tell you what, this weekend, let's go to the Japanese Gardens. You and your mom always love it there."

"Sounds perfect."

"Knock 'em dead." Her father ducked inside his car and the engine purred. Harper watched the vehicle disappear around a corner before she turned and headed for the bookstore.

Harper tugged her jean's waist back into place and inhaled a deep breath of the sweet air. Must be roses blooming somewhere. Beautiful day. A fun weekend with her family, fantastic friends; her life was perfect. *But it's not yours.*

A woman's voice with a rather odd accent called to her. She sounded far away, like she was calling to her down a long tunnel. "Harper! Harper! You're so strong, I feel your mind fighting it. I can't keep this link open for long. Keep pushing! Come back to us."

Harper spun around on her heel. Only groups of students and visitors milling about, minding their own business.

"Harper, you have to fight it." A male's voice this time, deep and resonant.

She snapped her head behind her, breath rising in shallow pants. People were stopping to stare at the apparently crazy person, but none of them had called out to her. She grimaced and focused on her sneakers.

"Harper, none of this is real." Still another male voice, higher this time.

Then all three voices shouted at her simultaneously. Calling her name, warning of danger. She clapped her hands over her ears and squeezed her eyes closed. *They aren't real. They aren't real. They can't be real. It's just stress.* She repeated it like a mantra whispered under the breath to ward off evil and then the scent of eastern spice and apple wafted into her nostrils.

# CHAPTER 39

It surprised Eileen how well she'd slept in this strange place, but Hieronymous had explained to her what this pub was. Fògradh. Exile. The word resonated with her.

For the past fifteen years, grief and the spell Gwyn ap Nudd cast to shatter her memory had exiled her. From others. From Harper. Even from herself. And like all who return from exile, she only returned bodily. While she'd languished, everything else moved on, leaving her out of sync, isolated and paralyzed as if she'd relocated to a foreign country without learning the language.

At the Lodge, refugees and outsiders from all Fae courts, Fomorian, Tuatha, anyone not human, gathered. Weapons and conflicts stowed at the door so everyone could enjoy a slice of their respective homelands in peace.

Outside Fògradh Lodge, however, war brewed, her only child in the center. And evil stalked her adopted family.

She ran through the list of Fir Bolg and the Green World Court Fae she'd met, trying to suss out whether any were the sort who'd betray them to Badb.

Lord Ezrynhivar was the obvious suspect. King of dark Fae,

arrogant, and utterly unbothered by killing. But he'd done more than most defending the village from Sluagh attack, and he'd melted her terror with glamour. On the other hand, Fae manipulated ruthlessly, so his apparent heroism was equally likely a long con.

That left Queen Serotina and her Dawn Court Fae, who'd been nothing but kind to everyone. Surely none of them would be an informer.

With a groan, she pressed the pillow over her face and drew up her knees so the flats of her feet rested on the supple mattress. These same ruminations chased their tails like puppies, exuberant and naïve.

Perhaps Hieronymous was wrong about the mole, but Eileen's instincts screamed he wasn't. In the miles and miles of untouched forest around Mount Hood, the chances were vanishingly small that the Sluagh had simply stumbled upon a race so expert at hiding that modern humanity hadn't conclusively documented a single encounter. Ever.

One more deep sigh and she tossed the pillow aside, rising to her elbows to blink the sleep from her eyes. Then she crawled from under the silky golden blankets, grasped the carved post of her bed, and slipped into the green brocade robe Hieronymous had provided. Her room held riches that would make the ritziest five-star accommodations seem like a roadside roach motel.

She was up early, well before the meeting, at least according to her watch. The suite was underground where the sun couldn't reach. That could have felt oppressive, but the entire wall opposite her lush bed comprised a woodland mural with a jet-black spire in the distance that changed with the time of day. When she'd first fallen into the bed, the painting showed a dark blue sky covered in wispy clouds, and cool light bathed the trees. The painted forest now shone with the soft blush of dawn, and tiny birds fluttered among the treetops.

After she dressed, she explored part of the vast library bordering her room. The Sólás Atheneum, Hieronymous called it. Before alcohol had taken over her mind, she'd loved libraries. She read anything and everything she could find, but volumes about spirituality captivated her above all else. The Sólás Atheneum stretched for thousands of feet underneath Forest Park. She could spend a lifetime plucking books from the ornate mahogany wood shelves and still barely scratch the surface.

The library seemed in some magical way to discover what she most wanted to study, because she chose a pair of very ancient looking Taoist texts from a top shelf. In the vastness of this repository, what were the odds of her standing before that which she most loved to read?

She carried the books to one of the claw-footed tables perched atop an ornate carpet. Reading promised relief from the looped recording of her fears. With an anticipatory grin, she snuggled into the puffy chair and flipped the first book open.

Rats. The volumes were written in Chinese, but she found the drawings interesting enough to leaf through several pages. Just like a kid; only looking at the pictures.

"You might find these helpful if you're planning to read those." Hieronymous's velvet deep voice rumbled behind her. She twisted around to discover him dangling a tiny pair of round, wire-rimmed glasses between his fingers. She reached out and took them, folding apart the filigree legs.

"My eyesight is about the only thing that still works well."

"Try them, anyway."

Eileen slid the spectacles on and flipped the book open once more. She laughed and clapped her hands. Right before her bespectacled eyes, the unfamiliar squiggles melted into plain English. "Wondrous," was all she could think to say. She glanced down at the thick black leggings and oversize red plaid flannel shirt that had been left for her to change into. "The outfit is perfect," she said, careful to not utter the thank you on her lips. "I'm surprised you kept human clothes here."

"They belonged to my ex-wife. Goblin seamstresses altered them, for she is much larger than you."

"You married a human?"

"Do not look bewildered. Romance between Fae and humans is as old as time."

Eileen remembered enough of her grandmother's old stories to recall that dalliances were common between mortals and the Fae, but marriage was decidedly not. "She must be one hell of a woman."

"That she is." The ogre's lips drooped, but he shook it off with a curt smile before fussing over the plates and silverware at a thick, carved conference table tucked into an alcove.

Childlike winged Fae trooped in and laid out a lavish breakfast along the center of the table while goblins dusted and cleaned every inch of the enormous room.

Eileen was lost in her book when Phelan entered, grinned at the spread of food, and started piling his plate high with sweet cakes, sausage, exotic fruits, and slices of ham. She closed the volume and slipped the magical glasses into the front pocket of her flannel shirt.

"Good morning," he called in a cheery voice.

"Morning." Eileen's stomach growled when she caught the hearty scent of caramelized sausage and the fresh aroma of strawberry. She tried not to notice Phelan's muscled chest beneath another long-sleeved Lovecraft Film Festival shirt, this time featuring a blue demon with several appendages. And she definitely did not allow her attention to linger too long on his shining, tousled hair.

"We're only waiting for Giselle to arrive and then we can begin." Hieronymous sat in the largest seat, primly slicing off small hunks of pancake. He dabbed each exactly once in a little puddle of lavender syrup and lifted the fork to his lips, refined despite the tusks jutting up from his bottom lip.

"Who is this Giselle?" Phelan asked with his mouth half full of sausage. He hunched over his plate as though guarding it from interlopers.

The ogre wiped his lips with a lacy napkin, tilted his head, and smiled. "One of my many informants."

"Do you have spies everywhere?"

The ogre steepled his clawed fingers and gazed at Eileen. "What my staff don't overhear from Fae coming to my magnificent lodge, I hear from others I send outside my territory."

"This guy probably knows more about every Court than the kings and queens themselves."

"Indeed." Hieronymous swirled his morning cocktail. "And trading that knowledge provided the gold required to build this little fiefdom."

Eileen's thoughts drifted back to her daughter. The familiar lump of worry wrapped itself deep in her intestines and knotted her shoulders. Echoes of Ezrynhivar's subtle shot of glamour whispered of instant relief. "Have you heard anything more about Harper?"

"Careful. Did you learn nothing from your encounter with Black Annis last night? Bargaining with the Fae is dicey business, especially with the ogre." Phelan jabbed toward her with his fork.

"I seek no bargain with either of you. I labor for the interests of all." Hieronymous smoothed the lace doublet inside his purple brocade vest. "The mists cloaking Sauvie Island are impenetrable to outside observation. No more of the emissaries I've sent through the mist have returned, or contacted me, so I regret the lack of credible intelligence to soothe your fears, Eileen."

The color drained out of Eileen's face, leaving a leaden cold in her limbs.

"That likely means little," Hieronymous added. "As Nuada

informed us, that island is metamorphosing, becoming more similar to the Underworld with each moment. Maybe their journey has simply become an excessively long one."

"Also makes finding Harper like the proverbial needle in the haystack." Eileen picked at her strawberries with her fork, appetite gone. "She may already be dead." Her breath stalled in her chest.

"She's not dead," Phelan said, pushing back in his chair. He clasped his hands behind his head and looked at Eileen down his nose. A smug grin curled his lip.

Hieronymous paused with a forkful of food on the way to his mouth.

"And how would you know that? Got a crystal ball or something?" Eileen said rather snappily.

Phelan let the front two legs of his chair fall back to the floor. His hand disappeared into the pocket of his leather jacket, and he produced a white, crystalline stone about three inches in length. The center of it glowed faintly. Plopping the rock on the table, he slid it over to Eileen.

She studied it. It was smaller, but otherwise like the Lia Fail piece Nuada had shown them in the Fir Bolg village. She lifted her face to meet Phelan's gaze.

"Because, were the heir dead, the Lia Fail would be dark." Phelan leaned forward, a flush coloring his cheeks.

Hieronymous laid his knife and fork aside, interest riveted on the faintly glowing stone. "I have rooms burgeoning with treasures I'd trade you for that."

"I'm sure you would, but if I traded it to you, how would the Clan Baiscne carry out our sacred task?"

Eileen stared into the heart of the stone, drinking in its sliver of inner light like a withered plant soaking in water. She was alive. Reluctantly, Eileen placed the shard of the Lia Fail onto the table. Her fingers hung poised to slide it back to Phelan when he held out his hand. "Can we use it to find her?" she asked.

Phelan and Hieronymous shook their heads in unison. Phelan's shoulders drooped. "No way I know of, lass."

"Though I'll have Twitch begin an inquiry immediately."

Eileen felt the icy anxiety creep back into her bones.

"Why don't you hang on to that for me. At least for now. Seems unfair for me to know more about the state of your daughter than you." Phelan smiled at her and dropped his gaze to stare at his food.

"Thank you. I can't express what this means to me." Eileen clasped the shard to her chest. Underneath his flippant exterior, the Fianna had a heart full of compassion. Not to mention a dashing smile.

The flap of wet feet slapping on stone pulled Eileen out of her moment of reverie. In seconds, a green creature with the lower parts of a frog and a mostly human-looking torso hopped inside.

"Ah, Giselle. Welcome." Hieronymous made introductions while the Fae slipped into the last chair. The two Fae shared idle chat about who was favored and who had fallen among the gentry, talked about the weather plenty, and eventually Hieronymous slid his breakfast plate to the table's edge where a pair of goblins retrieved it and scurried out of the room.

"Now then, to business." Hieronymous placed the Sphaera Indicens near the pitcher of water. "Giselle, I was not altogether surprised at your suggestion of a mole within the Fir Bolg ranks. Have you ascertained who?"

"No, my lord. Only rumors of shifting alliances and hushed talk that the forest village was discovered again. With the two locations so distant from one another, that flies in the face of reason, making the intel unconfirmed."

"But we were. I mean, they were," Eileen said. She relayed the events of the last few days with her friends. When she finished, the little nixie dropped back in her seat with a wet squelch.

"Then my sources were right." Giselle poured herself some mead and took a gulp.

"Do your sources know whether Fae or Fir Bolg betrayed the village?" Phelan asked.

The nixie shook her head, green hair fluttering around her face. "No. They gleaned the knowledge from gossip. Many rumors from multiple sources. Nothing confirmed. Until now." Giselle glanced sidelong at Eileen.

"Hieronymous, you have to do something," Eileen said. Her leg jounced up and down.

"I'm afraid I cannot be directly involved. If the solitary Fae return to the Fir Bolg, any hope of discovering the mole would vanish."

"But why?"

Giselle answered her. "Because the solitary are independent. Hieronymous is not like their kings and queens, he's more like the president. Scapegoating solitaries is a long tradition among both Seelie and Unseelie, an easy way out if the mole happens to be Fae."

Hieronymous nodded. "Precisely. And if we mysteriously returned, we might tip our hand as to the extent of our knowledge. The best we can do is to station a contingent around the secondary village as reinforcements in anticipation of subsequent attack."

"They're not there anymore," Giselle said.

"That's true." Eileen told of Glani's letter. Her pulse quickened. She envisioned Glani and the others captured by the Sluagh, marched off to be drained or forced to fight in a war. "Did they escape?"

"Rumors say yes." Giselle hung her head. "And report of heavy casualties, even among both visiting Fae Courts. Mount Hood Forest crawls with Sluagh and Badb Catha's hunters. Both the Dawn and Dusk contingents remain with them, I'd guess, because no one dares to leave and be the next ones hunted down. The survivors hide, and no one knows their whereabouts."

Phelan looked pale. "Until the mole betrays them again."

"You have done well, Giselle. The remainder of this congress must continue without you." Hieronymous gestured toward the door and the nixie plodded out.

Eileen lowered her forehead to her hands to slow the spinning. "This is hopeless. Why did you call me here to hear this if nothing I can do changes it?"

"I called you here, Eileen O'Neill, because you possess two assets none of us does. Both attributes instrumental in ferreting out this mole. The Fir Bolg accepted you. And you're human."

"What does being human matter?"

"Because only you can lie."

# CHAPTER 40

Harper's neglected cereal solidified into a slurry of mushy goo while she hunched over her third steaming cup of coffee. Her mother sat to her right, scouring the business section of the newspaper, a ritual designed to help her stay on top of her game in pharmaceutical marketing.

Eileen folded the paper down and wrinkled her nose at the bowl of congealed cereal. "Not hungry today?"

"I was. But I just feel too exhausted to eat." Her listlessness increased every day, like a battery slowly draining.

"College is a hard adjustment, Rabbit." Her dad slid his toast and coffee onto a tan placemat and plopped down across from his daughter. "You should rest up this weekend. Emilio can hit the dance clubs on his own for once."

Harper draped her napkin over the mushy glop in her bowl. "It's been almost two months. I think I'm adjusted. Maybe I'm coming down with something."

"I'll make my super-secret chicken noodle soup for dinner. That'll cure anything." Her mom pushed her chair squeaking across the wood floor. She smoothed the wrinkles from her navy blue suit and twirled a set of keys in her hand. Leaning forward, she kissed her husband. "Best shake a leg, honey. You're going to be late."

"I better get going too. Biology beckons." Harper gulped down the last of her coffee and grabbed her uneaten cereal.

"Man! I can sure clear a room," her father said with a smile. "Take some of the vitamin C above the sink. It'll help."

"Thanks, Dad." Harper took two for good measure, packed up her books, and headed out to her car.

She navigated the usual weekday gauntlet of traffic snarls and assorted delays, but the goddess of parking smiled on her, bestowing on her a space within an easy stroll to her first class. She snatched her backpack out of the back seat and checked the time. Just enough to snag another cup of coffee before class started. That should help.

"Damn, girl. Third time this week with the executive parking spot." Emilio had changed the colored streaks in his shiny black mane to purple and blue. They perfectly matched the royal blue glitter-covered sneakers and jacket he wore. He rubbed his knuckles over her hair, pulling some strands from her ponytail. "Let's rub some of that luck off on me. Big chem test today."

"You don't need any luck. You're like a savant with that stuff. Probably why you landed that internship at Erimus."

Emilio pulled his face into an asymmetrical smirk of disbelief. "Internship? I'm not even through my sophomore year."

Harper scrunched her features. It had seemed so true when she said it, like it had already happened. But of course Emilio was right. What had pushed that strange notion into her mind? Must be one of the strange dreams she'd been having every night. Her friend's eyes creased with concern.

"I slept like crap. Weird dreams, like we'd graduated from college and odd things were happening in the city. Must have come from that."

"Pass me some of whatever you're smoking." Emilio laughed and headed toward his class. When Harper didn't follow, he halted and turned around. "You coming with?"

"I'm going to grab a coffee or I'll never stay awake. Come with? My treat."

"Twist my arm." Emilio held out his arm. She took it and gave a gentle twist.

"Another sunny day. That has to be a record. Three weeks in Portland and not a cloud in the sky." Emilio spread his hands and lifted his face to the warm sunlight.

"You're welcome."

Emilio giggled. "What?"

"Betcha my parking mojo rubbed off on the weather."

"O.M.G. I bet you're right." He came close and whispered into her hair. "We better keep this between us before you end up in a government lab somewhere."

"The only reason I'll end up in a lab will be for how much coffee I've consumed today. They'll want to study why I'm not having a nervous breakdown about now. No matter what I do, I can't wake up."

In the coffee shop, Emilio squinted at the menu. "Better get the large."

"Make it two."

The barista bustled about, fulfilling orders. He must be new. Harper came here at least twice a week and had never seen him before. The man had very long, thick dreadlocks and deep black skin. But it was his eyes that drew her attention. Piercing yellow, like they'd glow at night.

The barista's oddness was outmatched only by the girl perched at the end of a short stretch of brown leather barstools flanking the counter. She had deep green hair, skin the color of Emilio's, and bright yellowish green eyes that drilled into Harper.

Harper elbowed Emilio in the side and jerked her head toward the barista. "Look at the server and that girl. Their eyes are creeping me out."

"Seriously. Colored contacts creep you out?" Emilio crinkled his nose and scanned the menu. He always got a mocha but read the entire menu every time anyway.

"Right." Contacts. Of course, that had to be it. They stood behind at least a dozen other students, but the moment he saw Harper, the barista nearly dropped the espresso he'd decanted into a small paper cup. A little sloshed on a name tag that read 'Robin G.' He recovered fast but continued to cast furtive glances at her as she scurried about making sweet caffeinated drinks.

Emilio tapped his cheek as though he pondered the truth of the universe. "I think I'll have the mocha."

"Of course you will." Her words came out flat. "The barista keeps staring at me."

"He's probably just bummed at how slammed this place is."

"No, watch him. He keeps looking right at me, that green-haired girl too."

The strange girl looked like a dancer the way she stretched her long legs across the stool beside her. She flicked her eyes toward Harper several times in the course of a minute.

Meanwhile, the barista's long-fingered black hands flew over the complicated machines, brewing their stimulant delights. He at least tried to hide his interest, a sidelong glance while frothing milk, a dropped spoon affording him another look.

"Hmm. I think he's into you. You should talk to him, he's pretty hot."

Maybe Emilio was right. But Harper couldn't shake the idea she'd met both of them before. She was sure she'd recall meeting someone with green hair and yellow-green eyes and a handsome black man.

Harper's shoulders rose as she stepped up to the counter.

Robin G. turned those gleaming yellow eyes to her, and a white, toothy smile broke out across his face.

"What'll it be, Harper?" His accent was faintly Jamaican.

Harper's left hand gripped the edge of the counter while her right slid into her pack, scrabbling around but finding only pens. *Why did I just do that?* Some instinct had driven her to seek something, but why grab a pen because the staff made her uneasy?

"How do you know my name?"

"I know all my customer's names." The man shrugged, but his eyes narrowed with the faintest grin.

Emilio pressed against Harper's shoulder and grinned. "And it's on your backpack."

Harper clawed her olive drab backpack off and gawked at her name embroidered across the top. *I never had my name on my stuff before.* She ran a hand over the silky white threads, verifying it felt real. It was a reasonable explanation. She chalked her anxieties up to tiredness and sighed.

Harper ordered a large coffee for her and a mocha for Emilio, and they slid down the counter to wait for their order.

The moment the drinks were done, the barista pulled them in front of him so his back blocked what he was doing for several seconds. That looked odd. Harper's hands clenched until he reached over her head, grabbed a pair of lids, and put them on the cups. *He just wanted to make sure they didn't spill. I gotta relax.*

"Large coffee and a mocha." The man placed the drinks on the counter with a broad smile. The green-haired girl placed her palms over the lids. Harper thought she saw a flash of light before she slid them down toward Harper and Emilio. "Might want to take a sip of that coffee now. Make sure he put the right amount of cream in there. He's a terrible barista." The girl shot a smirk at an indignant Robin G.

Harper nodded and took a sip. "Perfect." She smiled back at the barista.

The walls started melting. Harper staggered backward, collided with the stool, and fumbled the drink.

"Harper! What's going on? Are you all right?" Emilio's face was transparent.

A ring of people clustered around, murmuring to each other and pointing. A bunch of them pulled out their phones and started filming. She could see completely through them all. Behind them, a woodland canopy stretched, where the moon shone through the branches. Wispy fuzz, like mold, coated the backs of her arms. With a grunt, she wiped it off.

The barista called to her. "Harper. Harper. Over here."

Beside him, the green-haired girl beckoned.

She turned her face toward him and gasped. They were the only things other than Harper that wasn't rippling and transparent. But most terrifying was the strange woman's shaggy brown goat legs, and Robin G. looked like a patchwork of other jet-black animals. Part rabbit, goat hooves, horns, and glowing yellow eyes.

Harper screamed and more smartphones whipped out.

"I'm calling campus security. They'll take you to health services." Emilio punched a number into his phone. Behind him, wind rustled the tree branches.

"Harper. It's me, the Phooka." The monster jerked a thumb at the animal girl. "And this is Melinoe. You're in a dream sequence and, I know you don't remember, but we're friends."

How could she be friends with things like that? *They're not real. What's happening?* Dizziness sent her crashing to all fours. The assembled students muttered and continued to film, but no one offered to help, and anyway, they'd almost faded away. Emilio's voice trembled as he told emergency services she was having some kind of episode.

"I don't know you. Don't know what you are."

The warm sensation bloomed on the crown of her head. She

could swear she saw a puff of smoke rolling down her face, filling her nose with the scent of spices and fruit. Her muscles slackened as a scintillating tingle crawled down the back of her neck. She smiled.

"No!" Melinoe screamed and held out her hand. "Harper, listen to me now. Take my hand. You *have* to take my hand. It'll help you break the spell."

Beside her, Robin G. hopped over the shimmering half-there counter, rabbit ears twitching. "Harper! Fight this! Even with Paegrinn's mycelium spreading underneath you, breaking through Santaigh's enchantment is difficult."

*Enchantment? Who the hell is Santaigh?* The scent of eastern spices and sweet fruit tickled her nostrils. Another wave of smoke cascaded before her eyes and the coffee shop thickened. The onlookers slowly became opaque.

The pair had morphed back into their human shapes. Melinoe flung a tan hand toward Harper. "None of this is real. He's killing you. Right now. You have to break free of his magic soon or you'll be dead."

The strange pair flickered and disappeared. Only the ring of curious faces remained.

# CHAPTER 41

A massive cramp like a huge hunger pang sent Emilio crashing down. The fatigue had grown worse and slowed his reaction time, but the cramping was new. "Stand and fight, half-breed filth." Callon loomed over Emilio, a booted foot prodding him in the side, right where his muscles had spasmed.

Emilio had learned to keep his face impassive while entertaining visions of slicing the elf to shreds. Even when he begged Callon for mercy, the vision of his bully's broken body tasted sweet. Hatred, once a strange feeling, had taken up residence, rearranged all the furniture, and propped its dirty feet on the dinner table. Who was Callon to treat them this way?

His evening in the draining cage had given Emilio one thing. Now he saw his transformation in a new light. Of course, the awareness of what he'd lost and his status as an eternal outcast brought periods of rage and despair, but being Netherfae gifted him with power. The power to slice that smug superiority off Sidhe faces. Since they'd made him a monster, he planned to play the role. That meant applying himself to his lessons. Both in combat and in his clandestine studies with Breas.

Frustration creasing his face, Callon stepped forward to kick him in the ribs again. Just when the Sidhe shifted his weight to unleash a firmer kick, Emilio flipped to his hands and knees, sweeping his wing up with the flats of the feathers facing his attacker, careful not to draw blood for fear of the consequences.

A sound like a dozen swords clanging against Callon's breastplate rang and he flew several feet before slamming into the ground. Too hard. Not good. His fury had blinded him to the long game they all played: reveal as little as possible about their abilities; look for an opening to escape.

Callon pushed himself to his elbows and stared daggers at his reluctant student. Sparring had stopped. Every face was riveted to Emilio and his trainer.

A woman's laugh turned Emilio's blood to ice water. Oh no. *She* saw. Badb Catha summoned Breas and Dr. Jones to her side as Emilio shakily got to his feet. He watched them whisper behind their hands, his feet shuffling nervously.

Damage control time. Emilio reached a hand down to Callon. "Just trying to apply your lessons. Surprise. And leverage," he said at a volume he hoped reached the observers.

Callon smacked his hand away. The warrior leapt to his feet and gripped Emilio's arm, wrenching it underneath his wings and up between his shoulder blades. Pressing his face close to Emilio's hair, he whispered, "You ever do anything like that to me again, and I'll make you pray for death."

"Like I don't already?"

The Sidhe wrenched his arm even tighter. "You will not speak to me in that insolent tone."

"Or what? You'll pop me back in the cages again?"

The red gemstone flamed and crackling agony lanced through all the limbs and sinews in his body. Hatred gave him a new power. He refused to let this pretty demon see a hint of his suffering. He clenched his jaw, spine straight, and stared right into the eyes of his tormenter. Every muscle cramped, each nerve screamed, yet he stood still and silent.

"Callon. Enough." Badb Catha positioned herself between the elf and his student, her voluminous dress swirling behind her.

The Sidhe lowered their weapons and pivoted to face their leader while Breas meandered through the Netherfae. He stared down his nose at them and stopped beside Emilio.

"Today is a graduation day, of sorts." Breas smoothed an imagined wrinkle out of his tie and smirked at Emilio. "Your basic training is at an end, and your internship begins."

"What? We've been training for days, not weeks," Selina said from behind Emilio.

"And now it's time to see how you fare in a real-world setting, controlling stronger human cattle." Badb's crow companion squawked from her shoulder.

Breas beckoned to an escort of goblins and trolls. They lumbered forward, herding a dozen muscled men in identical prison blues, all wearing the same blissed-out expressions the indigent abductees wore.

Badb must be running low on the poor and festival abductees if she'd already taken the risk of pilfering the jails, Emilio thought. They'd probably make more lethal human weapons for the Netherfae to control, and more of them might survive the Abraxas process.

Emilio peeked over his shoulder to soak in the shocked expressions on the faces of his Netherfae companions. A slow nod from Selina suggested her mind was also working on turning this field trip to their advantage. Though just how promised a mountain of problems, their pain collars prime among them.

Fiach flapped his wings and muttered from Badb's shoulder as she sauntered along the line of Sidhe. "The numbers of enemy Fae in our dungeons grow few. Soon, keeping the gateway open will be difficult, yet so many remain suffering on the other side. We cannot allow it to close before the heir of Niall makes it everlasting."

The Sidhe and other Fae all bowed their heads and placed a hand over their hearts.

Badb came to rest just as the prisoners and their escorts arrived behind her. "Because of their extended proximity to human cities, the solitary Fae can tolerate longer excursions into the polluted iron wastelands than my allies. A small band of very powerful solitaries have hidden deep within the city where the Sidhe cannot effectively reach them. I need those Fae to power the gate."

Callon dropped to a knee and lowered his head. "My lady, if I may be so bold. My Sidhe will be useless in a fight there and using the Netherfae may be unwise. They are willful and—"

Breas rolled his eyes. "You will conserve your energy because it is they who will do the fighting." Breas gestured both at the Netherfae and prisoners at the same time.

"You need only use the torques to force compliance," Badb said.

Callon dipped his head further. "You are wise, my lady."

A deep, slow moan rose to Emilio's left. Alan had slipped to the ground and clasped his knees in his arms. He rocked back and forth with unfocused eyes. Emilio stepped beside him and laid a hand on his shoulder, while Tamika dropped on his other side and whispered something that brought the sharpness back to his gaze. Whatever the Fae believed, they weren't ready for this.

"You will each pilot three prisoners." Breas bustled about, moving the groups of prisoners in place beside their assigned Netherfae. "Callon's Sidhe will accompany you and take custody of the enemy Fae. Your objective is to subdue the Fae, not kill them. They can't power the gateway if they're dead."

Selina snorted. "And just how do we do that?"

Badb fixed her cold, black gaze on the Romani woman. "You better hope you can figure it out. I'm guessing this assignment will reveal more about your powers than we've yet discovered." She flicked her head to the contingent of servants shuffling about with their empty grins. "And if you fail, I'll kill a dozen cattle."

The air evaporated from Emilio's lungs along with any hope of using their time in downtown Portland to escape. A shiver ran over his back and tinkled his feathers together.

The white smiles and fanged grins leering around him told him they were well aware of what their choice would be. The cold willingness they showed to exploit basic compassion hardened his heart a little more. He bit the inside of his cheek to keep any expression off his face. *And when my heart turns fully to stone, I'll hurl it at you.*

Breas clapped his hands and beamed. "Well, you have your orders." He brought a languid hand to his lips and blasted a shrill whistle.

Roars as loud as thunder rumbled in the forest. Short gusts of wind from every direction blew through Emilio's hair and plumage hard enough for his primary wing feathers to clang together like several gongs sounding at once.

Tamika screamed and clutched Selina's arm. Beside her, Alan stared up blankly, not registering the majestic sight above.

"Dragons," Selina said with wonder scrawled on her face.

Breas placed his hands on his hips and bent backward to gaze overhead. "Yes. Many solitary Fae died to get these rare creatures through the portal."

In unison, the four dragons touched down from their low flight. The ground shook and a cloud of dust caused Emilio to shield his face. Each beast was a different color: gold, black, red, and green. Long, thin faces bristled with teeth. Pairs of Sidhe guided the glamoured prisoners and their Netherfae pilots onto the beast's broad backs before one elf hopped in front, and the other behind the last prisoner.

All except Emilio's black dragon. Because of his wings, he rode in the back to avoid slicing to ribbons whomever perched behind him.

His stomach lurched as the dragons roared and threw themselves at the sky, leathery wings jerking them higher with every flap. They flew low, perhaps twenty feet above the surface, to avoid the barrier.

In a couple of minutes, they slowed, and the elves held glowing hands overhead. The air shimmered and parted like someone drew aside a curtain of diamonds. Once through, the dragons banked vertically. With a yelp, Emilio clenched his legs as tight as he could.

He laughed at himself. Why was he freaking out? He had wings. Astride the blue dragon, Tamika lifted her face toward the stars, now visible above the clouds stretched below them. She radiated serenity. He couldn't see Alan, but Selina looked like she was about to pass out. She held on to her dragon with both her legs and her arms, and the group soared over the sparkling Portland skyline.

# CHAPTER 42

Fortunately, the half-strigoi was spared a long flight. They spiraled lower in the sky, homing in on a small pocket park visible between thick, tall buildings. Another few moments and they touched down.

Emilio guessed the elves had glamoured them invisible because none of the pedestrians hustling up and down the night sidewalks paid them any mind, even as the wind from the dragon wings flapping hard against the ground buffeted them, whipping hats off and lashing hair across their faces.

The prisoners still wore the vacant stare of the glamoured when Callon herded groups of three to their Netherfae commanders. The elf kept the entire team hiding behind the shrubs and tall grass of the landscaping, a sleeve clamped across his nose and mouth. "Take hold of your soldiers."

Alan's face fell and he lurched back a step. A grunt was the only sound he made. One of his Sidhe escorts gripped him by the arm and gave him a shake. Loud enough for all to hear, she said, "Fail us and dozens of stinking humans die."

With a whimper, Alan dropped his mossy head. The lifting of

their chests and grim set of their mouths were the only signs the accountant had taken control of his contingent.

Emilio shared his disdain for treating these poor people as his puppets, but other lives depended on his willingness to endure the dirty feeling sullying his heart.

With a breath, the gemstone glowed. Red tendrils of his thoughts snaked through the stagnant night air and wormed into the minds of his three charges, bending their will and seizing control of their muscles. Because part of him was in their consciousness, he sensed their terror as the effects of Dust faded slightly in the wake of his grip. They fought against him, especially the tall man with the sleeve of tribal tattoos, who attempted to steel himself to prevent the takeover. But it was useless.

Emilio sent thoughts to them. He didn't know if they could understand him, because he couldn't hear their thoughts, only feel their physical pain and emotions. *I don't want to do this, but many lives depend on completing our objective. I'll do my best to keep you safe.*

He assumed they at least sensed his regret and hope for their safety, because their postures relaxed a little, and he noticed their pulses slowed ever so slightly.

"Good." Callon led them past a stand of trees and into a clearing. He raised a single palm inch by inch over his head. At first, Emilio wondered if he was praying, then the cords on the elf's neck popped out and his teeth clenched. The other Sidhe circled a massive, unmoving concrete cap.

"Woodstock Park. I think I know where my ex-husband's people are hiding," Selina whispered beside Emilio.

*The Mystery Hole.* The park was the former site of an underground amusement he'd avoided because of mild claustrophobia.

Barron Mind had been the eccentric proprietor of the Woodstock Mystery Hole tourist attraction. Harper had wanted to go, but Emilio always diverted her into less tightly cramped options for their outings.

One day, the illustrious Barron packed up his rowboat treehouse "fun generator," dissembled the mystery pole, and capped the Mystery Hole before riding into the sunset, and Emilio had breathed a sigh of relief.

But thick concrete wasn't the reason for Callon's difficulty levitating the cap off. The Fae inside likely had it sealed with magic.

Emilio leaned his head to Selina. "I sure hope the Fae hollowed out the inside further. It always looked cramped on the YouTube videos Harper made me watch."

Callon grunted, and the other elves planted their feet wider. All twisted their upturned hands into claws and strained, but the cap on the Mystery Hole refused to budge.

"We need to plan our escape," Tamika whispered behind him.

"Can you do *the thing*?" Selina asked.

Tamika shook her head. "Don't think so, too much focus piloting my three." She grimaced.

Even the redcaps had joined Callon now. Emilio was beginning to believe this field trip to abduct innocent creatures would be over before it began.

Alan stared straight ahead.

Emilio was sure the man would go along with whatever they planned, but with Alan, the fear he'd snap and be the unwitting cause of human death loomed large. "We can't escape now. Too many will die."

"How many will die if we don't?" Selina asked.

"I don't know, but I agree with Emilio. We can't sentence those poor people to death for our own selfish reasons." Alan's voice was constricted.

"Selina, you said these are your ex's subjects, right?" A loose plan was forming in Emilio's mind.

"Yes, Hieronymous has been elected leader for over a hundred years. I see where you're headed with this. Badb is rounding up solitaries, so it's a safe bet they won't fight for her. If we can manage to spare one of the Fae hiding out in the Mystery Hole..." Selina's gaze roved to the former opening of the odd attraction.

"Maybe we can get a message to him to rescue us." Emilio finished the thought and noticed the concrete cap jittering, clattering enough to draw attention if it continued.

With a loud bang, the concrete levitated five feet up and shattered. Everyone ducked and waited to be pelted with debris, but Sidhe magic forced the shrapnel to fly straight down a safe distance from the hole.

The Sidhe slumped, some of them resting hands on thighs.

"Netherfae. Into the opening." Callon and the Sidhe reached into their cloaks and withdrew handfuls of collars identical to the ones clamped around Netherfae necks. So that was how they planned to subdue the solitaries. Pain. Not surprising actually; it seemed to be how Badb's people solved all their problems.

A thin female warrior, taller even than Callon, gestured to the Sidhe. They fanned out, encircling the opening, collars clasped. "Your job is to capture them and drag them to the surface. If you cannot, flush them out and we'll do the rest."

Emilio frowned. "How do you expect us to accomplish that?"

Callon refused to even look at them. "That's up to you. Part of the test. Useless as battlefield leaders if you're unable to improvise a strategy."

Beside him, the woman, his second-in-command, tapped her foot and jerked her head toward the Mystery Hole. "Do hurry, the air here is burning my lungs."

"Emilio." Alan finally spoke, a tremor in his voice. "I- I can't go down there. In the dark."

Tamika tilted his chin and her oversize eyes radiated warmth. Her smile melted some of the tension out of Alan's body. "We have to, sweetheart." Her voice resonated with the warm overtones of deep stringed instruments.

Emilio gripped the accountant's forearm, careful not to let his feathers slice him. "You should be the last in. That way, you don't have to go very far from the light. Think you can manage that?"

Alan nodded once and swallowed hard.

Selina patted him on the back and repeated, a little too loudly, "That's a splendid plan, Alan. You're the biggest, you go in last. Prevent their escape." Then more quietly, "You can't show them this weakness. Stand straight, stare ahead. We don't know what they'll do if they believe you held back."

Emilio opted to go first, even though the walls allowed barely enough space for his wings. The elves laughed when he chose to be the shield to keep his prisoners safe. Despite their derision, Emilio thought they were wrong. His plan made some sense. In such tight quarters, his wings and feathers could be deadly to his allies. He needed to ensure distance between them.

Emilio paused at the bottom of the stairs and pulled out the lantern the Sidhe had given him. Strange carvings in concrete adorned the lip and circumference of the tubelike entrance. The proprietor may have packed up the stuff on the surface, but he had left the Spock action figure and his plastic friends tucked away in their concrete nooks.

He dropped over at the waist and took a few steadying breaths, legs quaking like jelly. Rationally, he knew the walls weren't shrinking, but that wasn't the source of his weakness; rather, it was more like the lethargy that accompanied hunger. And it was happening more frequently. He stamped his feet and willed vigor back into his limbs as his prisoners dropped off the last rung and moved aside to allow the rest to cram in.

Soon Selina and Tamika were admiring the odd features the strange Barron Mind had meticulously added. Emilio lifted the over-bright lantern. A rustic arch of river stone resembled a small fireplace but served more like an altar, covered in esoteric carvings. Where the concrete design work of the hole ended, the Fae had vastly expanded the tunnel system of the Woodstock Mystery Hole.

"I don't like it here, Emilio." Alan had his back pressed against the last step.

"It's okay, buddy. Remain by the ladder, but duck behind it so the elves can't see you. We got this."

Selina squeezed around Emilio's feathers. He'd drawn them so tight against his body, rivulets of blood sprouted along his sides. Selina's jaw slackened when she stared at the splotches of red. "There's a lot more space down here than we guessed. It makes the most sense I take point. If they recognize me, we can solve this without a conflict."

Tamika chewed her bottom lip. "You think they'll voluntarily accompany us to be imprisoned, tortured, and killed?"

Emilio's wing scraped a deep cut in the wall when he sidled in front of his humans. "We may still have to fight them to show them it's hopeless. But we might convince the solitaries to join the Fae using my feathers to weaken their prisons. More recruits means improved chances of escape. It's the only strategy we have."

Selina already had the lantern in hand and edged step by step into the dark. Safely shielded from a frontal attack by his wingspan, Emilio noted his prisoners' heartrates increase. He pushed as much compassion and goodwill along their connection as he could, hoping it salved their fear. He planned to fight himself, not use them at all.

Progress was agonizing. The Fae must have expanded this tunnel a quarter mile, but the walls still allowed only single file movement. Up ahead, Selina froze.

Only silence greeted Emilio, then a rhythmic scraping, very faint. They were close.

"Tamika, can you try the mindspace trick, with just Alan?

Advise him to watch for the Sidhe?" Emilio's voice carried in the cavern even though he used his softest whisper.

Tamika's eyes unfocused for several seconds, then she nodded. "Coast is clear."

Selina lifted the lantern high. "Solitary Fae. You know why we're here, but we mean you no harm."

Feet scampered, then the scrape of metal on metal. Someone drew a weapon.

Emilio's blood rushed in his ears. "We aren't hoping to fight, but this ends only one way. Badb's Sidhe outside will capture you, with or without us, but if you work with us, we might all survive."

Selina clenched a fist. "Even strike back at them."

"I smells humans. Humans lies," a thin, wavering voice came back.

Selina took a hesitant step toward the sound. "At least one of you may remember me. I lived at the Lodge with my then-husband, Hieronymous, your leader."

A whispered conversation, then a pause.

"Then what is your name?" The woman's voice was clear as a bell.

"Selina Leanabel. Is that you, Dewberry?"

"It is you." The Fae that emerged into the circle of light would have reached seven feet tall if the tunnel allowed her to stand upright. Her face was tiny, delicate, and looked composed of layers of rose petals. Green skin covered pencil-thin limbs peeking out under a glimmering aqua gown.

The Fae's smile fell when she saw her old friend.

Selina lifted her palms and shrugged. "More like Fae now. We all are."

Shuffling feet scraping over gravel emanated from the back of the tunnel. Emilio dropped into a defensive stance. His prisoners mirrored his move.

Dewberry recoiled. "Are you *glamouring* them?"

"You could say that," Emilio said.

A ring of strange faces appeared in the light, eight of them. A little leathery-skinned hobgoblin with a bat's face clutched Dewberry's leg. Beside him, a creature with a humanlike torso, dragonfly wings, and frog legs stared at Emilio's plumage.

He recognized Seelie elves, some sylphs, and goblins.

Suddenly, everyone froze. Something approached up the tunnel. Tamika's hand curled into a fist.

A flat voice emanated out of range of the light. "Alan says the Sidhe grow suspicious there hasn't been fighting." The footfalls receded.

"Shit." Emilio had hoped they'd have more time. "If we fail to exit the tunnel with you, those Sidhe are coming in."

Dewberry turned her nose up in the air. "Maybe it is you that joins us, not the other way round. We can take them together."

Selina's full lips drew into a thin line, and she pointed to the collar. "Afraid not. These aren't for pretty. One false move and we're a heap of pain on the ground. A set of these awaits you too."

Dewberry slouched forward, pressing her face inches from Selina's neck. The Fae hissed. "Réabadh Torques. Barbarians." She raised her eyebrows. "Why haven't you sprung them? Or are you affected by iron the same way we are?"

Tamika's face went from hopeful to the brink of tears all at once. "We're not, but there's hardly any in the tower."

A rail-thin, chartreuse goblin hopped to Emilio. "There's iron in the park bench arm rests. Let the Alicanto eat them."

Emilio's jaw dropped. "What? Eat metal?!"

Dewberry's laugh was musical. "You didn't know? If you haven't been eating metal, how do you have the strength to stand?"

"We've only been this way for a couple weeks."

"Well, you need to eat metal every few days to maintain your strength and keep your feathers tough."

The little goblin chimed in. "And whatever metal you eat, that's what your feathers will contain."

Emilio smiled broadly for the first time since his abduction and transformation. Not only did his plumage slice, if he devoured the bench, his touch would kill Fae. Old Emilio's escape plan had failed, but Netherfae Emilio would prevail and save every one of Badb Catha's victims.

Tamika shattered his reasoning. "How do iron feathers break the collars?"

Dewberry smiled at her. "Fae magic locks the Réabadh Torques. Slide an iron-infused feather in the clasp and the spell breaks. They'd pop right off."

Alan's prisoner shuffled closer. "Guys, they're listening and preparing to come down there," he said, then continued shuffling in a lazy circle.

Dewberry's lips pursed. "We can't become their prisoners. We have to get word to Hieronymous about what they're doing."

Emilio inhaled a deep breath. He was losing them. "The only way we live and eventually win is to join forces. I won't leave you behind. I've already got some of the other Fae prisoners in the cages plotting escape. Now that we know we can spring these torques, we can all escape together."

The little bald goblin looked at him sideways. "Humans lie, even half-Fae ones. It's their only talent."

Emilio dropped to a knee and looked the goblin in his brown eyes. "Not me. I want to get every victim of Badb Catha off that island. Human and Fae."

Selina met the eyes of every Fae in the Mystery Hole. "He's speaking the truth."

"We leave someone free to get help. We'll say there were only seven of you," Emilio said.

Selina smiled. "Should be you, Dewberry, you're the fastest."

The Fae hesitated for a second, brow creased as she scanned

her companions, and nodded. The tiny, bat-faced Fae spoke first. "What do we do now?"

Emilio took a deep breath and let his hands fall to his sides. "We stage a noisy fight."

The solitary Fae wasted no time launching themselves at Emilio and his friends with a chorus of yells.

# CHAPTER 43

Harper slumped to the coffee shop floor. The white noise of murmuring voices droned as a larger audience gathered. How did she end up down here? She remembered ordering a drink, a golden-eyed black man and an odd girl telling her this was all just a dream and she was dying, then the smell of spices and fruit.

"There she is." Emilio's button-crusted shoulder bag dropped as he pointed campus security toward where Harper rolled herself to her feet, wavering.

"Harper, my name's Dave and this is Nadine." The stocky woman next to him waved. "Let's sit down and you can tell me what happened."

Emilio retrieved Harper's backpack from the floor and followed Dave and Nadine to a small table.

"Okay, folks, give her some space. Nothing more to see here," Nadine shouted at the crowd, which retreated but didn't disperse entirely.

Heat bloomed on Harper's cheeks. She'd given them quite a show.

"Hey!" She jerked her head away from the pinpoint of light Dave blasted in her face.

"You fall today or get hit in the head?" Nadine asked.

"No."

The pair took her temperature and looked her over, asking questions as they went. She told them she'd slept poorly, but that was about it.

"How much coffee have you had today?" Dave asked.

"What, you want me to walk a straight line now and touch my nose?" Harper asked.

"Too much caffeine might explain why you got light-headed and passed out." Dave's voice was soft and patient.

"Three cups at home and about two sips of this one. I think someone drugged it."

Nadine and Dave leaned in simultaneously. "Someone here drugged your coffee? Who?"

"The new barista or the girl with the green hair. Melanie or something. They both handled the cups."

"Harper, there was no one here with green hair. The same barista who's always here served us." Emilio pointed at the short redhead with the face piercings. "Lauren works here every day."

"You messing with me? The black guy had yellow eyes. You told me they were contacts. He handed you that mocha." She dipped her chin at Emilio's cup while the blood pressure cuff deflated.

"Lauren handed me my mocha." Emilio's voice radiated concern.

"Well, Harper, you seem fine, but you should head to the health center. Both too much caffeine and insomnia can cause hallucinations." Nadine rolled up the cuff and stuffed it in a case.

Harper launched herself up, knocking the chair over in her haste. "I'm not crazy." But even as she said it, doubt whispered that perhaps everyone else was right and she was midway to a psychotic break.

Nadine held up her hands. "No one is saying that. But you fainted in a coffee shop. You should get checked out further, just to be safe."

"They're right, Harper. Come on, it's on my way to class. I'll walk you." Emilio wrapped a gentle hand around her elbow and guided her toward the door. Harper looked back over her shoulder at Lauren. She would have sworn the black man and green-haired girl had been real. That couldn't be, though. No one else had seen them, and they'd said some pretty crazy crap.

Emilio walked her to the health center and then left for his class. Both of them were already late, and Harper was probably going to miss her first class completely. Bio could wait a day, she supposed.

The staff found nothing obviously wrong, but they concurred with the first responders. She needed rest. Harper promised to get a good night's sleep and cut back on the coffee.

"Well," said Emilio later, "you don't look like you're seeing phantom men with yellow eyes. They pump you full of Haldol or something?" When Harper didn't laugh, Emilio switched gears. "Seriously, they find anything?"

Harper shook her head. "Just exhausted. And apparently you actually can overdose on caffeine. It causes hallucinations. Who knew?"

"So you going cold turkey? Cause I don't think I could do it."

Harper laughed. "I don't have to never drink coffee again."

Emilio grabbed both of her hands in his own and adopted a grave expression. "Because you can stop anytime you want, right?"

"You should only worry if you catch me snorting lines of instant on my makeup mirror."

"That's it. I'm coming over tonight and your dad and I are staging an intervention."

They both laughed, because a coffee intervention is exactly the sort of thing Gerald O'Neill would run with. Before long they'd be crank calling rehabs asking if they had an espresso detox unit.

"Seriously though, I'm fine, so stop looking at me like that."

"Okay, but if you hallucinate green-haired women again, I'm checking you in."

"Deal."

Both she and Emilio had signed up for Literature of the Romantic Period because it fulfilled their English requirement, sounded easy, and gave them a class together. Dr. Horvath taught the course, and he was everything she expected in someone teaching sappy Victorian stories. Thin. Pale. Nerdy.

But it wasn't Dr. Horvath who greeted the students today. As Emilio and Harper entered the classroom, a short, olive-skinned woman with waist-length green hair greeted them. She scrawled her name across the chalkboard: Melinoe Caprica.

"Melinoe. What an odd name." Emilio slid into a desk in the last row.

"Emilio. Look at her hair."

"Yeah. Cool color. Might work that into mine next time."

"The coffee shop. You said to tell you if I see women with green hair, you're checking me in to psychiatric services."

"Well, except this time I see her too, so she's real."

"You saw her the last time." *At least, I think he did.* Harper twisted her pen in her hand, unwilling to look at Melinoe for more than a few seconds. She flicked her eyes around the room, expecting the black man with the Jamaican accent, but he wasn't there.

"Good morning, class. I am Dr. Horvath's graduate assistant. He sends apologies; he's feeling under the weather. Today we'll be discussing one of the cornerstones of the Romantic Period. Fairies." Professor Caprica ambled down Harper's aisle and paused at her desk. "In my research, I've been studying a particular class of fairies that figure into stories of infidelity and women going mad, unleashing their sexual desires in a time where suppression of anything deemed sinful was lauded."

After a pause, she pivoted and returned to the front. Melinoe scratched out two words on the chalkboard underneath her name. 'Incubus' and 'gancanagh.'

"Now the gancanagh was known by another name. The love talker. And he survived by consuming strong feelings, usually those linked to his victim's heart's desire."

Every student, including Emilio, stared at her with rapt attention, slackened faces like they had fallen under a spell. Everyone except Harper, whose eyes wandered everywhere. She thought she was losing her grip on reality.

"Emilio," she whispered and kicked his foot under the desk. When he didn't respond, her breathing became fast and shallow.

"Harper. You have some personal experience with the love talker. Care to share it with the rest of the class?" Professor Caprica meandered down the aisle toward the classroom's rear.

"I, um. What?" Harper kicked Emilio's leg even harder. No response. He and the rest of the students were frozen like someone had pressed a pause button. She and the professor were the only animated people. Then the classroom faded, and behind it, the wooded clearing came into focus. Both images overlapped, just like before.

An iron hand coiled around her wrist and jerked. Hard. Harper looked down at Emilio, his face contorted but eyes unfocused, an expression she'd never seen him wear. "You need to come with me, Harper. Now." He yanked her to standing, something Emilio would never do.

Melinoe leapt forward and drew a design in the air with her finger. Emilio vanished. Her best friend *vanished*. Harper pressed herself against the back wall of the classroom when she noticed her new professor had goat's legs, same as in the coffee shop.

"Harper, don't be afraid. We're the best of friends, I promise. You don't remember right now because of him."

"Emilio?"

"The gancanagh. Santaigh. None of this is real. If it were, could I make your friend disappear or the walls fade?"

"You're the one who's not real. Green-haired goat people aren't real. I'm going crazy." A lump burned at the back of her throat.

Melinoe's eyebrows tilted. When she slid toward Harper, her lips parted. "Sweetie, you're not, but you're running out of time. Only I was able to come this time, but that's for the best. You cannot trust the Phooka. I need you to listen to me. I may not have the strength to fight Santaigh's enchantment a third time, even with the mycelium growing beneath you connecting us. When this ends, you could be on your own."

"Enchantment? Mycelium?" Harper slid a step to her right, planning to edge past the goat-legged girl and run for it.

Melinoe stepped to block her route. "Relax, Harper. I'm not here to hurt you. Just a simple favor and I'll go. I have to, anyway. I'm growing weak and Santaigh is pushing back hard."

Harper nodded. "A favor and you leave me alone?"

"Yes. Take my hand. Just for a second. Touching something from reality will help you pierce through some of his enchantment."

The scent of fruity spices wafted in. Harper sniffed the air.

"Spiced fruits. That's what you smelled just now. That's his smoke. It makes you experience the life you hungered for, and what the gancanagh wants you to see. You're about to feel warm, heavy, euphoric."

Harper nodded. "How did you—" That sensation of the warmest sunlight bathing her started. Exhaling, Harper dropped into the nearest chair and slumped forward, a smile creeping onto her face.

Melinoe lunged and grabbed her hand. When the euphoria of her perfect life collided with the feelings that touch brought with it, it was turbulent, like a lightning storm unleashed.

In that moment, two realities existed simultaneously in her mind, just like two physical realities overlapped before her eyes. In one of those lives her father lived, her mother was happy, and Harper had a bright future. She couldn't discern the specifics of that other existence, other than the cold certainty that Gerald O'Neill had died. Other details remained fuzzy, but the paralyzing fear from a life that brimmed with despair caused her to pull away.

This life, right here, had to be the real one. The devil's in the details. Her mother always said that.

"No, this is real, this life. Right now. I remember what I ate for breakfast, Dad's silly jokes, the carpet in my room. In seventh grade my dad..." She had no memories of her dad during her seventh-grade year. "I remember when we moved to Gresham..." Her family had never lived in Gresham.

Harper sank her head in her hands and screamed, clutching handfuls of hair.

Melinoe sighed and patted Harper's shoulder. "Don't you see? That's how he works. He gives you the life you always wanted, erases the rest, feeds on your feelings. That's why your memory has holes. You're strong, which is why pieces of your real life keep punching through."

Harper shoved the desk careening into a wall. "No! Go away. This life is the real one. Not you. Not that other place." Spit flew from her lips as she screamed at Melinoe. "This life is the real one, it has to be."

The surrounding forest faded like someone turned down a dial. Melinoe flickered like a radio tuned between stations.

"Harper, you have to fight it. You're the only one who can.

Wake yourself up. You must want to leave this alternate life, desire reality more than what Santaigh offers. Time grows short. In the real world, you're almost dead."

"Tell me one thing." Harper looked straight into those shockingly bright yellow-green eyes. "If I die, do I get to die in here? Happy. With my family?"

# CHAPTER 44

Emilio sidestepped the goblin and sent his trio of prisoners into the fray, shuffling around recklessly, banging their weapons against each other's and bellowing. The solitary Fae clanged their blades on the walls and screamed.

"Grab the little one!" Emilio shouted.

The bat-faced hobgoblin grinned and squealed. "Get your filthy hands off me, mongrel scum!" Emilio bashed his wing against the wall, with a sound like a dozen swords clashing.

The group made a fairly convincing fight as long as the Sidhe only heard the faux battle and did not peek in on them.

"Tamika!" Emilio shouted. "Tell Alan we're coming. He needs to make his man return to the steps."

Tamika threw a softball-size stone at the wall, and the red-haired elf next to her yelped and shot her a grin. She nodded at Emilio. She stilled, purple eyes slipped closed, and Alan's prisoner shuffled toward the entrance.

Emilio was strangely proud of his trio of fighters. Maybe it was his influence, but the fear had left them. The entire process still revolted him, but controlling them became like managing his own limbs. Effortless. Seeing through so many eyes at once made him a little dizzy, but he kept them moving smoothly.

Selina called, just loud enough for the Fae to hear. "Run for the entrance. We're supposed to flush you out."

Dewberry scowled and pointed to the fighters. "Not a scratch on any of us. Those Unseelie will be suspicious unless we cause at least light damage."

Tamika's face scrunched. "She's right."

The Netherfae had no time to respond before the Fae were on them, biting and punching. Pain lanced Emilio's cheek. His hand flew to his neck on impulse, checking for a wound that wasn't there. Dull aches bloomed over his arms before he fully realized the contusions and lacerations weren't on his body, but his fighters'. He hoped they felt nothing, and he'd gladly endure their pain.

He maneuvered his people through a series of strikes and used just the tips of his wings to make some superficial slices on the solitary Fae. When they looked sufficiently beat up, the Fae fled for the entrance, screaming.

The Netherfae bellowed and chased behind them.

Emilio cast a backward glance at Dewberry. She hunched, her upper back wedged along the top of the tunnel wall, her floral face drawn with worry. Emilio offered her a reassuring smile before sprinting behind his forces, wings clamped between his shoulders.

Alan's prisoner increased his pace, loping ahead. The Fae and their clandestine allies rounded the last curve to discover Alan with his prisoners, positioned to maneuver the fleeing solitary Fae toward the waiting Sidhe with their collars ready. Emilio's group pressed them relentlessly forward and up the ladder.

Where the solitary Fae had held back in their cosmetic scuffle with Emilio and his companions, they attacked the elves full force, and the Sidhe leapt into the Mystery Hole. Bright flashes of magic as blinding as lightning illuminated claw swipes, knife stabs, and bites like a strobe light.

Emilio's mind raced. If his friends were ever going to get these collars off and mount their escape, he had to figure out how to break free, then eat part of a park bench. He smoothed his tongue over his teeth. They felt like normal teeth that would shatter if he bit down on a big hunk of decorative metal.

Maybe this was all a Fae prank to damage him without having to fight. No. Fae couldn't lie, nor could they have known how each day he was more and more listless. Instinct agreed with his new allies.

Selina and Tamika's prisoners mounted a half-hearted attempt to join the fray and aid an elven woman. It looked dangerous but the solitaries only took swipes at them they could easily dodge, and their magical spells sailed wide every time they targeted human or Netherfae. Emilio spread his puppets along the tunnel's rear to give the appearance he was penning the solitary Fae in by preventing retreat, but mostly he wanted to look for a way to get to the metal legs of the bench before the Sidhe noticed.

The little hobgoblin met his eyes and jerked his chin up the steps. The skirmish moved to the left toward a stone arch filled with more action figures, clearing a path to the ladder.

Emilio paused a half second to push a command to his fighters. *Hang back, block the tunnel, and avoid injury.* Then he rushed forward and flicked a wing feather at a goblin who battled a couple steps away from Callon. He twisted the feather at the last second to thump the creature in the sternum, not to cut but to send him staggering backward.

Callon jerked his head around, blade poised to strike, and met Emilio's eyes. He grimaced.

"You're welcome." Emilio faked his most dazzling smile.

The little bat-nosed hobgoblin scampered through the

scuffling feet to the base of the ladder. With a wink at Emilio, he darted for the surface.

Callon's mouth opened to shout an order.

"I'll get him," Emilio called and dashed up after the hobgoblin who was almost to the lip. He didn't pause to check if they bought his ruse.

His head crested the opening to the Woodstock Mystery Hole and met a trio of blades. The Fae already sat, looking dejected, with a torque clamped around his neck. Their scheme had to succeed now. The Fae down there were sacrificing themselves for nothing if his plan didn't work.

"Hey, guys." Emilio held his hands up, fingers wide. "Um. Good job catching that little bugger for me. Dang, he was fast!" He faked a chuckle.

The blades didn't drop and elven eyes remained narrow.

Emilio swallowed hard. "So, yeah. Anyway, it's going pretty badly down there and you all are needed as reinforcements."

"Then get back down there, Netherfae."

Emilio flicked his wings out. They clacked against the rim of the hole. "Yeah, it's tight down there. Lots more enemy Fae than we thought. They're all right by the ladder and my guys are guarding the tunnel, so none can run into the depths. If I fight in that crowded, narrow passage, I'm just going to tear everyone to shreds." That was at least the truth.

The Sidhe woman poked the hobgoblin with the toe of her boot. "I'll guard the prisoner."

"I'm useless down there." Emilio tinkled his wing feathers again. "I can watch him."

All three elves shook their heads. "You'll try to run," the tallest man said.

Emilio hopped off the top rung, hands still up as he stepped aside, and relaxed his wings. "Where would I go?" He indicated the choker. "I bet you could zap me from anywhere in the city with this thing." There it was. The bench. Ten feet away. If the elves all climbed inside the Mystery Hole, he could get to it, chow down, and be back before the elves surfaced.

"The thing's got a point," the woman said.

Her shorter companion lifted a hand and a jolt of electricity skittered down Emilio's neck and along his limbs. "Try to flee, and your agony will never end."

The woman clamped a small chain to the hobgoblin's collar and handed it to Emilio. Behind her, the other Fae were already jumping through the opening.

Emilio grinned and flapped his free hand at them. "Have fun storming the castle."

The instant the last raven-haired elven head disappeared down the shaft, he dropped the solitary Fae's leash and raced for the seat. The little guy beat him there.

The bench was comprised of slats of wood held parallel by an ornate cast-iron back that flowed into an armrest and legs. Emilio dropped to a crouch beside it and placed his palm on the armrest. The scent of rust made his stomach growl. That was weird.

"Eat," the hobgoblin's squeaky voice commanded. He kept a fair distance from the metal.

"How?"

"Open your jaw. Wrap your mouth around the edge. Bite down."

His tongue slipped along his front teeth. The hobgoblin nodded and gestured toward the bench.

Still doubtful, Emilio slid closer, tilted his head, and took part of the armrest into his mouth. He didn't have to will himself to shatter his teeth as he'd feared. The moment the coppery taste of iron met his tongue, ravenous hunger roared. His jaws clamped down hard on their own and the armrest splintered, filling his mouth with broken bits of cast iron.

He chewed and side-eyed the hobgoblin.

The creature winced. "How is it?"

"Crunchy." Bits of bench fell from his lips, causing the Fae to hop back. Emilio gulped down his first mouthful of metal. "Better than Grape Nuts."

Emilio swallowed another couple mouthfuls of the armrest and his hunger slaked. "How much of this do I need to eat for my feathers to become iron laced?"

The Fae shrugged.

Emilio nodded and bit off a few more bites of the bench's scrollwork. When he could stuff no more iron into his stomach, he rose and brushed the shards off his clothing and wings. The bench looked terrible. No hiding the bite marks. He supposed that would be a fun mystery for city workers and park visitors.

The sounds of battle slowed, and boots thudded against the ladder. "We better get back." Emilio picked up the leash. The little hobgoblin's ears twitched and his eyes widened.

"I promise not to abandon you. I'll fight to free all of us, even if it kills me." Emilio had never set out to lead a rebellion, but his new power had thrust him into the role. He smiled at the hobgoblin and they sprinted for the hole.

Emilio skidded to a halt a moment before two Sidhe emerged. Behind them trooped the solitaries, all in their fab new chokers, fear in their eyes. It resonated with his own.

The remnants of the raiding party crested the hole's lip, Callon last of all. Emilio searched the group for Dewberry. She'd be pretty obvious, but she wasn't there. Emilio blew out a quiet breath.

Callon brought a hand to his lips and whistled. Seconds later, the dragons spiraled out of the clouds and settled in the park. The Sidhe loaded their charges onto the backs of the dragons while Callon stepped up beside Emilio, fingers hovering over his breastplate.

"Just what was that back there?"

Emilio slouched like a sullen teenager. "Looked like success to me. Did we pass, Teach?" Emilio gestured to the solitary Fae being loaded onto the dragons. "Because it seems we should all get an A-plus on our field trip."

Callon paced in front of Emilio. "And yet you disobeyed orders and came up alone. Why?" Sodium lights reflected in the elf's black eyes made them burn like embers.

Emilio imitated one of Breas's favorite dismissive gestures and lifted a hand, picking at his nails without meeting Callon's narrowed eyes. "Strategy."

"What?" Callon was close enough to Emilio for the elf's breath to stir the hairs on his neck.

Emilio exaggerated a sigh and purposely spoke slowly. "My super-sharp wings. Like I said before, a tiny tunnel packed with solitary Fae and my cherished handlers. You should be glad I came up here, or you'd all be in pieces."

"I don't trust you."

"I don't care."

The chill blade of a knife slid into Emilio's midsection. He grunted, and a trickle of blood seeped from the corner of his mouth. The dagger slid in again and again, while Callon stared right into Emilio's eyes with a smile as though he was savoring a great delicacy. The Réabadh Torque flared to life, filling every cell in Emilio's body with searing heat.

"I know this won't kill you. You'll heal soon enough, but internal wounds will slow you down in training where I'll be waiting for you." Two more quick stabs and the torque darkened.

Blood stained Emilio's clothing, and he slumped. The pain from the collar and blood loss overpowered the boost from consuming the iron.

His vision flared to a bright yellow like an overexposed picture, and the murmur of city traffic sounded muffled in his ears. Emilio fell like a cut tree.

The impact forced the air from his lungs. He rolled onto his side to collect himself and found himself inside a child's room. He lay on the same tan carpet that blanketed affordable apartments from Portland, Oregon to Portland, Maine and stared up at the Stepford smiles of black-skinned Barbie dolls. Tamika sat on her pink comforter, while Selina and Alan perched on opposite ends of a desk. He knew they had just seconds in the mindspace before Callon came at him again to punish him for being slow to board his dragon.

"Emilio, he's going to kill you." Selina's voice was soft with concern.

"He's already tried. Stabbed me at least a dozen times," Emilio said while his body spasmed in agony.

"We'll rush him together and save you," Tamika said.

"No. That would put you all at risk."

"Take your shirt off."

Emilio faked a smile. "I thought it was obvious, but I don't swing that way."

"Just do it. I've got an idea to stop his abuses."

"What are you driving at, sweetheart?" Selina asked.

"Badb—"

Agony lancing through his ribcage jerked Emilio out of their shared mindspace before Tamika could finish her sentence. Instinctively, he rolled out of the way of the next flurry of kicks to his abdomen. He pushed himself to his feet in one fluid movement.

Callon sneered. "You're babbling. Get up."

"One sec." Emilio worked his white shirt over his shoulders and down his legs. All other methods of removal resulted in shredded clothing. He tossed the garment to the side. "Much better." His breath was visible in the chill air.

"What do you think you're doing?" Callon's face showed genuine bewilderment.

"Woo!" Emilio shouted and slapped his naked chest. "Damned invigorating." He raised his arms in the air and spun around, catching sight of the Sidhe's faces echoing the confusion on Callon's.

Callon kicked him in the leg and smiled. "If you think showing my mistress how badly I've damaged her prize will result in some kind of punishment for me, your wounds have already closed. Pick it up."

"As you wish." Emilio faked a bow that made the internal injuries shriek with agony. A shaky hand grabbed his shirt, stuffed it into the waistband of his pants, and he followed Callon to the dragon.

The flight back to Sauvie Island was swift, and soon the party and their prisoners gathered in the gate room of the citadel. Badb and Breas circled, assessing their new living batteries while Dr. Jones bustled around the Netherfae, checking for damage.

Tamika nodded at the bloody tank top in Emilio's waistband. He smiled and pulled it free, dropping it.

"Your Highness. The leader of our guard attacked Emilio." Tamika's musical voice rang out as she stepped toward Badb, sweeping the shirt into her hand.

A line of Sidhe closed around Badb Catha as Tamika continued forward, but she dropped to the floor on one knee and held the shirt forward. "One of you should examine this," she said as she laid the garment down.

Callon's face contorted with rage and he lunged at Emilio, striking him with blow after blow on his aching chest.

"Stop!" Badb shouted, waving the bloodied shirt.

Callon ceased immediately, bowed, and clasped his hands behind his back. "Yes, my Queen."

Emilio bent over, his palms resting on his knees, trying to catch his breath. From the corners of his eyes, he caught the rest of his friends and their handlers drawing into a semicircle. To his surprise, a pair of shiny black business shoes appeared beside him. Breas rested fingertips on a safe spot on Emilio's shoulder and pressed a bottle of water into his hand. He tipped his head back and took a long pull. Dr. Jones scuttled around him, eyeing his chest, feeling along his arm bones, looking for signs of injury.

"Well, Doctor?" Badb refused to even look at the human.

"H- h- he looks undamaged, but I must check him for internal bleeding."

Her horned headdress trembled with barely suppressed rage. "What part of not damaging our creations did you fail to understand?" The gleaming black cloth of her cloak cascaded along her shoulders, pooling on the lavish floor.

Callon stared at his boots. "No lasting damage was done, Highness."

Badb held the tattered shirt up to Callon's face. "This was a cowardly act. Something I'd expect from them, not from you."

"I was teaching him, as you commanded. They have to learn to fight as one with us under all circumstances if we are to be victorious. This filth has an attitude problem that requires correcting."

"Is this true, Netherfae?" Badb swept her flaming red hair back from her face and stepped directly in front of Emilio.

"I don't pretend to understand his training methods." He found it much more difficult to maintain his flippant facade before Badb. He'd seen far too many incidents of her casual cruelty. Behind his queen, Callon stared daggers at Emilio.

"Let me be more direct. Your garment would seem to suggest he stabbed you repeatedly. Did he?"

"Yes."

The rage flaring in Badb's eyes made Emilio cringe.

Breas smoothed the lapels of his suit and picked stray lint from his lapel with an expression of utter boredom. "After all our efforts, we can't have rogue elves damaging our Netherfae."

"No. We cannot." Badb jerked her head and a contingent of Sidhe and kelpies surrounded Callon. The elf bent forward and hissed into Emilio's ear. "I know you four planned this somehow. I aim to find out how and when I do—"

"Zalille." Badb beckoned behind her and the wispy sylph glided forward and bowed her head.

"Yes, my Queen."

"Until I can drill into Callon's thick skull that our experiments are not to be harmed, you will oversee his training."

"You honor me, my Queen." The sylph turned her head toward Emilio and winced.

# CHAPTER 45

After a quick stopover at Eileen's home to pack everything they'd need for a hike into the wilderness, Phelan said they had to gather his clan because they'd be key protectors of the remaining Fir Bolg. He assured her many of the Fianna were long-time friends with the Fir Bolg and he knew where they'd gone to hide.

"So you're telling me the Fianna's big secret hiding place is in Boring, Oregon?" Eileen couldn't be completely sure Phelan wasn't having a joke at her expense. She gave him the side-eye, checking for a telltale twitch at the corner of his mouth that would betray his ruse, but he remained focused on the road as he steered his black Wrangler down the highway.

"No place better. Way I see it, the big mistake all the other secret societies made was popping their headquarters smack down in some fancy tourist trap church in the heart of Europe somewhere. Just begging for discovery at that point. You want to remain hidden, you hunker down in a town in the middle of nowhere with a name like Boring, Oregon, or Tightwad, Missouri." He waggled his fingers against the wheel.

"Now I know you're taking a piss." Eileen put her feet up on the dashboard and set her seat back a notch. "Tightwad, Missouri?"

"The piss. Taking the piss. And the Primitive Olde Crowe Winery has the best pizza in Missouri. Perfect town for a secret society, if you ask me. All the chanting and clandestine shenanigans really work up the appetite, so being close to great pie is a definite prerequisite for a secret base."

He glanced over at Eileen, and their eyes met. His mouth twitched at the corners and utterly ruined his serious expression. A silent chortle rushed from her nose, and that was it. The pair of them cracked up.

"Sweet Eileen, someday when this is all over, I'll take you on a whirlwind tour of the other two international cities in the Trinity of Tedium."

"Oh, really?" She stifled another round of chuckles.

"First, we'll explore the misty Highlands of Scotland when we visit the charming town of Dull. Then I'll whisk you down under where we can enjoy all the delights the great city of Bland offers. I hear the food is spectacular."

"Those are actually places?"

"On the honor of Clan Baiscne. Proper places. They've even formed an alliance. You'll see it at the town line in about an hour."

It had been a long time since Eileen had smiled, much less laughed like this. She felt light, expansive.

Phelan shared with Gerald the skill of pulling Eileen out of herself and bringing delight through the most ridiculous of things. Memory of Gerald erased the vestiges of her grin. She knew he'd want her to feel joy, move on with her life, but that didn't stop the sense that enjoying Phelan's company was betraying him. A better person wouldn't be laughing it up with a handsome stranger when her husband had been brutally murdered and her daughter was facing monsters.

Not long after exiting the highway, Phelan pointed to the welcome sign for the town. "See? Sister city to Dull, Scotland."

Eileen nodded and looked out the window without really seeing anything.

The Jeep rumbled past The Bigfoot Center. Phelan nudged Eileen on the shoulder and gestured to the small building housing the attraction. "If they only knew, right?"

Eileen's smile didn't touch her eyes. "Yeah, for sure."

Phelan leaned forward. "Hey, if I said something to offend you..."

"You didn't." She inhaled a slow sigh and forced her muscles to release before turning to Phelan, shaking her head and clasping the Lia Fail shard in her pocket. She wanted to be honest with him about how she felt. Her mouth opened and closed a couple times like a goldfish in a bowl. Years of drinking away every emotion made it difficult to find the words. Instead, she offered a half-truth. "I'm just worried about Harper and the Fir Bolg."

She pulled out the piece of the Lia Fail and checked to see if it still glowed. In the bright outdoor light, she had to cup her hands over the stone to detect its faint radiance.

The Wrangler wound through the residential streets of Boring in a series of turns. "Let me share a bit of advice earned from over a hundred years of rough living and coping with danger lurking around every corner. Moments of bliss and happiness are more necessary in the darkness than they are in the light. Enjoying a laugh or good company..." His expression was dreamy. "None of that means we don't care deeply about the suffering we carry. Because we've suffered, joy is even more precious."

Chewing the inside of her cheek, Eileen focused intently on twisting the little stone fragment in her hands. "You're over one hundred?" Deflection was a skill she'd picked up when Harper had drilled her about medication adherence or eating three full meals a day or a hundred other things.

Phelan pursed his lips and nodded once. Then that casual smirk returned. "One hundred and ten last year."

He pulled the car into a long driveway already packed with assorted vehicles ranging from a lovely white Mercedes to a tie-dye Volkswagen van.

"You're taking the piss." Eileen enunciated every word, making Phelan laugh again.

"Afraid not." He checked his shiny wild hair in the rearview, running a hand through it and tilting some ends up close to the glass. "Started getting a few grays at seventy. Early. Just like my dad."

Eileen swung the door open and hopped out into the damp, still air. With a thump to the top of the Jeep she said, "Well, you don't look a day over ninety-five."

The modest home blended perfectly with the others. Unremarkable. Grey stone fascia spanned both stories, slate-blue shutters hung over utilitarian landscaping. The simple home certainly didn't appear to house a secret society.

Phelan stepped around the front of his vehicle and maneuvered in front of Eileen. Placing his hands gently on her shoulders, he looked down at her upturned face. "We don't normally welcome outsiders, so don't expect a warm reception from everyone. Shane and Michael shouldn't be much of a problem, but Lorna and Declan are the oldest, most set in their ways. The rest will follow the prevailing winds, so to speak. Neither of them has quite figured out the clan's survival rests in being open to newer possibilities."

"Great. This diversion is all for eight more people?"

Phelan's eyes never left her face, and his hands lingered on her arm. He shrugged. "Ten total, maybe fewer. Whatever goes down in there, understand I won't let anything happen to you. I promise."

Her mouth dried. She swallowed hard and nodded, studying

the laces on her brown hiking boots. "You make it sound as though they'll attack me or something."

"Not physically, but they can bluster and intimidate. I just don't want you to worry. If they respect you, you'll learn a lot about my people and what we're facing." He finally let his hands slip from her shoulders and swept one toward the winding walkway to the front door.

Eileen flinched when Phelan threw his head back and howled at the top of his lungs.

"Don't stare at me like I'm nuts. It's how we greet each other. Come on, join in. They need to know there's two of us out here. Count of three."

He counted out the numbers on his fingers, spread his hands wide, and howled at the sun. Eileen joined toward the end, letting out a weak *owoooo*. He dropped over at the waist, arms dangling, head shaking.

"That was the weakest howl I've ever heard. An asthmatic Chihuahua could do better. From the diaphragm. Come on now." He rested a hand along the back of her neck and nodded out one, two. On three, they raised their faces to the sky and howled as loud as they could.

"There you go, lass. That's more like it. Gets the blood pumping." He shook out his limbs, placed a hand on Eileen's shoulder, and guided her up the front steps.

They emerged into an open concept living area studded with couches, bookshelves on every wall. The shades and blinds were all drawn, so the room was bathed in the soft glow of lamplight.

"What the hell was all that racket about?" A stocky man with curly brown hair pushed himself up from a puffy recliner and clapped Phelan on the back.

"Teaching Eileen here the secret greeting, just like you taught me, Patrick."

"Aye. Where were you when you made a damned fool out of yourself?" Patrick's eyes twinkled, and he winked at Eileen.

Phelan laughed. "Museum of Natural History, as I recall."

Imagining the scene, Eileen smiled in spite of herself, and some of the jitters faded.

A woman with hot pink hair, shaved on the right side, half stood from her seat on the plaid couch and extended a can of beer toward Eileen. Phelan's hand intercepted it and popped it on an end table. "Didn't know we were supposed to bring a plus-one to this shindig, or I'd have brought my Janey." She had the same accent as Phelan.

Eileen's mouth watered at the sight of the beer, but she maneuvered herself so she brushed Phelan's shoulder. The resulting flush of warmth more than made up for the forbidden drink.

"She's the designated driver, Aisling. And once she shares her story, I think you all will be very glad I invited her."

"Fine by us." A lanky red-headed man sat next to a shorter boy with hair so blond it was almost white. "Too many old fuddy-duddies as it is. Welcome. I'm Michael. This lunkhead is Shane."

"Nice to meet—"

"Phelan, you need to get this woman out of here right now."

The admonition cut from across the room, the speaker draped over half a couch. Her posture conveyed a studied nonchalance, but her eyes carried a sharp edge. She reminded Eileen of Harper, though she was far, far older. The even older looking man next to her nodded. These two must be Lorna and Declan.

Eileen tensed every muscle as she scanned the ring of faces scrutinizing her. It jangled her nerves worse than that panel job interview she went on when she'd applied for a leadership role at Erimus Pharmaceutical, and it would probably end as disastrously for the same reason. She was out of her depth.

Phelan squeezed her shoulder gently.

"Well, since we've already started the introductions. You've met Patrick Campbell. The lady with the fashion sense of a high school girl intent on making her parents cry is Aisling McCarthy." Aisling gave Phelan the finger but raised her beer to Eileen. "These two scalawags are Michael Geddes and Shane McKenna, the two musketeers." The red-haired man and his young companion smiled and waved.

Phelan gestured to a pair of recliners to the left occupied by a plump older woman and a bodybuilder with a shaved head and a thick brown moustache. "This is Grianne Bell and Oscar Doyle."

Both merely nodded at Eileen, so she returned the gesture.

"And giving their trademarked warm greeting from the far couch are Lorna MacCool and Declan Rees." The pair of them were still, but they continued to stare daggers at Eileen.

"Everyone, including the naysayers, this is Eileen." He paused for dramatic effect. "Eileen *O'Neill*."

"That changes nothing," Lorna said.

"It does if I say it does." A very old man sauntered into the room and everyone sat up a little straighter. Declan and Lorna dropped their gazes and softened their expressions.

The old man meandered along the brown carpet and stopped in front of Eileen. His skin was a network of fine lines and wrinkles. Creases and his grey hair and beard were the only things that betrayed his age, which Eileen suspected was far greater than he appeared. His blue eyes sparkled with wit and quick intelligence. He stood tall and well muscled.

Phelan kept a reassuring arm draped over her shoulder.

"Breaking the rules, again, Mr. Kane." He studied Eileen. She felt like a lab sample. Assessed and measured by those sparkling eyes.

Phelan lifted a hand as though he swore on a stack of bibles. "I solemnly swear I'm up to no good."

Eileen silently groaned. This guy didn't know when to tone

down the silliness. The old man, clearly their leader, drew his lips into a fine line and nodded slowly. Anxiety pushed her unconsciously a step backward toward the door. But then the man threw his arms around Phelan and clapped him on the back.

"Good, laddie. Just like I taught you." He laughed.

"Ms. O'Neill, I am Fintan mac Bochra, at your service." He lifted her hand in his own and his white mustache and beard tickled her knuckles as he pressed his lips to her skin and bowed deeply.

"You can call me Eileen."

She couldn't help but return his radiant smile. She'd have thought she just gave him a million dollars instead of mere permission to call her by her first name. "Welcome to my home, Eileen." He turned and smiled at Lorna and Declan. "You are most welcome here."

Declan and Lorna tapped their feet and refused to acknowledge their guest, while everyone else raised drinks and bellowed a hearty welcome. Phelan guided Eileen to another short couch next to the pair of recliners.

"Who is he?" Eileen whispered into Phelan's ear.

Fintan swiveled to answer Eileen's soft question. "I'm the oldest living man in Ireland. Well, Oregon now."

"Oy. Here it comes." Michael smacked his hand on his forehead.

"He'll be at this for an hour. Time to grab snacks." Aisling toyed with a black ring through her nostril, stretched, and stood. "Anyone want anything? Popcorn? Sleeping pills? Icepick for your ears?"

Fintan shook his head. "Youth these days. So impatient. So little respect for their elders."

"Youth? I'm seventy-one." Aisling waved him off and stomped into the kitchen. She slipped off her studded jacket, and Eileen noticed an intricate blue tattoo of a howling wolf done in winding Celtic knotwork on the outside of her left shoulder. She noted the same design on Shane, visible beneath his t-shirt, and on Oscar to her right. They probably all had them.

A twinkle formed in the old man's eye as he walked a slow circle in the center of the room. He paused in front of Eileen.

"It has been long since I've stood before one of the O'Neill clan." His voice was deep.

Eileen leaned over to Phelan. "Technically, I'm from the Anderson clan."

He caressed her shoulder with a grin. "Won't matter, it's story hour. Just run with it."

Fintan raised his arms high like he led a campaign rally. "And the last time I stood before the line of kings was like this time, a shifting in the Great Peace. And the assembled kings sought my wisdom, for none of them could recall the proper order of things, both within the land and inside the hearts of men."

"As it is now when the prophecies of Badb Catha are coming to pass," Grianne said, a sadness softening her harsh features.

"Aye. And it's a good thing old Fintan still haunts the Green World to remind us of the proper order of land and soul." He thumped his chest and laughed. "For Ireland was my home eons before she became a home to men, long before her hills and valleys teemed with squabbling kings. I was made wise with the knowledge of air, earth, and sky because the land herself tutored me in the magical arts of this world. She renewed me in life and death in the sacred waters of the Boyne, and I laid to rest a thousand times over in her caves and lochs."

Across from her, young Michael and Shane feigned sleep and snored dramatically. But Fintan remained undaunted. His voice boomed.

"I am Fintan, son of Bochra. I have been the wise salmon. I have been an eagle. I've been a hawk riding the wind. I have been a man of verse. I know of every people who occupied Inisfáil for I have survived flame and flood. Spear and sword."

"Boredom and blowhards," called Patrick.

"Bullshit and exaggeration," added Michael.

Unfazed, Fintan leapt up to stand in Aisling's former seat. In a half crouch, he met every eye, with a grave expression.

"I lived among the Fir Bolg of the dark wood. I was there when the Fomorians rose from the seas to occupy the islands around Inisfáil. I welcomed the coming of the Tuatha de Danann from the Undying Lands, and I bore witness to their war with the Fir Bolg at Moytura and later their victory over the tyrannical Fomorians in the Second Battle of Moytura, when the Tuatha drove those misshapen louts back under the waves."

Fintan slashed the air with his hands as though he wielded a sword. He paused then, features draining from excitement to sorrow.

"And I witnessed the dark times when the Sons of Mil stole Ireland from the Tuatha, the only time I lifted a weapon, for I fought beside the Tuatha against them."

Fintan's voice lost all its bluster and he sank slowly to his seat. Around him, most of the Fianna mirrored faraway expressions. Even Shane and Michael stopped their clowning. Fintan sighed and focused on his hands, his tone dropping almost to a whisper.

"I have seen the rising and falling of kings as waves on the sea. And now the world shifts beneath again. Souls feel thinner every generation. The land weeps and a reckoning is coming. In this new Moytura so far from Inisfáil, the final battle is upon us."

# CHAPTER 46

Nearly a week passed with no sign of the strange green-haired woman or the yellow-eyed man. There'd been something odd about them, something shocking, but Harper couldn't remember precisely what. The details receded, becoming fuzzier with each passing day, but she remembered they'd wanted to take away her family and, for that, she despised them.

"Harper, honey, it's your day to take out the trash," her mother called from her upstairs workspace. The clickety-clack of her keyboard didn't even slow with her gentle nagging.

"I know, Mom, getting it now." She wasn't, but she laid her biology book on the coffee table, stretched her arms overhead, draped across the couch's arm, and yawned. Rubbing her hand on the nape of her neck, she shuffled into the kitchen and worked on collecting any missing refuse and stuffing it into the wastebasket.

Wrinkling her nose at the acid yet earthy scent of decaying coffee grounds, she held the bag at arm's length and hopped down the steps. She'd hauled the garbage halfway across the lawn when she saw him. Skin the color of night made the amber eyes glow. He didn't move, but his edges shimmered and looked fuzzy.

Harper gasped and dropped the trash bag. The man shrank into a nondescript blob before popping into the form of a large black dog. Only the piercing golden stare told her it was the same being.

The canine opened its tooth-filled maw and a long pink tongue rolled out. With a hop, it started across the street.

"Harper, it's me. This is the shape I took when you first met me, remember?" the dog said.

Harper shrieked, pivoted, and bolted for the house. The plastic loop of the garbage bag caught her ankle, and she sprawled on the front lawn.

"I told you not to do that!" the green-haired woman bellowed, suddenly beside Harper. "Frightening her only feeds the gancanagh, or was that your plan, shapeshifter?" The woman flung a hand forward and the dog flew, disappearing in midair.

Harper scrambled away, clawing the grass, half on her side. "Stay away from me!" How did the woman even know where she lived?

"Harper! Harper, wait!" Melinoe shouted, waving her hand frantically.

"I don't want to talk to you. Leave or I'm calling the cops." Harper put her father's Mercedes between herself and Melinoe.

"Harper, sweetie, this is your last chance." Melinoe started down the driveway, tan fingers spread wide and held in front of her.

Harper dropped, picked up a stick that had fallen next to the car, and hurled it at Melinoe. "Stay off our property. Don't get any closer." She didn't want her parents to come out and discover the scene, so she kept her voice just short of a yell.

Melinoe dipped her head and stopped. "Harper, you're nearly out of time. You only have minutes now. He's almost drained you. People outside this dream world are depending on you. Emilio. Your mom."

"My mother is inside the house, and I just talked to Emilio on the phone." She'd had enough of these lunatics trying to destroy her family. "None of this is real." Then she remembered Melinoe's goat legs. "You're not real. Dogs don't talk and there's no way you have goat legs." Her eyes flashed, blood rushing in her ears. Harper twisted the ring on her finger. *But I don't have any rings.* She looked down and a filigree ring circled her right middle finger. It glowed with a blue light, and power like electricity surged.

Melinoe beamed. "That's it, use your magic. Wake up."

On instinct, Harper hurled her arm, fingers outstretched, toward Melinoe. A lance of crackling energy caught the stranger and flung her to the middle of the road. She disappeared exactly where the talking dog had.

Breathing ragged, Harper gaped at her hand before the sweet fruity smell rolled in on the wind and warmth melted away all tension, like she was immersed in a hot bath. She dropped to one knee on the grass, individual blades prickling against her palm.

"Rabbit, what happened? Are you okay?" Her dad's hands wrapped around her shoulders and pulled her upright.

Harper tilted her face to him. "Daddy, I think I'm losing my mind."

"Nonsense."

"No, really. I keep seeing a woman with green hair and she has this dog." Harper didn't dare tell her father the animal talked and started out as a man, or he'd lock her up in the same psych ward her mom went to. *Mom was never in a psych ward.*

"It's Portland, Rabbit." Her dad chuckled and helped her up. "Come on inside. I'll make us some hot chocolate."

"That sounds really nice." And it did. When Harper hadn't been chosen for the lead in the Christmas pageant in first grade, her father made hot chocolate and pointed out all her other talents. When she'd skinned her knee falling off her bike, hot chocolate and her dad's jokes had distracted her from the pain. And now the simple promise of sugary cocoa melted away the fears that she was losing it.

"What's happening out there?" Harper's mom padded down the hall, face drawn with concern.

Gerald O'Neill rubbed his wife's shoulder. "Nothing some hot chocolate won't fix."

"Make three. I could use a break. Sales reports." Her mother stuck out her tongue.

While her father hummed to himself and bustled around the kitchen, Harper sat across from her mom, chewing at her fingernails. Eileen leaned her head to the side and reached a hand over the table, grasping Harper's fingers in her own.

"Come on, sweetie. Spill it. What's going on with you lately?"

Harper relayed what she remembered about Melinoe at the coffee shop and then discovering she was her substitute professor who'd now shown up at their house. "I think she's following me, and, I don't know, I feel sick when she shows up. It's hard to explain."

"I worked a campus job when I was in school. She probably works at the coffee shop to pay her bills. Maybe she lives in the neighborhood and that's why you keep seeing her." Her mom patted Harper's hand.

"When you're stressed, sometimes coincidences can seem like something more," her dad said. The clinking of the spoon along the edges of the mugs sounded like the most comforting music in the world.

Her dad gripped all three steaming cups in his hand and walked across the kitchen like a tightrope walker in the circus. He slid Harper her drink. She inhaled the rich chocolate scent deeply and took a sip. The sugary warmth was a balm that soothed all pains.

"Maybe you should talk to this Melinoe. Clear the air." Her

dad sipped his drink, purposely leaving a hot chocolate mustache on his face.

Harper smiled. "Clearing the air won't help. I just want her far away. She scares me."

With his foamy sweet mustache, her dad held up a finger and adopted a serious expression. "It's like I always tell you, Rabbit. Nothing in life is to be feared. Only understood."

The floodgates broke. Harper shoved herself up, the dishes rattling together on the wooden table. With a grunt, she hurled her torso forward and clasped her head.

"Honey, you're scaring me," her mother said, a hand reaching toward her.

"Harper. Rabbit, just—"

She shrank from her father's reach and brought an arm across her eyes. He was dead. Melinoe was right. She'd seen his pallid face from the farmhouse. The real Gerald O'Neill was a prisoner and lived an existence of endless suffering. Her life here was a sham. The smoking Fae. Memories fell into place like dominoes.

The telltale scent of spices and fruit came from nowhere. She knew the warm bliss would follow, then she'd forget again. Harper leapt for the table, grabbed the spoon in her chocolate, and jammed the handle into the back of her hand as hard as she could.

"Oh my God! Gerald, stop her!" her mother shouted as she leapt up, sending dishes and her chair careening.

"Rabbit, what are you doing?" Her dad crushed her to his chest and held her tight.

But the pain anchored her, drove away all that obliterating warmth.

"I know you don't understand." Her breath hitched as her parents stared at her with concern. "But none of this is real. As much as I want it, it's not real."

"Rabbit, what's wrong?"

"Sweetie, we'll get you all the help you need." Her mom ran her fingers through Harper's hair. Harper closed her eyes and drank in the feeling of her father's arms keeping her safe and her mother's soft hand reassuring her, both here together like it should have been. The life she should have had. The life Badb Catha stole from her.

But if she claimed this dream life, Emilio was lost, her father would be drained away, and everyone else in the real world would remain in terrible danger.

She turned to her father, drinking in each detail of his face. His warm eyes. Tousled hair. His love for her etched in every line of his features. The woman he would have raised her to be would not let others suffer for her own wish fulfillment. Nor would he prefer her to waste away in a fake perfect life, serving no one.

Santaigh may be devouring her, but he'd also given her something precious: time with her father, even if it wasn't real. In this fantasy world, she revisited all the lessons he'd taught her in their short ten years together. Above all, her father prized compassion and rationality.

His greatest gift was to plant the seeds of empathy in Harper, and fifteen years of crawling through hell on her stomach had grown those seeds into the conviction to come to the aid of those around her. If she stayed here, those gifts would die on the vine, benefiting no one and disappointing the real Gerald O'Neill. She had to break free. She had people to rescue, including her dad.

Harper edged around the table and reached her hands up to cup her father's chin in her palms. The stubble of his beard prickled and scraped her skin. With trembling lips, she smiled as a tear slid down her cheek.

"Dad, in another life, you died. And in that life you're suffering, and I can save you. I love you, Dad, but I have to go now."

"Rabbit, I—"

Harper shook her head and soaked in the warmth of his rich brown eyes one last time. Melinoe said she had to want to leave this place, had to desire something else even more. She pulled in a deep breath, lifted her face to the ceiling, and shouted.

"I want my pain back."

And just like someone paused a movie, the world froze.

# CHAPTER 47

Silence descended on the gathered Fianna as each pondered Fintan's meaning. Eileen's thoughts dwelled on her daughter and her friends deep in the Oregon woodland, hoping Hieronymous's plan would both ensure the safety of the Fir Bolg and collect enough reinforcements to help Harper. Her hand stroked the bit of Lia Fail in her pocket, her anchor in the storm.

Phelan broke the silence. "Come now, old man, you're just being dramatic."

"Damn straight. I pop off for snacks and you all go maudlin." Aisling settled into a slipper chair close to the kitchen door with a fresh ale and a bowl full of popcorn.

"I can feel it in my bones. Even as the last of the Fomorians sank under the ocean, King Lugh and I knew after the Second Battle of Moytura a third Great War was inevitable."

"Fomorians and Milesians?" Eileen had heard Nuada mention Fomorians, but Milesians were new.

"Milesians. The Sons of Mil. Humans," Phelan said.

"Fomorians are the Children of Domnu, Danu's sister.

Misshapen and evil. They ruled over the Tuatha for a time, extracting their labor, tearing what they wanted from the land without giving back," Declan said.

Fintan lowered his weight to the arm of a recliner and looked at Eileen. "If you're going to help us in our sacred duty to protect your daughter, you'll need some background."

"So you've unilaterally decided this stranger is trustworthy, without so much as a vote?" Lorna crossed her arms in front of her chest.

Heat bloomed across Eileen's skin. "You want to sniff my ass, then go ahead."

Shane and Michael burst out laughing. Several others, including Fintan, hid smiles behind their hands. Beside the scowling Lorna, Declan tapped his foot and crinkled his nose.

"Oh come on, you two, look at us. There's literally nine of us left, plus the old man. If someone wants to join this hopeless quest, let them." Grianne's voice was raspy, like a lifelong smoker.

"I say we vote right now." Shane stood up and threw his arm in the air. "You had me when you asked Lorna to sniff your arse."

Michael grinned. "I second that."

Phelan stood, one hand high, the other clasping Eileen's shoulder. Followed by Aisling still crunching her popcorn. Soon all except Lorna and Declan were on their feet.

Even Fintan raised his glass to Eileen. "Blood relation or not, the mother of the heir joining our sacred quest is auspicious indeed."

"Bloody old curmudgeons," Shane said as he sat back down.

"It's decided then. If she wishes it, Eileen O'Neill can join us for this mission." Phelan smiled beside her.

Declan growled. "She's as ignorant as a bairn."

"You all are compared to me, and I still tolerate you." Fintan laughed. "But there is truth in your words. Before you decide, you need to know more about the events leading to war and the forces we face."

Eileen nodded. "Nuada told me about Badb Catha, that she murdered her sisters to gain the power to punch through the Veil between the worlds, and her sister, Macha, somehow donated the last of her magic to Harper."

Phelan pointed to the mushroom necklace Eileen wore tucked inside her shirt and circled his finger. She looped a finger around the woven cord and fished it out.

"And I learned a bit from the Fir Bolg," she added.

Almost in unison, jaws slackened, eyes widened, and everyone leaned in for a closer look.

Declan flopped back in his seat. "But that—"

"Means she's Fir Bolg. She's even got the official bag out in the car," Phelan said, looking every bit like the cat that swallowed the canary.

Eileen rotated her head toward him and tossed her hands up.

"What? I thought you knew," he said.

She wanted to cry. How could she have not trusted Glani and Aeld? She'd assumed they'd abandoned her, dumped her like an unwanted pet, when all along they really were trying to keep her safe. They were family.

Phelan looked around at the assembled group. "The Fir Bolg choose their allies with the greatest of care. I think we can trust her."

Fintan clapped his hands, rubbing them vigorously. "Right. Before we were interrupted, we'd been discussing Fomorians." He cleared his throat. "The Fomorian King, Balor, had a single massive eye. So huge it took several men with staffs to lift the lid. Whatever fell within the gaze of that devouring eye was scorched, consumed utterly. Balor's grandson Lugh destroyed the eye during the Tuatha's uprising, by lobbing his spear into its core. Their leader dead, the Fomorians lost and the Tuatha reigned."

"But why would the Tuatha abdicate after fighting two wars just to remain in the Green World?" Eileen asked.

"That, my esteemed guest, is a question no one has ever been able to answer. The Tuatha ruled for merely four hundred years before Milesian invaders drove the magical races to the Underworld and the Tuatha agreed to never contest humans for the land of Inisfáil."

"What I've always wanted to learn is how a band of humans defeated essentially a race of gods. That bit never made sense to me." Grianne tapped her grey hair with a single finger.

Fintan nodded. "How the Tuatha lost the war to mere humans, no one can be sure. But in the absence of Fae and Tuatha, the damage wrought to the earth by humanity sealed the worlds from one another. With the Fir Bolg and the Fomorians trapped here in the Green World with humanity, and the Fae and Tuatha trapped in the Underworld, the Tuatha believed no final war could come."

"But Badb Catha opened a gateway. That's what started all this, right?" Eileen's forehead creased. "What led to my husband's death and all the rest?"

The ring of Fianna mumbled their agreement.

"And why several tasks lie ahead of us if we are to prevail," Fintan said. "The last piece of your crash course in Celtic legend concerns the four treasures the Tuatha brought with them from the Undying Lands."

Eileen gripped the Lia Fail shard in her pocket and drew it out, where the stone glowed faintly. Lorna and Declan frowned.

"Mother Danu, Phelan, you trusted her with the Lia Fail?" Declan scanned him from head to toe as he spoke.

"If something told you your daughter still lived, wouldn't you want it close?" Phelan fired back.

Declan winced and swallowed hard.

Fintan nodded toward the glowing rock in Eileen's hands.

"Two massive pieces of that lie in the Underworld. The fourth piece was with Nuada."

Eileen filled the Fianna in on details of Nuada's journey with Harper and the attack at the Fir Bolg village.

"Those giant hairy pacifists still won't throw in their lot." Patrick's curls shook with his head.

Aisling laughed. "Aye, almost as stubborn as Lorna, they are."

"Perhaps with our intervention they may join the fight before it's too late," Phelan said.

"Before Harper can come into her full power and battle Badb Catha, she will need to be tested by the Lia Fail. And that means she'll have to bring the pieces of it back from the Undying Lands and we will mend it." Fintan took a sip of beer, dragging a hand across his mouth before he continued. "Two of the treasures were weapons. The Cliamh Solais, the Sword of Light, once drawn on an enemy, always prevails. It has seldom left its scabbard and has known only one master, Nuada."

"After the attack, when Harper was taken by Gwyn, the blade was gone too," Eileen said.

Exclamations of despair mingled with Gaelic cursing, and many of the Fianna blanched.

"Well then, we can only hope the fact the stone says she still lives means she also possesses the Cliamh Solais, and it obeys her if called to strike in this battle. The blade chooses its masters carefully." Fintan nodded gravely. "So the Cliamh Solais is out of our reach, along with parts of the Lia Fail and the Dagdha's Cauldron."

Fintan continued. "The Dagdha was the father of the gods, and he possessed a great cauldron that, during periods of peace, produced an abundance of food and then magically refilled. Potions brewed in it could imbue knowledge, fighting skill, almost anything. But during times of battle, its role became far more pivotal. Soldiers fallen in combat and laid inside the great cauldron were reborn to fight another day. This is how the outnumbered Tuatha evened the score in their fight with the Fomorians."

Eileen's thoughts strayed to Nuada, suspended between life and death. The Fir Bolg had said he could be reborn in it. She wondered if it would have worked on Gerald. "Where is the Cauldron?"

"No one knows. Some rumors have it in the Underworld with another of its former masters. Some say it was cracked and no longer works, lying abandoned somewhere. It might be anywhere."

"Looks like we're zero for three, here," Eileen said.

A slow smile spread across Fintan's face. "Lugh was among the few Tuatha who remained in the Green World after the Veil fell. Though his tragic fate is a tale for another time, the Spear of Lugh is the weapon that blinded King Balor and won the day in the Second Battle of Moytura. It lies in the Green World still, and I've spent decades following leads to determine its location." He swept his hands around the bookshelves lining the walls of his den.

"Ya prolly could have just googled it, old man," Shane said with a laugh.

"What makes you think I haven't?" Fintan waggled an iPhone across the room at his hecklers.

Eileen suppressed a laugh. The idea of someone more ancient than the Bible or even the Ice Age using a smartphone was comical.

"I've narrowed down the possible locations to three. But I believe our best chance is in the last place it was seen: The House of the Red Man in Ireland. So we will begin our search there."

"Da Derga's Hostel? It was destroyed a thousand years ago when King Connaire died." Lorna waved off the old man's suggestion as though it were a pesky fly.

Fintan shrugged. "Yes. And your point?"

"De-stroyed," Shane spelled out like he spoke to a five-year-old.

"Bring. A. Shovel."

Oscar slapped his palms on his thighs and hopped to his feet. "I'll go. Been too long since I walked in the motherland."

"Some of us must remain here to accompany Phelan and Eileen to help our Fir Bolg brothers and sisters, then locate the heir. The rest of you, search your connections because an artifact near identical to the Spear was located in a remote corner of Peru." Fintan swigged the last of his beer and crumpled the can. "I plan to pay Hieronymous a visit. His prices are robbery, but if anyone can confirm my theories, he can. Plus, he just volunteered to be our backup for the Fir Bolg mission."

"I'll go with Oscar," Lorna said. "Ireland calls me home."

"Excellent. Patrick, you're from the area, you'll join them along with the rest," Fintan said.

"I'd like Aisling and Michael with me," Phelan said.

"High five, Pinky, we're going Squatching." Michael air high-fived Aisling from across the room and she fist pumped her enthusiasm.

Eileen drifted to the back of the room as the Fianna laid their plans said and their goodbyes. The band around her ribcage was so tight she became dizzy. She fiddled with the Lia Fail piece, which was still glowing. This entire plan rested on her ability to deceive the Green World Courts. Fail, and Harper was on her own. For the past fifteen years, inadequacy described her every action as a parent. *I can't do anything right.* And now the stakes were astronomical.

She lurched, bashing into an end table and barely catching what flew off it in time. A half-full bottle of beer. In her palm. Pivoting her back to Phelan, she lifted it but stopped short when she caught sight of the cigarette butt swirling inside. Throat tight, she replaced the bottle on the table and walked with shaking legs to Phelan's side, where she stared at the floor while he conversed with Fintan.

*I can't do this. Harper needs a fighter, not her failure of a mother.*

# CHAPTER 48

"Callon seems to have forgiven you." Tamika took a sip of the sweet fruit juice that accompanied each meal.

Emilio eyed the redcap pair at the door. "Yeah, we're the best of friends now." Two days had passed without an attack from Callon, but Emilio knew the instant the Sidhe found a way, he'd be in for a heap of pain.

Selina leaned over the table with a sidelong glance at their guards. "So how do you know when your feathers have soaked up enough iron to spring the Réabadh Torques?"

Emilio shrugged. "I'm hoping the next time I'm in the lab, I can test them somehow, but that's a long shot."

"I think I'm choosing vanilla as the warning I'm pulling you in." A wistful yearning passed over Tamika's's face. "Wish we could sneak out and get some ice cream. Vanilla's my favorite."

"Everyone knows the sole reason vanilla exists is as a substrate for candy topping, or chocolate sauce and a mountain of whipped cream. If you have to eat it straight, peanut butter chocolate swirl is where it's at, girl."

The silly conversation was an oasis, and Emilio was grateful Breas had kept his word and let them enjoy meals together.

Selina wrinkled her nose. "Overrated. Strawberry cheesecake. That's the best ice cream and should be our secret word."

Tamika made a figure eight with her fork. "Nope, vanilla. One word. Easy to remember. What do you think, Alan?"

Emilio studied Alan. Not that any of them had adjusted well to their predicament, but Alan struggled with panic each time he caught himself in a reflection. "You okay, big guy?"

The accountant shook his bearded head slowly and poked at his meal with his fork.

"Alan, sweetie, you need to eat. Keep your strength up for"—Selina rotated her head over her shoulder—"training."

"We're all worse than dead, anyway," Alan said, the branches sprouting from his forehead rustling.

"What's worse than dead?" Tamika's voice sounded like music, even when tinged with sadness.

"Being just away." Alan slumped forward, resting his chin in his palm, long twiggy fingers coiled around his scalp. "Not living life because anyone you loved is without you, not really dead because you keep breathing. My family must be searching for me and my eldest daughter, wondering if we're alive. I don't even know if she escaped. They'll never have closure because I'm here. Just. Away."

Selina nodded. "I understand what you mean, big guy."

Emilio squeezed his friend's woody shoulder. "Remember what we talked about. My new project." He eyed the guards, both of them had propped themselves against the door, looks of boredom on their pinched little faces. "Our escape to the real world." Emilio caught Alan's eye and waggled his eyebrows with a single nod.

"You must feel it in your bones, same as me. There's no way back for us." Alan's voice cracked.

"Then we fight." Selina's red hand clenched into a fist. The redcap guards scowled over their shoulders at the table. "This war. We fight this war." Satisfied, the redcaps returned to their idleness.

"Good evening, my young apprentice. Dr. Jones wants you in his office for some. Um. Samples." Breas, clad in a navy-blue suit and lavender tie, pushed past the redcaps. Hand outstretched, he waved Emilio toward the door.

Emilio patted his friend's back as he stood. "Hang in there, Alan. We'll talk later."

Once they were out in the hallway, Breas motioned Emilio into a room kitty-corner to where they'd just exited. Emilio furrowed his brow. His secret lab within a secret lab was down several floors, not in some side chamber.

Breas looked both ways along the long corridor, then pulled the door closed behind them and pushed the button on the doorknob to lock them inside.

"What are we doing in here?"

"This is Dr. Jones's office."

"I know that, but aren't we going where your experiment is?"

Breas signed and rubbed his forehead with his palm. "For such a brilliant mind, you're sure thick sometimes."

Emilio swatted the air.

"When I told you no one must find out what we're doing before it's complete, I meant it. I said you were going to Dr. Jones's office, and that is where we are. Can't just go waltzing somewhere else with all these Fae milling about."

Breas hustled Emilio to the room's rear, where a large mahogany storage closet hulked beside a pair of wooden tables crowded with beakers and test tubes. Opening the closet door, he motioned Emilio inside.

"Yeah, unless we're going to Narnia to meet Mr. Tumnus, I'm not getting back in the closet. Especially not with you. Bad for both of us." Emilio ruffled his wings.

Breas sighed and opened the other door so the wardrobe stood fully open. Shoving aside the doctor's collection of lab coats, he gestured at the back wall.

Emilio gaped at the suddenly transparent back. It was like looking through a window into the lab he'd seen with Breas a couple of nights ago, but from the opposite side of the room. The office beyond held the enormous steaming round tub and was lined with a mixture of modern lab equipment and what resembled a potions class from Hogwarts.

"After you." Breas bowed slightly as though Emilio were a visiting dignitary.

Emilio folded his wings as tight as they would go against his back, hunched forward to clear the top of the door, and stepped through into a laboratory far larger than it looked from the other side.

Breas emerged behind him, framed in an ornate mirror standing on brass feet. The moment he cleared the threshold, the view into the doctor's office closed and only a pretty, full-length mirror remained.

Emilio's chest tightened. He'd only glimpsed his reflection from the shoulders up and avoided his reflection whenever possible. The person—or more accurately, creature—staring back at him was simultaneously beautiful and heartrending.

In his teens, he'd devoured X-men comics. They were freaks and outsiders, too, but they drew power from what made them unwelcome among people. Dreams of flying like Rogue thrilled him. The fantasy became real, although he resembled the Morlocks now. So bizarre, they lived underground safe from the jeers of the masses. Emilio was a monstrosity who'd never have a home again, but he was a powerful freak, and perhaps one of the few who could stand against these demons.

"Oh, come on. Don't look so morose." Breas's blond head appeared hovering above his shoulder in the mirror.

Emilio's shoulders tightened and his spine drew straight.

Breas pointed at the colored streaks lancing through his hair. "You clearly never wanted to be merely normal."

Emilio rounded on him, the tips of his wing feathers gouging an arc in the floor. "I didn't want to be a monster, either. What gave you the right to—" He lurched away from Breas but kept his gaze on his feet and away from the mirror.

"Power." Breas shrugged as though what happened to Emilio was meaningless to him. "Happens every day. The powerful few determine the destinies of the powerless. This conversation is boring and pointless. You are what you are now." He fidgeted with the knot on his tie, then brushed a stray bit of lint from his lapel. "I have a much more pressing issue that requires your keen eye for genetics and tissue culture."

Emilio swallowed his fury and swiveled to face the enormous bubbling tank in the room's center. In the distance, the murmur of traffic and honking horns dropped his jaw. "Where are we, exactly?"

Breas sighed. "In my secret lab. Did Callon thump you on the head? Cause brain damage?"

Emilio's lips clamped into a thin line. "Is your workshop on the island, because I hear cars."

"Your hearing must be enhanced, because I detect nothing." Breas paused and lifted an ear before flashing Emilio a wicked grin. "Would be poor strategy to house a secret this big under Badb's nose."

Emilio eyed a sculptured oak door on the opposite side of the laboratory. Portland. He was in the city. No landscape of monsters to crawl through and lots of pollution and iron to repel the Fae.

To discover an escape hatch from the tower into the heart of Portland set his mind ablaze with possibilities. He dismissed most of them immediately. To shepherd humans, Netherfae, and Fae through a single door into another defended citadel was an incremental improvement.

Breas wagged a finger. "Don't even think about it. Your torque would kill you the instant you left the room. Focus on your task."

Reluctantly, he approached the tank. Vapor cascaded down the thick black sides and crept along the marble floor.

Breas motioned him forward. "Come. It won't bite." He smiled and smoothed his hair. "At least not yet."

Emilio inched up to the edge, careful to duck under the rigging that suspended a massive metal disk several feet from the surface of the roiling liquid. He fanned some vapors aside and staggered away, retching.

"Ach." Emilio bent forward with his hands on his thighs and choked back a wave of nausea. It smelled of rancid pork and it looked like a single, large, misshapen lump of pulsating flesh. "What is—"

"It's an insurance policy." Breas rifled through some papers on the workbench behind the tank. Cabinets of glassware, odd bits of creatures Emilio guessed had been Fae, and swirling potions stretched to the ceiling.

Emilio choked back his gorge and steeled himself for another glance. The *thing* was about five feet across and made of pink and white wet scar tissue, with blue veins crisscrossing beneath almost transparent skin. Tubes entered the flesh from either lip of the tank. Red liquid that Emilio guessed was blood flowed into and out of it. He didn't wish to ponder where the blood came from any more than he wanted to contemplate what the blob would eventually become.

"Insurance against what?"

Breas turned just enough to catch Emilio in his peripheral vision and paused before answering. "Defeat, of course."

Emilio didn't believe him. "From betrayal by your queen, more likely."

"Partner. She is not my queen."

"Right." Emilio's tone was sardonic. "If I learned anything from the movies, it was that evil always betrays itself." He clapped his hands together and rubbed. "How can I help with that?"

Breas thumbed a thick book of papers, discarding some and slamming others into a slapdash pile on the corner of the table, unconcerned with Emilio.

*"Vanilla,"* Tamika's voice whispered in his mind. Within seconds, the familiar shapes of her childhood bedroom resolved into focus, but everything appeared fuzzy, like a TV channel broadcasting from far away.

"Emilio. Where are you?" Tamika walked the periphery of her room as though avoiding the middle. The others sat on the edge of her bed. Selina leaned on a windowsill.

"Secret laboratory. Can't stay long, Breas is here. You can see this?" He spoke in the mindspace. To the outside, he'd appear still as a statue, eyes unfocused. Hopefully, the bubbling tank provided enough cover so Breas wouldn't notice him just standing there looking vacant.

"Yeah, I can. What's in that tank? I can see something pink, but everything's fuzzy."

"We just ate. You really don't want to know." Emilio noted the others lacked the grossed-out expression on Tamika's face. "Alan, Selina, can you see anything in the room I'm in?"

"Not a thing, sweet," Selina said. "Only Tamika can see through our eyes."

"Yeah. Choosing only one to look through at a time is tricky."

"Tamika's getting better at it. We've never been able to hold everyone together with you five floors away." Alan smiled for the first time since any of them remembered.

"Plot twist. I'm in Portland, in the building I worked at for my internship."

"The city!" Selina and Tamika exclaimed simultaneously, while Alan's jaw dropped.

Tamika smiled. "My power must be growing."

"We can talk about that later. Tamika, you think you can dial it down a little? All I can see is your old bedroom. I'm blind here," Emilio whispered.

"Never tried that before." Tamika rested her hands on her desk and bent somewhat forward, her eyes squeezed shut. "I'm going to attempt pushing you out. You try to stay here. That ought to work."

Immediately an invisible hand shoved him toward the bedroom's white door. He dug his heels in and resisted. Tamika's bedroom faded slightly while the secret lab came into more focus.

"That's good, I have the feeling now. I can keep it there."

Seeing two places at once was weird. Breas bent over the workstation, still sorting papers and oblivious to his unwanted guests. Right next to him Selina smiled, while behind Emilio Alan sat across the tank. Tamika moved beside Breas and peered over his shoulder.

"I have no idea what any of this means, Emilio."

"Just read as much as you can, try to remember."

"What?" Breas glanced up from his desk and stared at Emilio, coming face to face with Tamika.

Crap. He said that out loud. "Nothing. I meant just get me what you can. I'll work on it when Callon isn't pummeling me."

Breas gave him an odd look and turned back to his work. "Nearly finished."

Tamika smiled and pointed down at the cell phone in her hand. "Don't know if this'll work, but won't hurt to try." She pointed the phone over Breas's shoulder and snapped pictures every few seconds.

Emilio tried not to gaze at the thing growing in the tank. It unnerved him, so he picked at the hem of his white top and fiddled with the drawstring on his scrubs. He noticed a long purple hair with looping curls and plucked it from the bottom of his shirt. The instant his fingers released the stray hair, Tamika's childhood bedroom vanished, leaving only the dimly lit lab.

# CHAPTER 49

Harper wasn't sure how long she hung in the black between worlds. It seemed a day or more, while her heart insisted only a few seconds had passed. Her head felt like someone had taken an axe to a watermelon. She winced and clasped her hands on the sides of her ears like she could push the pieces back together again.

A tall figure flickered into the blackness. Curved horns stretched forward and up from underneath a short top hat, and a brown hand held a smoking pipe. His bright eyes were riveted on her face as he brought the pipe to his lips, inhaled, and let the smoke billow up under the brim.

The gancanagh. She crouched low and edged back a step.

Santaigh blew another stream of smoke into his palm and a picture of Harper and her father hung suspended, framed in a gleaming filigree frame. In it, she was six years old, laughing from the tops of his shoulders. One hand clasped around his head, the other holding a stuffed giraffe by the neck.

She inhaled sharply and clamped her palm over her mouth.

The gancanagh inhaled another toke of his pipe and blew a high arc of smoke across from the picture. More photos materialized of family trips they never took, a graduation she never attended, and places she never went.

"My, my, you are a strong one. It's been a thousand years since someone shattered the perfect world I built for them."

He edged forward. She frantically scanned the blackness for a weapon, even squeezing her eyes shut and imagining a blade in her hand. But nothing formed. This was his world, not hers.

"Testy, aren't you? Did you just try to wish a weapon into your hands? Been even longer since anyone tried that." He chuckled and lifted the pipe to his mouth. "Fighting this is useless, Harper. You might break free, but I'll merely glamour you again. Your desires are far too delicious..." He licked the clawed tips of his fingers.

"My friends will come for me." Lame, but her mind was still sorting itself out.

Santaigh bit his bottom lip. "At the moment, they've got their hands full with Ashley and the other mist-changed. Why fight this? Why go back to the miserable, broken life you had before?"

"Because people depend on me."

"For what?" He laughed long and hard. "You must know your little quest only ends in your death. You won't save your friend, and eventually the Fae will slaughter everyone else. I'm offering you a gift few of your kind will get."

"You're killing me." The allure of a life with the family she should have had tugged on her heart like a siren's song.

Santaigh smiled and waved his hand. "Yes, yes, that small thing. But what I offer in exchange is so much more. In these last hours of your physical existence, you'd experience months, even years of the life you should have had, the life stolen from you. Then one night you drift off and just never wake. Only happiness. No pain." His electric blue eyes pleaded with her to accept.

Harper looked at the first picture of her dad hanging there in the blackness. That one happened. Her father had taken her to the zoo that day. She'd spent all her money buying crunchy crackers to feed the giraffes from atop his shoulders and had none left to buy anything from the gift shop. At first her dad had pointed out she'd need to budget better if she wanted to shop.

"Okay, Daddy, but can we come back when I save some more? We'll come to the shop first so I don't give too much to the giraffes," she'd said.

Gerald O'Neill had looked at her with a warm smile.

"You know, Rabbit, on second thought, it was a pretty nice thing you did, spending your entire allowance on feeding the giraffes when you could have spent it on candy or ice cream." He'd bought her a stuffed giraffe, the one she cradled in the picture.

In the wake of his murder, she'd clutched that little plush toy like it was a life preserver, and loneliness receded with it by her side. The giraffe appeared now at her feet. Without thinking, she reached down and hugged it. The flood of tears she'd been damming up broke, and she wept.

All she had to do was accept Santaigh's offer and her struggles in the real world ended. No more desperately holding things together. No more of Nuada's hopeless quest. Everything she ever wanted was inside the gancanagh's dream world.

But although her heart yearned for more time with her happy family, she knew if she remained in the pretty delusion, thousands of other children would lose their parents. She was all that stood between the Fae invasion and countless innocent lives. No one else was coming to save the taken, or the rest of the city, even the world. Through some cosmic joke, it fell to her.

Her fingers tightened around the giraffe, and she studied the picture of the zoo trip. She was so small. She felt that insignificant now. What resources did she have to rescue Emilio and the others, much less fight a war?

Santaigh flashed a grin with gleaming, pointed white teeth.

Another smoke cloud rose underneath the brim of the hat, cloaking his face so that only the glowing blue eyes were visible.

"Yes, Harper, it's hopeless. The destruction of humanity is both richly deserved and certain, but, in a sense, I can save you. Your empathy and the sweet ache it produces is rare, delectable fruit. Stay here. I'll devour you slowly. You can live an entire lifetime in my dreamtime. Just surrender to me." The Fae glided forward and ran a supple hand down her hair and along her shoulder, trailing it softly all the way down her arm. When it reached her wrist, he curled a warm hand around hers and squeezed.

Harper's features twisted as she lunged back, snapping her hand from his grasp. "No! That's horrible—" Her throat constricted.

The line of pictures floated forward and surrounded her. A carousel of happy moments, promised to her if only she abandoned her friends. She sucked her lips between her teeth and bit down to keep from crying out. How many times had she curled into a ball inside their tent on the streets, again in foster care, and every night since in their Gresham home? Knees clasped to her torso, chin clamped against her chest while she wished she'd wake up and her beautiful life would be there once more. Her dad would toss her in the air, catch her and spin a circle and everything would be okay. Barring that, she'd hoped to fall asleep and never awaken.

She hated that his offer tempted her.

Santaigh's ice-blue eyes flared. "Yes, that's it. If you return to this cruel world, you will fail, exactly like you have all your life. You're a small, weak human. Just let go. Stay with me, Harper. Give yourself to me."

*You are stronger than you know, Harper O'Neill.*

More and more family photos of memories that never happened winked into existence, surrounding her. In one, she had grey streaks in her hair. Beside her stood a wild-haired boy, about thirteen, and a mischievous looking six-year-old girl made rabbit ears with her fingers behind her brother. A broad-chested man with shoulder-length wavy brown hair and a trim beard draped an arm over her shoulders. He looked familiar, but she couldn't make out the details of his face through her watery vision.

She stared down and the tears fell, shimmering into nothingness.

Nuada had believed in her. Entrusted her with the Sword of Light, even if it refused to work after his death. He'd thought her kindness made her fit to be his queen, would give her what she needed to win this fight. Selina. Her mom. Emilio. Nuada. They'd all talked about her strength.

Never would she have labeled herself as strong, but perhaps she wasn't looking at it from the right perspective. Much of the goodness in her life was stolen when Badb cut down Gerald O'Neill, but it hadn't broken her. She'd steeled herself, risen the next day, and solved the next problem. Though it meant she got a fake ID so she could work full-time hours at fourteen. And along the way, a lonely, difficult life had filled her with compassion. For Abraham, who had shared what little he had with them. For Emilio, picked on because he was different. Abandoned outsiders just like her. She wanted to defend them.

On the night the Wild Hunt swept Emilio and so many others away, Selina had seen those aspects of her heart. Beautiful things. Strong things. Rare things in this world, according to Nuada. A single, silent laugh escaped her lips. "Seeds need the dark to sprout."

With a shaky laugh, she crouched and sat the little giraffe back down. It rippled in her vision, either due to Santaigh erasing it or her lens of tears.

The pictures faded from their points of suspension in the emptiness. A half-smile formed on her face, the same kind the peaceful Fir Bolg had all worn.

"A life of only happiness is no life. My pain created me, somewhere in my own darkness, and suffering guided me to something deeper than the easy pleasure you offer: a purpose and the tools to meet it."

A shadow passed over Santaigh's face, and his body trembled. He slashed the air with his upturned hand and the pair stood at the dining room table next to Harper's parents. The cloying scent of fruit and spices filled her nostrils, while that familiar warm, floaty sensation tried to push into her mind.

"Hey, Rabbit, I'm glad you're home."

"Harper, honey, what's wrong?"

"Your resistance is useless. As you can see, I'll simply glamour you again." Santaigh exhaled a jet of smoke in Harper's direction and bay windows, shelves filled with books, and a slate couch formed.

Harper stood inches from the gancanagh now and tilted her face up to his. "I don't think that's how it works. I think a part of me had to want what you offer. And now I don't."

Fury contorted his handsome features. "Then you can waste away in here with nothing." He spat every word through trembling lips. The house in Portland, along with its occupants, blinked out of existence and then there was only blackness.

Harper laughed and stared into those faintly glowing eyes. "But I already know how to escape. I figured it out with the help of my friends. It's the desire for my truth."

Harper turned her face and focused on a point over Santaigh's shoulder, where a bright red door materialized.

He snarled, crouched, and bellowed. Beneath the hat, his eyes blazed. "No! You *will* be mine." The fire in his eyes dimmed when he attempted to lunge for her, but his feet were glued to the spot. He thrashed side to side and his clawed hands flailed so violently golden buttons popped from the orange brocade vest and skittered, glinting through the blackness.

Harper strode purposely to the red door, grasped the cool brass handle, and pushed it open. On the other side, green grass rippled and pine boughs swayed.

Halfway over the threshold, she turned her head over her shoulder and smiled at the slavering gancanagh. "No. I won't. You have nothing I want."

She slammed the door on his shriek, and a blinding flash brought her arm across her eyes.

When the light receded, Harper found herself lying beneath a great oak tree, pillowed in the gancanagh's embrace, his face and body frozen in a look of surprise. The Fae made moaning sounds, but it seemed like he couldn't move with his mind still in the dreamworld he'd woven for her. He'd break free fast, she was sure of that, and then he'd kill her.

She scrambled backward and grabbed her sword, pack, and clothing from the nearby rock they rested on. A patch of fuzzy mycelium created a silhouette, a milky afterimage of where she'd lain. *Paegrinn. So that's how they reached me.*

Dizziness brought a fuzzy sensation pulsing over her skin. Already the Fae stirred. No sign of her friends in the clearing.

Her entire body was noodley from lack of food and what Santaigh had drained from her. She needed help fast. She shoved her feet into her studded boots, clutched her possessions to her chest, and staggered into the forest. After a minute, she risked calling out.

"Melinoe? Paegrinn? Help me."

# CHAPTER 50

Internal tremors threatened to unleash the same hyperventilating panic attack in Eileen that had always required alcohol to fix. The weight of what rode on her shoulders compressed her heart like a pile of stones. Her near miss with the abandoned ale merely added another rock.

Eileen strode up the hall from the bathroom, paused with her back against a wall, and traced the spiraling stems of the mushroom necklace... *and now you must make room within your soul for a new you. A bigger you. One brave enough to do whatever is necessary to defend others...* Glani's words played like a recording in her mind.

Eileen was the only person who could carry out their plan and keep the Fir Bolg safe, and achieving that was the best chance to get help for Harper. Glani believed in her, and she'd made it this far.

*Get a grip. You can do this, Eileen. Besides, what choice do you have?* "Thank you," she whispered to her necklace, slipped it inside her shirt, and shook out the jitters before joining the others in the vestibule.

Fintan shoved his jeans into tall brown boots, shouldered a pack, and with a bow, swept an arm, beckoning Eileen and Phelan down the steps to where Michael and Aisling waited on the lawn.

Phelan leaned down to whisper in her ear. "Now, lass, listen well, because what I'm about to relay is of paramount importance."

Eileen's forehead creased, and she nodded with a gulp.

"The Fianna are bound by many ancient rules, none as sacred as the one I'm sharing."

Remembering her potentially deadly blunder with Black Annis, Eileen's ears perked up, and the newly banished nerves crackled beneath her skin again. "Okay."

"The four of us are going to walk up to my Wrangler. The others will pause near the back, waiting for me to open the door. That's when you strike."

"What? Strike at what?"

"Not what. Who. I cannot stress this enough, lass. It's pivotal. Fail, and life for the next several hours will be unbearable."

Eileen pressed her lips into a line.

"Keep those lovely green eyes focused on my hand." His face was solemn. "The second you see me lift the handle, and not a millisecond before, I need you to shout something." He dropped his voice almost to a whisper.

Eileen leaned forward. "Shout what?"

"Shotgun."

Phelan's serious expression never lapsed. Eileen pursed her lips and blew a stray hair out of her face. "You smartass, you had me on edge for—"

Fintan gave a deep chuckle. "Oh, lassie, he's deadly serious. Under the Fianna Code, the sacred rules of shotgun can never be challenged."

Phelan's smile cracked. "I'm sincere about one thing. Michael or Aisling in the front seat will drive both of us insane, so, for the love of all that's holy, just shout shotgun."

Phelan strode for the Jeep. Michael and Aisling already hovered by the rear bumper. Eileen's eyes were glued to his hand, and when she detected the slightest lift in the handle, she struck. "Shotgun!" she called, standing on her tiptoes.

"Cheater!" Michael threw his head back with a grin.

"Who told you?" Aisling smacked her palm to her forehead.

"Maith thú, Eileen. Good on you." Fintan's booming laughter drowned out wails of mock protest. The old man lifted a hand. "Safe journey."

Phelan waved. "You, too."

Michael's and Aisling's banter filled the car almost nonstop. Eileen enjoyed their wit and mirth, but she periodically pulled the Lia Fail shard from her pocket. Relief filled her each time the glow confirmed her daughter still lived.

A sea of pine trees whizzed by the window. Every mile marker brought her nearer to the Fir Bolg and closer to the tools to come to her daughter's aid. It felt good to finally take action.

When she wasn't compulsively checking the shard, she fidgeted with the mushroom necklace. She really hadn't known what the gift meant, and Glani's note didn't explain much. They'd been so adamant about hiding from the outside world, she couldn't fathom their motives for folding her into their society. She guessed it was the healer's influence. Eileen sensed not all the Fir Bolg wanted to stay out of the brewing conflict, especially after the second attack on their people, and that gave her hope she could complete her task.

As if reading her thoughts, Phelan risked pulling his eyes from the road to peek at her. "I've known the Fir Bolg a long while and never have I seen them make an outsider a member of their culture."

"Yeah, you're far too pretty to be one of them, wouldn't you agree, Phelan?" Michael punched Phelan on the arm.

"Aye. Too short for a Sasquatch," Aisling said.

"And not near as hairy," Phelan added.

"I don't know, you should see me the week before shorts season," Eileen said.

Michael and Aisling's laugh was infectious. Michael leaned all the way into the gap between the front seats, his flaming red hair brighter against the cloudy sky. "Ah, Phelan, she's a funny one too. I see—"

Phelan cleared his throat and squinted at the road. "We're coming to the end of the line. We'll have to continue on foot in about another mile."

Eileen fiddled with the Lia Fail, suddenly wondering if saving her from the chatter of the other two was the only reason she sat upfront with Phelan. A scintillating warmth started in her ribcage and spread to her cheeks.

She lifted the stone close to her face when it flared to life, glowing brighter than before. She held it toward the center of the Jeep so all could see. "How does this thing work? Is it like a tracking beacon that glows brighter the closer it gets to Harper?"

"Naw, don't think so, but it must mean something. Maybe her power is growing," Phelan said.

"Or maybe she's in a fight," Michael said.

Eileen gasped and hugged the stone to her chest.

Aisling smacked Michael on the shoulder. "You git. Don't say things like that with her mum present."

"Eileen, it probably means nothing terrible." Phelan sent Michael a scowl in the rearview mirror.

"Guys, it's fine. It's still glowing, means she's alive. That's all I need, and I'm glad all of you are helping her."

Aisling squeezed Eileen's arm. "It's our sworn duty."

"Well. End of the road, folks. Literally," Phelan said.

Michael poked a thumb over his shoulder at the dirt road behind them. "Ye call that a road? Deer path more like."

Ahead, the tiny unpaved lane they'd been traveling on simply ended. Nothing past it except deep, pristine woods and the snow-capped Mount Hood jutting above all.

All four car doors opened simultaneously, and everyone hopped out. Eileen placed her hands on her lower back and arched backward. Michael and Aisling swung their arms in circles and rotated stiff necks.

"How much farther?" Eileen asked.

"On foot, about two days."

Eileen's heart fell. Two days. From what Hieronymous said, they may be too late. And from the leanness of the Fianna, they were in top shape. She'd definitely slow them all down. She glanced at the shard. The longer they took, the more danger Harper faced without backup.

"Don't look like your dog just died, lass." Michael smirked and sidled up to Phelan. "We going to show her, boss?"

"Lorna and Declan will be furious if we do this." Aisling rested her hands on the Jeep's roof and focused on Phelan on the other side.

"Sounds like another good reason to bring her in. I trust Eileen. And if Fintan felt otherwise, she wouldn't be here." Phelan motioned Eileen to join him at the opposite side of the Jeep. "You two, get the packs ready. I need a word with my friend."

The damp in the air sent the chill right through her clothing to bite at her skin. She pulled on her brown insulated jacket and grabbed her backpack from the car floor. Belongings in hand, her footfalls crunched the pine needles as she moved over to Phelan.

If she wasn't so comfortable in his presence, she'd be quite worried about the cloak and dagger routine they all suddenly fell into. Phelan leaned against the SUV and made arcs on the forest floor with his boot. He inhaled, and it seemed like he'd speak, but he performed a few more revolutions with his feet. This went on for half a minute before Eileen broke the silence.

"You're making me a little nervous here. What's so terrible none of you can't just spit it out?"

When Phelan lifted his head, he grabbed her hands and pulled her around in front of him. Those deep brown eyes searched her face, and he swept a lock of hair from her forehead. Electricity crackled where his fingertips brushed her skin, and she leaned closer. His features were drawn like he was about to express something dreadful, and she braced herself.

"Eileen, the Fianna may look human, but we aren't. Not anymore."

"I gathered that when you told me your age." Her heart skipped a beat at the crease in his brow and the way his eyes darted everywhere but at her.

"It's just. Well, we just met and I don't want you to..." He licked his lips and paused.

"Want me to what?" Eileen whispered. She lifted her hand to his cheek and nudged his face down so his eyes would once more meet hers. He looked genuinely frightened.

"Think less of us." His hand covered hers, pressing it tighter against his cheek. "Of me."

The notion she could judge him when she was the one cracking under pressure. What would he think of her if he knew how close she'd come to giving in to alcohol and endangering their mission? Heart hammering in her chest, she pressed herself closer to him.

"Probably easier to show her." Aisling tossed her backpack aside.

Eileen leapt back and Phelan jerked his hand away and straightened his hair. Both of them stared at the pebbles and pinecones strewn everywhere.

"You git, Pinky." Michael dropped his pack and crammed his jacket inside the big pocket on the front with a broad grin.

"Craic on with your tender moment. We'll wait." Aisling

shoved the sleeve of her shirt high, revealing the wolf tattoo. She pressed a hand over her wide smile.

Phelan dusted imaginary detritus from his pants. "Get on with it then."

Michael's and Aisling's tattoos flared with a bright, warm light. Eileen gasped and she lifted her eyes to Phelan. His breathing came shallow and fast.

Brighter and brighter, the light blazed until it was so blinding, Eileen turned away. When the brightness faded, where Michael and Aisling had been, a pair of silver wolves paced, one with a smear of pink running by her ear.

Eileen crouched beside the wolves and ran a finger along the pink streak. "Aisling?"

The wolf nodded once. They were much taller and stockier than their wild cousins, backs reaching Eileen's waist. She looked over her shoulder at Phelan. He hovered beside his Jeep, elbows clamped at his sides, arms crossed across his chest.

Eileen pushed herself to her feet and rested a hand on Aisling's back. She shrugged and returned to Phelan's side. "You all aren't my first shapeshifters. Turns out my cat was a phooka."

The two wolves yipped and capered about, tossing their heads. Phelan's jaw hung a little slack, and the tension melted from his body. She didn't want to admit to herself how charming he looked. Like a high school kid surprised his prom date had said yes.

Phelan drew in a deep, slow breath and smiled down at her. "I think I know what the Fir Bolg see in you. Thank you, sweet Eileen. The Fianna don't find acceptance much of anywhere."

"That's hard to believe."

"Living for a couple hundred years and transforming into wolves isn't a recipe for human approval. And the Fae aren't very amenable to 'half-breeds.' So we live as we always have, on the fringes." He shrugged with a one-sided grin, perked up, clapped his hands, and placed them on her shoulders. "I have a job for you."

Phelan tasked Eileen with strapping Aisling and Michael's packs onto their backs. She slipped their legs through the armholes and cinched them tighter, then looped the waist strap around their midsections. When she was done, she dusted wolf hair from her sleeves and admired her handiwork.

The pair of enormous wolves wearing their blue and black backpacks struck her as funny. She stifled a laugh. "You two look ridiculous."

Aisling tossed her head and her tongue lolled out. Michael lowered his neck, raised his hackles and growled before doing the same.

"So you guys got a sled to pull like the Iditarod? Because I don't see another way I'm getting through these woods with you."

Phelan smiled. "Nothing so complicated. But you'll have to wear both of our backpacks. I tried to pack light." He handed her his bag.

She shrugged it on and worked the two packs side by side between her shoulder blades, using the waist belt of hers to stabilize it since she slung it over only one shoulder. It was uncomfortable, but doable. "Now what?"

"Now you ride."

Aisling and Michael capered around them, pawing the air.

"What?"

"I'm sorry, but it's the only way. Grab onto my neck and lie as flat along my back as you can. Ever ridden a horse?"

"When I was a kid."

"Great, then you know to grip with your legs since in no universe am I wearing a saddle."

Eileen swallowed hard. Straddling Phelan brought a surge of warmth, a flutter to her heart, and the constricting sensation of guilt at somehow betraying Gerald. "That'll raise some shaggy Fir Bolg eyebrows." She gave a nervous laugh.

"Not my first choice either, but if I've got to suffer the indignity of carrying a passenger, might as well be the mother of the heir."

A blinding flash of light flared beneath his sleeve, and a gigantic wolf stood. Phelan tipped his furred head toward his own back and Eileen crept up beside him. Slinging a leg across him, she rested her stomach flat, folded her legs against his sides, and wound her hands through his neck ruff.

Phelan yelped gently, nodded, and lurched forward, Michael and Aisling close behind.

Eileen shrieked and wrapped her arms all the way around Phelan's neck. Drizzle whipped her face, stinging her cheeks. Beneath her, Phelan fell into a steady pace and the trees whizzed past nearly as fast as they did on the highway, far faster than normal wolves could race. Beside her, Aisling's canine face pulled into a wide grin, her ears pinned back to add to her aerodynamics.

Even uphill, their stride never slowed. The Fianna wove in and out of trees and hopped over creeks and stones. She'd never liked horses much but felt thankful she'd learned to ride or she'd be miserable right now.

Any feeling of awkwardness melted away, soothed by the hypnotic rhythm of Phelan's paws striking the ground. His fur was downy and smooth beneath her hands, and she rested the side of her face on his neck to watch the woodland slide by, soaring and silent like a cathedral. Though they raced to root out a traitor, her thoughts stilled and she enjoyed the moment. Soon she'd be with her new family and then, with or without them, she'd travel to the island to find Harper.

Dusk sent a warm glow bathing the wood. They'd been racing for the majority of the day when Phelan slowed to a halt next to a moss-covered stone that was taller than Eileen. Other rocks, some even larger, clustered around a small rise.

Aisling and Michael sat, tails thumping the earth while their earls swiveled. Phelan pointed with his long nose toward them as Eileen slid off his back.

"We have to get their packs off before they can transform," he said, once more in human form.

"Oh, right." Eileen dropped to her knees beside Aisling and fumbled with the bags. The wolf nudged her playfully.

Aisling shook out her pink hair and stamped in place. "Woo! That was invigorating."

Michael bent at the waist with his head dangling between his legs. "Lassie, some of us don't live in the gym. I could sleep for a year."

Eileen circled the edges of the little clearing. There was nothing to suggest anyone had ever camped here, Fir Bolg or human.

"Are we resting before we continue?" Eileen turned to Phelan.

The Fianna averted his eyes but studied the stone.

"We've arrived. This is their most secret and sacred of places. We only need to let them know we're outside."

"And just how do we do that? Knock?" Michael ran his hands over the stones as though searching for a hidden entrance. Phelan said, "You've lived with them, Eileen. What do they do morning, noon, and night?"

"Chant."

"They chant." Phelan motioned Aisling and Michael closer. "Follow along. There're no words, so it's pretty easy."

Phelan closed his eyes and toned a deep sound in his chest. Parting his lips, he started the shifting vowel-laced improvisational mantra of the Fir Bolg. Beside him, Eileen raised her voice.

Michael stood with his hands on his hips, and Aisling wore a matching dubious expression.

"This one of your little pranks then?" Aisling tapped a foot and flashed a sly smile.

"No, he's right. This is what they do," Eileen said.

"Gah, she's in on it. Like peas in a pod, those two." Michael elbowed Aisling, who nodded her agreement. "You'll have to try harder to trick us into looking stupid."

Phelan let his hands slap against his thighs and rolled his head back. "Don't need to trick you for that. I'm serious, this is how we gain passage."

Phelan began his chant again, and all joined in this time. Eileen and her new Fianna friends wove a lovely sound deep in the Oregon woods. For several minutes, they sang, and the boulder winked out of existence. Aeld and Glani stood framed in the fading light of the day.

"Phelan Kane," Aeld said, as the voices of the Fianna died away. "Why did you bring Eileen back to us?"

<h1 style="text-align:center">CHAPTER 51</h1>

"Aeld." Glani laid a hand on the chieftain's hairy arm. "She's going to think she's not welcome."

Aeld sighed and bowed his head. "We know killing incubi for us was hard on you, and we feared more battles loomed. We took great pains to protect you from danger and pain, ensuring your safety."

"I'm not a child. Shouldn't I have had a say in what was better for me?"

Glani smiled. "That's just what I told him." The healer rushed forward to clasp Eileen in a crushing embrace.

"You killed an incubus?" Michael appraised her with wide eyes.

"Five."

"Bloody five?" Aisling gaped at her. "How?"

Eileen grimaced. "Shot them mostly." She tapped her pack where the Mossberg nestled inside.

"Damn, Mrs. O'Neill. You're hardcore," Michael said.

Phelan held up a hand. "We can swap stories later." He looked at Aeld and Glani. "Hieronymous sent us. We're here because your people are in great danger. Are the Dusk and Dawn Fae still among you?"

Aeld nodded.

"One side are traitors. It's why the Sluagh keep finding us," Eileen said.

"This news is troubling, though we wondered the same thing after we fled our second village." Aeld's shoulders slumped. "But you could have brought the message without involving Eileen."

"Well, I am glad he involved me. He explained what this means." Eileen fished her mushroom pendant from beneath her jacket. "And if what Hieronymous said is true, I am uniquely qualified to discover which Court has betrayed us."

"This cave has two entrances, right?" Phelan said.

Aeld nodded.

"No, it doesn't. There are three. This one, the western rear exit, and an eastern passage just wide enough to crawl through."

"But only Aeld and I know of the east exit. How did you find it?" Glani asked.

Phelan tapped his nose. "Fianna. I sniffed it out forty years ago when we last hid here. The more important question is, are the Fae aware?"

"No." Aeld shook his head. "The near-invisible threads of mycelium across the side entrances remain unbroken. They've not discovered them."

"Good. Then that is why Eileen is here."

Both Fir Bolg looked utterly lost.

Eileen shrugged with a tilt of her head. "I'm the only one who can lie."

Neither Aeld nor Glani seemed any less bewildered. Phelan motioned the Fianna into a close huddle with the Fir Bolg.

"Michael and Aisling here will each watch a side exit. They'll appear as wolves hunting, and the Fae would have to draw really close to sniff them out."

Aisling snarled. "They won't come that near."

"You'll bring me inside now with Eileen. Tell them Hieronymous sent them to deliver the Lia Fail shard for safekeeping."

Eileen dug the stone from her pocket and held it for the Fir Bolg's inspection. The shard glowed steady, not as bright as before, but constant.

"She's still alive," Eileen said.

"Phelan, why can't you lie to the Fae?" Glani asked.

"Because I'm not a part of this like she is." Phelan inclined his head toward Eileen but refused to meet her eyes.

"So how does Eileen's ability to be dishonest help us?" Glani asked.

Phelan scanned the skies above and nodded to Aisling and Michael. "Make sure we're alone, you two."

Light flared from their tattooed arms, and a pair of wolves sauntered off in either direction, sniffing the earth as they went.

Phelan waited a moment, glancing after his companions. "Tell them, Eileen."

"I think I have a plan. Before Badb killed Gerald, I worked for a pharmaceutical company."

Both Fir Bolg cocked their heads. Eileen gave a half laugh. Sasquatch hadn't a clue what a company even was.

"Let's just say I was with a group and there was this other group who wanted some secrets we had. The best way to get the secrets was from the inside. One of our own was stealing our secrets and selling them to the enemy group."

Eileen's eyes traveled from one Fir Bolg face to the other. She raised her eyebrows and nodded once. Both mirrored her slow nod. Satisfied they understood, she wiped her hands on her jacket sleeves and continued her story.

"We didn't know who it was, but we suspected two, and one of them was in my, shall we say, party? So we crafted two unique pieces of material to draw them out. One suspect got one piece, the other the second.”

Glani and Aeld nodded their understanding.

“So when our competitor received the intelligence and acted, we knew who the mole was.”

“Because you lied,” Glani said.

Eileen nodded. “Because I faked information to protect our interests.”

“Fir Bolg don’t lie.” Glani reached out a long finger and touched the necklace around Eileen’s neck, her expression grave.

“They don’t shoot guns either, but aren’t you glad she did?” Phelan said.

“Your plan will bring the Sluagh down on us. This is our final safe place.” Aeld’s frown couldn’t hide the tightness of his posture. The Fir Bolg Chieftain was scared.

Eileen empathized with them. For thousands of years, they lived their bucolic lives, moving deeper into the forest to remain in their self-imposed isolation, and now they were pursued, hiding, and facing a sea change in their way of life. A way of life that had healed Eileen and one she’d grown to love.

Eileen softened her voice. “I don’t like it either, but eventually, the Sluagh will come. Better on our terms, right? You don’t want to hear this, but war is on your doorstep. It has been since Paegrinn’s disappearance. The way I see it, you can fight with your friends, or be hunted because both sides desperately seek your alliance.”

“Just our side doesn’t want to drain the life out of you,” Phelan said.

“Assuming your plan works and we discover who’s in league with the Sluagh, we still have no more places we can hide from those who wish to do us harm. And when the Sluagh attack with their allies from inside, we’ll be at a disadvantage.” Aeld’s face held a faraway expression, his eyes unfocused.

“Leave that to us. Fintan is on his way to join Hieronymous.

Reinforcements will arrive early morning. My friends will watch the exits until then and discover anyone trying to leave," Phelan said.

"But where do we go afterwards?" Glani's voice was soft and small despite her size. "We have no safe home anymore. No place hidden."

Eileen laid a hand gently on her arm. "One thing at a time. First, we make sure you escape the Sluagh. Then we figure out the rest."

"Well, do we have a plan?" Phelan leaned toward Aeld.

Exhaustion had etched lines into the Fir Bolg leader's features. "We have little choice, it would seem."

Aeld passed his hand across the looming boulder, and the mouth of the wide cave appeared. The tall Fir Bolg had to crouch slightly to navigate the cavern, but Eileen and Phelan could stand comfortably upright, their heads far from the ceiling.

Row upon row of softly glowing shelf mushrooms lined either side. Eileen counted at least five different species, from huge ones the size of her head that cast a warm orange glow to clusters of tiny lichen-like fungus with a blue tone.

Phelan's breath rasped rapid and shallow, and he frequently wiped his hands along his thighs. Eileen recognized the symptoms of early panic, like the words to an old song. Soon as someone cued it up, it played itself on a loop. A sweet ache filled her heart. The flip devil-may-care exterior the Fianna worked so hard to cultivate got brushed away by the threat of an enclosed space.

Eileen slowed to give the Fir Bolg more of a lead. Phelan startled when she drew alongside him, and she twined her fingers through his. For the first time since he'd retaken human form, he looked at her. Wide brown eyes flicked to the ceiling and his body folded inward like he could shrink.

"Hey. Take a deep breath and let it out slowly."

He gulped and drooped his head, but Eileen ducked down and met his gaze.

"You're claustrophobic."

He nodded. Up ahead, the Fir Bolg paused but didn't return to join their guests.

"That obvious?" He gave a nervous laugh.

"That why you've been acting strange since we got here?"

He licked his lips, unlacing their fingers, and rubbed his palms on his pants again. "Little bit. And you…"

"Did I say something wrong? Violate some unwritten Fianna rule?"

"No. Nothing like that. It's just…". He dropped his head back and swept a stray hair away. He stood there with his mouth hanging half open.

"Just what?"

With another deep breath, Phelan rested his hands on her shoulders, looked down into her upturned face, and squirmed. Beads of sweat peppered his forehead despite the cool air inside the cave. Eileen clasped his hand again and pulled him away from the wall. "And now the big brave wolf man doesn't want anyone to see caves make him nervous."

His fingers closed around hers. "Doesn't want *you* to notice he's terrified of this place."

The way he fidgeted, the drawn brows… Eileen felt echoes of his anxiety in her own body. Phelan struggled with the same fear she did, his from the cave, hers from alcohol and failure.

She held his hand to her heart, and her eyes watered. "Want to know something I never thought I'd admit to anyone?"

Phelan nodded.

"I'm scared shitless right now. My daughter's life, the potential destruction of my Fir Bolg family if I screw this up. I've been a total train wreck for fifteen years—"

Phelan wove his fingers through the back of her hair. "Oh, my sweet, what you endured—"

"Broke me. Hours ago at Fintan's." Eileen's throat closed. She rubbed her hand on her sternum, voice thick with sorrow. "I'd have gulped down half an abandoned beer just to relieve this relentless pressure, but there was a cigarette in the bottle. I don't think I can do this."

She trembled all over, and Phelan crushed her against his chest, stroking her lower back, the heat of his hands like the refuge of a campfire in the cold. The scent of woodsy soap and leather tickled her senses, and she breathed deep. Phelan's voice was thick. "Oh, lovely, yes you can. One impulsive moment doesn't erase the heroic things you've done."

"And claustrophobia doesn't change how I feel about you." She hadn't been aware of the depths of her loneliness until Phelan's bright light illuminated it. All she wanted was his blazing nearness.

"And how's that, lass?" he murmured.

Eileen snaked her arms around his neck, pulled him down to her, and their lips met. All other emotions dried up in the heat of Phelan's lips and the searching of his hands.

One perfect moment of bliss was shattered by a deep cough.

Reluctantly, Phelan drew back. Eileen's insides quaked as she smoothed her hair and clothing. Glani and Aeld flashed them that content half-smile and waited.

Phelan bent and whispered, "Best cure for claustrophobia I've ever had. I'll return for another dose when it wears off."

Eileen blushed and strode to their guides. Her retort to Phelan died in her throat. Aeld and Glani withdrew to either side of the tunnel's end, giving Eileen a view of an underground dome so vast several football fields would fit inside with room to spare.

She bet Phelan's claustrophobia would melt away without

another kiss when he glimpsed the wonder before them, because the ceilings towered twenty feet tall at their lowest point. Off to the right, a stream wound its way along the wall, around tall stalagmites jutting up from the floor like teeth. High above, more conical stalactites hung, covered in the same glowing mushrooms lining the walls.

Round wooden huts similar to the ones the Fir Bolg built in the trees studded every open space. The cavern buzzed with day-to-day activities, much the same as their arboreal life, except the slumped postures and plodding gait of the inhabitants signaled fatigue. And the silence, their fear.

"Space is limited down here. You two will have to share my hut. It's this way." Glani beckoned Phelan and Eileen.

"Thank you, Glani." Eileen shifted her pack and Phelan followed close behind, his hand periodically brushing her arm and waist.

Aeld raised a hand in farewell and strode down the middle of the massive cavern toward the biggest structure in the back, while Glani led her guests along the winding path next to the creek. Eileen was surprised to see bushes growing on the bank covered in fat white berries. Other vines wound down from shelves in the cavern walls.

They passed several Fir Bolg, who each smiled and nodded to their guests. Both Eileen and Phelan returned the gesture.

"Did you make this place?" Eileen asked.

"No. Mount Hood, as you call it, is volcanic. These caves were formed millions of years ago by the lava."

Phelan pointed up at the stalactites. "Any of those ever fall?"

Glani shook her head. Phelan did not look convinced.

The Fir Bolg healer's temporary home sat one row from the creek. Once inside, Glani pulled the door shut and sat on a bunk. "Aeld will spread the word for our people to be prepared to leave in a moment's notice."

Eileen dropped her pack on the cot next to Glani's. "I better go search out some Fae and lie like a rug."

Glani paused while pulling a tray of herbs and mushrooms out from underneath the bed.

"Just an expression." Eileen stood framed in the doorway.

"The Dusk Court is staying in a group of houses adjacent to the great hall," Glani said. "The Dawn have decorated theirs with fabric and gems. It'll be easy to spot."

"I best go alone. Not sure how Fae respond to Fianna." Eileen shoved the shard into her front pants pocket and stretched.

"Depends on the Fae," Phelan said with a warm smile.

Glani's hands danced over the tray, dropping items into a bowl and grinding them. "I'll make Phelan some tea to calm him. He's not coping without the sky."

"That obvious?" Phelan said and dropped onto the last open bed.

"I'll find you when I'm done." Eileen waved and slipped out into the subterranean city.

Voices rose all around her. The rumbling croon of the Fir Bolg chant was made even more beautiful by the acoustics in the cavern. Tonight, she didn't join them but listened, her eyes half closed. In the formlessness of their toning, eddies formed, temporary patterns coalesced and released. Joined others in conversation, then fell away. Like life itself, dynamic, surprising, and beautiful.

Soaking in the musical healing, she rounded a corner and nearly slammed into Lord Ezrynhivar. She scrambled to the side out of instinct, braced for an attack. She may have shared an adventure with the Dusk King, but he could still be the mole.

His usual bored smirk gone, his eyebrows shot up. He hopped back a step with his wings half unfurled.

"What are you doing here? I thought Aeld had you dumped

like a stray dog back wherever it was you came from." And the smirk returned to his pale face.

"I should ask you the same. Before I left, you went on and on about how you were going to vamoose out of the ultra-dull village the first chance you got, and yet here you are. Couldn't you have simply gone when the Fir Bolg moved?" She didn't trust him. It was a safe bet he was the one leading the Sluagh to them. Yes, he'd seemed to help Harper with the ring, but what if that was a way for him to track her, to lead Badb's minions to their prize?

"Badb is hunting down any Fae not siding with her. What were we supposed to do? Waltz out of the treehouses unprotected and go home to New Orleans? Badb would be on our doorstep in a heartbeat." His hands made dramatic gestures as he spoke.

His story was weak. She'd seen him fight. Probably he and his entourage could handle themselves. There had to be another reason he was still here, and Badb Catha was likely it, but not because he was avoiding her.

"So you're here because you're afraid to leave? Phelan and I got here all by our lonesomes with no big bad Sluagh chasing us."

"So you came with a Fianna? Interesting choice, but I suppose it explains how a human could find this place." He leaned back against the wall of a hut and crossed one hoof over the other. "The biggest reason I'm still here is because Serotina also remains. She says to help the Fir Bolg, but the light Fae are all duplicitous."

As if the dark weren't probably worse. "So, peer pressure then?"

Ez laughed. "That's why I like you so much, Eileen O'Neill. You're funny, and not afraid to kill a Fae or five when it comes down to it."

Eileen's stomach twisted, but only for an instant. Disappointment flickered across Ezrynhivar's eyes when his goad failed to produce the same result it had a few days ago.

"The more interesting question is why you're here," Ez said.

"Figured I'd make it six," she said with a forced smile. She had to be convincing or the ruse wouldn't work.

"Deflection, sweetheart. You're not as good at it as we are."

Eileen matched his smirk. "If you must know, Hieronymous sent us with this." She drew out the Lia Fail shard and held it up in front of the dark Fae's face.

"Another piece has been found." Ez's voice softened with awe.

"He figured the best place for it was with the Fir Bolg, experts at hiding and such. Plus, too many Fae in the Lodge and no reliable way to be sure where their allegiance really lies."

"Fascinating."

"And the Fianna believe there's another way out of this cave. We might be able to escape without the Sluagh or Badb tracking us. You could return to New Orleans, be finished with this, and the Fir Bolg would be free to return to hiding somewhere new."

Ezrynhivar remained draped against the side of the building, but his gaze sharpened.

"Off to the west, I would guess where the stream enters, is a small passage leading outside. It's far enough away from the main entrance that anyone watching it wouldn't see us leaving. Aeld is making plans to move soon through that exit. It's our best chance of not being discovered."

"Is he?" Ezrynhivar tapped a hand to his lips and let his eyes rise to the ceiling.

Well, the seed was planted. Now she needed to find Serotina and hope they really did hate each other enough to not share information.

# CHAPTER 52

A groan followed by rustling leaves meant the gancanagh already stirred. An anguished, inhuman scream sliced through the evening air. Deep in the restless woods, a dozen half-animal, half-human screams rose in answer.

Too weakened to hold her weight, Harper's knee buckled, sending her tumbling to the hard earth. She sucked in a hissing breath between clenched teeth. Bruised, but nothing sprained or broken. She swept her leather jacket on and shoved her arms through the straps on her pack.

The smallest movement took effort like moving through thick syrup. The gaps between trees and patchy fog revealed nowhere she could hide. Her best chance was to find her friends. They had to be close, or they'd never have reached her in Santaigh's constructed world.

Dragging herself up, using the Cliamh Solais like a cane, she only crumpled partway when a head rush caused the world to spin. A small sound escaped her lips, but she shook it off and shoved off. Each lurching step made her body feel heavier, forcing her to stop every few feet, making progress only by floundering from tree trunk to tree trunk.

"Big mistake, Harper. If you come back to me right now, I'll let you die peacefully inside your dream life. Defy me and, well, let's just say fear isn't my favorite flavor, but in your case I'd savor each drop." There was a playful lilt to Santaigh's shouted taunt.

"Phooka, where are you?" she whispered.

The gancanagh sounded far away, as though he hovered at the edge of his grove, but that might be the ringing in her hears obscuring his whereabouts.

"Ashley and her friends will find you. Your little game is fruitless."

The rustle of dried vegetation and snapping twigs sent her heart hammering. The mist-changed ferals had already tracked her; this weak, she'd never outrun them. Her eyes crawled along the earth and into the treetops, searching for any advantage, a place to hide or launch a surprise attack.

Up ahead, perhaps twenty feet, a dead oak offered some protection. Ashley and the mist-changed didn't seem versed in stealth. Maybe Harper could take some out from the relative safety of the tree. Harper crouched low and stumbled into the shelter. Around her she collected a pile of softball-size stones and held Gwyn's sword ready. She strained her ears for sounds of approach.

"Dumb move. Heading toward the water will only get you trapped." A voice she didn't recognize called to her left.

Water? Harper leaned forward as far as she dared and scanned all around her, but there wasn't any water. She held her breath and listened but heard not even a trickle. But the pitter patter of footfalls faded.

"There she is." Ashley's nasal drone cut through the night air like a foghorn.

"Told you this little adventure was useless." Santaigh's voice had also receded, following the feral's taunts.

Harper wasted no time. Another ten feet of progress and lightheadedness sent her careening into a tree. It was more exhausting to keep standing back up, so she hung over at the waist and let her head dangle between her knees. That's when the tiny green light buzzed in from her right.

"Alina!" She nearly cried with relief.

The will o' wisp squeaked and fluttered off just ahead.

"Alina. Come back." Harper whimpered. Sorrow sapped the last of her will to press forward, so she sank to the ground. She waited for one minute. Then two. Ears straining for signs of pursuit, eyes scanning the woods for a little green light. Nothing.

Ahead, a dull crunch-crunch, like slow footfalls, froze her breath. *Snap. Crunch.* Closer now. Harper slipped the pack from her back with deliberate slowness and laid it on the ground. Her palms sweaty, she wiped them on her pants. Adrenaline sharpened her senses and gave her body an extra kick. Ducking behind a tree, she held Gwyn's sword ready to strike when whatever it was strayed near.

*Click-click. Crunch.* Five feet away. Now or never. Harper hurled herself forward and rushed her attacker.

If her pursuer had been human, her attack would have landed, but Melinoe danced out of the way, sending Harper tumbling, arms wheeling to regain her balance.

"Harper! What are you doing," Melinoe whispered while Alina zoomed circles around Harper's head.

"Melinoe! You found me!"

The glaistig's face lit up. She gripped Harper's shoulders and pressed her face inches from her friend's. "I knew you'd break free. I told Paegrinn there was no way a gancanagh could best you, even if that horrible shapeshifter was actually helping him."

"He wouldn't do that. Where is the Phooka?" Harper asked, her voice barely a whisper.

"We split up to find you. The Phooka wanted to destroy the

gancanagh, or so he says." Melinoe's smile faded, and she shrugged a shoulder. "I asked Paegrinn to stay with Alina and me, but he insisted on going with the Phooka."

"Well, we don't know how many of those half-human things Santaigh has. The Phooka might have needed the reinforcements."

"Or having two gifts for Badb Catha would curry more favor. A Fir Bolg is a handsome prize."

"He wouldn't betray me. He's helped me from the beginning. Killed Badb's Fae for me."

"Your trusting nature is one thing I love about you, Harper, but you understand nothing of Fae games. We play the long con, and sometimes to be convincing, that means the loss of a few on our own side."

Harper shook her head. "No, it isn't like that." But then again, she hadn't known the Phooka long, and Melinoe had a point. Fae culture eluded her. "He had plenty of opportunity, so why not just hand me over to Badb?"

"Before Gwyn's attack on the Fir Bolg, Nuada guarded you. Not even Badb would go directly against him, at least not yet. As her power grows, she'll get bolder."

Harper didn't want to believe her friend was a traitor. "Nuada would have never left me alone with him if..." Even Nuada had challenged the Phooka's faithfulness sometimes.

"How many people have warned you about him? I'd guess pretty many."

Harper ran through in her mind Selina's reaction to the Phooka, Aeld's, and others. Each had warned her. Even Ezrynhivar seemed shocked that she traveled with the shapeshifter. And then there was the fact he'd kept a captive in a lantern. But the thing that raised the most suspicion was his dodging her questions about his motives.

That first night as Gwyn's prisoner, she'd swear she saw his glowing yellow eyes up in the trees. The Wild Hunt held her captive for days. Even tortured her. With Alina, the Phooka could have tracked her, saved her when the Sidhe abused her. Now that she really thought about it, the Phooka didn't add up. She swallowed hard and slumped deeper.

"Oh, sweetie, don't fear. I'll keep you safe." Melinoe smiled her most compassionate smile and rubbed Harper's back.

The clarion call of a hunting horn and the far-off howl of Gwyn's Gabriel hounds silenced the crickets. Harper's heart plummeted. Gwyn must have found their trail.

"Get behind me." Melinoe drew her blade and crouched between Harper and the path.

"They're not close any—"

"Something else. Shhh." The Fae held a finger to her green lips and edged forward.

Harper poised the sword across her chest and scanned the periphery. The blade's tip trembled in her anemic grip.

Footsteps, likely two beings, approached. Moving slowly, in an attempt at stealth, Melinoe motioned Harper to the side to flank their guests when they came nearer. The Fae ducked behind underbrush on the other side.

A tiny green light zoomed overhead and circled around Harper, who exhaled with relief. A couple of seconds later, the familiar yellow glowing eyes of the Phooka flashed in the mist, followed by the hulking shadow of Paegrinn.

Harper stepped from her cover and slid down the trunk of a tree, suddenly too exhausted to stand. "Phooka. Paegrinn. Am I glad to see you. You too, Alina."

Melinoe emerged from her hiding place, her usual bright smile replaced by pressed thin lips and narrowed eyes. She lowered her dagger but maintained her ready stance.

Paegrinn grabbed Harper in a crushing embrace, nearly lifting her up off the forest floor. "You made it out! We were worried."

"Hard to believe you'd be tempted by that bougie Stepford

hell I saw in there." The Phooka sauntered over to her. "I have to admit, I lost a little respect for you." His words were harsh but his smile playful.

"I missed you, too, Phooka. At least eventually." Harper searched the shapeshifter's face for something, anything that might indicate he'd betray her. But all she saw was her wisecracking trickster sidekick. "Did you kill the gancanagh?"

"No." Paegrinn said. "The changed humans were faster and more of an immediate threat. We disabled all but their leader. She fled. After that, the Phooka suggested we find you again." Paegrinn's face fell. The Fir Bolg teen still struggled with violence, even when it was the only option. He rummaged in his bag and brought out a handful of orange dried mushrooms. "Here, eat these. They'll give you some energy."

Harper sniffed them and crinkled her nose at the scent of mold and dirt. Paegrinn flapped his hand at her, and she tossed the whole handful into her mouth. Their flavor was identical to the wretched smell, but some of her strength returned almost instantly.

Melinoe hovered protectively near Harper. "So the Phooka decided to let the most dangerous enemies get away. And now the Wild Hunt has picked up our trail. I wonder why that is?"

Paegrinn lowered his weight to the fallen log and sat. "I don't think it's like that. Alina showed up, showed us the way back to you."

The Phooka let his horned head drop back with a palm resting on his face. "With only the gancanagh and the feral leader left, we'd be safer together in greater numbers. Ever heard of strategy, glaistig?"

Melinoe's eyes flashed. "You let a hungry gancanagh escape."

"Clearly it must be because I'm a dark Fae. Or because I'm a trickster. Or whatever flaw Miss Goody Two-Hooves has dreamed up now." He glowered at Melinoe. "And the Wild Hunt is close by. Again. Isn't the fastest, most bestest tracker in all the three worlds supposed to have covered our trail so our enemies couldn't locate us?"

He changed into the same form as Melinoe, only in shades of grey and black. He tip-toed around Harper, miming overly proper curtseys and exaggerating the glaistig's smile. "Oh Harper, you're just the most greatest awesome brave phantasmagorical human I've ever met. There aren't enough superlatives to describe your magnificence. Harper, the Phooka's bad. Harper, what you did back there was so splendiferous it changed my whole life." He batted his eyelashes and capered about.

Then he popped back into his usual form and stuck his tongue out at Melinoe. "The light usually lay it on thick. Right before they stab you in the back."

She ignored him and stared into the woods, sniffing the air.

Paegrinn covered his ears and looked at Harper. "It didn't get any better when you were with the gancanagh," he said. "I thought about slipping them valerian root so they'd fall asleep and stop bickering."

Alina tittered from the treetop.

More baying from the spectral dogs quieted them immediately. Much closer than before. Gwyn had picked up their trail.

The companions stared at each other, wide eyed.

"The Wild Hunt is never far behind the Phooka. Still think he's innocent?" Melinoe jabbed a finger at the shapeshifter.

# CHAPTER 53

Eileen had wandered for over an hour before the Fir Bolg began meandering along the paths between dwellings to the great hall for their nighttime meal. A single pixie had remained in the Dawn Court's temporary abode, and he'd said the others were out exploring. Eileen walked through most of the cavern, but she found no sign of the Dawn Court Fae.

Her stomach growled at the earthy scent of cooking wafting from the hall. *Well, the Fae have to eat too. Perhaps I'll find Serotina there.* Overhead, incandescent mushrooms swept along the ceiling like multicolored stars. Smiling up at them, she quickened her pace.

The resonant murmur of deep Fir Bolg voices droned in the dining hall. Not as vast as the round structure where they'd taken their communal meals in the forest, the hall still shared the trademarks of Fir Bolg architecture. Conical roof, rustic wooden furniture, and artwork formed from items gathered from the woodland made the structure inviting.

On the far right side, Serotina was whispering into the ear of a tall, red-haired elven man. Eileen took a deep breath and racked her brain for a way to proceed that wouldn't seem utterly awkward and suspicious.

From the opposite side of the hall, Phelan raised a hand and beckoned to her. She waved and pointed to the table laden with food at the end of the oblong room before lowering her head and assessing her approach to the Dawn Queen. The clip-clop of hooves rescued her from further deliberation. She turned just as Latreus, the white satyr, scuttled to her side.

"Eileen!" He beamed and made a deep bow, a hoof placed elegantly in front of him. "I am happy to see you, but I thought you'd returned home."

"Latreus, good to see you too." The nervy satyr clearly hadn't forgotten how she'd defended him from Ezrynhivar's taunts. She inhaled and let her hands fall to her sides. "Part of the plan. I couldn't tell anyone, but I went to find some help."

She was surprised at how easily the lie flowed from her lips. A second ago, she had no clue how she'd explain her return or make a pretense to get to Serotina. As long as the Dawn Fae snubbed Ez's people, she doubted her ruse would be discovered before the trap sprung.

"From whom?" Latreus wrung his hands, eyes narrowing slightly.

"The Fianna." She wagged her head at Phelan's table.

"Oh! My goodness! That is help, indeed." The little satyr rubbed his throat while he swallowed hard. He rose to the tips of his hooves to scan the crowd. He looked decidedly jumpy, especially at the mention of the Fianna. She supposed the satyr would be skittish about people who could become wolves. Then again, perhaps he kept tabs on Lord Ezrynhivar's whereabouts. The Dusk King loved tormenting him.

"One of their leaders is here with me now, the rest are on their way."

"Come. You must share your news with the queen."

Eileen followed him, weaving between benches laden with dining Fir Bolg. When the pair reached the Dawn Court table, Eileen dropped a low curtsy.

Serotina waved her up with a warm smile. She wore a pale-yellow dress with golden leaves and vines embroidered in a sweeping pattern along the bodice and down the full length of the garment. Her green hair wove in and around the leafed branches reaching up from her head. They rustled with every movement, as if blown by an unseen wind.

"Your Majesty, Eileen has news. We may soon be able to leave this place in safety." Latreus's hands clasped behind his back so hard his knuckles turned white.

"Really? And what change in our fortunes has brought this about?" She swept a languid hand to a seat across from her.

Eileen slid onto the bench and hunched forward, eyes sweeping over first her left, then her right shoulder. When she spoke, it was barely a whisper. "The Dawn Court so graciously helped Harper. This is supposed to be a secret..." She paused for dramatic effect.

Every light Fae inched nearer. Serotina's smile dazzled as she rested her branchlike fingers on Eileen's forearm. "The Dawn's interests are for the greater good. You can tell us."

Eileen hung her head and inhaled a long breath. "Aeld sent me to bring reinforcements. Tomorrow, between dawn and noon, more Fianna will arrive. That should give us the cover we need to escape through a secret exit to the east of these caves, not visible from the outside. Then we can all go home and prepare for whatever comes next. The Fir Bolg plan to scatter until the heat dies down, then rebuild their village somewhere new."

The Fae flanking their queen shot her sidelong glances as though waiting for her reaction to decide their response. The red-haired elf dug at his plate with his spoon, while on the other side of the queen, pixies whispered in each other's ears.

Serotina's smile blazed. "This is wonderful news. You have brought such relief to my people."

"Just please don't let Aeld know I told you. His people are frightened and are keeping information close to the chieftain."

Serotina dipped her head. "Of course not. We shall keep your secret."

Across the hall, Phelan's eyes had never left her. Eileen nodded once to him, hoping he'd understand her task was complete. He tapped Aeld on the shoulder. The chieftain bent his ear to the Fianna, then caught Eileen's eye and nodded.

After some pleasantries, Eileen took her leave of the Dawn Court, grabbed some of the hearty food, and seated herself across from Aeld and Phelan. The tightness in her chest eased somewhat. She'd done what she could for now. Still, so much could go wrong. Her heart skipped a beat.

"It's done. Ez thinks the plan is for us to escape to the west, Serotina to the east."

"Now we watch where the Sluagh and the Hunt gather and our mole reveals themself." Phelan said.

"I will spread the word among my people to ready themselves to flee this place, well away from the eyes of our Fae guests."

"I told them both midmorning, to give Hieronymous enough time to arrive," Eileen whispered while twirling the food on her plate.

"They'll be here, and in the meantime, Aisling and Michael guard the exits."

They passed the rest of mealtime in idle conversation, feigning casualness. Later, Eileen slept fitfully on the Fir Bolg cot, while Glani and another snored more softly that would seem possible. Phelan returned to the forest to watch for Hieronymous's approach.

She'd barely fallen asleep when Phelan's hands shook her gently awake. "It's time."

She wiped a hand over her face, her stomach suddenly full of butterflies. Glani and her friend were already gone.

"Where are the others?" Eileen whispered as she followed Phelan along the tunnel leading to the front entry.

"Aeld is at the front entrance. The Fir Bolg are poised and ready to escape the instant the battle begins."

Battle. Eileen hadn't thought of that part, so focused was she on planting her intel. Her success eliminating the Sluagh previously seemed like a fluke, and the familiar internal jelly sensation returned. Suddenly, she wished Ez was there, just for that little boost of glamour to calm her nerves so she didn't royally screw up and cost lives. *No, that's the same as drinking. You can't fight blissed out on Fae glamour. Grit it out.*

Her mouth dried while she strapped the shotgun to her hip and fastened the second strap around her thigh. She crammed a dozen birdshot shells in her pockets and crept along the cavern wall behind Phelan.

The moment she and Phelan emerged from the cave, the undulating calls of something terrible and the clash of weapons grew louder.

"They're attacking from the east," Aeld shouted.

The Dawn Court was working with Badb Catha. Eileen felt the color drain from her face. "Melinoe," she whispered.

Her daughter was in terrible danger.

# CHAPTER 54

"You shameless lit—" The Phooka's yellow eyes flared, and he launched himself at Melinoe, shifting into a wolf's form midleap.

Paegrinn, ever the peacekeeper, stepped between them and grabbed the Phooka by his scruff. The Fae hung in the Fir Bolg's massive hand and shifted back to his natural shape, hooves dangling two feet from the ground.

"You see? When the truth is spoken, what else can he do but attack?" Melinoe spat each word like they were bitter. "Harper, I care what happens to you. Please come with me and leave this dark Fae behind." She held an amber-tinged hand out to Harper. "Come, the Wild Hunt is close. They'll catch us soon."

"He did nothing wrong here," Paegrinn said, his voice calm, ignoring Melinoe's urgency.

"I was in Santaigh's grove for days. Gwyn had plenty of time to track us while you all tried to reach me," Harper said, but in her mind she reviewed the litany of warnings and all the red flags. She didn't even realize she'd taken a step away from the Phooka until she pressed close to Melinoe.

"No. Gwyn probably tracked *him* here." Melinoe jabbed her

finger at him. "It was he who ran off. Supposedly to chase after Santaigh's mist-changed servants. Plenty of opportunity to signal his true master. To follow you here. Kill you or capture you himself. Badb Catha would reward him with a lot of power if he laid you at her feet, but he's not powerful enough to accomplish that alone. He'd need all his trickster talents to make you believe he's your friend, all while leading your enemies to your doorstep."

The Phooka screeched and flailed his hooves, slapping his hands against Paegrinn's grip. "That's the most preposterous thing I've ever heard. From the moment I found you, I've protected you. Please. Harper." A new wave of thrashing sent him spinning impotently in Paegrinn's grasp. "Put me down, you galoot. I've got a glaistig to kill."

"Phooka!" Harper's jaw hung open, and she looked at her friend as though seeing him for the first time. The Fae's eyes blazed, and drool slipped from the corners of his mouth. She feared if he got free from Paegrinn, he would kill Melinoe. And he was capable of it. Just morph into a dragon again. They'd all be toast.

Harper took a steadying breath. "Phooka. Melinoe. No one is attacking or killing anyone. Or turning anyone over to Badb Catha. Is that clear?"

Melinoe averted her gaze. "All the time he's been with you, even with Nuada there, I'll bet danger was never far away. He found you because he's probably been hunting you for a while."

"See! She wants to harm me, she dodged the question."

Harper squinted at the Phooka. "What aren't you telling me? From the moment I met you, you seemed to know me. The way you stared at me in that alley... Like you'd been searching...". Harper chewed her bottom lip and her pulse quickened. If Melinoe was right, the threat to her life and her family had always been greater than she'd known.

The Phooka's hands fell to his side and his rabbit ears hung limp around his face. "Harper, please, this is—"

Harper took another step back from him. "Answer my question."

The glaistig's yellow-green eyes glittered, and she stepped beside Harper, positioning herself sideways between Harper and the Phooka.

Some of the fire flickered out of the Phooka's eyes and he stopped straining in Paegrinn's clutch. "Harper, you know I'd never harm you. After what we've been through together, how could you think—"

"Everyone, we can't fix this until we're all calm." Paegrinn let the Phooka's hooves touch the ground but maintained a firm grip on the scruff of his neck.

"And you see how artfully he dodged answering you, Harper. So masterfully he appeals to your feelings." Melinoe bared her teeth at the Phooka. "This is what he does. He'll manipulate you right to Badb's tower and hand you right over."

The Phooka growled. Black fur rippled and ballooned out. His muzzle jutted forward and broke out in scales while he sprouted black, leathery wings. Harper gasped. He was going to do it, change into something big and nasty and attack the glaistig. Her too, for all she knew.

"Oh no, you don't." Melinoe dug into her dress pocket and flung a handful of sand at him.

With a pop, the Phooka snapped into his normal form, gnashing his teeth and shouting words none of them understood. Paegrinn surged forward to hold him back.

"Phooka! Leave Melinoe alone," Harper said. "I can't believe it." But suddenly, in her heart, she did. She pressed a hand to her abdomen to suppress the churning.

The Phooka dropped to his knees and sat on his hooves. His back curled so that his head hung almost to the ground. Beside him, Paegrinn maintained his hold on him in case he lunged at Melinoe again, but the Fae looked utterly dejected.

After a couple of seconds, the shapeshifter lifted his face. "Harper. Listen to me, you can't believe her. I've been by your side. After all this time I found you." His voice was strained, and he looked genuinely stricken, but that could just part of the act.

"You see? Like I suspected, he's been hunting you for a long time. Did he tell you that before now?" Melinoe didn't wait for an answer. "Of course not. It's either a meaningless truth or as close to a lie as he can get."

Paegrinn shook his head. "I don't think he'd do that."

"No offense, but you're a teenager with no past interactions with Fae kind." Melinoe's voice was gentle, like she explained something to a small child.

Paegrinn's expression was unreadable as his head swiveled between the two Fae.

Harper stepped to the Phooka. Paegrinn was holding him, so she felt it safe. She peered into his bright yellow eyes, trying to scry the truth from them, but she couldn't. The Phooka's chest rose and fell in a rapid pant.

"Harper." His voice was almost a whisper. The long tail lashed, leaving tracks in the dry pine needles.

"Phooka, just answer the question." Harper kept her gaze on his eyes.

"He won't answer because he probably swore to Badb he wouldn't," Melinoe said.

"That's not true. In time, my motives will become clear. You see, we—" The shapeshifter scrunched up his features and formed his lips into an O shape. His neck strained forward several times, and short grunts were all that came out.

Harper tilted her head. That was odd, even for the Phooka.

Melinoe cackled. "He just tried to lie."

The Phooka scowled and picked up a stick, swiping the pine

needles aside. The stick scraped at the dirt as the Phooka scrawled a message. *No betray you because—* The makeshift pencil froze. He coiled his other hand around it and pushed, straining, but no more words appeared.

Melinoe scoffed. "Can't write a lie either, everyone knows that."

The Phooka sagged. "I want to tell you, but I can't because I made a promise. Please trust me, Harper. I've defended you since the day we met." His eyes misted over. Long fingers toyed with the tuft at the end of his tail.

Melinoe snorted. "For himself."

Harper slashed an arm to silence her. "Promise to who?"

The Phooka only shrunk further and shook his head.

Harper squeezed her eyes shut. Fae couldn't lie. And the Phooka couldn't tell her what she wanted to know, probably because he'd been working for Badb all along. The lengths he went to, to pretend to be her friend, fake rescues from their enemies. She didn't want to believe it despite the damning evidence Melinoe lined out against him.

She supposed his trickster mojo was really that good. How he'd bamboozled Nuada would probably end up a ballad in the annals of phooka trickery.

"There it is then. You will never get a straight answer out of him. Question is, given all the warnings, all you've seen, do you trust him?" Melinoe smiled at the Phooka.

Harper slumped and avoided the Phooka's eyes. "No."

"Harper, please." His voice squeaked. His front feet lifted off the ground as he tried to crawl toward Harper, but Paegrinn held him in place.

"Harper, this is a misunderstanding. We all just need time to cool down. You've been through a very confusing ordeal," Paegrinn said.

"No, Paegrinn. Melinoe's right." Harper looked up at the poor will o' wisp prisoner perched on a high branch above. "I can't risk trusting him. Even if part of me wants to."

She turned to face the Phooka again. He let his forehead fall forward to rest on his furry knees. "I'm sorry, Phooka, but here is where we part ways. Maybe once I find Emilio..."

The Phooka's shoulders hitched, and he refused to meet her eyes. "You don't understand any of this. But I forgive you, Harper."

"Forgive her, for what?" Melinoe sounded incredulous.

"For being naïve." His eyes flashed at Melinoe. "And for trusting *you*. I'll never forgive you, Melinoe, and I'll stop you." His hackles stood on end and his hands formed claws, scraping tiny trenches in the dirt. He didn't try another attack, and Harper was glad. That was a conflict she hoped to avoid.

Melinoe drew her blade and pivoted toward the shapehifter.

Harper skidded between them. "Oh no. No one harms him."

"But he'll follow us. Betray you again."

Paegrinn hovered protectively over the shapeshifter. "You'll have to go through me."

"Fine. Your mistake." Melinoe nodded and beckoned. Harper pushed herself up and straightened her pack. "Come on, Paegrinn. Tie him to that tree and we'll get out of here."

The Fir Bolg shook his shaggy head, his eyes pools of sadness. "I have to stay with the Phooka. It would be wrong to leave him in this place alone and undefended."

"Paegrinn..." Harper reached up a hand toward his cheek.

"I only came to find you, and we did. My dad probably misses me, so I should head home, anyway. I'll take care of the Phooka."

"We could really use your help." Harper didn't want her Fir Bolg friend to go, but she supposed the choice was his.

"Well, I can tell my dad that Nuada was right about all of it. Maybe then he'll join you."

"When this is over, I can sneak you into the city and take some videos of us." Harper's smile came out more like a wince.

A broad grin crept over the Fir Bolg's face. He reached into the outer pocket of his bag and pulled out the tiny Lego Batman. "Hopefully we can see a Batman movie. The Phooka told me of his legendary feats."

Harper nodded and flung her arms around her furry friend. "Thank you, Paegrinn, for everything."

"Harper, we need to leave. It's not safe here." Melinoe was beckoning her from the other side of the clearing.

"I know you'll save your friend," Paegrinn said as Harper drew away.

The Phooka sat nearby, legs clasped in his long-fingered hands, forehead resting on his knees. All the defiance and anger had drained from him and he just looked small.

"Goodbye, Phooka." Then Harper turned and followed Melinoe into the woods.

# CHAPTER 55

Eileen sprinted behind Phelan, the shotgun unholstered and pointed safely at the ground but ready to fire. As they neared the cave's entrance, he motioned her against the cavern wall. The Fir Bolg would soon arrive and flank Serotina's contingent from both sides.

"Slow now. Be ready."

She nodded. Her stomach clenched and her heart pounded. Her new family depended on her. None of the Dawn Court could be allowed to escape or the Fir Bolg's last haven was lost. Ahead of her, Phelan whipped a short sword from beneath his coat.

Eileen copied Phelan's low stance and slid behind him. The rock wall scratched her clothing as she crept, back pressed against its fortifying solidity.

The mouth of the cave yawned and the clang of battle carried through the forest from the wrong direction. Serotina and her people had moved west. Any outside reinforcement she called should be to the east. A skirmish meant something had gone terribly awry, and she was going into battle for a second time.

Phelan's eyes focused ahead, but he lifted his palm to halt their approach, then motioned her to his side.

"We don't want to linger in the cave's mouth. No idea what's out there," he whispered.

"What do we do?"

"Stay tight to the wall. I'll go to the other side. When I give the signal, I'll step out and drop behind the boulder at the front. You cover me." He held his hand and made a quick chop. "Once I say it's clear, you do the same on the right."

"Got it."

"Any baddies come at us, shoot them."

She nodded with a wince. Sweaty hands made the shotgun feel like a bar of soap, slippery and cold.

"Look, if this is too much, stay inside. I'll come for you when it's over."

"Nope. Let's do it."

Phelan checked behind him, loped across the cavern, and pushed his back up against the other side.

Eileen took a deep breath and held it for a moment before exhaling slowly through pursed lips. Her hands steadied slightly.

The pair hovered just inside the cave. The illusion of the boulder was all that stood between them and the shouts and ring of metal on metal growing outside.

Phelan gave the signal and shot out of the cave mouth, hugging the wall, his blade across his body.

"Clear," he said.

Eileen mirrored his movements, dropping behind a fallen tree. The din of battle echoed from the far side of the hill. She stretched her neck so just her head showed over the log and searched the clearing.

No Sluagh or Wild Hunt. A high whistle rang out in the forest ahead. She dropped back down and clutched the gun.

To her left, an answering whistle came from Phelan. Aeld

and a trio of Fir Bolg strode out of the underbrush. Aeld nodded at Phelan. "Sluagh attacked us the moment we ran for the woods."

Eileen inhaled sharply. "Anyone hurt?"

"No, we defeated them."

"Get anyone who can't fight back into the shelter of the cavern entrance," Phelan said. "By the sound of it, Hieronymous has confined the rest of the fight to the west."

Aeld nodded and motioned his friends into the cave. He gripped his spear and joined Phelan.

"The Fae will think we fled into the woods. Most of my people can fight if we must, so we'll be ready to serve should the battle demand it."

"It's a good plan." Phelan turned to Eileen. "Care for another ride, milady?"

Eileen scanned the trees above before joining them. She nodded and holstered the Mossberg.

"Better take this." He handed her the blade. "Anything comes close, slash them with it."

The tattoo was hidden beneath his leather duster, but she knew it sprang to life when Phelan the wolf bounded to her and she leapt onto his back. One hand gripped his ruff, the other held the sword. With a lurch he took off. Aeld, Fengre, and five others loped beside him, spears in hand.

They'd covered a lot of ground when screams erupted behind them. Aeld was wrong. The Sluagh must have hidden, and now they were attacking the hiding villagers.

Aeld growled and spun to race back to the front entrance, his fighters close behind. "We'll join you if we can," he bellowed over his shoulder.

Phelan yipped and skidded, legs cartwheeling beneath him with the sudden change in direction. Apparently, they were backing up the Fir Bolg. Eileen lurched, her leg came free and she slid partway down Phelan's back. He slowed, giving her a chance to regain her grip.

Her stomach plummeted with every stride he took. A trio of screeching birds dove for her just as she righted herself on Phelan's back.

She shrieked and pressed herself down against the Fianna's fur. *Very brave. You're useless, Eileen.* Without breaking rhythm, Aeld swung his spear and caught the nearest avian Sluagh. It screamed and slammed to the ground.

Eileen slashed blindly with the sword. The other two stopped dive-bombing and soared ahead.

Dozens of Fir Bolg were clustered at the front of the cave, ringed by Sluagh, banshee, and incubi. The Dawn Court must have some way to remain in communication with Badb's forces for them to already be here.

Phelan careened to a halt and Eileen hopped off his back. Her legs felt rubbery as she tossed human Phelan his sword and unholstered her shotgun.

Aeld bellowed and charged the line of gaunt Sluagh. He moved fast for his bulk.

"That gun full of birdshot?" Phelan clasped one hand around Eileen's wrist while the other brandished the blade.

"Yeah." Eileen clicked off the safety and froze.

Phelan shook her. "Focus. You stay back here. If you get a clear shot, you take it, understand."

Wide eyed, her head bobbed once. Her voice refused to come.

Phelan nodded and sprinted into the skirmish. The Fir Bolg were outnumbered, but the bulk of the Sluagh's forces were shambling former humans, easier to neutralize.

A piercing ring filled Eileen's ears, and her breath rasped like sandpaper in her mouth. *Not this.* She was panicking. The Mossberg's barrel trembled. *It'll be my fault if we fail, and Harper will pay the price. Again.*

A deep scream snapped her focus to her right. One of the spectral women slashed long claws across the throat of a Fir Bolg warrior. He fell, gurgling, to the ground. The Sluagh swarmed him, some in their bird shapes, some in human shape. Mouths wide, they inhaled shimmering spirals of light from the man.

*Oh God, this is how they feed. I'm so sorry.*

"Eileen!" Phelan yelled and pointed to a cluster of incubi and the ghostly women screaming straight for her.

Time slowed. Everything but her attackers faded away. Like she moved underwater, she brought the gun up, sighted to the center of the approaching horde, and pulled the trigger. Once. Twice.

The shots echoed off the surrounding mountains and bellows of rage and screams of agony rose from the Sluagh's ranks.

In front of her, bodies stretched like rag dolls tossed carelessly. Next to them, the wounded writhed and screeched and clawed deep gouges in their own skin in a vain attempt to dig out the steel before they died.

More Sluagh snarled behind them, taking a run at her. Hot tears streamed down her cheeks, this time not from regret for her kills, but from surging adrenaline. Everything in her peripheral vision darkened, and every muscle twitched.

"You're dead, human," an incubus bellowed.

Hysterical laughter tumbled from Eileen as she cracked the shotgun open and fished out a fresh pair of shells. "You first," she shouted and snapped the weapon together, but wet, tremoring hands caused her to fumble it and it clattered to the ground.

Two giant wolves rushed into the incubi, teeth gnashing. Eileen clawed for the gun, her vision blurry.

An incubus bore down on her. She leveled the Mossberg at the creature.

"Really? You're going to shoot me? We don't all look the same, you know."

"Ez?" Eileen shuddered and lowered the weapon.

Behind him, his entourage swept over the ridge and into the fray. The ones who could fly joined the solitary Fae in taking to the skies to dispatch the escaping birdlike Sluagh.

He shot her a dazzling grin. "You're a wreck."

She clutched handfuls of blue sparkling fabric. "Glamour me like last time. I'm crawling out of my skin." Even as she said it, monstrous guilt broke free of its cage.

The King of the Dusk Court flashed her a hungry smile and pulled her close. "Delighted." The effect was instant. The paralysis cleared and her hearing returned to normal, but it was the gentle euphoria that melted all the tension of the battle away, just like a double shot of Smirnoff's.

Eileen shoved her guilt back down and pulled out of Ez's embrace. "Your Court joined the conflict?"

"I'd wager you're shocked it isn't my people joining the Sluagh." He tossed his arm over his chest and drooped before flashing her a toothy grin. "It's become more of a pursuit." He pointed to the fracas.

Mercifully, the battle was mostly over. Fintan and Hieronymous had defeated their foes and flanked the Sluagh from the other side. Now vastly outnumbered, the Sluagh scattered into the forest, pursued by wolves, Fir Bolg, and every shape of Fae imaginable.

"Shall we see how many notches you can add to your belt?" Ez said.

"At least twenty. How many did you get?" Eileen still didn't enjoy the brutality of her shooting, but rage at the duplicitous Serotina and grief for the fallen Fir Bolg were enough of a moral compass. She was a protector now, and that suited her. She hadn't truly needed Ezrynhivar's hit of glamour at all.

"Half that, but you cheated." He lifted a black long sword. "I had to kill mine one by one. Fascinating change of heart. May I ask what caused it?"

Eileen smiled. "Just some things I had to work through."

"You think she cares for you, incubus?" Phelan stepped beside her and rested a hand on her shoulder. Aeld followed behind.

"King. And yes. Eileen and I became quite close during the harrowing experiences we've shared." Ezrynhivar's red eyes sparkled.

"Well, *King* Incubus. Eileen, Aeld, and I have much to discuss. Alone." Phelan pulled her away from the Dusk King.

"Eileen, my sweet, tell your dog to heel—"

Phelan closed the distance between them in a flash. His face hovered inches from Ez's and he snarled.

Eileen pushed her arms between them and levered them aside from each other. "Really?"

"We have no time for bellicosity." Hieronymous strode to join them, festooned in shining silver armor over a velvet tunic. He held a long chain in one of his paws. At the other end, Queen Serotina sulked.

"You?" Eileen looked at the bedraggled queen. "I truly believed it was him." Eileen pointed over her shoulder at Ez.

Phelan laughed and smirked at Ezrynhivar.

The Dusk King feigned indignation. "If you'd learned anything, I thought it would be dark does not always mean evil."

"Nor does light mean good. It wasn't my intention to offend you, Ez."

Eileen's heart skipped a beat. She pulled out the Lia Fail shard and held it up to her face. Still it glowed. She clenched the stone in her fist hard enough to hurt and rounded on the Dawn Queen, eyes flashing.

"Melinoe. Did you send her to kill my daughter?"

Serotina focused her gaze over Eileen's head and shifted her weight.

"Answer me, or I swear to God, I'm coming back here with a chainsaw."

Serotina held her chin in the air and refused to look at Eileen, but she tilted her head toward Ezrynhivar. "It's still not too late to join us."

"I serve no one." Ez's eyes darkened. "You're a traitor."

"I made this deal to preserve *my* people. No one from the Dawn Court will be killed to keep the gateway open. Meanwhile, Badb will hunt and drain the Dusk Court alongside the solitaries. At least then you'll finally be of service to your people."

Eileen felt her face flush. "You sold us all out just to save yourselves?"

Phelan laid a hand in the center of her back. "You won't get any answers out of her."

"How many of your people were lost?" Hieronymous asked as he passed Aeld a canteen.

"Six. Between all these clashes with the Wild Hunt and Sluagh, a quarter of our village has died. And we have nowhere else we can go that hasn't been compromised." The Fir Bolg took a long pull of water and handed it back to the ogre.

"Then come with us to Sauvie. Maybe Paegrinn is there, and we'll stop this now." Eileen marked her words with a clenched fist.

Aeld's face softened. "Our time for fighting is past."

"After all that's happened, how can you still say that? The lass is right. The only choice you have is whether you bring the fight to them, or if it comes to you," Phelan said.

"Aeld, I'm begging you. Help me find my daughter. She's in even more danger now that the Dawn Court has betrayed us all."

Aeld shuffled his feet, the conflict evident on his thick features.

"Uuuugh!" Eileen half yelled through gritted teeth. She kicked a rock. She was angry with herself for the tears that brimmed in her eyes. This was no time to project weakness.

"Well, let no one say that the dark Fae have no sense of honor."

Lord Ezrynhivar flicked his leathery wings, brought a long whistle to his lips, and blew a high tone. "I'd shudder to think this vegetative bitch would be on the same side as the Dusk Court. Any of my people in answering distance of my call will join your crusade to rescue your charming daughter."

Hieronymous drew himself straight and beckoned to his people. "I don't have many warriors among the solitary Fae, but we, too, shall join you. You are right, Eileen, Badb Catha threatens us all. We must protect the heir at all costs."

Eileen's heart soared. Finally, she could do something to help Harper.

All eyes fell on Aeld. "Old friend, you can change your mind."

The chieftain pressed his lips together. "I cannot pledge to enter this fight." Groans rose all around him. The Fir Bolg held up a finger. "But a contingent of my warriors will accompany you to Sauvie to bring back Harper, and my son if he still lives. We cannot ignore your service to us, Eileen."

Eileen smiled through her tears. "Thank you, Aeld."

She had accomplished what she feared was impossible. She had raised a small army; now she needed to find her daughter.

# CHAPTER 56

Sweating and exhausted from more drills controlling ever-larger groups of Dusted humans, Emilio savored his lunch. Not just the rich flavors, but the chance to sit and allow his mind to be empty, not filled with the slow thoughts of a dozen drugged-out puppets.

A pair of goblins guarded the door from the outside, and a redcap and kelpie leaned against opposite walls, not even bothering to hide their disdain each time they glanced at their wards, between rolls of their game of dice.

At least they were far enough away, and engrossed in whatever game they played, not to overhear the Netherfae's discussion. All four friends slumped over their plates and leaned close to talk in low tones.

"You sure you were in the city last night?" Tamika's eyes glimmered in the bright overhead light.

"Yes, I heard traffic, and Breas confirmed our presence at Erimus's downtown headquarters."

Alan perked up. "Can we find the door to Portland and get out?"

Emilio swallowed a mouthful of sweet bread. "Doubtful. We'd

trade one problem for another. They'll guard the Portland office too, then there's the difficulty accessing the passage from the island and moving many people through."

Bright bluebells bloomed in Tamika's purple hair. "Don't worry, Alan, we'll escape some other way."

"You maintained contact that whole time? That's a gigantic leap in your range, Tamika." Selina's dark hair tumbled into her face when she shifted her weight on the bench. Her clawed hand worked it back into place.

Emilio grinned. "Yes, and I may know why." He lifted his chest a little to check that the redcap and his kelpie friend were still engrossed in their dice game.

Alan edged out of his usual slumped posture and leaned closer to Emilio. "Is Tamika getting stronger?"

"I don't think that's it." Emilio stirred the bread pudding on his plate. "We thought her ability to draw us into the mindspace was because of our, I don't know, *spiritual* connection. Or potentially our proximity."

"It feels like I can reach you because of our emotional bonds." Tamika took a bite of the mixed vegetables and glanced over her shoulder at the Fae arguing over some game element.

"When I was with Breas, I found a strand of your hair on my sleeve. When I picked off, your kiddie room disappeared." Emilio's fork poised over his plate.

Selina hunched her shoulders, hiding her face from the guards. "A physical connection is stronger?"

Emilio bobbed his head. "That's my working theory."

Alan pinched his features and scratched his mossy beard.

"We should test it," Emilio said. "Maybe if we all trade bits of clothing, strands of hair, things that have touched us, we can extend Tamika's range."

"Do we each need a piece of all the others?" Alan asked.

"I don't think so," Tamika said, shaking her head. "Each

connection is separate. Not dependent on the others. At least that's how it feels."

Selina's eyebrow inched up. "Has the iron made it into your feathers yet?"

Emilio shrugged. "No way to tell without tipping my hand. We have to hope they can break the torques when the time is right."

"We should hurry and finish our lunch before evil Legolas out there gets suspicious." Emilio tipped his head to the hallway.

"So we simply pass off our little talismans surreptitiously," Selina said.

Emilio checked their guards. "Shouldn't be too difficult."

"And what did you discover in the secret lab, boy genius?" Selina scraped the last drop of savory sauce from her plate with a bit of bread.

"Not sure. Best guess, they're resurrecting something."

All three of his friends widened their eyes.

"What sort of thing?" Alan mumbled.

Emilio glanced at Alan. "No idea. I couldn't see through the vapors coming off the tank. But whatever it is, the sample is degraded. Breas must have an alternate source of DNA to fill in the gaps or the culture wouldn't grow."

"Why would he do such a thing?" Tamika looked like she was about to gag. She'd been the only other one capable of seeing into the tank through Emilio.

"It's a weapon. It has to be," Selina whispered.

"And one Breas does not want Badb to discover," Emilio added. "There has to be a way to use that information, but I haven't figured out how."

"Trade it to Badb for our freedom." Alan's eyes looked sad.

"Pffft!" Selina waved her hand and rolled her eyes. "She'd only betray us. She won't let her new weapons waltz out of this tower."

Tamika risked another look at their wiry guards. "Looks like their game's done. They'll be coming for us soon."

They finished the rest of their meal in silence. The creak of the brass hinges meant training session number two was about to begin.

"Slop time is over, Netherfae hogs." Callon, always so charming.

Emilio levered himself to his feet and stretched. Across the room, Tamika clicked her butterfly wings and ran fingers through her gleaming purple hair.

Emilio shuffled past her, rubbing his forehead. As his hand swept to the edge of his hairline, he snapped out one of his tiny feathers for Tamika. When she bumped into him, he slipped it into the pocket on her scrubs while she pressed a strand of purple hair into his palm.

Emilio paused. He hadn't worked out how the pieces fit together in Escape Plan: The Sequel. Everything depended on a coordinated effort between Fae prisoners and Netherfae. Destroying the secret weapon would be a great bonus.

Perhaps Tamika could pull Alphine into the mindspace if he exchanged bits of their clothing or hair with her. But with his movements so tightly controlled, he doubted they'd be able to get to Alphine. Emilio's temples throbbed like they always did when he chased his tail over some irascible mathematical proof or scientific roadblock. For now, his best bet was to learn what he could, then sabotage Breas's secret project as an added bonus. Hopefully, in a way that didn't end in his own death.

# CHAPTER 57

Harper's mind warred with itself. Minutes after she sent the Phooka away, the look of utter despair on the little Fae's face melted her resolve. She plodded silently along behind Melinoe as they wove their way through the sprawling wood, the good times with the Phooka replaying in her mind.

Their first meeting in the alley when he'd leapt between her glamoured self and the kelpie. His actions shattered the glamour and denied Badb her prize. He'd fought off the Wild Hunt with her more than once. Would he really do that if he was working for Badb Catha all along? Maybe. Perhaps the shapeshifter was a double agent. When her magical power blossomed at Mystic Island, her capture may have seemed far less certain, so, better to have an insurance policy on the inside.

With that thought, the lens through which she sorted her memories shifted again, and she recalled the parade of warnings about the Phooka. Yet Paegrinn chose to remain with him. She couldn't imagine the Fir Bolg youth misjudging someone so completely.

She drew in a long, weary breath, and the cycle began again.

"Oh Harper, you're such a sweetheart. Worrying about him, aren't you?" Melinoe slowed their pace and strode shoulder to shoulder. Her eyes radiated concern.

"I'm not one hundred percent certain I made the right decision is all." Her hand flipped the zipper on her jacket up and down.

"Then let me be sure for both of us. Dark Fae are never to be trusted."

"Without Paegrinn and the Phooka, how will we free Emilio once we get to the tower? You and I won't be enough to accomplish anything." She had to face the reality that she had no plan. Her every move across this cursed land had been survival. She'd had little time to figure out what she'd do once she arrived. Two against a host of Fae and a demigod. She really missed the Phooka now. This would be the time he'd make a wisecrack or cook up a crazy plan.

"Please don't be sad, Harper. Two more of us wouldn't make a difference."

Harper wasn't sure she agreed. The Phooka's shapeshifting ability and Paegrinn's strength were definite assets.

"I'm Fae, remember. I could use my glamour to control some humans and sneak your friend out, or fight our way in through a less guarded entrance. There's a way and we'll find it." Melinoe's hand started toward Harper's shoulder but drew back when the glaistig glanced at the steel spikes bristling along the leather.

Harper managed a slow nod. A wave of exhaustion caused her leg to buckle and she staggered, catching herself against a particularly twisty and vaguely familiar tree.

Melinoe dropped beside her. "Please forgive me. I've been horribly insensitive. In my rush to get you away from the Phooka's betrayal, I forgot about your weakened state."

"Paegrinn's mushrooms helped. Um, haven't we passed this tree before?" Harper looked up at the thick, lumpy trunk and scanned the top. A part of her hoped to discover two yellow eyes gleaming back at her, but only darkness and patches of mist hung.

Melinoe's eyes narrowed and the cheery visage fell for an instant before she beamed wider than before. "I don't think so. There were a lot of trees like that in the Underworld. I know just where we are. When you were captive, I scouted ahead when I could."

"I guess you must be right." But Harper wasn't certain. At all.

"After that horrible ordeal with the gancanagh, you still need rest. We've probably put enough distance between us and the Phooka that we can breathe for a moment. There's a clearing just ahead, about a quarter mile."

Melinoe was at least right about that. Rest sounded perfect. Harper clambered to her feet and rubbed her hands on her pants. The backpack had shifted when she stumbled. With a hop, she centered it between her shoulder blades and trailed behind Melinoe.

The creak of branches and rustle of leaves followed, despite the still air. From behind, a high, clear howl sent goosebumps racing across Harper's flesh. It sounded more canine than Fae. It sounded exactly like the Gabriel hounds.

Melinoe froze and craned her neck, green hair sweeping backward over her shoulder. "Hurry. We need the high ground ahead so I can weave a spell to keep us safe." She jabbed a finger toward the tree line behind Harper.

"Sounded like Gwyn's dogs."

"Banshee? Wolf? Something else?" Melinoe shrugged and quickened her pace.

Harper had to jog to pace the Fae.

Snap.

Crack.

Breaking branches to each side. Another howl rang out. Harper's hands shook. Now she had to sprint to keep up with

Melinoe. Farther and farther ahead the glaistig pulled, brown-furred legs like pistons.

"Melinoe," she called in a harsh whisper, but Melinoe disappeared around a slight bend in the animal trail they'd been following. The Fae must have forgotten Harper wasn't near as fast as a glaistig.

Breathing ragged, legs burning, she raced down the path. Less than a minute passed, and the trees gave way to a small clearing. She skidded to a halt and yelped. Her fingers scrambled for her weapon, but pale hands seized her from either side, pinning her in place, covering her mouth and nose.

Harper thrashed and tried to yell for the Phooka and Paegrinn, but only a muffled scream whistled between the hands of the two black-haired elves who held her fast.

"You're late, glaistig." Gwyn ap Nudd stood, his leather boot resting against a boulder, brown cloak rustling behind him.

# CHAPTER 58

Everyone looked expectantly at Eileen, as though she should be the one to decide what to do next. None of this was within her wheelhouse; the parts that were she'd already completed. She'd used her limited corporate espionage background to root out the betrayers and had maneuvered the Fir Bolg one step closer to entering the war.

And essentially relapsed on Fae magic. She was doubly not the one to be handing out advice.

"Um, well... I think the next step has to be getting onto the island. After that I'm fresh out of ideas." She lowered herself to sit on a fallen log before her quaking legs gave out. Phelan rested a comforting hand on her shoulder. She couldn't look at him. Ez's glamour still eased the hard edges of battle, reminding her that Phelan admired her, and that she'd crumbled.

Hieronymous beckoned a thin Fae with rose petals framing her face. She stood taller even than the ogre. "Time may be shorter than we believed. Dewberry, please relay to the company what you told me."

The slender Fae stepped into the center of the assembly.

"Badb's Sidhe elves and creatures we'd never before seen attacked one of our city sanctuaries the night before last." Dewberry told them about the Netherfae and how Badb's lab experiments had betrayed their overlords by sending her back to Hieronymous.

For once, Lord Ezrynhivar's flippant exterior fell completely. "If this is true, Badb Catha has overcome all the weaknesses of the Fae around iron and city warfare. They'll have an instant army wherever Dust has touched."

Dewberry's petals shuddered. "And they're growing more by the day. If we can't stop them now, the world, human and Green World Fae, will fall. The Netherfae told me as much as they knew about where her tower lies on the island. I can guide you close."

"Time is of the essence. Sauvie is more than a day on foot," Aeld said.

Eileen's heart constricted. She hadn't thought of that. How were the huge Fir Bolg going to pass through the more urban parts of Portland that stretched between them and the island?

"I've got that covered." Hieronymous placed his clawed hand to his lips and let out a shrill whistle that echoed off the mountains.

The ground beneath their feet trembled, and a chorus of roaring and screeching arose from all directions. Eileen ducked, throwing her hands over her head. Massive forms flapped overhead, circled, and landed between the trees and boulders.

Beside her, Phelan smiled and whooped, fist pounding the air. "We're flying in style, lass!" He laughed.

Eileen's jaw hung slack. The woods filled with dragons and smaller beasts. Some with feathers. Others looked like a collage of different animals. She couldn't imagine flying on the backs of those things.

"What are they?"

"Dragons, wyverns, and griffins. Too big to fight in the woods but sturdy enough to carry all of us to your daughter." Phelan pulled her along behind him near a shimmering grey dragon that had to be bigger than a barge. He ran a hand along the beast's scales, and the dragon let out a low rumble.

Phelan smiled. "Aw, she likes me."

"Don't suppose she has seatbelts?"

Hieronymous smoothed the wing feathers of a griffin. "This won't be easy. The island is more like the Underworld now, far vaster than it once was. In addition, Badb Catha has it bound with protections and wards."

Eileen's heart skipped a beat. "What does that mean?"

"It means first, we may be swimming the last few feet to the island, because nothing that flies can get close without Badb's permission. And second, once we arrive on the island, finding Harper will be akin to searching for the proverbial needle in a haystack."

Eileen's shoulders drooped. "We can't have come this far only to fail."

Aeld twitched his fingers and a thread of mycelium arced from the earth to wind itself around his hand. "The fungal network stretches under the earth like a nervous system. We use it to heal but also to communicate. Once we're on the island, we might be able to use it to locate Harper."

"That's a big if." Fintan's grey beard face flashed a mischievous grin. Behind him, the other Fianna nodded. "Given the sudden growth of the island, the network may not be continuous."

Eileen dropped her forehead into her palms.

"But we can track anything, even in the Underworld," Aisling said, and tapped her nose.

"But don't you need something with her scent?" Eileen lifted her face to her pink-haired friend.

Phelan tapped his own nose. "Picked it up when I was in your house, but if you have anything of hers for my friends, it would help."

"I do." Eileen rummaged in the bottom of her backpack and

pulled out a small stuffed giraffe. She smoothed its fuzzy mane before handing it to Phelan.

One by one the Fianna brought the toy to their noses, then passed the doll to the next. When all had her scent, Phelan passed it back to Eileen.

The Fir Bolg warriors were already perched on the biggest dragons, three or four deep. The Fae without wings shared the smaller griffins and wyverns, while the Fianna climbed aboard the creatures with the fewest other passengers.

Eileen clutched the Lia Fail shard so tight her knuckles were white. She hadn't realized she'd slid a few steps away from the grey dragon. Jagged teeth and long claws were things she wanted to avoid.

"Come now, Eileen, it won't bite...much." Lord Ezrynhivar's silken voice behind her caused her to jump and yelp. She shot him a frown. Phelan leapt onto the dragon's back and held a hand down to her. He placed her trembling hand in his and hauled her onto the beast's back.

"Just hang on to me, Eileen. I won't let you fall," Phelan said over his shoulder. Not that she needed to be told. She already had his waist in a vise grip.

"And if he fails, I'll catch you." Ez unfurled his leathery wings and gave them a languid flap.

She didn't get the chance to answer the Dusk King because the dragon crouched low, then hurled itself at the sky. Her stomach lurched, and she buried her face in Phelan's jacket to stifle a scream.

Beneath her, she felt the dragon's muscles work with every stroke. The creature's wings flapped faster than Eileen thought something of its size would, then slowed. She felt their ascent level off the way she had in an airplane. The cool wind whipped her cheeks and sent her hair swirling over her face.

"You okay back there?" Phelan called over his shoulder.

Eileen nodded, eyes still pressed closed.

"You really should look below. The city's beautiful from up here."

Eileen tilted her head to the side and opened an eye. The Fianna was right. She didn't know how high up they were, but it was far enough that the city looked like a jewel glimmering in the twilight. Wisps of cloud hung like cataracts over the brilliant lights.

Ez folded his wings and did a corkscrew twirl, maneuvering as close as he could above them. His tunic and long hair flowed behind him. "Any idea where we should land?" he yelled over the wind.

"She'd be heading to Badb to rescue her friend. So as close as we can safely get to her tower," Eileen called back.

"I'll relay it to the others farther back, in case they lose you in the mist." He pointed behind him.

Eileen risked a glance over her shoulder and gasped. It made sense that she and Phelan took the lead; they rode the biggest dragon. But what she saw behind her lightened her heart. Dragons, wyverns, and griffins, all carrying passengers, spread out across the sky. Between them flew Fae of every shape and size. All coming to protect Harper. Eileen's limbs glowed with the warmth of her gratitude.

After a half hour of flight, the dragon banked slightly north, heading toward the narrow tip of the island.

Ezrynhivar swooped beside Phelan and Eileen. "Dewberry says we should head to the lighthouse near the northern tip of the island."

The dragon rumbled her assent. Another twenty minutes of flight brought them to the easternmost edge of the island.

They hovered on the Washington side and waited for the stragglers, who arrived shortly after Ezrynhivar returned. "I should take your passenger for now, Fianna."

"The hell you will." Phelan's tone was incredulous.

Hieronymous and Twitch glided up to them, followed by a large blue dragon carrying Aeld and two other Fir Bolg.

"The Dusk King is right, Phelan," Hieronymous called. "You won't be able to keep Eileen from leaping off the dragon's back."

"Wait, what?" Eileen's eyes flew wide.

Phelan sighed. "The warding spells protecting this place will make you do anything to avoid going near. It'll start off with the thought that you don't want to be here. When you keep going, you'll become more and more anxious until the terror of this place becomes too much to bear and you'll be desperate to avoid it."

"Why—"

"How else would Badb keep tourists away?" Hieronymous said.

Lord Ezrynhivar hovered so close to Eileen's right shoulder she could have reached out to touch him. He held out a pale hand to her and smiled a devious smile. With a gulp, she passed Phelan her gun and pack.

"You harm her, dark Fae, and there will be no place you can hide," Phelan all but growled at the Dusk Court ruler.

"Eileen and I have been through much together. I'd sooner lose a member of my Court than allow her to come to harm." With an arrogant, lopsided grin, he pulled Eileen to him. She clasped her arms around his neck while he gripped her waist. "Just like last time, sweet. Hold tight and don't let go."

Phelan's eyes were shooting daggers.

Beneath them, the flying army banked and dove for the strip of sandy beach on the island below. Ez plunged after them, sweeping low across the water.

The effect was instant. Eileen's heart pounded. Something terrible was going to happen on that island if they kept going. A cold sweat bloomed over her whole body.

"We have to go back!" she screamed at Ez.

"It's just the wards. It'll be over soon." Ez's voice was measured and calm.

"No. No, it isn't. If I go there, I'll die." Eileen released her grip on the incubus.

She had to get away, swim for it if she could. She thought her heart would burst. Terror shredded her mind. She shrieked and pounded Ez with her fists. He only clutched her tighter.

"Think of Harper, just another few seconds."

"Fuck you, let me go!" Eileen flailed and kicked. She was almost out of time. If this monster wouldn't let her go, she'd die. She opened her mouth and sank her teeth into Ez's shoulder. He let out a yelp.

"You bit me!"

Eileen shrieked and bit him again, all rationality lost.

And in the next instant, the Dusk King bellowed and threw his weight forward, releasing her. She went sailing a few feet and slammed into a sandy beach. The panic receded like it had never been there at all, and she lay panting while winged beasts wheeled and flapped away from the island.

Once everyone splashed to the shore, they regrouped. Ezrynhivar arrived at her side at the same time as Phelan.

"You still think you could have held on to this panicked hellcat, Fianna?" Ez rubbed his shoulder. "She bit me. Twice."

Phelan chuckled. "Better you than me, I suppose. You'll heal faster."

Eileen winced. "I didn't mean to bite you."

"It wasn't all bad. Someday I may return the favor," Ez said, looking right at Phelan as he spoke.

Hieronymous and Aeld strode over, both dry. The Fir Bolg scanned his surroundings, jaw agape. Despite his expression of awe, the furred giant dropped to a knee and spread his fingers over the ground under the patchy, low mist.

For a moment he remained before pushing himself to his feet, great head shaking from side to side. "It is as I feared. The island's rapid expansion has shredded the mycelial network beneath. Harper is north of here, an hour, perhaps two, but the Fianna will have to pinpoint her location."

Eileen fished out the Lia Fail shard out of her pocked and held it close to her face. The comforting glow made her sigh with short-lived relief. If Phelan and his friends couldn't pick up Harper's trail... A hundred horrible thoughts vied for attention.

"We'll find her, Eileen." Phelan's voice was soft.

The wolf tattoos shone so brightly they were visible beneath the Fianna's shirts. A blinding glare forced her to shield her eyes. When it died away, Fintan and the transformed Fianna circled, sniffing the ground.

"Not joining the other mutts?" Lord Ezryhnivar smirked at Phelan, backed by his contingent of Fae.

Phelan wrenched his eyes from the other Fianna fanning out through the underbrush and clenched his fists at his side. "You'll be glad I didn't. Hundreds of dark Fae have felt my fangs clamped around their throats."

Ezrynhivar unfurled his wings partway, puffing up like an angry cat.

*Men are the same no matter the species.* Eileen rolled her eyes and stepped between them, meeting Hieronymous doing the same from the opposite direction.

The ogre sighed. "We have no time to battle amongst ourselves."

The three wolves cantered back to the clearing, pink tongues lolling. Aisling bounded up to Eileen, yipped, tossed her head, and trotted off to their left. Fintan and Michael joined her. Together, they dashed through the mist.

"Luck smiled on us. They've found her trail. She's close," Phelan said, and the supernatural army followed the Fianna into the dark wood.

# CHAPTER 59

"Bastards." Harper twisted her head from one side to the next at the black-haired elves who held her fast.

"The fly finally found its way to my little web."

How she wanted to wipe that haughty grin from Gwyn's bearded face. Harper shuddered at the approach of two dripping wet kelpies. Their dull grey eyes met hers and they hissed in unison as they returned Gwyn's blade to its master. The vile monsters pawed her, searching for more weapons. One of them grabbed Nuada's sword and passed it to Gwyn, while the other gingerly wrenched her backpack off and tossed it to another cluster of Sidhe.

This is why Gwyn's hounds always arrived after the Sluagh. He had an inside Fae. "So the Phooka didn't betray me." Harper glared at the glaistig.

Gwyn answered. "Well, not yet. Given the chance, he would."

Melinoe batted her long eyelashes and put on the same starstruck grin she so often wore when she interacted with Harper. "Oh, it's just so wonderful to be the one to deliver you to Badb Catha." She dropped the sappy act and her gaze turned cold. "My success will guarantee my queen gains the favor of Badb and our people will be safe from her death squads."

Harper jerked her arms in a vain attempt to break free. She forced fast, deep breaths into her lungs to kindle her anger and magic. But it wasn't rage stirring, it was shock, humiliation, and guilt. She couldn't reach Melinoe, but in her mind, she saw herself punching the glaistig senseless. Her face felt hot. How could she be so stupid? To come so far and be captured yet again was almost too much to bear. And she'd rejected the Phooka. No ace up her sleeve to get away, and anyone who depended on her was shit out of luck.

The glaistig minced around her with her delicate nose in the air. "I swear, one more day of pretending this human filth was my *bestest friend* and I'd have thrown myself over the nearest cliff." Melinoe put on a sappy grin and batted her eyelashes before her face sank into an expression of disgust.

The Sidhe and other Fae took up sentry positions, not taking any chances Harper would flee again.

Harper sneered up at Gwyn while Melinoe bound her wrists. "I should have killed you when I had the chance."

He dropped onto his haunches a few feet from her. Those copper-flecked eyes roamed over her face, finally settling on her eyes. It would have been easier if she found malice there. Instead, she saw bewilderment.

His brows flicked together and one corner of his mouth twitched into what tried to be a smile. "The fact you did not is a mystery that has kept me awake for several nights. I've hunted you from the start. Whether I desire it or not, I must escort you to Badb. Why spare me?"

"A moment of weakness I deeply regret." Harper slumped. From now on, she vowed to do that opposite of what felt right. Every choice she'd made turned out to be the wrong one.

"I still get to bring her in," Melinoe chimed in. "The Dawn

Court apprehended her, and the Dawn Court shall present her to Badb Catha."

"You vile, nasty little viper." Melinoe's voice ground Harper's last nerve to a nub. She lunged at Melinoe, but Gwyn's powerful hands held her. The ring of Fae closed like a noose. Only when Gwyn lifted a hand and motioned them back did they revert to their original positions.

Melinoe stuck her tongue out and skittered behind Gwyn. He gestured for her to join the Wild Hunt and crouched back down, inches from Harper. When he spoke, his voice was soft. Sadness radiated from his eyes.

"When we arrive at the citadel, offer to give Badb what she wants freely. Ally with her. It's the only way to save your life."

"Never." Harper spat the word at him like venom. "Badb took *everything* from me. She's planning genocide against humanity. Against my people."

"You're part Tuatha." Gwyn scanned the elves and Fae around him. Melinoe narrowed her eyelids and tilted her head to regard him out of the corner of her eye. The rest of the Fae eyed him with suspicion. When he continued, his voice had hardened again. "I believe Badb's best interests are served with you at her side."

"You think I could live with my choices if I saved myself and let everyone else die?"

Gwyn pressed his lips into a line and held his body perfectly still, but his sharp intake of breath betrayed how much her words had affected him. He leaned close to her so the others couldn't overhear him. "It is not my wish to see you dead. You must know it's the single card you have left to play. The Tuatha blood in your veins and Macha's magic are valuable to her, but be very specific in your bargain. Like the Fae, she enjoys finding loopholes."

"If you really don't want to see me dead, then let me go. She'll simply steal my power, not bargain with me. If you bring me to your master, you'll live with my blood on your hands. But you murdered your own father, so what's one more?"

His face contracted and for a moment Harper thought he was going to break into tears, but he clenched a gloved fist and shot to his feet. "Bind her, but someone keeps a watch on her at all times. She's resourceful. And guard the perimeter. Her friends may yet attempt something foolish." Gwyn strode away from her.

Melinoe fell in behind him, galloping to keep up. "I'll watch her. She is *my* prisoner."

"Doesn't matter who watches me. Soon as Donn shows up, I'll slip away in the fight just like last time."

An elven woman wrenched Harper forward.

Emboldened by her bindings, Melinoe skipped beside her. "Oh, by the way, the Sluagh are hunting those animals, the Fir Bolg. Donn may still be on the island searching for you, but his Host should route out the last of them soon, along with your pathetic mother."

"No!" Harper kicked at Melinoe.

She tossed her green hair and laughed, hopping around and around Harper while a pair of Sidhe men shoved Harper down, her back to a log, and stood over her, palms hovering over their weapons.

Gwyn crouched in front of her again. "They won't be stupid enough to harm your mother. Badb will want leverage to force you to relinquish Macha's magic willingly."

At his words, she rubbed her fingers across Ez's ring. It helped her channel her magic, but she still needed to spark it. Her eyes bored into Gwyn's face. She rehearsed all the terrible things he'd done, hoping to trigger her rage. She squeezed her eyes closed and willed it to bubble up, but only stillness answered.

Then everyone in the camp dropped low and froze, responding to the rhythmic crack of... Was that gunfire? Here?

The distraction gave her the opening she needed to push herself to her feet again before the Sidhe opted to bind her legs.

She searched for her weapon and bag as a second round of shots rang through the forest, followed by shouts. Gunfire meant humans, and humans meant allies. She bounded toward her pack.

"Oh, no you don't." Melinoe advanced, a knife in her tan hand.

Harper shifted her weight to one leg and kicked detritus into Melinoe's eyes. The glaistig screamed and clawed at her face, dropping the knife.

The Wild Hunt streamed into the woods to back up their scouts.

Harper half hopped, half jogged toward the din of battle. But a broad hand smacked down on her shoulder, shoving her low.

"Not this time," Gwyn whispered into her hair.

# CHAPTER 60

The unlikely company of Sasquatch, wolves, and Fae had made good time through the dark forest. The only resistance they'd encountered had been a pack of solitary hobgoblins, and a couple shots had scattered them. Phelan eventually had to transform because it took all four of the Fianna to track the threads of Harper's trail. Ezrynhivar had appointed himself Eileen's guardian in Phelan's stead, and he trudged along at her side.

"I can sense your fear, and my glamour ebbing away."

Eileen chewed her bottom lip. "And how could you know that?"

Ezrynhivar's sultry smile accompanied a long inhale. "Natural skill. An incubus senses any change in his partner's physiology, and we play them like a fine violin."

"And drain their victims."

"Lovers. Lovers, my sweet. Yes, we gain something we need, but it is no less orgasmic for that, perhaps more so."

Eileen scowled and rubbed her forehead. "Seriously?"

The Dusk King's chuckle was low and flirtatious. "I wasn't offering that, only to take the edge off."

Saliva flooded her mouth the same way it did when she poured a drink. Ez was perceptive. The last shot of his glamour had all but faded away, and her skin prickled, heart raced. If she fell apart or hesitated, her anxiety could cost her daughter.

Her fingers strayed to the mushroom pendant. *You're thinking about the poison again.* But this time was different. Fae magic wasn't booze, and she wasn't trying to avoid anything. Quite the opposite.

Far ahead, a warm light flickered. Ez clasped her shoulder. "Campfires. We found them."

Bushes quaked, and the patter of a dozen tiny feet accompanied guttural snarls. A tight pack of redcaps burst from the undergrowth.

To her surprise, Eileen didn't hesitate but swung the rifle up and squeezed off a shot. All but two redcaps dropped. They'd stilled when Ez leapt on the survivors, claws flying, and shredded them both.

"We need to surround that camp," Eileen said, and the solitary Fae and Fir Bolg split into two groups and raced to either side of the campsite. She paused, cracked the rifle open, and slid another shell into the barrel with trembling fingers.

"My offer still stands. No strings." Ez hovered at her back, bending over her neck so his lips brushed her ear.

Phelan trotted up beside her, the other Fianna in tow. The wolf's lips curled over canine teeth, slavering jaws snapped, and guttural snorts and growls sent Ez backing away.

A flash of white and their heads turned in unison to the crest of a hill that sheltered the campfires. Eileen spotted three white dogs with glowing red eyes and bright red ears racing to flank their forces.

With a howl, the other wolves rocketed after them. Phelan's ears drooped with a single high whine as he lifted his muzzle to Eileen. She stretched a hand to him, but he already loped after his friends, leaving Eileen and the incubus king to sprint for the campsite alone. She dreaded trying to explain this to Phelan later.

They halted, dropped behind a log, and Eileen's heart leapt. For half a second, illuminated by the ring of small campfires, she'd glimpsed her daughter before an elf shoved her toward the ground and out of sight. She'd found her. Despite the danger, her face cracked into a smile.

"I wish they'd hurry. No telling what they'll do to Harper," Eileen whispered.

Ez's lips pressed close to her ear. "If the Wild Hunt wanted to harm her, she'd be dead. Patience. If they need us, they'll signal. Wait for it and we'll pick off any of the Hunt trying to escape."

Less than a minute passed before shouts, howls, and clanging blades from the far end of the camp broke the silence of the shrouded wood. Eileen resisted the urge to run for her daughter, and focused on the deep, slow breaths that kept the ringing in her ears and the hammering of her heart under control just enough. She glanced at Ezrynhivar.

The tremor returned to her hands, more and more each moment. She desperately wanted to run to Harper and damn the consequences.

Most of the sounds of battle stayed confined to the opposite side of the Wild Hunt's camp, so she risked slinking closer to Harper. Step by shaky step, she sought the shelter of the next broad tree trunk.

"Eileen, where are you going?" Ez hissed.

She paused and glanced over her shoulder. "Just getting closer."

The creak of branches sent gooseflesh spreading over her body. No wind stirred, yet branches creaked and moved. Her dry tongue stuck to the roof of her mouth as she crouched and searched the trees for an animal. Or worse. But nothing was there, only the trees.

With another deep breath, she edged forward. A stick snapped beneath her foot, and a tall, bearded man shoved her daughter behind him and brandished a sword.

But it was the green-haired Fae with the goat's legs that stabbed the hot knife of fury into Eileen's heart. Serotina's little toad with her saccharine smiles and deferential words.

Every nerve screamed at her to rush the foul little turncoat, but Eileen fought against it. No way she was faster than Melinoe, and a wrong move could get Harper killed, because the Dawn Court Fae rounded on her daughter, pressing a long knife to her throat.

"Melinoe, stop—" The bearded man smacked the goat-legged Fae aside.

"Was this your plan? How did you get reinforcements?" Melinoe brandished the knife at Harper, attempting to slide past the man.

Eileen wasn't certain what prompted her to do what she did next. The battle raged on all sides of her now, and no one else was available to protect Harper from the green-haired demon.

Eileen leapt to her feet and charged the few yards to the camp. Leaping over the outermost campfire, she yelled her daughter's name.

"Eileen, what—" Ez's wings unfurled behind her as she landed six feet from Harper's captors and leveled the gun at Melinoe.

The Dusk King's wing caught on a branch and he touched down, half teetering at her side. By the time he recovered his footing, the bearded man had a blade trained on him.

"Mom?! Lord Ezrynhivar?" Harper gasped, staggering backward.

"Harper, honey." Eileen jerked her head, beckoning her daughter to her side. Her hands maintained a steady grasp on the Mossberg.

"Eileen O'Neill, *Lord* Ezrynhivar. You are quite literally the last people I expected to see." Melinoe flicked her knife in her palm, tightening her grip, and stared at Eileen from the tops of her eyes, fists clenched, chest heaving. "You'll not steal this day from my queen." The Fae advanced, and Eileen pointed the weapon at her abdomen.

"Steel shot shells. You touch my daughter and I'll pump you full of them. Drop your weapons," she snarled. For the first time, she truly wanted to kill. Melinoe and the man exchanged a quick glance and dropped their blades.

"Kick them over here." She only said that because she saw it in movies. The pair obliged.

Melinoe smiled a nasty grin. "Glaistig are fast. You—"

"Faster than steel shot? Go on, twitch. Try me."

Ezrynhivar had already settled into his usual languid slouch. He flashed a toothy smirk at Melinoe. "I'd do as she says. She's pumped a couple dozen Fae full of iron in the last few days."

Melinoe exhaled and frowned at her captor.

"That's what I thought. Now over by the Fae with the brown hair."

"I'm no Fae," the man said.

Eileen's gaze never left Melinoe. "I'm betting guns will still kill you."

"Mom, you're truly here?"

"Yep. And I brought an army."

"How- How on earth? The Fir Bolg?"

"Safe. Some joined us."

Harper dropped and worked the bonds around her wrists against a craggy rock.

Across from Eileen, the man smiled and the Fae glowered at her while the shouts and clanging echoed ahead.

"For what it's worth, I wasn't the one who killed her father. Badb Catha did that," the man said.

With Harper freed and protected by Ez, Eileen risked a

glimpse of the man and froze. Her breathing became a rapid pant. That face. The blue spiral tattoo. She'd seen him before. He was the one who scrambled her memories, broke her. And he'd been there when the dark lady murdered Gerald. The earth listed beneath her and the gun's barrel trembled.

Time slowed to a crawl. Grey-clawed hands seized her shoulders as the gun slipped free and clattered to the ground.

"Eileen!" Ez shook her out of her momentary shock in time to see Melinoe grin and dash for the underbrush and the man lunge toward the campfire.

He paused then, brown eyes fixed on Harper just as her bonds snapped. The trees behind him warped, and he was simply gone.

Harper rushed to clasp her mother in a fierce embrace and they collapsed against each other. Hitching breaths made the words Eileen sputtered into Harper's hair barely intelligible.

"I'm so sorry. I froze. Let them get away. Harper, forgive me."

"Mom, it's okay, it's okay." Her daughter ran a soothing hand between her shoulder blades.

Ez patted Eileen's back. "Gwyn's a Tuatha. We'd never have captured him, anyway." The Dusk King brought his lips to her ear. "If you need another boost, just ask."

Eileen shook her head. Through every step of this long journey she'd feared not being enough. Not strong enough to battle the Fae. Not stable enough to be for once what her daughter needed her to be, but she'd prevailed. Vodka. Glamour. None of that was necessary anymore.

Grey wolves bounding into the clearing were barely visible through Harper's hair. Two of the Fianna tore off after Melinoe, while the others glowed brightly before reverting to human form. Behind them, the members of the makeshift army strode out of the woods.

Fintan and Phelan rolled their necks and stretched, and

Phelan took one look at Ez hovering beside Eileen and busied himself chatting with a Fae.

Eileen drew away from Harper and swallowed hard to force her feelings back under the surface. Harper gaped at the ring of Fae and Aeld's people.

Hieronymous stopped beside Fintan. "No sign of Paegrinn. He's probably in that tower. Several Sidhe escaped. Any hope of a surprise attack is gone."

# CHAPTER 61

Emilio hunched over a set of tissue samples under a very fancy microscope. Breas had come for him right after dinner. He'd only just tied the strand of Tamika's hair into his own when he'd been summoned.

Breas hovered around the roiling tank in the room's middle, reading dials and adjusting them, fully immersed in his own work. Emilio guessed it wasn't going well because Breas cursed under his breath and his eyes held a fierceness he'd not seen before.

*Vanilla.*

Emilio snapped into the little girl's bedroom, his friends in their usual places. He couldn't see the lab at all anymore.

"Turn it down," he said inside the mindspace, then Tamika's room winked off and he stared at the tissue sample again. "Holy crap," he exclaimed out loud. The sudden change disoriented his senses, so he closed his eyes and focused on the feel of the floor meeting his shoes, the vent blowing on his scalp, and breathed.

"What'd you say?" Breas barked from the other side of the tank.

"Oh. Um, I was talking to myself."

*Vanilla.*

Emilio took a deep breath and lowered his head to the microscope, a position he hoped would give him cover if he was suddenly whipsawing between realities again.

But he wasn't. At least not completely. Tamika's room and his friends were faint but present. Like a transparent film of another reality laid over the lab.

"Can you hear me?" Tamika said.

"Mmm. Hmm," Emilio said in the child's bedroom.

"Look around. Show Tamika the exit, any windows," Selina said.

Emilio straightened his back, pivoted to the rippling pool, and continued a slow revolution. He rubbed his eyes for effect.

Breas popped his head up from the basin. "You find something, my brilliant intern?"

"Not sure yet, just stretching my legs a little." Emilio swiveled back to face the sample. To his right, Tamika sat on her bed, clapping her hands and smiling.

"No windows, a single door."

"That probably leads to armed guards. The traffic is very faint. Either we're near a top floor or deep within the building," Emilio muttered.

Selina let her head loll forward. "Or both. You were correct, not a viable escape hatch."

"I'll be over in just a sec to see what you've uncovered. I hope it's good news," Breas said.

He could hear Tamika describing what she saw through his eyes to the others. This was going to be weird. And hard to keep track of. His palms started to sweat. One false move and they'd lose their advantage if the Fae suspected they could communicate with each other regardless of their proximity.

"Try to get close to the tank Tamika described. I'd like to know what he's growing," Selina said.

Emilio grabbed a clipboard and paced the full circumference of the festering vessel. Bubbles squelched and popped. Emilio's nose crinkled with each wet, slimy burst, but it was the smell that raised his gorge. Like a fresh can of Spam and something just turning rancid. The thing was even a Spammy pink.

"Oh God, it's disgusting." Tamika covered her mouth with her hand. Emilio met her eyes and nodded.

He needed to confabulate some sort of revelation and fast, or Breas would wonder if he was stalling. Once he completed his circle around the tank, he returned to the microscope. Scrunching up his face, tongue clamped between his lips, he hunched over it again.

The tissue was clearly degrading, but why? He drew back and flipped open the genetic profile. The patterns were like nothing he'd ever seen. Most genetic sequences on Earth shared at least ninety percent of their DNA, but he guessed this sample shared seventy, maybe less. And it didn't even look like the Fae DNA from the Abraxas files. This was something entirely different.

Emilio pored over the genetic sequence as he took a few tentative steps back toward the tank. Lighted panels placed along every third of the tank's circumference flickered beneath the roiling mist falling to the floor. More displays flashed from the dome hovering above it.

He paused. "What you're growing in the basin, it's not Fae or human, is it?"

Breas straightened his tie. "Very good, my young intern. No, it is not." Then he disappeared back down to the instrument panel he'd been working on.

"Well, then what is it?"

Emilio wasn't sure Breas had heard him. For nearly half a minute, the only sounds in the room were the tank's bubbling and the tap-tapping of his former boss's fingers on the panel. Emilio returned to the microscope with a shrug aimed at Tamika, who appeared to teeter on the vessel's lip.

"You might as well come over and observe. I've brought it as far as I can, time to wake it and see if it fares better than the others." Breas stood and motioned Emilio to his side.

"What nightmare is he creating in that thing?" Tamika asked, grimacing.

"He's making something? Is it more like us?" Alan asked.

Breas squatted behind the panel for a split second, and Emilio made a cutting gesture across his throat and hoped Tamika understood his mimed request for their silence. He needed his full concentration to maneuver around his 'boss.' He squinted at the surface, but the roiling of the liquid had increased and mercifully obscured whatever grew within.

"The same sample from that file you hold grows in this tank. It is very, very old."

"And very, very degraded. How did you fill in the missing sequences?"

"All in due time. If this works, I'll not be needing your help." He handed Emilio a helmet with a tinted face shield and a lead apron. "Put these on."

"Is that thing radioactive?"

Breas shook his head.

Emilio slipped on the headgear, careful not to cut it too badly on his plumage. The sleeved apron proved more difficult. His wings made it impossible to tie properly, and the feathers on his shoulders sliced into the fabric. He ended up half draping it across his chest and arms. The visor tinted everything blue but with a halo of orange ringing any bright light. Beside him, Breas slipped on his own protective equipment.

Tamika leaned forward to get the best vantage she could, chewing on her fingers.

"When I press this lever, the liquid will drain from the tank.

The shield should protect your vision, but do not stare directly into it for more than a couple seconds."

Emilio nodded and Breas pressed the lever down, tucking his hands inside the apron. He flicked his chin at Emilio, who did the same.

The level of the roiling liquid dropped inch by inch. The face shield fogged and obscured the lumpy mass that broke through like a small island.

"Eew. What is that?" Tamika stuck out her tongue. "It looks like a giant head."

Emilio swallowed hard. His palms and forehead grew clammy. The fluid's surface stilled somewhat, and he squinted to make out what was growing within. Fleshy tendrils connected to the tank's flashing panels.

The thing filled almost the entire tank. Emilio estimated it had to be at least seven feet long.

"Okay, Dr. Frankenstein, what am I looking at here?" Emilio asked, more for Tamika's benefit.

"Just wait. All will become clear." Breas wrung his hands.

The fluid had all but drained away, and what lay at the bottom made Emilio's stomach lurch and his heart pound. Tamika's wide lavender eyes darted over the scene.

Across the oblong mass ran a slit about three quarters of the way down. Thick black hairs sprouted along the edges.

"Oh my God, it's an eye. A giant eye." Tamika smashed a pillow over her face.

Emilio gasped. She was right. Breas had grown a single enormous eye. He leapt back and yelped when the thing moved. The tentacle-like terminations connected to the panels and writhed even when the eye stilled.

Breas laughed and clapped his hands. "This is the longest it's ever made it before tissue decomposition. Now to bring it fully to life. Be ready to duck."

Breas turned a small dial on his console and the eye jolted, jiggling and quaking, under the current flowing into it.

"What. The. Hell." Tamika looked as horrified as Emilio felt.

The lid snapped open. The iris was a putrid yellow ringed with an even fouler green. It flicked back and forth in the tank like it searched for something.

"Isn't this the part where you shout *It's alive!?*" Emilio turned his head yet kept his gaze on the monstrous eye.

Breas had his fingers crossed on both hands. "Please work this time. Please work." He leaned forward and flipped a small switch.

The eyelid snapped completely open and a beam of white light shot from the thing, blinding Emilio even through the shield.

Tamika shrieked, and their connection dissipated.

When the light faded, all that remained of the giant eye were its charred remains sticking to the bottom of the tank. Breas tore off the helmet and threw it across the room, cursing.

Emilio removed his more deliberately with shaking hands. He didn't think anything could be more horrific than what Badb had turned him into. He was wrong. Whatever Breas had cloned was far worse.

The lid swung loose and crashed into the tank. At least it covered part of the charred horror beneath. Emilio edged closer to inspect it. The blast from the eye had reduced metal to ash anywhere the eye's fiery gaze fell. Even the ceiling sported a gaping hole, through which the night sky twinkled with stars. Emilio removed the lead apron, doubtful it would have protected him.

"What the hell was that thing?"

"That was the seventh Eye of Balor." Breas rubbed a hand over his face and straightened his slumped shoulders.

"Eye of what?"

"Balor. A long-dead Fomorian king. Perhaps the greatest of our leaders."

"Were his eyes as big as this one?" Emilio's curiosity overwhelmed the sheer magnitude of his revulsion.

"Eye. Single. And the original was far larger. I hoped had this one survived, it would've eventually grown to size."

Emilio imagined a titan, taller than the tallest building in Portland. The question of how Breas had procured an ancient genetic sample of long-dead Balor could wait. Though it explained why the genetic profile was so degraded.

"How huge was this dude?" Emilio drifted to a wheeled armchair. Draping his wings across the back, he sank into it.

"Not as tall as you'd think. Most Fomorians have no uniform proportion. Balor was mostly skull." Breas sank into the chair next to Emilio's and let his head drop back, spinning a lazy circle.

"Did his eye set everything on fire all the time?"

Breas chuckled. "Yes. And no." He pulled himself up so that his elbows rested on his knees and fixed Emilio with his icy blue eyes. "The Children of Danu, the Tuatha, believed the eye scorched all it looked upon. And indeed it did. But that wasn't all it did."

"Jesus."

"Before the Tuatha invaded Ireland, we ruled the seas and, at times, the land. The Eye of Balor allowed us to. For whatever it gazed upon, Balor would instantly know how to turn it to our benefit. Trees became lumber for our ships, grassland a place for crops, and humans the labor to grow them. His gaze taught us to dominate the earth and use every last shred of it to our advantage."

Emilio rolled his eyes. "Let me guess, the Tuatha came and ruined all that."

"Indeed they did. The Second Battle of Moytura, fought on the plains of Inisfáil—what you call Ireland—ended our reign of supremacy. At least for a while."

"With the power of the eye, how could you fail?"

"Prophecy. You see, it was foretold Balor would be killed by his own grandson. So he locked his only child, a beautiful daughter named Eithne, in a glass tower and forbade any men to visit the island where it stood. But one of the Tuatha discovered her there, and they fell in love. Nine months later, Lugh Lhamfada was born. Half Tuatha, half Fomorian. Just like me."

"And this Lugh killed Balor."

"Yes, by lobbing a magical spear through his eye. And thus the Tuatha turned the tide and drove the Fomorians back beneath the seas. We bore the rest of our great king under the waves, to be interred in our capital at Tor Inis. I took the last of it."

"And you used it to make a new eye."

"To once again turn the tide of war, if it came to that. I have just enough material for one final try."

"Or if you wished to betray your mistress." Emilio craned his neck at the hole in the ceiling. Clouds had moved in.

Somehow, this revelation had to be useful. He just didn't know how.

A slow smile spread, and Breas gave Emilio a sidelong glance. "But I'd never betray my queen."

"Partner, you said earlier. So Badb is Fomorian?"

"Tuatha."

The answer smacked Emilio in the face. He lowered his gaze and toyed with the tie on his green scrubs. Sharing what he'd figured out with Breas promised the destruction of all he loved. The last thing humanity needed was additional super-weapons in the hands of the evil seeking to destroy them.

"I saw that." Breas wheeled his chair across to Emilio and clasped his hand, pulling his torso down so their faces were inches apart.

"What?"

"You just figured something out. It was all over your face."

"No. I'm just trying to soak in what you've told me."

"Liar. I've seen that look before. You've figured it out and you don't want to tell me." He smiled and leaned back. "How's this for motivation? You tell me what you just discovered, and I won't kill one of your friends."

Emilio pressed his lips together and curled his scaled toes into the floor. He'd had enough of being manipulated by these asshats. "You wouldn't. We're too valuable."

Breas wagged a slow finger in front of Emilio. "Surely you've seen the busloads of prison inmates arriving daily, just like the ones you piloted at Woodstock Park. Young. Strong. Pre-screened. Why, the Abraxas success rate is up to eighty percent. You and your friends are not nearly as special as you were a week ago, so I can spare one or two if it gets me what I want. Now spill it."

He let out a long breath. No way he could sentence any one of them to death. "Well, I don't know what a Fomorian looks like, but I haven't seen any creatures who all look different as you described."

"Your point?"

"The sample is missing a lot of sequences. Where did you get the DNA to fill in the missing pieces?"

"I used my own." Breas's brows furrowed.

"And you just got through telling me you're half Tuatha."

Breas hopped to his feet and punched the air. "It's so obvious! I knew my intern wouldn't fail me. Genius. All I need is a pure Fomorian sample and my problem is solved. The CEOs of any American company should suffice. Beaxzos and Aelahn both owe me favors..."

*Vanilla.*

"Emilio." Tamika slid from her bed and raced for the bedroom door. Alan's and Selina's eyes widened.

"What is it?" Emilio whispered accidentally aloud.

Breas waved a dismissive hand. "Not what. Who. Nearly all the Fortune Five Hundred are run by my people, and I helped every one of them get where they are."

Tamika tilted her ear toward the door. "There's commotion in the hallway. Elves, goblins, all gabbing with each other. Most are running for the stairs."

A few seconds slid by while Emilio pretended to examine the charred remains of the Eye of Balor. In the mindspace, his friends poised, listening, worry written over their faces, and Breas scribbled notes into a folder beside him.

"Emilio! It's your friend. They think she's on her way here, with fighters."

*Harper. If she's coming, we need to make contact with our Fae allies. We're going to have to fight our way out.*

# CHAPTER 62

The gobsmacking fact her mother stood not three feet from Harper shoved all other thoughts aside. For a fleeting moment, the notion that Eileen O'Neill was a figment of some new Fae glamour brought a chill.

"Mom? I can't believe you're here." She swept her mother into another embrace. After her imprisonment by Santaigh, the line between truth and delusion was thin. Only when the scent of the strawberry cream shampoo Eileen always used tickled her nose did Harper allow herself to accept reality.

"Of course I am, sweetheart. I'm your mother and it's my turn to save you," Eileen O'Neill whispered into Harper's hair.

Gwyn hadn't lied. Somehow, her mom and the Fir Bolg had escaped the Sluagh. "Mom. What are you doing here? It's not safe. How did you find me?"

Eileen stepped back and wiped Harper's tears from her cheeks. "I had a lot of help." Eileen swiveled and both of them greeted the small fighting force she'd assembled.

Harper let her arm linger across her mother's shoulders before walking a slow circuit along the line of rescuers. Aeld,

Hieronymous, a wall of Fir Bolg with their thick staffs, a diverse contingent of Fae, but what surprised her most was a very tall horned Fae with long black wings.

Harper resisted the urge to rub her eyes. "Ezrynhivar?"

The King of the Dusk Court gave a dramatic shrug and smoothed a lock of his waist-length dark locks back into place. "Yes, your mother suckered me into this hopeless cause."

"That and you want to make Serotina pay for betraying you." A tall man with wavy, near-black hair and a stubble beard led a trio of wolves to her mother's side.

"Yes, all of that too, I suppose." Ez leaned against the trunk of a tree and flicked his wings.

"Harper, this is Phelan. He and the Fianna helped me find you."

Behind him, the wolves glowed blue, sat up on their haunches, and when the light faded, they were human.

With all she'd seen, wolves turning into people shouldn't have fazed her. And in truth, their glimmering transformation didn't shock her. But when all four of them stepped forward, dropped to their knees, and lowered their heads at her feet, she raised her eyebrows and swallowed hard.

"Um, Mom? What the hell is going on?"

Eileen clasped Harper's hands, nodded at the frontmost shapeshifter, and a pained expression passed over her features. "They're the Fianna, and they led us to you."

Harper squinted and part her lips to speak, but she lacked the words. So she snapped her mouth shut. The Fianna remained kneeling, heads bowed. "I... Um... Mom?" She pointed at Phelan and his friends.

"May I rise, Your Grace?" Phelan said into his knee.

"Sure?" Harper said, more a question than a command.

Ezrynhivar laughed, his eyes sparkling. "Congratulations, Harper, you've got pets. A grand total of ten mangy dogs to order around as you see fit. Don't let all that power go to your head."

Harper stuck out her hand. Phelan grasped it and studied it reverently.

"Tha— I'm happy you helped my mom, though I'd rather you'd kept her out of this."

"You can thank me. We aren't Fae."

Harper nodded, a single slow dip to her chin. They acted like she literally was royalty and not just someone bumbling her way ineffectively through this misadventure. It was weird. Really weird. "Um, no offense or anything, but what are you? And why are you doing..." She waved a hand over the kneeling shapeshifters before her. "That?"

Phelan smiled. "For centuries, we Fianna have served the High Kings of Ireland. We are and ever shall be at your command, Heir to the High Throne. It is our sworn duty to protect you and carry out your wishes."

"Umm. Hmm." Harper's eyes pleaded with her mother, who shrugged her shoulders.

Harper stared at the group of kneeling forms, then scanned the faces of the Fir Bolg and Fae behind them. Hieronymous and Aeld both grinned from across the sea of bodies assembled in the moonlit woods. Harper waved and offered an awkward smile.

It was Hieronymous who spoke. "They won't stand until you tell them it's all right to do so." The ogre tucked the end of his lace doublet into his purple brocade vest.

"You can stand. Do...whatever it is you do and stuff." Harper motioned for the Fianna to rise.

"Thank you, Your Highness," a woman with bright pink hair said, then dropped her eyes.

"Don't call me that. I'm just Harper." She spoke to all the Fianna.

The woman bowed and smiled at her. "Thank you, Harper. You honor me." Then she averted her gaze.

Harper laughed. "No, no. This isn't going to work for me." Confused glances passed between the Fianna. "I don't want followers. Only friends. And friends are equals. No bowing. No staring at your feet instead of looking me in the eye. And absolutely no Your Grace and Your Majesty. And I'm the one who owes you humble gratitude for keeping my mother safe." *Besides, if these Fianna only knew what a screwup I am at making any decision at all, they'd head for the hills.*

In unison, they rose and moved to flank her, scanning the edge of the woods. The woman with the pink hair stuck out a hand with a smile that stretched across her whole face. "I'm Aisling."

Harper gripped her palm and pulled her into a quick hug. "Glad to meet you, Aisling."

One by one she introduced herself to the Fianna, and each seemed over the moon to make her acquaintance, embracing her or shaking her hand before returning to patrol the perimeter.

Aeld ambled over, the corners of his mouth down-turned. Guilt stabbed at her. Since she'd sent the Phooka away, she didn't know what had happened to Paegrinn. How was she going to tell Aeld she'd lost his son because she trusted the wrong Fae?

"Harper, we're delighted to find you safe. We owe you our thanks for what you did protecting our village." Aeld bowed his head.

"I'm happy to see you, Aeld. And I'm sorry it wasn't enough. The Sluagh told me they'd found you." She swallowed, unsure where to begin. "I... uh... Paegrinn followed me here and rescued me. When I thought the Phooka had betrayed me, I sent him away and Paegrinn stayed with him." She winced, ready for anger from the towering man.

But Aeld sighed and a weary smile softened his face. "Thank

you, Harper. News that my son still lives…" The Fir Bolg clasped both open palms across his chest.

"I hate to break up such a chain of touching moments, but we need to keep moving. Might I remind you Gwyn knows where we are." Lord Ezrynhivar and Hieronymous joined Aeld. "We'll be discovered if we remain here."

They all looked at Harper expectantly. Problem was, she had no clue where to go or what to do next. She turned to Phelan.

"You tracked me, so do you think you can track where Badb is holding her prisoners?"

Phelan tapped his nose. "Not without a scent."

"And flight is out of the question. My wings still ache," Ez added.

Aeld thudded his spear on the ground. "We need to find my son."

Lord Ezrynhivar rolled his eyes. "With all due respect, young Paegrinn, if he has any sense at all, has already escaped the island. We waste valuable time searching for him. We've found Harper. We should leave."

"I promised to free the human Sluagh, and I'm not leaving here without Emilio." Now that she had a small assault force, Harper might actually pull off the rescue. Paegrinn had joined her quest to save her friends. If he remained on this island, he'd be a welcome addition. "I agree with Aeld. First, we find Paegrinn, then we go to Badb's tower."

The eldest of the Fianna, Fintan, gestured at the malevolent trees with one hand while the other rested on his hip. "How do you propose to do that in these infernal woods?"

"If he's close, the mycelium might be connected enough to locate him." Aeld dropped to his knees, spreading his broad hands over forest detritus. Even through the patchy mist, Harper watched tendrils of fuzzy white shoot off in all directions, branching and racing along every possible path.

Aeld squatted there, eyes closed, chin lifted. A low rumbling chant bubbled up the back of his throat. The other Fir Bolg joined in, deep voices toning, rising and falling while the mycelium twisted and waved.

The circle of Fae and others watched in wonder. All except the dark Fae, with Ezrynhivar miming a dramatic yawn and looping strands of his hair around a finger. "Are we quite finished? Every hungry shade and spy of Badb probably heard that abysmal crooning and will be flocking to us any—"

"Shh." Harper cut him off. "Look." She indicated a branch of the fungus that sparkled and lit up brighter and thicker than the rest. Its glow visible beneath the drifting fog, the shimmering line arced to their right.

"Paegrinn is that direction." Aeld rose and gestured along the wispy white path.

Hieronymous fell in behind him. "From what Nuada's intel about this place revealed, Badb's citadel may lie in a similar direction."

Harper swallowed hard. "He's on the way, so let's go find him." She felt relieved to search for her Fir Bolg friend, but she also feared the Phooka might still be with him. She wasn't ready to face the little shapeshifter yet, after she'd rejected him.

And she still hadn't told her mom about the horrible things happening to her dad. Suddenly Harper's heart weighed in her chest like a stone.

# CHAPTER 63

The company trudged through the misty forest, following the gleaming fungal pathway.

Eileen stepped up beside Harper, laced an arm across her shoulders, and pulled her into a side-hug as they walked.

"What's wrong, sweetheart? You look like you bear the weight of the world."

If she only knew. "So much has happened since the village..." Harper relayed her flight from Gwyn, watching Donn feed on a soul, and the siege in the farmhouse. She forced the lump back down her throat before blurting out. "Dad's a Sluagh now. When I touched him, what remained of him woke, and he helped me escape."

"What?" Eileen whispered, her face drained of color.

"He told me to tell you he loves you very much. And I told him the story about how he followed you to the silent retreat, and that made him happy, because Donn had already eaten that memory. I got to give it back to him." Her breath hitched.

Her mother's palm clamped over her mouth and tears

glistened in her eyes. Harper told her the rest of her story and about the dream world.

When she had finished, Eileen swiped at her eyes and ran a hand down her daughter's hair. "You're amazing. I'm not sure I'd have had the strength. Losing myself in dreams where Gerald hadn't died was all I did for fifteen years. But I'm trying to do better. Make up for being a terrible mom." Eileen gestured to the small army.

"Mom, we both did the best we could." Harper paused. "I'm afraid that I can't do this. Not without Nuada and now without the Phooka. How am I supposed to fight a goddess and save the world? I'll be lucky not to get you all killed."

"Yes, you can. I've never met anyone with the mental strength to resist a gancanagh." The pink-haired Aisling drew up beside the O'Neills. She tapped a finger to her ear. "Super hearing. Goes with the wolf thing."

Harper managed a small smile.

"The most important trait of a High King, or Queen, is sovereignty, which you showed when you defended the Fir Bolg village, with your oath to liberate the Sluagh, and your defeat of Santaigh."

"I thought sovereignty had to do with countries and borders." Harper rubbed a kink from her thigh as she walked.

Fintan joined Aisling. "Aye, it does, but it used to mean so much more. It meant a king ruled for the good of all, human and nature. The measure of a leader was the flourishing of the land. And *all* its people, not merely a few."

"That sounds like a fantasy utopia," Harper said dryly.

Aisling sighed. "Humanity has largely lost touch with the whole concept."

"And that's what created the enemy you face." Fintan indicated the ominous wood.

"Badb?" Harper asked.

Fintan nodded. "Thousands of years ago, Badb Catha and her sisters, Anand and Macha, were tasked with keeping the balance between the needs of people and the needs of nature, of maintaining sovereignty. It was they who represented the land in granting a High King dominion over it. In a prophecy, Badb beheld a vision of the future, the modern world, and vowed to wipe out humanity so that life could flourish."

Eileen barked out a single, mirthless laugh. "Some people would agree with her on that point."

Phelan drew up next to Eileen, arms across his chest. "The Underworld Fae believe Badb Catha is humanity's reckoning for their crimes."

Fintan shook his head vigorously. "And they'd be just as wrong as she is. In seeking to free the non-human worlds from Homo sapiens, Badb has fallen as out of touch with sovereignty as humanity itself has."

Before the lack of money forced her to drop out of college, Harper had taken a handful of philosophy classes, and struggled. Emilio loved pondering all those big questions, thinking Buddhism held all the answers. In high school, he'd prattled on and on about the latest book from the Dalai Lama. God, she missed him. More of his spiritual soliloquies must have sunk in than she thought, because she muttered, "The middle way is always the better path."

"Exactly!" Fintan beamed and clapped his hands together. "Balance is what the world and humanity need to heal themselves, and sovereignty is about balance. Balance between the needs of the people and the land. Balance between destruction and creation. Too much of either begets trouble."

Aeld had fallen back to listen to the conversation. Harper tilted her head and studied the thick yet rounded features of his profile. The Fir Bolg lived in harmony with all that surrounded them. She was sure they deeply loathed the destruction of nature wrought by her kind.

"Badb seeks to save the natural world by eliminating humans. Is that why the Fir Bolg wouldn't join Nuada's cause?" Harper asked.

Aeld grimaced. "No. Badb's cause may be just, but we do not approve of her methods. Death and suffering are not solved by more death and suffering. What I said at the council still stands. My people no longer fight wars because of this simple truth."

Ahead, Hieronymous and Ezrynhivar had paused, peering high into the branches of a towering pine tree, seemingly untouched by the magic that twisted this island.

Harper drew up alongside them. Beneath her feet, the thread of mycelium gleamed bright enough that she shielded her eyes. She lifted her face to sight along Ez's pointed finger.

"Up in the treetop, something flashed. Green. Just for a second."

Aeld crept to the gentle ridge almost on all fours and leaned so close to the strand of fungus, it touched his nose. "We're nearly there, the mycelium is brighter."

"There it is again," Hieronymous whispered.

Only one thing Harper knew glowed like that. She stretched up on her tiptoes as close as she could get to the tiny pinpoint of light. "Alina?" she whispered.

As though called, a miniature green light zoomed toward the group. She zipped around Harper's head several times before lighting on her shoulder and tittering in her ear.

"Harper, honey, what is that?"

"Alina, Mom. A will o' wisp. She lived in the Phooka's bag. Long story." Her happiness at seeing her miniature friend turned to stone in her stomach. If Alina was here, that meant the Phooka was nearby. No telling how he'd react to her now.

"Well, there's a rare sight." Ez managed to make leaning against a trunk look luxurious.

"Will o' wisps are rare?" Harper followed Alina's serpentine flight.

Hieronymous's face wore an expression of longing. "Most stayed in the Underworld because here they're a supreme delicacy. The goblin gangs would pay a hefty price for her at my Lodge."

Was that why the Phooka kept her? Was he planning to eat her some day? Harper shuddered. "No one is eating my friend."

Eileen rubbed a palm between Harper's shoulder blades. "The Phooka'll forgive you, honey."

Ezrynhivar picked at his claws. "Unlikely. Fae have delicate sensibilities and extensive memories." He flicked his leathery wings. "But losing that little turncoat is to your advantage, Harper."

Harper wasn't so sure. She'd been wrong about Melinoe. Perhaps her distrust of the Phooka was incorrect. The way he'd pleaded with her not to send him away suggested he was loyal.

Alina fluttered from Harper's shoulder and zipped a few feet ahead. She bobbed up and down before continuing along the same path the fungus illuminated.

The group followed her for several minutes. Ahead, the mycelium faded and the fog grew thin, but that wasn't what took Harper's breath away.

In the distance loomed a tower at the edge of a broad lake. Fae of every shape and size milled around a concrete plaza, guiding humans in prison blues into the building. In the trees hung oblong cocoons of mist stretching deep into the surrounding woods.

Paegrinn sat with his back against a looping, twisted tree, munching some of the Sasquatch trail mix he favored, and the Phooka perched on a high branch overlooking Badb's domain.

# CHAPTER 64

Callon pounded on Emilio's door, then shoved his way inside. The customary look of revulsion spread across his perfect features.

Emilio groaned. He'd only just dozed off. Between his late evening with the vile cloned Eye of Balor, and his anxiety about Harper being caught as she approached the citadel, he'd tossed and turned throughout the night, drifting off as the eastern horizon first started to glow.

He let a long breath blow through puffed cheeks. "More lessons already?"

Callon's cold smile revealed perfect white teeth. "Not for you. My queen has a special assignment for you alone today."

A special assignment from that red-haired psychopath. Wonderful. Any lingering drowsiness evaporated with his growing fear. Adopting a nonchalant tone, he yawned, stretched, and pressed his feathers flat to his back. "Great. I'm bushed. A day off sounds perfect."

Callon laughed low and long. "By the time Mistress is done with you, you'll yearn for training." Callon flung the door wide and flicked his raven head toward the hallway, where two lumbering trolls waited to escort him. "Come. Badb loathes waiting."

This had to be about Harper. Had these miscreants captured her? What would she think when she saw what he'd become? And now there was going to be face time with Badb Catha. Competing fears warring in his heart, he rustled his gleaming feathers and followed the elf.

More than river trolls lined the hallway outside his room. A half dozen goblins bared their teeth and fingered short swords. More elves flanked every doorway at the ends of the hall and on the center stairs.

"Why the defcon five?" Emilio asked.

His reluctant mentor ignored him and strode gracefully up the hallway.

Emilio glanced at each of the passing windows, straining to see if his companions would be joining him. *Vanilla*, he said in his own mind, but there was no answer. Anxiety ramped up. He chewed the inside of his lip. They're probably fine. Only Tamika ever initiated her mindspace. It apparently didn't work both ways.

Trolls and the goblin regiment slouched along behind him. The gurgling breath of the massive trolls made his skin crawl. The hulking mouth breathers disgusted him on a good day, so he pressed as close to Callon's back as he dared when the group descended the stairs.

Emilio couldn't help feeling as though he was marching to his death. Flight by flight, the steps passed under his slippered feet, and with each one, his breathing quickened. As he rounded the corner to the final set, his knees buckled.

The grubby troll clamped a hand around his arm, hauled him back up, and bellowed. Hot blood from the slices his feathers made through its leathery skin spattered Emilio's shoulder, but he barely noticed.

Badb Catha awaited his arrival beside a cage, a fierce set to her jaw. Next to her was a ring of elves, blades pointed at his chest, and Breas focusing on his fingernails, refusing to meet Emilio's eyes.

"Bring the Netherfae." Badb's voice rang through the plaza. Behind her, the portal shimmered. The crates had all been pressed back against the far wall, leaving a row with a pair of side-by-side vacant cages. Alphine curled in the third spot and held up the feather he'd given her. Several others along the wall did the same. Too bad he didn't get a chance to collect more of Tamika's shimmering hair, because he was about to get the opportunity to give one to Alphine.

Emilio gulped. Every very well-armed Fae eye focused on him. The insane idea of making a run for it clawed through his mind. The huge double doors hung open, the forest visible outside, but if they didn't slaughter him before he reached the exits, they'd hunt him down in the woods.

Callon shoved him sprawling at Badb's feet.

He thought of using what he knew about Breas's clandestine experiment to bargain for his freedom.

Emilio lifted his face to fix Badb in his gaze. "Your Highness, your associate—"

Breas crouched in front of Emilio, blocking Badb Catha under the pretense of helping him up. His lips hovered an inch from Emilio's ear. "Be very careful. The game is not yet over, and you may still require my help to survive. I certainly need yours to complete the Eye." He helped Emilio stand, then resumed his post beside his partner.

The swirling horns of her headdress dipped as Badb looked down at her captive. "What about my associate?"

Behind her, Breas narrowed icy blue eyes at Emilio. "He. Uh. He needs samples of my blood to perfect Abraxas."

"When I'm through with you, he'll have full access to your

blood." She beckoned Sidhe sentries, who jabbed thin swords at him. "We have no demand for a consultant. But we find ourselves in need of bait."

The guards seized him and dragged him to the cage.

"Bait? For what?" But he already knew. Harper. She was coming for him. She always had.

"For a little thorn in my side. Your friend Harper. And if you attempt to call out to her. Warn her. Do anything except lie helplessly in the bottom of that cage, not only will I enjoy killing her, but I'll slaughter every one of your friends. Slowly." The crow cawed his agreement from her shoulder.

"Majesty." A broad-chested man with a cropped beard and a blue spiral tattoo beneath his eye thudded across the floor.

Badb sneered at him. "Gwyn. After your failures, you had better have good news for me."

Gwyn dipped a shallow bow. "Harper's forces are on the lake's far side. I observed a contingent of the Dusk Court, including Lord Ezrynhivar himself, with them. And you should know, Donn nearly killed her. We should bar him from the island—"

Badb snarled. "He will be punished, but for now we need the Sluagh." She paused and her smile returned. "How thoughtful of the Dusk Court King to deliver his people to my doorstep. Saves me the trouble of hunting them."

Callon glided over to bow before his mistress. "Shall I dispatch a regiment to capture them?"

Badb's bitter smile broadened. "No. The plan remains the same. Let them come. Pull half our forces from the eastern doorway. Their numbers are few, so they'll choose the least defended entrance. And we'll be ready for them. I'm actually impressed the little whelp managed to muster her pathetic army. If we can capture them, we'll have enough Fir Bolg and Fae to power our gateway for a year."

The tips of elven swords prickled against Emilio's back, a

swarthy goblin swung the door open, and Emilio crawled inside, meeting Breas's indifferent eyes as the grate slammed shut. Knobby fingers scrabbled over his neck and arms where metal feathers weren't. He felt a pinch as they inserted each lead into his skin. Then he screamed.

<h1 style="text-align:center">CHAPTER 65</h1>

"Son!" Aeld called.

Paegrinn's head shot up and he leapt to his feet, bits of food scattering in every direction. "Father? Harper! How?" He raced for Aeld, and the pair embraced, clapping each other on the back.

Harper's mouth had dried out. The Phooka would probably never be her friend again, but she had to at least try to make things right between them.

"Everyone, can you give us a moment?"

Her mother squeezed her hand, then followed the company out of sight into the woods.

The Phooka dropped flat on his stomach along the branch, and golden eyes flared with a surge of magic before dimming to their usual soft glow.

"Oh. It's you." He tipped back on his haunches and focused on pulling the long tuft of hair at the end of his tail through his chimpanzee-like fingers. "Where's your new best pal?" He refused to meet her eyes.

She gulped. Twigs snapped underfoot as she made her way to

478

stand beneath the craggy tree. With her neck craned up and a quivering lip, she shook her head.

The Phooka pivoted so his shiny back faced her, but he kept his face turned to the side.

"She's gone. The Dawn Court betrayed us all, and I couldn't see it." Harper's shoulders sagged and she stared at her steel-tipped shoes. "Phooka, I don't know where to begin or what to say that'll make what I did right, but Melinoe's manipulations clouded my thinking."

The Phooka sniffed and pulled his tail close to his eyes.

"I think how I felt about Alina gave her the opening to work a wedge between us. You kept a slave, Phooka, and I—"

He hissed and turned his body the rest of the way from Harper, hiding his face.

"The customs of Fae are so alien to me." She paused. So far, her apology sounded like more judgment. "But none of that is the point. You've protected me. Guided me. Made me laugh when I needed it. I'd never have made it this long without you, and even though we've only been friends for a short time, I can't imagine my life if you leave my side."

The Phooka shifted, dropped his tail, and swiveled his head to regard her again, finally meeting Harper's eyes. The corners of his mouth sagged, matching the lines of his drooping ears.

"I should have trusted you." Harper's voice choked and her face pinched. She rested her palm against the tree and cradled her forehead with her other hand. After a deep breath, she continued. "What I'm going to say next will probably trigger some dark Fae debt and I'll end up stuffed in your satchel like Alina. I don't care. Phooka, thank you. And I'm sorry."

He rounded on her then, already changing form. His head wove side to side while his spine stretched and scales rippled along his body. Amber eyes blazed like twin fires above a fierce, reptilian grin. The black Chinese dragon Phooka skittered down the tree in tight spirals, his talons scrabbling along the bark.

Harper hoped the others could hear the commotion and would burst into the clearing. She doubted she could subdue him on her own.

The Phooka landed inches from Harper and reared up on his hind legs. A swirling wind blew the shaggy mane in whorls. He was looming over her now, claws pointed at her chest. Harper stumbled away to clutch a narrow fir tree, her back pressed flat against its trunk.

The Phooka arced over her and cackled with his talons digging the air. "You'll wish you lived jammed in my magical bag when this is all over!"

Harper froze, slack-jawed, and clutched the tree's bark. Then she yelped and brandished the sheathed Sword of Light. She waited for his jaws to snap over her and the accompanying agony of torn flesh. One second passed. Then two. The black dragon loomed, his tail lashing like an angry cat and a single talon a millimeter from her face.

"Boop." The Phooka tapped the talon to her nose.

Harper's mouth opened and snapped closed while her brain caught up.

Fianna and Ez's people came crashing through the woody brush. "Harper!" several yelled in unison.

The dragon rolled onto his back. His clawed feet pedaled the air as he shrank to his original form. Transformation complete, he clutched his sides and rolled back and forth, braying like a high-pitched donkey. "You should see your face. Wait." His hand shot into his bag and brought out a cell phone. "Shoot," he said, and the shutter clicked. The Phooka looked at his phone and guffawed while he slapped his knee. "Look." He flipped the phone toward Harper, wheezing the final strains of his laughter.

"Honey, are you okay?" Eileen raced toward them, Phelan and the Fianna behind her.

Harper finally let herself relax and smiled at the Phooka. "We're fine. I think."

"The others are scouting the view of that tower from the other side. They'll be back soon." Phelan and the other Fianna stood beside her mom and all dipped their chins in deference.

It was the Phooka's turn to stand with a slack jaw. "I'm gone for a day and you get minions?"

Harper dried her eyes on her sleeve and dropped to pull him into an embrace. His fur felt silky like a cat's, so she buried her face in his neck ruff.

"So you didn't kill me. What bargain have I landed myself in by thanking you?"

She felt his hand wrap around her shoulders and he relaxed into the hug. "No bargains."

"But I thought—"

"There's nothing more you can give me than you already have. Believe me, the balance sheet remains strongly in your favor."

That was a strange thing for him to say. What on earth did he mean?

The Phooka drew back from her and pointed at the cluster of Fianna. "Greetings, sweet Eileen. Who are your friends?" He sniffed the air. "They smell like damp dog."

Harper wanted to find out more about his strange comment, but Aeld, Paegrinn, and Hieronymous arrived.

"Paegrinn!" Harper hauled herself up and pulled the young Fir Bolg into a hug. "I'm sorry I left you guys." She clapped him on the shoulders.

"Melinoe influenced you. Besides, we never left you," Paegrinn said.

"I'm afraid reunion time must cease, as charming as it is." Hieronymous beckoned for Harper and her friends to join him around a broad, flat rock. "We must decide on a strategy because that citadel is heavily fortified."

"Not to mention we have no clue where the portal even is inside it," Phelan said beside him. Fintan dispatched Aisling and Michael to prowl the forest.

Harper paced, face scrunched in concentration. "Back at the council in the village, Nuada said the portal was in the center of a tree on the ground floor. That shouldn't be too hard to find."

Hieronymous rumbled an affirmative. "But the location of the prisoners eludes us."

"And Dewberry said Badb created the Netherfae from the prisoners. We have to stop this." Eileen reached for Harper's hand and squeezed it.

Harper gave her mom a forced smile. The possibility that Emilio was one of the Fae hybrids was too horrid to entertain. Almost as gut-wrenching, he could be one of the Dust-addicted people the Netherfae used as puppets.

Harper sagged onto the rock like a wrung-out cloth. Rescuing the stolen was a tall order, but only half of what they needed to accomplish. "And we've got to keep that gateway open long enough for the Sluagh to go through, and Nuada's dying wish was for me to get to the Underworld and find his people. Convince them to fight with us."

Aeld's massive head shook. "That will be nearly impossible. Donn won't relinquish the source of his power. Besides, their minds are bent to his. They couldn't leave if they wanted to."

"But Harper's dad fought his influence. Maybe he can break Donn's control," Paegrinn said.

Phelan's features pulled into a frown. "The likelihood he'll get close enough to the portal is slim. Badb hates the Sluagh. She won't invite them inside the citadel unless her situation is dire. On this island her strength is the Underworld Fae."

"Regardless, our focus must be on preventing any more reinforcements from the Underworld arriving." Phelan pounded a fist against his palm. "Otherwise we'll be overrun, even if we rallied every Green World Fae to our cause. We can't delay for the Sluagh to escape. We'll be lucky to just get Harper and the rest of the Fianna through."

"This just went pear-shaped," Fintan said.

"Never thought I'd agree with a mongrel." Lord Ezrynhivar drew himself to his full height. "If we do decide to attack, we should make this a recon mission and return with greater numbers. I am loath to admit it but, my friends, we are completely outclassed."

"Emilio and the stolen can't wait that long," Harper said. "Plus, won't we take a bite out of Badb's numbers now if the Sluagh escape and we prevent more Fae from coming through?"

Her mother rested her palm on Harper's back. "The longer we wait, the more Badb's ranks grow. It'll never be easier than it is right now to knock her down a few pegs."

The company lapsed into a heated debate about next steps. Harper didn't try to stop them. She shifted from foot to foot beside her mom, while the Phooka chowed down on a bag of hot Cheetos. He blamed his stress eating on all the bickering.

While fantasies of striking Badb Catha down with her magic and Nuada's sword brought a warm glow to her chest, the truth remained: Harper's priority had to be to free everyone inside and help her father find peace. A journey through the gateway to the Undying Lands seemed impossible, but perhaps closing the gateway would hamstring Badb's strength and end this now, saving her the trip.

She pressed her palms to her temples and let out a groan. The debate regarding the plan remained in stalemate, and the voices were intensifying around her.

"Stop!" Harper barked. The chatter fell still, and all eyes

focused on her. "If we abandon the Sluagh, we're no better than Badb Catha. We'd be dooming our race to a slow decline."

Hieronymous lifted his shaggy, horned head toward the tower and stroked his chin. "Your ethics are correct, but they vastly outnumber us. We will be fortunate if we can even free your friend and destroy whatever magic powers that portal."

Ez slumped. "I've developed a fondness for hopeless causes, and a taste for vengeance, so the Dusk Court is at your disposal." His spine lifted again, and he focused his red eyes on Harper. "But I can't help you infiltrate that fortress."

Harper's brow creased. "Why not?"

"Serotina's subjects would sense a Dusk Fae instantly. Any of my people would get you discovered the second we set foot inside."

Hope retreated before Harper like the tide. Well, screw hope. She'd not had any in her adult life, and she'd accomplished the improbable.

Hieronymous twitched his ears and stroked his chin. "We lack the forces to destroy the tower, so this is must be a surgical strike. That being said, my solitary Fae won't be detected by the Dawn Court inside. We're the logical choice to infiltrate the tower, search for prisoners, and destroy the gateway."

Eileen turned to Aeld and the Fir Bolg clustered around him. "Harper needs your help. After all you've seen here, after being hunted in your own woods, isn't now the time to join the fight?"

Paegrinn stretched tall. "Father, she's right."

Aeld nodded and sighed. "Since we are already here, we shall repay your defense of our community in kind. Though we have the same problem as Lord Ezrynhivar's people. We can only help from the outside."

Phelan stood close to Eileen and smiled broadly down at Harper. "There's only four of us here, but we'll follow you, Harper."

Fintan's brogue rang out through the clearing. "By my reckoning, that leaves more of our forces outside that tower than in. That gateway and your friends will probably be more heavily guarded than those doors."

Hieronymous rubbed his lace doublet. "And if we can't get enough of us inside to accomplish our task, we may as well save our forces to fight again another day."

They'd argued themselves full circle. Harper's fists clenched at her sides. Emilio and her dad may not have another day. Any delay and she'd lose the Dusk Court and the Fir Bolg. Even if she made it across this island a second time, Badb's ranks would have grown, making a second rescue attempt impossible.

Her jaw clamped tight, matching the tension in her hands. To have come so far, only to have it all fall apart at the tower gates, was more than she could bear. Despair slithered down her spine.

*Emilio. Abraham. Dad.*

Suddenly, she jerked upright.

"Honey?" Her mother tugged on her arm.

*Of course! The answer's been staring me in the face the whole time.* "Our army's on the inside. We just have to release them." Badb had been stealing people from the streets for months, at least, maybe longer. There had to be hundreds of people in that tower.

"Did you get into Twitch's crazy pills?" The Phooka wound a finger in circles about his long ear while the goblin shot her the thumbs-up from beside Hieronymous. "I mean, I approve, but..."

Lord Ezrynhivar tossed his hair back and bent toward Harper. "Although I enjoy your hippy-dippy optimism, there is a glaring hole in your plan."

"Glamour." Hieronymous finished Ez's thought.

The Dusk King nodded. "This human army will be hopelessly glamoured. They simply won't fight for you."

Harper cursed under her breath and wrapped her arms

around herself, the steel studs of her jacket cold and jagged beneath her fingers. Steel. That's it.

She flung her pack to the ground, swiped open the zipper, and scrabbled around in the bottom for the last few shells she had. With a triumphant smile, she held one aloft. "There are a bunch of tiny steel spheres in here. If we could somehow give one to each person inside, they couldn't be glamoured."

Ezrynhivar appeared almost sad. "That's a tall order, would-be queen. Perhaps we can only shut down the portal. The best we can do. It's over."

"Over? Did you say over?" The Phooka marched into the center of the ring. His face bubbled and grew fat cheeks carpeted with sideburns. A red and black shirt materialized across his chest. "Was it over when the Germans bombed Pearl Harbor?"

He paused his pilfered speech. A ring of mostly confused faces surrounded him. Phelan and Eileen rolled their eyes, but Michael guffawed and slapped a knee.

"Hell no!" The Phooka pumped a fist. "Because when the going gets tough—"

"The tough get going!" Michael shouted. "My favorite movie."

The Phooka shook his jowls and pointed at the red-haired man. "There's my people!" He leapt up to the flat rock and scanned the assembly. "This situation absolutely requires a really futile and stupid gesture..." He scratched his head. "Wait. That's not my line. Eileen, you've seen *Animal House*, bring us home."

The smile faded from Phelan's face. "As hilarious as the Phooka is, and as difficult as it is for me to say this, I agree with Ezrynhivar."

"Good boy, want a biscuit?" Ez slapped his knees like he called to a dog.

Phelan scowled at him. "If we attempt to do too much, we'll spread ourselves too thin. We need a more streamlined plan, both for tonight and in the long term."

"No. It could work." Harper's voice was strong and confident. "The Fianna, the Phooka, a few of Hieronymous's people, and I can sneak inside in teams. The Fianna and I can hand out the steel shot—"

The Phooka's tail lashed like a cat ready to pounce. "With our new recruits, we save Emilio. Hopefully break that portal so the Sluagh can leave. Then the Dusk Court and the solitaries not inside cover our escape while the Fir Bolg do that fungus path thing to guide us the hell off this island. With the humans, we might be able to pull this cockamamie scheme off. Bloody brilliant."

Harper scanned the faces around her. Heck, she had huge doubts herself, but it was the only plan they had.

# CHAPTER 66

Ezrynhivar sighed and shook his head. "I still think the plan is doomed to fail, but the east entrance is the least guarded."

"Which is exactly why we shouldn't touch it." Phelan traced circles in the dust with his boot.

Beside him, Michael tossed his red head back and barked a single laugh. "You really want to hole up where it's most heavily guarded? You're daft."

Hieronymous nodded. "No. He's right. The glaistig and Gwyn have had plenty of time to warn Badb. The only reason we've not been attacked is because they already know we're here."

The Phooka's face popped into the shape of the fish-faced captain from *Star Wars*. "It's a trap!" he said before his face bubbled back to its normal shape.

Aeld dipped his head to Ezrynhivar's group and his own Fir Bolg. "The best approach is for us to keep the perimeter outside the citadel clear. Badb may yet be unaware of our numbers. Once Harper's team inside frees the humans and Sluagh, we can clear the way for our escape with the help of the will o' wisp and the Fianna."

It was a solid enough plan under the circumstances. Harper just needed to figure out how to sneak inside, given every Fae on this island was searching for her.

The Phooka lifted his face to the treetop where a faint green dot rested. He whistled and the little will o' wisp spiraled down to hover inches from him.

"Phooka, you promised to free her if she did her part," Harper said.

"Don't remind me. She'll probably not help us if I let her go. We may need her to guide the non-Fae races safely back to civilization."

"We still have the mycelium path, the Fianna, and plenty of Fae."

The Phooka just stared at her until Harper nudged him with her elbow.

"Alina, our bargain is concluded. You are free," he said, his voice barely a whisper.

The little Fae tittered and zoomed a few circles around Harper's head, while Harper dug out a bit of chocolate from her bag. With a gentle smile at the green glowing Fae, she placed the chocolate on a rock. "For the mice. No strings. You know what we're facing, and we could use your help if you want to join us."

Alina settled onto the rock and nibbled her chocolate. Harper thought she saw a tiny smile on the creature's face. Then she spiraled high and winked out. Harper's face fell. Looked like they'd have to rely on the Fianna to navigate the shifting forest. She'd turned back to the group when Alina streaked across the sky to settle on Harper's shoulder.

"Glad you stayed, Alina," Harper said. She squeezed her mom's hand. "Mom, you should get clear, it's too dangerous."

"Honey, I'm not abandoning you now."

"And me." Paegrinn thumped his chest. "I'm going inside with Harper."

"Son..."

"You cannot decide for me, Father. I am of age."

Harper patted Paegrinn on the back, gratitude warming her heart. "Thanks, Paegrinn, that means a lot." He returned the gesture, nearly bowling her over with the flat of his hand.

When she recovered, Harper fixed the others in her gaze. "I've got an idea." It was a lame idea and from one of the Phooka's favorite movies, but considering the stream of human prisoners guided inside by teams of Fae, it might actually work.

Harper shared the sparse details of her plan. "Our group will spread out in the forest around the tower's front and west entrances. They'll be our easiest escape if the east is a trap. We'll take fleeing humans or Alina's flight as our signal to either come to your aid to or cover your retreat."

"Good luck, would-be queen."

Harper smiled at Ez. When she'd first met the dark Fae, she could scarcely imagine working on the same side. "I'm glad you're with us. Best of luck to you too."

The Fir Bolg had already disappeared into the forest. Aeld held out a hand to Harper. She grasped it. "Keep my son safe, and when this is over, you and Eileen are free to reside with the Fir Bolg."

"I will, and thank you for helping my mom. And me."

The pale stone building loomed before them, taller than it appeared from a distance. How on earth had Breas built this here in such a short time? Harper was sure the building hadn't been there when she was a child. There were no roads in or out. It was as if it had just materialized on this spot. She saw the black and white chimaera holding its red double helix, standard elements of the Erimus Pharmaceutical logo. She rolled her eyes. Breas was certainly an egomaniac to need the sign here where no one would see it.

A large pond lay between them and the massive front gates.

Marble stairs stretched in every direction from the building and they crawled with Fae. Large and small, lumbering and lithe, they moved around the citadel, many guiding dazed humans between them.

Nuada's description of what hung from the trees couldn't prepare Harper for the sight up close. All around the building, cocoons of mist dangled. She thought of Emilio suspended in one and her heart skipped a beat. Above the mist cocoons, the branches were thick with black birds. Sluagh. Had to be. She squinted at them, wondering if one was her father.

The Phooka finished the last knot on Paegrinn's bonds. Beside him, Hieronymous and his solitary Fae bound the hands of her mother and the Fianna. Harper had already given them handfuls of steel shot to distribute.

With a final tug, the Phooka stepped back and crossed his arms over his chest. His eyebrows were cocked.

"Harper, look, you know how much I love a crazy plan. I don't like iron, but I was with you on the steel shot idea. But this is lunacy, even for me. It's never going to work."

Paegrinn looked down at the bright blue nylon cord that bound his hands and ended in a long, looped lead. "Why not?"

The Phooka interjected before Harper could begin. "She saw it in a movie once. Arguably the best piece of cinema ever made, but a movie nonetheless." He waved his hand dismissively as he spoke.

"Like a Batman movie?" Paegrinn beamed.

"Not like Batman." Harper said and clapped the Phooka on the arm. "I'd think with your passion for movies, Phooka, you'd be all over this plan."

"Oh, it's a fabulous plan, if you're on the bloody Death Star!"

Harper pointed to streams of Sidhe marching manacled Fae and dazed humans through the central door.

"Looks like we got here after some of their raiding parties

returned. It's actually a good plan considering our resources," she said.

"I have a bad feeling about this," the Phooka said, glowering at her from the tops of his eyes.

Eileen's eyes were like saucers. Harper pulled her close. "You can still wait here if this is too much for you," she whispered.

"Honey, I've let you down almost your whole life. I've had a little practice fighting these creatures recently. Once we're moving, I'll be fine." Harper's palm encountered the long bump in the center of her mother's back that betrayed the presence of the snubby shotgun.

"I love you, Mom."

"Love you, honey."

They exchanged a quick embrace, and the fake prisoners with their clusters of Fae guards departed for the main and west entrances. By now, Ezrynhivar would be massing a smaller force near the east entrance to keep up the ruse that they didn't suspect Badb had set a trap.

Harper's group included Paegrinn, Twitch, and the Phooka. The goblin earned his name because he startled at every sound and constantly flicked his nose. Several times, he asked the Phooka for drugs. Harper feared he'd blow their cover.

"We have a problem," the Phooka said.

Harper leaned her head close to the Phooka to avoid being overheard. "I know, he's not going to make it."

"Not him. He'll be fine. It's you. Gwyn and Donn will be in there, and Badb's crows have seen you before, so she knows what you look like."

Harper cursed under her breath. How could she have missed that detail? "What do we do?"

"Make you invisible." The Phooka brought out a purple stone and handed it to her. "This is a little Fomorian device I picked up on my travels. Makes a person see you the way you want them to.

Like a glamour but undetectable by Fae. I suggest totally transparent. Put it in your pocket."

Harper wrinkled her nose. Fomorian anything sounded like a bad idea. But she shoved the stone in her jacket pocket and envisioned herself as completely see through.

"Whoa, Harper. You just disappeared." Paegrinn smiled.

Twitch scratched his nose. "I can still smell her. They can too."

"But there's so many humans inside, they won't be able to tell," the Phooka said.

Twitch retched. "Ugh. You don't have any marijuana, do you? Mask the smell?"

The Phooka groaned and smacked his forehead. "For the hundredth time, I don't have any drugs. But if it's any consolation, we're about to break into a pharmaceutical company. I'm sure there'll be something to your liking inside."

The goblin's eyes glittered. He clapped his palms and hopped in place. "Lots more excited about mission now."

The friends crouched behind the undergrowth waiting for a lull in Fae traffic entering the building.

"It's time," Twitch said.

"Now or never." Harper was hovering a few steps behind Paegrinn. She craned her neck to catch sight of the two other teams of Fae escorting Michael and Aisling as their faux guards. Aisling's pink hair disappeared around the east corner, while Michael shuffled along behind an elf with jet-black skin toward the western entrance. Phelan and her mom were probably already inside. Two teams would each take a wing and start at the bottom. Harper and the Phooka planned to waltz right in the front door and proceed to the topmost floors, split up, and work their way down. They'd know they were done when they met in the middle. That is, if everything went according to plan.

The Phooka's shape began to fade. A black shimmer blurred

his edges as he grew in size and coalesced into a creature taller than Paegrinn. He was far uglier too. The Phooka's skin was still black, and he had a great barrel chest and short thick legs. His muscular arms dragged along the ground.

"What the hell are you?"

"Rock troll. Big. Stupid, but able to subdue a Fir Bolg. I'm going for realism here." His lump of a head sat directly on his shoulders. The only way he was recognizable were the golden eyes. The Phooka grabbed Paegrinn's leash.

Twitch wheezed a raspy laugh and grasped Paegrinn from the opposite side.

"Paegrinn, walk all slumped over like you've been beaten up," Harper said. He nodded and slouched almost in half.

Harper was invisible, but she swore anything in a ten-foot radius could hear her heart pounding. What if the plan didn't work? Her friends would probably be killed, drained in the portal or something, and her father would be doomed to being Donn's slow meal. Of course, she'd be killed a lot faster. Then who would save Emilio and the others? No. She had to push the doubt from her mind. It would work. It had to. The alternative was unimaginable.

There was a small concrete path up to the doorway. Paegrinn, Twitch, and the Phooka glanced around for signs of Fae before stepping out onto it from their hiding place in the undergrowth. Harper watched as the Phooka lumbered toward the entrance. He gave a periodic tug on the rope, causing Paegrinn to stumble and Twitch to claw for Paegrinn's arm. Each time, the Phooka turned around and roared at the young Fir Bolg. Spittle flew from his lips and his big ears trembled. Harper was impressed by their acting.

They arrived at the pair of glass doors, each bearing Erimus's lion-like chimaera logo and guarded by a pair of elegant red-and-black-clad Sidhe men. Their ears lanced up from unbound jet-black hair. They were beautiful in a cold way. Their heads inched up like an elevator in unison, scanning the towering Phooka. When they noticed Paegrinn behind him, their faces pulled into looks of undisguised disgust.

"Where did you find a Fir Bolg, troll?" a Sidhe asked, his voice low and cold.

"Wha?" The Phooka let a long string of drool dangle from his thick bottom lip. It flicked back and forth. His mouth hung open and his chest heaved with grunting breaths.

"What Fear Bulge?" Twitch knitted his brows and blinked rapidly.

"This creature." The other elf jabbed a finger at Paegrinn. "Where did you find it?"

The Phooka drew his lips into a broad smile to reveal yellowed teeth with bits of green gunk jammed between them. A laugh rumbled in his chest like rolling thunder. His great finger pointed at the nearest elf like he had told the best troll joke in the world. The Phooka slapped his knee with his huge hand. "Gots lots that in bag. Huh-huh-huh-huh." He pointed to a greasy-looking sack tied to his waist, elbowed the elf, and winked.

"Heh-heh-heh primo stuff too." Twitch tapped his nose and gave a conspiratorial wink. The pair of them sounded like the Fae Beavis and Butthead.

Both Sidhe took a step back. Their noses wrinkled. "Just take it up to the third floor for processing."

The Phooka wagged his head and winked again. "Huh-huh-huh." He presented two fingers at them.

"No, you great moron. Third floor. Three." The elf spat and waved three fingers at the Phooka's face.

Twitch snickered and held all ten of his fingers out.

The Phooka snorted and slapped his hand on his forehead. He held up his two fingers again and pushed a third finger up. "Huuuh?" The elves nodded, and the Phooka trudged toward the door. He pushed Paegrinn in first and paused to look back. It gave

Harper just enough time to slip inside unnoticed. He smiled again at the elves as he shambled through the door. He lifted a hand and waved at them with a broad, stupid grin on his face.

Both elves rolled their eyes. "Rock trolls. Dumber than rats," the tallest remarked. Just then, the Phooka let out a long, rumbling fart, sending both elves scurrying out of the way of the impending cloud of stench. Despite the stakes and the fact she was surrounded by superhuman enemies, Harper had to clamp her hand over her mouth to keep from laughing. And inhaling.

# CHAPTER 67

The place crawled with Fae, the team had been hustled to a side entrance far away from the shining, circular tree in the center of the ground floor. Elves in red-and-black armored regalia flanked every doorway, goblins and trolls circulated in clusters through the hallways, and delicate winged Fae hovered like dragonflies in the central stairway. Harper was grateful the Fomorian invisibility charm seemed to work. Her previous encounters with this many Fae in tight quarters had nearly ended in her death.

"Hey, you. Big, smelly, and dumb," a redcap jeered with his mouthful of needly teeth. His buddies snickered and punched him playfully on the shoulder.

The Phooka slapped Paegrinn on the back so hard he doubled over. "This Fur Bolt." He hovered his booger-crusted, bulbous nose over Paegrinn's head and inhaled with enough force to bring a wisp of his hair into a nostril. "He smell fine. Not that big." Troll Phooka slapped his chest and stretched to full height.

"Heh-heh, yeah. It's clever too." Twitch rubbed the tip of his long nose. "Say, you boyos know where they keep the free samples? The ones they hand out to doctors?"

497

Harper pressed her back flat against the wall as the redcaps scurried forward. Their leader tilted his head sideways and regarded the Phooka and Twitch from the corners of his eyes. "Everyone knows we don't make human medicine here."

Twitch looked crestfallen. "Dammit." He rounded on the Phooka. "You said there'd be good drugs here! We could trade the Fur Bulge for them. I feel cheated."

The Phooka inhaled a deep, gurgling breath, smacked his enormous hand on his forehead with a wet splat, and chuckled. "We no need catch Fear Bowl for ducks. Ducks everywhere."

While the Twitch and Phooka Show had the redcaps flummoxed, Harper slid along the wall and peered into a tiny office window. A dozen wood gurneys parked in neat rows, each bearing a human corpse in various stages of dissection.

She turned away and bit her lip. Too many rooms had been like this one, and the image of Emilio as one of the dead refused to recede. In their three-floor journey, they'd only handed out the steel shot to two rooms of terrified people. Hopefully, the other teams were having better luck.

The Phooka's performance ended the same way it always did. Enemy Fae telling them where to go, the Phooka playing dumb, and when that didn't get the Fae to leave, flatulence was his last line of defense. A rumble reverberated off every surface, and the redcaps scattered.

Harper crept close to the Phooka, sleeve pulled over her nose. "This floor might be a bust," she whispered.

The black-and-grey rock troll tilted his huge, round face down and nodded. Yellow eyes glinted with mischief. He was enjoying this.

At the end of the hall, elves sent the trio back into the stairwell with instructions to go down to the third floor. The Phooka dragged Paegrinn down half a flight before the Sidhe ducked back inside to guard their hallway. Then they tip-toed up a floor to the tenth level.

"What on earth are you bringing that reeking pile of hair up here for?" A lithe elven woman, her black hair coiled in a high bun, scowled up at the Phooka and pinched her nostrils together. "This floor is for the Abraxas experiments. Humans and Netherfae. Magical creature processing is on the third floor."

"Says one on door." A green-tinted string of snot oozed from the Phooka's nose, sending the Sidhe woman staggering out of the way.

"One-zero. That's ten, not one, you dolt."

"This where you keep the samples?" Twitch's eyes glittered.

While her Fae friends put on their disgusting spectacle, Harper slipped from door to door, peeking in the windows. Inside, most were creatures she'd never seen before housed in simple rooms like some kind of stripped-down college dorm. The occupants must be the Netherfae. Not that she'd probably scratched the surface of the different shapes and sizes of Fae, but absolutely none of them resembled any type of Fae she'd seen thus far. They all seemed to be different species entirely.

Each door revealed different beings. Not a single one looked anything like the last. *I have a bad feeling about this.* The Phooka's movie quote was the perfect expression of the sense of dread hovering over Harper like a dark cloud. Because she sought humans, she kept moving; no telling whether the Netherfae would be on her side.

She peered through the next tiny pane of glass. Inside, a Fae of exquisite beauty sat cross-legged on her simple cot. Black skin with a glimmering blue tinge harmonized with purple and magenta hair filled with flowers. Blooming flowers. As Harper gawked, buds opened and closed between shining locks of hair. Butterfly wings in matching colors rubbed together at her back.

But it was her roommate that made Harper gasp. Though

definitely not Fae-like beautiful, she seemed familiar. Grey skin, pointed ears, plump. Thick coils of black hair framing full lips, and a kindly face despite the sharp teeth. She evoked memories of the Romani woman who'd helped Harper at the Mystic Island Festival what seemed like ages ago. But that woman didn't have red, clawed hands.

Locks on the doors suggested these were prisoners, not residents, so she risked slipping inside for a closer look. All Fae eyes were riveted on the Phooka, Twitch, and Paegrinn and their performance. So she cracked the door open just enough to slide through and pulled it closed softly.

The beautiful Fae and the grey-skinned creature paused their conversation and focused on the exit. When no one stepped inside, they shared puzzled looks.

"Must have decided to check the commotion outside rather than escort us to the field," the purple-haired Fae said.

The other sniffed the air and squinted right at where Harper stood. "No. Something's here. I can smell their blood." She inhaled, smacked her lips, then her brows pinched. "It can't be."

"What?" the other Fae asked, wide eyed, her wings sliding back and forth like someone wringing their hands.

"Human." Curls bounced as the creature slid from her cot. "We're not Fae. We won't hurt you, but I'm curious how a human has used glamour."

That voice. Warm. Compassionate. It couldn't be, though. Before she caught herself, Harper whispered, "Selina?"

The winged Fae hugged her knees to her chest. The grey one smiled, the warmth of her face at odds with her appearance. "Yes. How do I know you?"

Harper rushed toward the Romani woman and clasped her hand. "It's Harper. From the Mystic Island Festival."

"Harper!" both said in unison.

"What did they do to you?" Harper's heart constricted at the sight of her friend.

"We're the first successful subjects of the Abraxas Fae hybrid experiment. Most of the power of the Fae, none of the troublesome allergy to iron or annoying rules about outright murdering humans."

"Plus, we can mind-control the glamoured. I'm Tamika Sani. Emilio's told us so much about you."

"Is…" Harper gulped. "Is Emilio like you?" She was glad she was invisible. Her hands clutched at her chest so hard it would leave a mark.

Selina's face fell. "I'm afraid so."

She was too late. All the delays in the Fir Bolg village. Her own failures at the farmhouse and under the spell of the gancanagh. It must have been a living hell to be here, to be changed into these things. Her best friend would never be the same, and it was all her fault.

"No." Harper's voice cracked, and a sob escaped. "I'm so sorry it took me so long. I've failed you all."

Selina's red, clawed fingers extended in front of her and searched the space. Once they found her, Selina pulled her into an embrace. Tamika drifted close with a compassionate smile. "No, you didn't, sweetheart. You kept safe, found help. Alone, you couldn't have stopped any of this."

"I guess the good thing is if we can get out of here, we can fight them. We're as strong as they are," Tamika said.

Harper drew back from her friends and fished out a bag of the stainless steel from her pocket, pressing it into Tamika's palm. "I have to go find Emilio, but others are with me. If you see any humans, give them one of these."

"BBs? What's that going to do?" Tamika caressed a few in her hand.

"Iron. It'll break the glamour and stop the Fae from re-spelling them."

Selina smiled. "But how are you invisible carrying these?"

"Fomorian magic. Once you hear a big commotion, head for the western exit. Friendly Fae will meet you in the woods and guide you off the island."

"Here. Take this." Tamika snapped off two flowers from her hair, a snowdrop and a bluebell, and pressed them into Harper's hand. "Now give me a strand of yours."

"What—"

"Tamika can communicate with us in a mindspace. It's how we've been able to stay alive in here," Selina said.

Harper didn't understand, but she broke off three strands of her hair and handed them to Tamika. The beautiful half-Fae tied them into her own hair and opened her mouth to speak.

The creak of a hinge snapped everyone to attention. Selina and Tamika scurried to their cots and Harper stood statue still.

"Hello, cousin." The smug voice purred from the doorway. "Did you think I'd not sense Fomorian magic enter my tower?"

The tall blond man wore a perfectly tailored blue business suit that looked completely out of place. He lifted a hand and made a pinching gesture. Harper felt a tug, like a sheet being dragged across her skin, and caught her reflection in the window's glass.

The sheathed sword already hovered between them.

"Please." The man flicked his hand, and the blade thudded to the floor.

"I'm not your cousin, asshat." Harper crinkled her nose.

Breas's blond hair swept back from his face as he laughed. He grabbed Harper by the neck and shoved her into the hallway, thrusting his fingers inside her pocket and drawing out the Fomorian stone. He smiled.

Selina and Tamika peered through the tiny window of their closed door.

"But you are my cousin. My name is Breas. Didn't Nuada tell you why Badb and I were hunting you?"

"He told me you were a traitor and that the Tuatha should have killed you instead of taking pity on you." Breas's hand flew across her jaw and sent her head smacking into the wall. She pulled herself back upright and rubbed her face, catching sight of the Phooka and Paegrinn who were ringed by weapon-wielding goblins and elves a couple more doors down.

Her eyes skewered Breas. *Well, if you're going to fail, at least make it spectacular.* She was too exhausted to worry much about herself, but she feared for her mom, Emilio, and all the others. She had to warn them to break off the attack, but she could barely hear herself think with the rushing blood rhythmically pounding in her ears.

Breas's lips formed a thin line. He leaned in to her and smoothed his hands down his lapels. "You are the last descendant of Niall, and Eriu is your ancestor. She is my mother." He jabbed a finger into her chest, sending her staggering back. "That is how we're related."

Harper's face flushed a deep red. Fists clenched at her side. A wave of anger and disgust soured her stomach. There was no way she was kin to this monster, no way her quest was to end like this. Her lungs were like bellows fanning the flames of her outrage. Watching the Sidhe strike Paegrinn and hold swords to the necks of the Phooka and Twitch added fuel to the fire.

That delicious sharp electricity hummed in her core, and she envisioned it flowing to the ring. *Focus on Breas.* In a flash, her hands whipped up. A savage scream erupted from her lips at the same instant crackling blue plasma slammed into Breas. He flew back and tumbled several more feet along the floor.

Harper relished the look of astonishment on his face, but she knew instantly it was a dumb and impulsive move. Breas was already on his feet, face contorted into a snarl. The Sidhe and other assorted Fae closed in to cut off any escape. She wished Paegrinn hadn't lost the shotguns because her mind played a delicious scene of a hall teeming with Fae writhing on the floor, full of steel shot.

Breas charged at her. His long strides echoed off the marble walls. Behind him, a pair of Sidhe pointed swords at her friends, ready to strike. Fear for them doused her magic and the crackly blue flames winked out. She raised herself from her defensive crouch and spread her fingers.

"Charming. I'd love to kill you myself. Slowly. But Badb has other plans for you. These days, the blood of Eriu is just too rare to waste. I wish Nuada had lived long enough to witness your failure." He grabbed her by the hair and dragged her staggering toward the stairwell. Harper's hands clamped over his and she half jogged behind him to keep up.

"Bring those three. We'll let Badb decide if they are grist for the portal or to be used for genetic extraction."

Breas was silent as he dragged her down flight after flight of stairs. Overbalanced, Harper fell many times, only to be wrenched to standing. Her head ached from his grip. Bruises flowered all over her legs and on her face where Breas had struck her. Harper heard the din of the Phooka, Twitch, and Paegrinn clattering along behind her with their goblin and troll guard.

"I told you this only works on the Death Star," the Phooka shouted. Even now he could joke.

"All part of the plan, Phooka. The Ewoks are on the way. Stay alert," Harper bluffed. She hoped Hieronymous's solitary Fae and their Fianna counterparts had distributed the stainless shot more than her group had, and she prayed Selina would slip the bits of steel to many others and pass her escape message along. Maybe, despite her failure, at least some of the kidnapped would be freed.

Breas jerked his grip and rattled her jaw. "Silence. Anyone who could save you now is long dead."

She risked a glance behind. Her friends trudged between the Fae, hands bound.

Breas rounded the last bend in the marble stairs and burst into the bustling portal room. Harper staggered behind. She twisted her head to the side and her heart dropped to her feet. Fae of every size and shape milled about in the large room. So many, she wondered if her reinforcements could even handle them.

The golden circular tree with its shifting, glimmering portal stalled her breath. Breas hurled her at the feet of a tall, pale woman with branching black horns spiraling from her headdress. She recognized the flaming red hair from the Mystic Island Festival.

Badb Catha.

# CHAPTER 68

"Harper!" called a familiar voice.

Still sprawled on the floor, she flicked her eyes along the rows of imprisoned Fae and a chill ricocheted up her spine.

*Oh God. What have they done to him?* All the whispered reports, Ashley's insinuations, were true. Harper had pushed those terrible possibilities away and chosen to believe that somehow her best friend had been spared. But the reality was almost too much to bear. "Emilio!" she shouted. She scanned the plaza, seeking Abraham, but he wasn't there.

"It's really you." Emilio wrapped his fingers around the bars and smiled.

"I came to save you," she called, voice pinched. There had to be a way to reverse the changes, because she couldn't accept she'd been too late. She hoped Emilio could forgive her someday.

"She failed," Breas interjected and stepped between them, passing the Cliamh Solais to Badb.

Badb's eyes traveled from Harper to Emilio and she ran her hand along the scabbard as she placed it on the armrest of her black throne. A wintry smile creased her porcelain features. "So much trouble caused by such a tiny whelp." Badb dropped to her haunches inches from Harper, still splayed on the floor. Pale fingers coiled through the hair at the back of her head and yanked Harper's face up. "So this is the one my sister hid from me all these years. How very unimpressive. Macha needn't have bothered. The child is clearly lacking."

The air around Badb Catha was several degrees colder, chilling Harper's clammy skin and bringing violent shivering. But it was the silky, resonant voice she recognized from the night that destroyed her life. The sound that woke her screaming from her sleep for over a decade.

*Well, if I'm going out, I'm not giving these horrors the pleasure of seeing my fear.* Harper nodded toward the Sword of Light. "The last time I drew that blade, this child wiped out half the Wild Hunt."

Badb wrenched Harper's head to the side and launched herself back to her feet. A lance of pain skewered Harper's neck and shoulder. Badb pivoted and slammed her boot into Harper's upper back. Her jaw clacked when she collapsed to the chill marble floor. She rolled aside and levered herself onto her forearm. The Phooka was uncharacteristically quiet. He'd adopted his natural form and stared at the ceiling next to Paegrinn and Twitch.

Badb followed her gaze and regarded Paegrinn. "It has been long since the Fir Bolg have left their villages. You honor us with your presence. Are your people planning to enter this war? You would have much to gain by joining my cause. Surely the human infection has overtaken more than a few of your ancient settlements."

Paegrinn lifted his chin and spoke in a measured tone. "My people have not gone to war since our defeat by the Tuatha at the First Battle of Moytura. We are content to deepen our knowledge of the worlds and live apart. Only I have joined this battle, and I am most definitely not on your side."

It was Breas who responded. "Unfortunate. Perhaps the Third Battle will see the wiser among you realizing we share a common enemy."

Harper laughed and drew her knees beneath her to look up at Breas. "That's pretty rich coming from a Fomorian. Nuada told me it's your people who profit from the mega-companies plundering the planet. With all the humans dead, who's going to buy your products and keep you wealthy? Seems to me the Fomorians have everything to lose. That makes you twice a traitor." The reward for her insight was Breas's boot slamming into her side. The air whooshed from her lungs and she dropped over, clutching her shins to her chest.

Harper focused on the filigree ring and probed her consciousness for the spark of her magic. She dredged her mind for thoughts of all Badb had destroyed, but her heart hammered more in fear than rage while despair at their likely failure brought a defeated listlessness. No tingle of magic followed, and try as she may, she could not summon it.

"I knew you'd come." Emilio's voice was strained. Harper managed a small smile. *Fat lot of good it did.*

Normally, the Phooka would've offered a snappy comment, but he stood statue still. The shapeshifter hadn't uttered a word since upstairs and he was avoiding her eyes.

"Phooka?" Harper said with a dry mouth. His eyes hopped to her momentarily and returned to Badb's face. What was wrong with him? Had one of the Sidhe glamoured him?

The baying of the Gabriel hounds wrenched her attention from her friend. The spectral dogs galloped into the plaza, followed by Gwyn and the Wild Hunt with Donn and a host of mostly Fae Sluagh. Gwyn and his rival both bowed to Badb.

Donn sneered down his aquiline nose at Harper and then inclined his head toward Badb while Gwyn avoided looking at her at all.

"Good of you to finally join us, Gwyn. The girl seems to have accomplished her capture with no help from you." Badb spat the words at him like they were the bitterest of fruit.

"Oh come now, Badb. Gwyn slew his own father, and for that, I am eternally grateful. I've waited ages for that pompous, self-righteous ass Nuada to be cleansed from the worlds." Breas clapped Gwyn on the shoulder. Gwyn did not return his smile. He cast his eyes down and clasped his hands. Harper had destroyed his mask, yet he hid behind another, one of studied impassivity.

Donn bowed even lower to his mistress. "The cocoons are all accounted for. If the girl's friends are still here, they haven't bothered to rescue the subjects in the trees."

While Donn sniveled and scraped, a single black shape soared for the portal like an arrow sailing toward its mark. With a ping, the avian Sluagh bounced off the shimmering lens and smacked the floor, lying in a heap, flapping broken wings.

Donn's high-pitched chuckle made Harper's skin crawl. Dark grey robes swirled aside as he lifted a gnarled hand and floated the struggling soul to his gaping mouth. He swallowed it whole.

Both Badb and Gwyn wrinkled their noses and focused anywhere but on Donn.

The corners of Badb's mouth drew down. "What of the Fir Bolg in the village? Did you capture them?"

Donn's nervous laugh scraped like nails on slate. "They escaped, thanks to the Dusk Court and a band of solitary Fae. I left a contingent of banshee to hunt the hairy louts down. They're nearly out of hiding places. They will be yours, Your Majesty, and then I can take my place at your side instead—"

Badb clenched her fist at Donn. Facing Gwyn, she gestured to Paegrinn and Twitch. "Well? Did you find the rest of her friends skulking in the forest?"

Gwyn bowed. "While the Hunt fortified the island's border, I walked the building's perimeter myself. I found nothing. There are likely a few others inside the tower, but if there were more Fae helping her, they may have all fled. Or betrayed her."

For an instant, a wistfulness flickered across Gwyn's face. Gooseflesh rippled across Harper's skin. Had they abandoned her? No. Impossible. The Dusk Court would probably betray her, but Aeld and Hieronymous would never leave her to her fate. Gwyn should have found them had he searched in earnest.

The Phooka's rough hands suddenly stripped off Harper's backpack. He paused for a moment, untangling a nylon strap delicately from around the jacket's steel studs, gingerly avoiding contact.

Her head whipped behind her. "Phooka, what the hell are you doing?" Her Fae friend's features were frozen in an uncharacteristically impassive expression. Time slowed as adrenaline pushed every nerve to high alert.

The bag finally swung free and the Phooka hugged it to his chest. Hooves clicked rhythmically along the white-and-gold marble floor as he minced toward Badb. Her ruby lips pulled into a crooked smile and her head tilted.

"What's this, Phooka?"

The shapeshifter thrust the pack into Badb's waiting hand. "You have claimed the Sword of Nuada for your own. I think you will find another treasure within."

"Phooka, you filthy little shit. Nuada trusted you. I trusted you. You're betraying me?" Harper's voice quavered.

The Phooka clasped his hands behind his back and took his place beside Badb. He shot her the side-eye but turned his face forward. "Oh, don't look so surprised. I'm dark Fae. We've always been aligned with the Dark Courts. Did you think we were friends?"

Paegrinn's sharp breath and dismayed shout echoed her feelings. Even Twitch yelped with surprise. Yes, she had thought they were friends, the momentary glitch in their relationship aside.

Nuada seemed to have known him for a long time, so the Phooka had successfully bamboozled a Tuatha in order to betray them now. She scanned his face again, seeking any indication this was a ruse. The dark queen seemed to share her reservations. Her eyes drilled into him.

"Well, Phooka, this is certainly a surprise after you've fought and killed so many of my subjects. Why should I not force you to share the same fate as this girl and her companions?"

The Phooka pivoted to her and bowed a deep bow, one hoof delicately crossed in front of the other. His long ears swept the floor. "My Queen. I long served on King Eveling's Court in the Underworld."

Badb's eyes narrowed. "You betrayed your king."

"Did I?" He flicked an ear toward Harper. "Or was I serving you even then? How did I turn up in the exact time and place the last heir of Niall would be discovered? It was my tip that led Nuada to locate her."

"And yet you failed to bring her to me."

He sighed dramatically and slumped at the waist. "Your Highness, I didn't know where you were. I wasn't sure the Aillen wouldn't kill her if she—"

"How convenient."

"Did I not lead her here? Didn't Gwyn find us outside the protections of the Fir Bolg village, giving him the opportunity to remove Nuada from the equation? I just gave you something precious inside that pack that will prevent another High King from ever ascending and opposing you. My allegiance has always been to my people. Sadly, there has been some, shall we say, collateral damage?"

Breas's face remained an unreadable mask. Harper wasn't sure the Fomorian believed the Phooka's story, but Badb seemed to. The corners of her eyes creased, and she picked up the pack.

Her expression fell when her gaze returned to Gwyn. He was

as unmoving as the statues that decked the plaza. His heaving chest was the only indication of emotion. Beside him, Donn giggled, his face lit with childish glee.

"Well, Gwyn. It appears your Wild Hunt was as ineffectual as I feared. This lowly solitary Fae has accomplished what you and your followers could not. Perhaps he takes your place at my side." Badb's voice was low and icy.

"But my Sluagh have never failed you, Highness." Donn's fingers clasped together beneath wild, bugged eyes.

Gwyn ignored both of them. "If this little rat is all he is claiming to be, then why did he and this Fir Bolg rescue her from my camp on this island? Why was it Melinoe who delivered the heir to me? No one should trust a phooka. Don't think he won't betray any of us the second it suits him. His race is without honor." Gwyn finished and his eyes returned to the floor, fists clenched at his sides, the cords on his neck taut.

The Phooka stuck out his tongue at Gwyn and blew a loud raspberry.

"Phooka, how could you." Paegrinn shook his head.

"Get the Fir Bolg up to my lab and take the goblin to the basement to await his turn powering the gate." Breas said. "They've outlived their usefulness here." Several elves seized Paegrinn's arms. He lurched and shrugged them off. The action made the blue cords cut into his skin and a small trickle of blood formed. The ring of blades suddenly pointing at his chest drained the rest of his resistance, but he still raised his head high. "Harper will save us."

Harper was barely hanging on. The notion she could save anyone now was ridiculous. Her hand lifted to Paegrinn. "I'm so sorry." She could add his name to the growing list of people who would have been better off never having met her.

Breas followed Paegrinn up the staircase toward whatever horrors awaited him. Eyes flashing, Harper turned to the Phooka.

Surely he would care about Paegrinn's fate, but his expression remained impassive.

"Well now. This distraction seems to be over," Badb said, her voice oozing with superiority. "The blood of Eriu and my sister's magic should stabilize the portal, perhaps even widen it, so more of our brethren can join this fight. Phooka. Take our little upstart and hook her up to the extractors. We'll feed the tree Eriu's gift first. Once she grows weak, I'll tear Macha's magic from her."

Gwyn dropped to his knee, inches from Badb Catha. "Your Highness, with the heritage of both sovereignty-granting bloodlines, the girl could be more useful to our cause alive. If she voluntarily—"

Donn cackled and crept to Badb's side, fingers interlacing beneath his chin as he leered down at Gwyn. "Fool." He gazed triumphantly at Badb. "The two of them are in cahoots!"

Gwyn leapt up and clutched Donn by the throat. "Lies," he hissed. "I rescued the girl from this unspeakable evil. He was moments from consuming her soul and denying you Macha's legacy. All for his own benefit, to prevent Macha's magic stabilizing the gateway. With the portal closed, his power grows."

Harper listened intently, but her focus was on the Phooka. Still struggling to believe he'd stabbed her in the back, she searched for any sign of internal conflict. Finding none, she risked a glance at Gwyn. He still knelt, face on his knee, features drawn with a mixture of sadness and frustration.

Badb Catha bared her teeth, and as her fist clenched, Donn lifted into the air, his shiny boots dangling beneath flapping robes. "You. Did. What?" Each word enunciated, low and deadly.

Donn flailed, lips pulled back in a desperate grimace. "A moment of weakness, my Queen, I'd have merely subdued her, never drank her all the way. You need me. Need my legions."

The fire dimmed in Badb's gaze, and she exhaled, tension draining. With lips drawn in a thin line, she released her grip on

Donn. "Unfortunately, you are correct." She raised a hand, summoning elven warriors to her side. "The Sluagh are to be watched at all times." With a look of utter disgust, she sidestepped Donn. "And get this vulture out of my sight."

Gwyn rose but kept his head lowered. "Highness, the girl—"

"Will serve out her usefulness to me when the last of Macha's magic and her disgusting human life are fed to the portal tree. Phooka, show our guest to her cage."

"As you wish, my Queen." The Phooka clicked over to where Harper knelt, eyes unfocused, breath stalled in her throat. She hoped her mother and the others had the sense to run and never look back.

Badb deposited her new treasures on the cages to confer with a line of Fae and human men in lab coats. She meandered to the opposite stairwell, engulfed in conversation.

As the Phooka approached, Harper shifted to one side, supporting her weight with her hand. Her foot shot out and slammed into the Phooka's chest, sending him sprawling.

"That was a mistake, would-be queen," he hissed, clawing himself back to his cloven hooves. His shape shimmered and lost its form. The rock troll shape was soon looming over her. The Phooka grabbed her by a leg, careful not to touch any of the iron-tipped boots, and dragged her to the empty cage next to Emilio.

# CHAPTER 69

Harper studied Emilio's transformation. Jaw clamped tight, she bit back a savage yell. They had no right. There must be a way to reverse the metamorphosis, and she wouldn't rest until she found it, but for now, anxiety for the future took a back seat. They had to escape. Fast.

"Don't tear them out," Emilio whispered. "They'll only put them back in and tie you up, which is far more uncomfortable."

The set of six gleaming cables wound from Harper's chest and shoulders, then peeked underneath her shirt. None of the Fae, including the Phooka, had wanted to touch her with the metal spikes adorning her wardrobe. So they simply made her push the terminal wires under her skin herself.

The Phooka's long tail swished over the marble tiles as he twisted the shining cables from her cage into a bundle.

Harper wrinkled her nose. She could hardly bear the sight of the backstabbing shapeshifter. "You're disgusting. I trusted you." The Phooka tilted his chin away and stared at his true master.

"From what I can see, you can't trust most of the Fae." Emilio rustled his wings. "I wonder how long it'll be until you can't trust me."

"I've kept your secrets, Netherfae," a Southern drawl oozed from Harper's opposite side.

Harper shifted in her cage to meet the aqua eyes of a purple-skinned succubus. Her breath caught. She held up her hand with the filigree ring. "Is your name Alphine?"

The Fae's jaw dropped and a hand with long nails shot through the bars to clasp Harper's fingers. "That's my ring! How—"

Harper dropped lower and gestured for the Fae to quiet her voice. Leaning close to the Fae's cage, she whispered. "Ezrynhivar lent this to me. I promised to try to free you if I found you." She gave a rueful smile at the jewelry. "He was right about it helping control my power." Harper started to pull the ring off.

"Keep it for now. It was my mother's engagement ring. You'll need all the help you can get if we're going to escape." Alphine revealed a shining feather, one of Emilio's, and nodded to a thin line running along the bottom of several of the wooden bars. "Emilio's already helped us all." She nodded her horned head at the row of cages, where other Fae surreptitiously revealed their metal feathers.

"I don't know how Gwyn didn't see them when he searched, but Ez and a bunch of others are here, both upstairs and outside the building. We need to get a signal to them and come up with a new escape plan."

Harper pointed at the collar around Emilio's neck and lifted an eyebrow.

"They control us with it. There's at least one advantage to my present state." He plucked a thin feather from his shoulder. "I hope I ate enough iron to spring the lock on this thing."

"You ate—"

Alphine tapped Harper's cage with her hoof and shook her

head. Harper fell silent as the Phooka ambled back to them, looping handfuls of transparent cord along the floor, humming a lilting tune while dutifully completing his appointed task.

The shapeshifter crept a full circle around the cage, testing the bars and top, then scampered around to the front and slipped a tiny lock through. It closed with a snick. His golden eyes met hers. A flame of anger scorched her heart. Disgusting little wretch. "Get out of my sight, traitor."

The Phooka held up a long finger and wagged it side to side. "Don't judge me too harshly. Check your back pocket, Harper." He pivoted and strode away, still humming his cheery tune. He stopped near a broad table where Badb sat with several Fae poring over a large map. Harper sighed when she caught sight of Nuada's sword, her sword, lying at the table's edge.

"Who is that ridiculous beast?" Emilio asked.

"I thought he was a friend," Harper answered. Her hand searched around in her back pocket. There was something in there. She dug it out and brought it close to her face. Her hand slammed instantly over the bright glow that lanced from it. "He slipped me the Lia Fail shard." Her eyes flicked up to catch the Phooka's golden stare from his new station beside his mistress. He winked at her. "He may still be a friend. I can't really tell."

"What's with the pet rock?" Emilio asked.

Harper reached an arm into his cage. Emilio's hand met hers and she squeezed it tightly. He may look different, but he was the same old Emilio where it counted. She had missed him terribly. "There's so much to tell you."

*Vanilla.*

Her head clanged on the ceiling. Tamika's voice. In her mind. The bustling plaza of Fae rippled and a new reality flickered before her. A child's bedroom?

"Emilio—"

"It's Tamika. Just lie down. The Fae don't know we can share this mindspace." Emilio curled into a ball, so Harper did the same.

Seated in a puffy chair was a creature that looked more tree than man. He had large, sad eyes. Tamika perched on a small bed and Selina leaned against a desk.

"Lemme dial it back a bit." Tamika closed her eyes for a second. When she reopened them, Harper saw both the cage floor and the child's bedroom like two interwoven realities. At least the dual worlds she'd experienced as Santaigh's captive gave her some experience with the sensation.

"Harper, this is Alan." Emilio stood next to her in the illusory room. "The four of us are a team."

Harper and Emilio exchanged the shortest versions of their time apart while the Netherfae listened intently, occasionally stopping her with questions. Harper relayed the briefest version of events about her mother, Nuada, and what she learned about her father's existence with the Sluagh. Emilio and his friends relayed their harrowing experience. Emilio told her about the attempts to resurrect the Eye of Balor.

'Wow," Emilio said. "I know royalty. This is so cool!" They shared a brief laugh despite the grave circumstances. "Harper, thank you for coming, to rescue us."

"You're welcome, Emilio. How does it feel to be rescued?" He smiled at her. She squeezed the piece of the Stone of Destiny until it dug painfully into her flesh. *This can't be how it ends.* The Phooka gave this back to her for a reason, but all the thing really ever did was sit there and glow when she was nearby. "I'm hoping we may have one last play. It'll be a Hail Mary for sure."

"Oh, no." Emilio's face drained of color. There were Fae coming through. "I've been through this before. It's going to be bad."

Harper twisted her head around to focus on the gleaming

portal. A rippling membrane barrier stretched across it, allowing Fae through but keeping the avian Sluagh from their freedom.

A low hum sounded from the tree that surrounded the shimmering surface of the gateway. "Something's coming through," came a shout from a Fae near it. The plaza erupted into activity. Creatures hustled for the controls that flanked the majestic tree. Shadowy figures, some small, some huge, approached from the portal's other side. A large palm pressed against it, stretching it.

Tamika yelped. "That's horrible."

Wails and cries rose from the cages around her and chilled Harper to the bone. Whatever happened next promised to be hell. Her hand clamped down reflexively on the shard. *Why did the Phooka give me the Lia Fail shard back?*

Badb stomped through the assembled Fae, who parted deferentially, with her open half-skirt swishing beneath a gleaming obsidian bodice. She stopped in front of Harper and bent at the waist to look into her cage. "Well, little girl, you're about to help several Fae cross over into this world. I'm only sorry Nuada isn't here to witness his failure."

"Anything is better than listening to more psychotic raving from you about the human infection."

"Defiant to the last. I like that about you, Harper." Badb's red hair fell back into place as she straightened up. "Lower the barrier. Begin extraction," she shouted and walked toward the portal, hands clasped together, with an almost matronly smile.

Emilio groaned and cradled his head in his arms. Blood seeped from tiny cuts between his fingers where the metallic feathers shredded his skin. Tamika reached out a hand to comfort him, but it passed through his shoulder.

Immediately, a surge of jagged power spiked through Harper's body, like an electric current, but instead of passing through, it was being sucked from every fiber of her being. She moaned and laid her head on the floor. The leads were like straws, pulling the vitality from her and sending little glowing pulses along the filaments. The same thing was happening to all the prisoners. Each creature lay listless as their life force was ripped from them. The bark of the great circular tree that formed the portal pulsed with new life. Their lives.

Emilio was curled in a fetal position with his head on his knees. She fumbled her hand until it found his, and he returned her comforting squeeze. Harper moaned again. Her heart clenched.

Alphine's screams mingled with the wails of the little hobgoblin in the next cell. An ache of pity washed over Harper; they didn't deserve this.

Badb's smug eyes bored into her from across the room. *I'll be damned if I'm going to let that fashion nightmare bitch see me shrinking like this.* It took all of her will, but Harper pulled herself up to sit cross-legged in the box. Emilio and Alphine did the same. Badb sneered and returned to her conversation with a cluster of Sidhe. The Phooka hovered near the end of the table and gave her a slow nod. His eyes focused on the hand that held the shard and widened. *That's it. The shard.* "The Lia Fail shard. Why—"

Selina gasped. "If you've got a shard of the Lia Fail, it'll amplify your magic. Then you can draw the Sword of Light and take Badb down."

Through gritted teeth, Harper replied. "Can't control magic and sword won't draw."

Selina's warm smile revealed her jagged teeth. "Human magic is exceedingly rare and different from Fae power. It flows from our feelings. Different emotions produce different results and the stronger the emotion, the stronger the magic. Try to intensify your feelings."

The hand gripping the shard was the only part of her body that wasn't hurting.

"Alphine. Tell the others it's time. Break out if you can. Let's torch this place," Emilio said beside her. His earnest expression of belief steeled her.

"Selina, it's anger, but right now…"

"When else has it manifested?"

"Only when I'm Incredible Hulk level angry." The hope of using her power receded. "Except when I fought Gwyn at the Fir Bolg village. It was different then." The last word came out in a short grunt as a wave of her life surged up the gleaming cables.

"What did you feel then?"

"Love. Ferocity. Like I'd die to protect everything I loved from Gwyn."

"Far stronger than anger, but harder to summon when you need it."

She had to. Everyone she had in the world was here, on this hellish island, and each of them needed her right now. But the emotions surging in her heart were terror and agony. Warm, fuzzy feelings of love were a distant memory.

Harper focused on images from Santaigh's delusion when her love for her dad had peaked and the desire to free him from his suffering unfolded in her heart. Echoes of the sweet ache that suffused her when her mother told her she was proud of who Harper had become. The joy Harper felt when her mother had charged to her rescue with her patchwork army. They had a lifetime of new, loving memories to build on top of the rubble from the past decade and a half.

Eyes ablaze, agony clenching every muscle, she watched Emilio contort in pain beside her. She'd always protected him, her constant companion. The only bright light in her dark adolescence.

Abraham had been brought here. She loved him too. If he lived, she owed him his freedom, or if he'd been killed, to honor his memory by doing what Sergeant Wilkes would: Protect the innocent. Fear receded and the spark of her power ignited, but it wavered like a match flame in the wind.

She'd spent so much time feeling rage, and protecting herself from loss by making her heart a fortress, it was difficult to hold on to anything else. Hope. Love. Those feelings seemed thin and weak compared to fury.

The protective membrane across the portal thinned and disintegrated with a bright flash. Soon, the creatures on the other side would muscle their way through.

She squeezed her eyes shut and concentrated on the shard. It would amplify her magic, so maybe she could charge it up like a battery. At least if she could channel her power into the stone, it was denied to the portal, then she'd unleash a blast with double the wallop.

The searing agony and growing weakness made concentration difficult, but it seemed to be working. The shard felt warmer and warmer against her flesh and pulsed like a slow heartbeat.

Emilio's eyes widened, and his body trembled. "It's working."

"That's it, sweetheart." Selina leaned forward. "Keep going."

"I love you so much, Emilio." She thought her heart would burst. The power rushing into the shard was like white water pounding it.

A staggering level of magic thrummed in the core of the Lia Fail and her thoughts strayed to the blue blast from Mystic Island. It had nearly killed her, then. Fear made the stream of magic sputter and almost flicker out, but she caught it just in time.

The only trick in her book was a barely targeted barrage. With human prisoners and her Fae allies scattered through the plaza, she couldn't risk it.

*Wait a minute. What would happen if all this power went to those machines all at once?* She remembered in physics lab in high school when she once sent too much electricity through their circuit and melted the whole experiment.

The Lia Fail blazed like fire in her hand. Her entire body hummed with energy. She opened her eyes and glanced at Emilio. "Get ready," she whispered. She turned to Alphine, who was kicking at the splintered bars with both hooves. "You too. Get ready to run."

Harper looked down at the blazing shard and focused her will on it, pushing the energy out of the stone and along the leads. She screamed as it tore through every sinew, shining white hot along the shimmering strands.

Shouts erupted, claws flailed at the blinding filaments, and the enemy Fae scrambled to save the machine. Too late. An explosion wrecked several instrument panels and sparks spewed from every cage. She used the burst of energy to channel the life energy back into the captive Fae, giving them the strength to shatter their weakened bars.

She leapt free, legs braced in a wide stance, and stared daggers at Badb and Gwyn who stood motionless with matching expressions of shock.

Harper's brown hair whipped around her head. The Lia Fail flamed white, sending sparks of magic leaping from spike to spike along the top of her studded jacket.

To her astonishment, kelpies, goblins, sylphs, trolls, and even the hobgoblin scurried from their cages and assembled behind her. Fae truly did abhor debts if they chose to stay and fight for her rather than do the sensible thing and flee.

Emilio crawled out and teetered at her side, his face pinched, tongue clamped between his lips as a shaky hand lifted a feather to the left of his collar. In quick succession, one finger glided over the edge while another slid the feather up from underneath. The stone in the center blazed and Emilio grunted, but the choker snapped in two and fell to the floor.

"It worked!" He kicked the collar aside. Before the mindspace faded, Harper watched Selina and the others pull out similar feathers and spring their own collars.

Badb and Gwyn recovered from their shock much more quickly than the minions buzzing between the tree and their commanders.

The cacophony of avian Sluagh pressing through the main doorway, winging for the damaged portal, was silenced by Donn. The Lord of the Dead lifted a palm, face pinched with effort. The flock banked and flew back for the forest just as the barrier flickered back into place.

Pandemonium overwhelmed the plaza. Badb and Gwyn had taken only a single step when their heads whipped toward the left stairwell where the thunder of footfalls filled the space.

"Selina! Paegrinn!" Harper called as her friends raced down the last flight of stairs, freed prisoners in tow. A green light zipped from the pack of humans and circled her head.

Her mother and the Fianna must be somewhere in the throng, but Harper had no time to search for them, because Badb's Fae forces had regrouped. They might have a fighting chance of escape, but it was a long shot.

# CHAPTER 70

Harper's forces panicked, visibly trembled, makeshift weapons dangling from loose grips.

Even with reinforcements outside, a few dozen terrified people, Emilio's friends, and some Fae wouldn't be enough to get everyone out and shut down that gateway. Harper cursed herself. She should have thought of that. Of course they'd freak out the moment the Fae-induced warm fuzzies melted away.

Furious buzzing grew louder before a swarm of tiny winged pixies swarmed down the stairwell and streaked for Badb. The Tuatha hurled tendrils of magic, and several of the winged Fae fell, but the whirling mass covered her.

For now, Badb's forces were surprised and scattered, but they'd regroup fast. Harper's new recruits were penned between the stairs they'd just raced down and the Fae massed behind them, while the Sidhe stationed on the ground floor covered the exits.

Harper risked a quick sweep of her eyes, seeking the Fianna and their solitary Fae escorts. They weren't there. *Please just be safe, Mom.* "Alina, find the Fianna and the others. We need them."

Alina streaked for the doors, unnoticed.

Harper flung out a hand and fluid white magic sent every advancing Fae tumbling back. One slapped into Badb, who was nearly free of the pixie storm.

"Emilio, get the barrier off the portal." Harper dropped into the defensive stance Nuada had taught her.

"You got it." Emilio was already flinging enemy Fae aside with broad sweeps of his wings.

A trio of Sidhe elves kneeled, fingers spread along the floor. Three lines of crackling dark blue flame sped toward Harper. She yelped and swung an arm over her face. The magic flames hit her and fizzled out. Harper threw her head back and laughed. "Stupid bastards!" She swept her hand at the spikes. "Iron. Fae magic isn't going to work." But the ring of blades flying from scabbards made her regret her bravado.

The lead elf snarled. "Insolent little girl."

Harper edged back, casting around for an opening. The plaza was engulfed in battle, her forces scattered, each fighting for their lives.

Time slowed.

The Netherfae may be powerful, but her new friends were outnumbered twenty to one. They were her responsibility. She started this. If she didn't stop it, millions would be turned into Netherfae or die. Her father's fate would await them. The Fir Bolg. The Fae who'd fought beside her, they'd be slaughtered. No one else was coming to save them.

Instinct took over. She thrust the Lia Fail Shard before the advancing elves. The stone flared, the magic surge vibrating every bone. The sensation sent her into a lower stance, her other arm bracing against the floor.

An arc of white lightning shot from the shard, lifted all the Fae nearby, and hurled them crashing into the advancing second wave. A haphazard pile of limbs and snouts lay in a heap at the edge of the cages.

She wheeled around, still crouched, and forced another blast at the trolls and goblins blocking the front door. A path cleared before them.

Behind her, the Phooka screamed, "Harper, look out!" She whipped around in time to see Badb's dark ball of shimmering magic heading for her. Her iron spikes wouldn't protect her from Tuatha sorcery. She directed another arc of white lightning toward the orb and flattened herself on the floor. The dark sphere weakened and dissipated as it sailed over her head.

A jet-black eagle with golden eyes soared toward her with the Claimh Solias clutched in its talons. Harper scrambled to her feet when the Phooka dropped the sword into her outstretched hand.

"What?"

"I never betrayed you, Harper."

She slipped the Lia Fail piece into her back pocket and clenched the Sword of Light in both hands. The Phooka had dropped to the floor and assumed his wolf form, snarling and circling around her legs between the ring of enemies.

He snapped his jaws and lanced arcs of amber magic at anything that came close.

Harper sprinted the few steps it took for her to stand before her band of fighters.

"Everyone! Fight your way out and run. Others are waiting outside to guide you home." She'd be no further help to them.

Badb advanced, face contorted in rage, blade in one hand, simmering black magic cupped in the other.

Tamika and a dozen people rushed her.

Badb shrieked and flicked a dark strand of power from her fingertips. The group howled and froze for a moment before staggering into Gwyn and his contingent, doubled over in pain.

The distraction let Harper sweep her eyes around the plaza, and her heart plummeted. Emilio pressed his company of Fae and humans closer to the portal controls, and Selina led the escapees within several feet of the exit, but Donn and throngs of Sluagh, some shambling, others flying, poured through the doors, cutting off the exit again. Several Sluagh flapped straight for the portal. The energy membrane lit briefly and emitted a *ping* when they bounced harmlessly off.

"No." Harper felt the color drain from her face.

Badb Catha laughed. "You see, little heir. It was all for nothing. Your friends will die. My gateway will be repaired and become permanent when I wring Macha's power from your corpse."

"No. Donn made a huge mistake bringing his Sluagh in here." Harper watched the Phooka shred a goblin. "Phooka, help Emilio. Destroy those controls!" she yelled. With luck, the portal would stay open just long enough for the Sluagh to escape. Without the life force feeding the tree, the gateway was already shrinking.

The Phooka bounded toward the control panels, shape already changing. "Hulk smash!" the greyscale Incredible Hulk bellowed. He bounded over the heads of the Sidhe, Gwyn racing behind him.

Badb charged Harper, ruby lips pulled into a snarl. Her black blade poised, dark magic dancing along the edge.

*I can't let this monster win.* Harper's hand curled around the hilt of the Claimh Solias. Sweat beaded her upper lip and memories of the sword not budging from the scabbard flooded her mind. *It has to draw. It has to. Nuada, if your spirit is out there, please make it draw. Please.*

She pulled on the sword. Time stopped. Badb's red hair lashed behind her as she sailed through the air, weapon overhead. All around Harper, weapons clanged and lances of magical energy flew. The Sword of Light slid from the scabbard with a clear, high ring and blazed like the sun.

# CHAPTER 71

Emilio spread his gleaming metal wings and rocketed up to hover over the plaza. The only humans not freaking out and getting themselves slaughtered were the few he and the other Netherfae could puppet. He'd need every bit of their help if he and the shapeshifter were going to get to the controls and destroy them.

He pushed off and soared to meet Tamika fluttering a few feet overhead. "The prisoners are panicked."

"I can fix that." Tamika glided high over the growing numbers of freed humans and smiled down on them. "My friends, we must fight. Let there be no fear in your hearts. Grab anything you can and follow us." Her speech was musical, amplified to fill the space. The people lifted the makeshift weapons they'd grabbed, determination settling into their features.

Selina lunged forward so fast she was a blur. When she came to rest beside Alan, six Sidhe lay bleeding to death at their feet. Emilio dove for the floor, sweeping his wing in a low arc as he landed, slicing through four more Sidhe and several goblins.

"You created us, now face your monsters." Emilio's bright red features contorted.

Selina licked a streak of blood from the back of her hand. "Get that barrier down, we'll do the rest." Behind her, Harper's army bellowed and plunged into Badb's ranks.

The Phooka landed in a crouch, then flung his limbs wide, sending Fae careening into one another. "Hey, Birdman, what's the plan?"

Emilio's eyebrows shot up. Normally, fighting beside the Hulk would have suggested he was dreaming, or insane. "We can't destroy the whole thing or the souls will be trapped." He dodged a swipe from a sylph, tilted, and caught her with the edge of his wing. "I need time to figure out what to crush."

The Phooka stomped around, squashing redcaps with each stride. The snap of bones and every wet squelch turned Emilio's stomach. The shapeshifter grasped a goblin by the neck and used his screaming, flailing body to smash a trio of elves. The path to the controls was clear for a moment. The Phooka bowed and motioned Emilio to the equipment. "I'll keep the Fae off your back."

The clang of weapons and screams of the dying were not conducive to concentrating. Lights flashed, tiny pumps connected to luminescent tubing leading to and from the circular tree. Probably not what Emilio was looking for, because that system looked like the life support for the tree. The barrier must be something else, but nothing he saw suggested a mechanism for keeping it in place.

"Emilio, Sluagh incoming," the Phooka roared.

Emilio's eyes flicked from his puzzle, and he wished they hadn't. Spectral women with clawed hands and gaping mouths shrieked above incubi bearing down on him.

Behind them, Donn lifted his staff overhead, lips moving in an inaudible chant. The grey staff kindled with a dark red light, and the Lord of the Dead fixed Emilio in his eyes. "Sorry, love. Can't let you destroy that barrier."

The Phooka tossed his goblin club aside and wrenched a

section of handrail free from the stairs. New weapon in hand, he hollered, "Now would be a good time. I can't hold off this many forever."

"Not sure what to smash yet. If I kill the tree, the souls are trapped for good."

"Just smash whatever isn't feeding the tree." The Phooka swung his improvised club with one hand, while with the other, he fired arcs of amber lightning into the banshee.

"That could work." Emilio sidestepped to a control panel that didn't seem to feed into the tree's life support. He raised a wing and curved his feathers toward it.

Then a grey-robed figure shrieked and slammed him aside. The red light of its staff clubbed him in the jaw. Stars burst in front of Emilio's eyes, and the staff crashed into the back of his neck, driving feathers into his flesh and bringing a trickle of blood.

"Didn't think I'd have to tell you again, love. The souls are mine." Donn's grating, wavering laugh carried over the ringing in Emilio's ears.

"Bigger problems on the way," Hulk Phooka shouted.

Emilio closed his wings around himself, ducked under them, and deflected Donn's overhead blow. From between wing feathers, he saw Gwyn sprinting straight for him.

Donn arced his staff low to sweep Emilio off his feet and expose him to another blow. He landed on his back, feathers clanking against marble. A pair of people from the prison tried to hide close by. Emilio's thoughts snaked toward them and pushed their way into consciousness. Without the torque, his control seemed weaker, but they responded. From either side, they lunged for Donn.

The Lord of the Dead parried their blows, which gave Emilio enough time to roll under one of the panels and pop up on the other side.

Gwyn banked and dove for Donn.

"What the hell?!" Emilio barked.

Gwyn spared a single glance over his shoulder. "Primary barrier controls are at the far end with a backup on the opposite side."

Emilio felt the tall, tattooed prisoner's life wink out as Donn bludgeoned him with the staff. Emilio's throat ached. Before he released control on the other, he thanked him and told him to run if he could.

Donn pulled a sword from his robes and whirled around to face Gwyn. "Traitor! I'll replace you by my queen's side."

"You'll be too dead to tell her, parasite." Gwyn's blade moved so fast it blurred, and Donn barely parried the blows.

Emilio scurried to the end panel and drove his wing feathers into it. The simmering barrier flickered, dropped for a second, then the failsafe kicked in. He glanced around, quickly assessing the situation.

The Phooka fought closer to the backup panel. Too many Sluagh stood between Emilio and smashing it. The battle was going badly in the middle of the plaza. He had a clear flight path to back up Tamika, and too many Sluagh rushed in to aid their master. He was cut off from the other panel by the overhang of the staircase. The Phooka was closer.

"Phooka, up to you. Smash the last panel and the barrier falls."

The Phooka shrugged and leapt over the goblins and redcaps blocking him from the controls. With a roar, he slammed his fist against the barrier control, missed, and obliterated two other banks of instruments. The tree shuddered.

"Hell yeah!" Emilio fist pumped.

"Not good. Damaged the gate more. Shrinking," Hulk Phooka hollered.

But Emilio's attention had already shifted to his friends, who desperately needed help. With a shout, he pushed off, flapping toward the heart of battle.

# CHAPTER 72

Harper danced back and Badb's strike clanged off the marble floor. Power hummed through Harper, both from the gleaming sword in her hands and from the Lia Fail piece in her back pocket. The same tiny arcs of energy that hopped over the studs on her coat swam across the blade.

With a savage yell, Harper held the sword low and level and launched herself at Badb. Metal clanged against metal, but it wasn't Badb's sword that met hers. One of the Sidhe snarled as he surged forward, flinging her blade aside.

Badb Catha growled and a black ball of magic swept the elf aside.

The Sword of Light whipped up on its own to block an overhead stab from Badb. Harper dropped her left hand from the grip and directed a blazing white blast at the Tuatha. Badb slammed on her back and four elves leapt between.

The intoxicating power of the sword sang in Harper's veins, guiding her through a low slice that hamstrung the nearest. The weapon continued her revolution to slash through the shoulder of another. The blade's fierce joy sang in her blood, urging her to its target hungrily.

Badb Catha swept the remaining two aside. "What part of she's mine eludes you?" she hissed, burying her black blade deep into the chest of the last disobedient Sidhe.

The Cliamh Solais refused to allow Harper to catch her breath, so she surrendered fully to its power and feinted low. Her enemy took the bait and blocked high. Badb realized her mistake too slowly and Harper sliced a gash along Badb's side beneath the black breastplate.

Rather than slow her, the wound enraged Badb, and she unleashed a flurry of strikes, driving Harper back.

Badb ducked Harper's next strike and slid a few steps away. She stepped a deliberate circle around Harper, sneering.

"I'd considered Gwyn's suggestion that we ally. I could have used your strength to save this world from destruction."

"You murdered my father, so, hard no."

"He was a sniveling fool like the rest. Pleading for his wife's life. At least he was smart enough not to tell me about you."

There was a clamor at the front doors. Eileen burst into the plaza on the back of a grey wolf, a shotgun pointed before her. Behind her mother, the Fir Bolg and the Fae thundered through.

In a second, they were swarmed by Sluagh. *Mom.*

Harper's focus snapped back to Badb, and she matched Badb's slow revolution around her. "Your own sister's power kept me safe from you."

"Not for long." Badb lifted her hand, fingers contorted into a claw shape, and every fiber of Harper's body filled with searing agony. She screamed and crashed to her knees, muscles spasming. Harper cursed. Only the cool thrum of the sword's power prevented her hammering heart from overwhelming her with terror.

"Too easy." Badb spun and brought her sword down. Harper

jerked sideways. The spiked leather offered some protection, but the blade sliced partway through and she screamed. Her left arm, now almost useless, dangled at her side.

No way she'd win this fight now. She gritted her teeth and clambered to her feet, the blade in her right hand. Badb pressed her advantage with raining blows that Harper barely blocked even with the sword's help.

Badb Catha drove Harper back toward the dwindling portal. Seeing it damaged seemed to enrage her more, and she lunged at Harper, pulled back at the last second, and kicked her in the sternum.

The air rushed from Harper's lungs. She couldn't inhale. Badb lifted the sword to strike just as Gwyn took a step that happened to shoulder Harper aside. Badb missed.

Gwyn took the full force of Donn's staff to his midsection. The sword in Donn's other hand was poised to attack. The Hulk Phooka flung a backhand strike and sent Donn smashing into a column.

Everything looked bright yellow in Harper's eyes. A tiny bit of air wheezed into her lungs as she directed another energy ball at Badb. This time, she concentrated on turning the magic into a net broad enough to blanket her enemy. Surprisingly, it worked. With a grunt, Harper clenched her fist and the net constricted, holding Badb in place. God, she was strong. The magic wouldn't hold her long, but hopefully long enough for Harper to breathe again.

Gwyn recovered and shot the Phooka a surprised look. He slid past Harper with a scowl as his mistress struggled against Harper's web. "Even with my father's sword, you can't win. Young. Untested. Badb will kill you."

"If... my death... means souls escape... and... friends safe... so... be it." Harper forced every word out through gritted teeth. Badb was already breaking through the net. "Sometimes one has to make a stand."

Gwyn shook his head and his features softened. "You really would have made a good Tuatha."

Beside her, the Phooka flung aside smaller Fae and lifted his enormous fist to smash the end panel, but Donn lunged for him, sword poised to deliver a deathblow. The Phooka hopped aside.

Then, with a fierce growl, Gwyn buried his blade in the instrument panel. The shimmering surface of the portal flashed and disappeared just as banshee and incubi swarmed the Phooka.

Harper had no time to process Gwyn's bizarre act, because only shreds of her magical net remained. Harper staggered back from Badb to give herself more time to breathe before Badb's next assault. She froze. Black, winged shapes shot through the portal. Beneath them lumbered the shade of Gerald O'Neill.

"Faaa—" Harper stretched a hand toward him.

Badb's magical blast caught her in the stomach, sending her tumbling. The Tuatha loomed over her, a boot crushing her sword arm. Neither moved, their attention riveted to the Sluagh horde.

The Sluagh stampeded through the gate on spindly leg and black wing. Behind them, Donn bellowed and opened his mouth. Wider and wider it yawned until his unhinged jaw stretched nearly to the floor. He inhaled and the retreating Sluagh, including Gerald, slowed. One by one, the Sluagh disappeared down the gaping maw of their master.

Harper's chest ached. Her father turned his face to her, and she saw a flash of recognition. He was still aware; he hadn't yet fallen back under Donn's control. Gerald stretched spindly arms to the portal and braced his legs, but Donn's evil gravity dragged him back inch by inch.

"No," was all Harper could manage with her searing lungs.

Badb Catha ground her heel into Harper's wrist. "I'd planned to give you a fast death in deference to Macha. But now you'll die slow."

Harper struggled uselessly against the boot on her arm.

Gwyn's face contorted into an anguished cry. He drew his arm back, sword gripped, and hurled the weapon. It tumbled end over end and lodged itself in Donn's slavering jaws.

The Lord of the Dead screamed and staggered back. Most of the Sluagh broke free and streaked for the shrinking portal, but others swarmed their former master. Donn shrieked and flapped his hands at the hoard, the sword lodged through the bottom of his face.

Harper's heart bloomed with a sweet ache as her father paused at the edge of the gateway and smiled. He lifted a knobby hand and a cloud of avian Sluagh flocked to his uplifted palm. He mouthed I love you. Then he jerked his hand toward Badb.

The flock careened into her. Clawed feet tore at her hair and raked her face. She howled and the dark, glistening magic in her palm flickered out. The torrent of wings lifted Badb high and smashed her into the far wall before banking and disappearing through the gateway.

Harper inhaled a deep breath, ignoring the agony in her arm as she dropped again into the battle stance Nuada had taught her in his single lesson. A sob escaped her lips, but it was a sob of joy. She'd saved someone. Her dad would finally be at peace.

"I've drawn the Sword of Nuada against you, Badb Catha. You die today."

Harper rushed at her enemy.

# CHAPTER 73

Emilio and Tamika hovered above the tumult. Tamika had steeled the humans, but they were still losing.

Alan fought, penned into the western corner nearest the entrance. They were split into two smaller groups and surrounded. The giant, shaggy reinforcements streaming in from the front door had no hope of reaching them.

Without a Netherfae to pilot the humans, they were disorganized and unskilled. As much as puppeting people revolted Emilio, it was their best chance of escaping with minimal casualties.

"Tamika, we have to pilot the humans. It's the only way we can punch through and form a new line with the reinforcements. Tell the others."

"I agree." Tamika's voice sounded in the four friend's minds. "Everyone, take control of as many people as you can. Join our reinforcements near the front exit." Tamika assigned Alan the left flank, herself and Emilio the center half, and Selina the right flank.

Alan looked like he was going to be sick. The poor man was covered in oozing green cuts, and his face held the vacant look of someone shutting down. But he nodded and soon the humans under his control fought as a single regiment.

Emilio sent his thoughts snaking into the minds of his own contingent. He'd never coordinated so many before. "I'm sorry," he whispered as he puppeted the limbs of his group.

A blast of fire slammed into his left wing and sent him whirling out of control. He clattered to the floor, rolling to his back with his hands braced in front of him.

"I've been looking forward to this." Callon's face was contorted with rage. "It's open season on Netherfae freaks."

Emilio drew himself tall and poised his wings. "Likewise."

Callon struck, twin blades spinning as he drove straight for Emilio's chest. Emilio's wing swept between them. As Callon's attack glanced off the metal feathers, sparks flew.

The elf dove under Emilio's wing like a baseball player sliding home. Emilio whipped his other wing around and caught the elf on the side of his shoulder. Callon screamed and his low assault sputtered to a halt. The wounds of the Sidhe normally stopped bleeding immediately, but blood kept gushing from this wound.

Emilio smiled and rippled his feathers. Even over the din of battle, their pleasant chime rang. "Ate some iron on our field trip to the park."

Emilio hopped back to give his wings room to strike a final blow but a sharp pain lanced through his diaphragm. Hands clutched at the wound in his chest, but nothing was there. From the corner of his eye, one of his human regiment fell forward with a chest wound. Emilio gasped as he felt the life drain out of the man.

His battle with Callon had pulled too much of his attention and someone else had paid the price. A strike to the back of his neck knocked him to his knees.

"You're weak, half-breed scum."

His feathers had protected him from a fatal blow. With a flap,

Emilio launched himself back. His feathered head slammed into Callon's face.

Emilio spun around, one wing spread low. Callon's perfect features were marred with dozens of cuts. Wing feathers sliced through armored boots and the elf tumbled back. Emilio focused his attention on pushing his puppets forward through a weak spot in the goblin ranks. They joined Tamika's group, where they had some more cover.

Blood flowed from Callon's injured leg, matching his crimson face. Wounds slowed his advance just enough for Emilio to put two more steps between them. Behind him, some of the smaller Fae took shots at his back, but their weapons slid off the metallic feathers.

Emilio staggered, hands flying to his neck. He'd lost another of his forces.

Callon laughed. "At least you're good at one thing, Netherfae. Your incompetence has killed more stinking humans today than I've slain all week."

Grief hardened into fury. For a split second, all of Callon's abuses flashed before Emilio's eyes. He'd been raised to be kind. Protect others. Turn the other cheek even when he was bullied. Attack wasn't in his playbook, but something deep inside him snapped. The world would be better off with Callon no longer in it.

"You aristocratic pile of shit." Emilio flicked his gleaming wings wide. "Your mad scientist may have created me, but it was you who made me a monster."

Before Callon could react, Emilio leapt into the air. Both wings pointed at the elf's chest, Emilio dropped. He stood over his tormentor with a dozen of his long feathers buried in the Sidhe's chest. Callon clawed at the air and gasped for breath.

"Yuck. You've dirtied my wings." Emilio yanked his feathers free and kicked the dying Sidhe out of the way.

His exhilaration faded when he saw Badb's forces pushing the Netherfae and freed Fae back toward the collapsing portal. To his surprise, he saw Eileen hopping from a giant grey wolf's back and pulling out a short shotgun. Last time he'd seen her, she was deep into the bottle.

Emilio lashed his wings from side to side to clear a path to his human fighters and watched Eileen lift the weapon and fire it into the enemy Fae closing in on her.

The crack from the weapon sent a dozen Fae falling dead and many more wailing and clawing at themselves. The battle paused. Eileen aimed the gun a second time. Crack. More Fae fell.

Badb's forces panicked. Surgical strikes became wild slashes.

"Tamika, Selina, there's an opening," Emilio said into the mindspace.

"We see it," Selina said, "but Alan's in trouble."

Emilio swept his wings and sent several redcaps sailing. In a corner of the room, far from the door, Alan and his remaining three human companions were fighting and losing.

"Alan!" Emilio shouted, both in the mindscape and the room. "I'm coming."

"No," Alan said. "I'm not going to make it. I can stop them pursuing you. Save the rest of my fighters. I've got one trick left I didn't tell anyone about."

Emilio blocked a sword strike from a Sidhe woman. "Alan, we'll get to you, just hold on." He pulled his wings tight around him and her sword glanced off.

"Emilio, I can't live like this, but I can save you all."

Emilio smashed a wing into the Sidhe woman's face and swung both wings wide. Bodies flew, and he ran the few steps he'd cleared toward his friend.

Alan flicked his long arm and blocked a goblin attack. He kept his remaining fighters behind him, but he was too late. Two Sidhe dragged them out and killed them.

Emilio couldn't push through the fallen. "Alan, we can figure this out. Whatever—"

"I love you guys," Alan said. His whole body glowed bright green. Fissures opened in the lines of his bark-like skin. Waves of glimmering spores erupted out of the cracks. "Get out of here. My spores will stun anything they touch, but not for long." And they did. An expanding ring of Fae bodies slumped.

"Alan! Run!" Emilio shouted.

"Can't. Too weak." Alan fell back into the corner. A kelpie covered his mouth with a dripping hand and with the other ran Alan through with a blade.

Emilio stopped just twenty feet from his friend. His chest ached with sorrow. Alan inhaled and a final wave of glittering green spores wafted from the fissures in his skin. He smiled at Emilio. The poor old accountant looked at peace for the first time since they'd met.

"Emilio, go!" Selina's voice boomed through the plaza.

Emilio spun. Alan's stun spores hovered inches away. He sprinted for Eileen and Selina. The Sidhe who weren't stunned fled up the stairs or toward the east exit.

"Harper!" Emilio skidded to a stop. She was locked in combat with Badb Catha a few steps from the portal. Green spores drifted between them.

"This is her fight. Have faith in her," Harper's mother said and fired another shot into the ranks of the remaining Fae. Beside her, a tall man with dark hair fended off a pair of redcaps. He glanced at Emilio.

"Son, she'll join us when she can. She wants us to save the people, and that's what we're doing."

Humans, Fir Bolg, Netherfae, and Fae streamed from the tower into the chill air.

A massive Fir Bolg and a furred Fae with horns and ornate armor beckoned the escapees.

"For now, the path off the island is clear, but it won't stay that way long," the horned Fae called.

Emilio paused in the doorway and cast one final look back at Harper. Her movements were a blur as she drove Badb Catha staggering backward. Eileen grabbed him by the arm, and they ran.

# CHAPTER 74

"You'll pay dearly for this," Badb hissed. The Tuatha lunged for Harper, the thin black blade aimed to slip under her defenses.

Harper waited till the last second, then dodged, grabbed Badb's forearm, and yanked her off balance. With a bark of surprise, Badb tumbled to the ground.

"Give up. Your gateway is closing, your forces are stunned or dead."

"Never! You are the only thing in the way of saving this world." Badb lashed out a leg to knock Harper down.

Harper arced her weapon down, planting the point into the marble. Badb's boot thumped into it.

"Murdering an entire species isn't saving the world. Humans are part of the world."

Badb was already on her feet and circling, seeking an opening. The Sword of Light surged power through Harper and she surrendered to it as it guided Harper's body into a whirling low feint followed by a kick to the Tuatha's exposed side.

Badb snarled. "Humans are a part of the world the same way

cancer is part of the body. This is hopeless. Even with your dead mentor's weapon, you can't defeat me."

Badb rounded on Harper and directed a blast of shimmering, dark magical energy. The force knocked Harper staggering back. Badb pressed the attack and forced Harper into a retreating dance of parried blows.

"I already have. Your experiments have revolted. The Sluagh escaped. I doubt you'll keep the gateway open."

"All you've done is delay me. Once I have Macha's power, I can rebuild all of this. Cliamh Solais or not, you cannot prevail against a Tuatha."

Part of Harper knew Badb was right. This battle was a stalemate, at best. Soon, Badb would tire of the game, and Harper was still outnumbered. The remaining few Sidhe ringed them, waiting for their mistress to give permission to attack, and the Phooka was fighting with Gwyn, who'd resumed his assault after the avian Sluagh escaped.

Nuada's dying wish was for Harper to journey to the Undying Lands and rally the Tuatha to enter this Third Battle. Until this moment, she'd only focused on saving her friends, but the only way to guarantee their safety was to fulfill her mentor's task, then return with more powerful reinforcements.

Despite growing exhaustion, her magic surged. She lunged forward, injured arm outstretched, and engulfed Badb in white flame. The Tuatha screamed and fell to the floor, her sword clattering away from her.

The Cliamh Solais radiated joy, bringing a burst of vitality, sensing victory. Hungering for it. Five Sidhe stepped between their mistress and her attacker before Harper advanced a single step. She took the moment to check the portal. Barely three feet across.

Visions of the perfect life the gancanagh had conjured replayed. Stolen. Rage surged in every vein. Harper could have her revenge right now. The sword sang its agreement to her blood. Victory and vengeance were at hand.

"Harper. It's closing fast." The Phooka slammed a fist into Gwyn's shoulder and the Tuatha skidded backward.

"Grab my backpack."

"Oh sure. I'm basically fighting a god, but I'll fetch your handbag."

Badb recovered and drew to her full height. Her green eyes blazed and her hair lashed around her, buffeted by an unseen wind. She flicked her fingers first to the right and then to the left, sending her defenders staggering out of her way.

"Let me guess, I'll pay for that too?" Harper said and raced forward, whirling the blade.

Badb held a hand in front of her, fingers spread, and Harper slammed into an invisible wall. She pushed against it, tip of the sword leveled at Badb's chest, but it held.

An unseen force lifted her from her feet. Surprise made her almost drop the sword.

"Now, little whelp, you will give me what I am owed." Badb yanked her elbow back and Harper flew, coming to rest inches from Badb's face. The Tuatha's palm hovered over Harper's head.

Immobilized, she felt a magnetic pull across her body and the gleaming bright energy shimmering over her hands traveled into Badb's open palm.

*She's draining my magic.* Harper squeezed her eyes shut and tried to stop the transfer, but her magic trickled into Badb. Her limbs were pinned to her side, useless.

"Let's see how long you last without the power of my family." Badb pulled her lips back from her teeth.

As Harper's magic weakened, the brilliant white glow winked out. She'd wished it wasn't hers plenty of times, but the power had kept her safe and gifted her the strength to free her friends.

Somehow Macha had chosen her. Nuada had chosen her. This power was *hers*.

An open door was a two-way passage. Harper clenched her fist around the sword and focused on the Lia Fail shard tucked in her pocket. *Well, magic rock, you glowed for me. Help me take my powers back.* She had no idea how to make that happen. So she formed an image in her mind of a vortex of her shining power disappearing into Badb's upturned palm. Then she envisioned it reversing, funneling through the Lia Fail and back into her.

Badb Catha shuddered and her jaw dropped. "No. You can't," she said with a gasp.

"I didn't think I could. But I am." Harper inhaled. The stream of magic became a torrent. The invisible bonds snapped, and Harper landed hard on one knee. Both Badb and her Sidhe covered their eyes, so intense was the light emanating from every inch of her skin.

With a savage yell, she hurled the Tuatha careening into her own throne. Badb sprawled across it with that same shocked expression. The Sword of Light sang in Harper's blood, sensing an end to its task. Harper flicked the blade in a quick circle and sprinted toward Badb.

"This is for my father."

"Harper, the portal! Now or never," the Phooka shouted behind her.

She skidded to a stop and watched the opening shrink another few inches. Another couple of seconds and it would be impossible to pass through.

"Big decision, little heir. Strike me down and pray Breas and the Fae don't finish what I began, or leave me and hope you can rouse the Tuatha from the Undying Lands." Badb laughed. "Either way, you can't win."

"You can if you're the High Queen," the Phooka said.

Harper wished Nuada was there. Or her mom. Or anyone

wiser than she was. She had a split second to decide. Nuada never stopped telling her she had to mend the Lia Fail and ascend to the High throne. She'd trusted him before, and she trusted him now.

Harper cursed and blasted another flash of her magic at Badb and the elves to ensure she had time to leap through the collapsing gateway. Then she bolted for the portal, legs and arms pumping.

"Grab my hand, we can't get separated." The Phooka, in his true shape, stretched his fingers to her.

Behind him, Gwyn's eyes flicked between his mistress and the closing portal. He leapt off the bannister and raced straight for Harper.

"Phooka, behind you!" Harper caught his hand and dove for the shimmering surface of the gateway. The Phooka matched her pace and the pair of them sailed headfirst through the portal.

The last thing she saw of the Green World was Gwyn ap Nudd behind them, reaching a hand out as he tumbled through the gateway into the Underworld.

And then she fell.

# CHAPTER 75

Eileen, absentmindedly winding strands of bleached hair around and around a finger, stared at the endless rows of ornately carved bookshelves. The rosy dawn had tinted the eastern horizon when they'd arrived at Fògradh Lodge. It had to be midmorning by now. Every muscle ached, and she felt the same wrung-out emotional state that usually accompanied her daily alcohol consumption.

All the Fir Bolg except Paegrinn had departed before the companions entered Hieronymous's Lodge. Her adopted family had to rebuild their arboreal city in a new location. They'd invited Eileen to join them again, but she'd refused. After what they'd witnessed at the Erimus tower, after the attacks on their home, they still wouldn't join her army, believing the crisis had passed.

The hum of conversation filled the room, her makeshift army and the escapees debating what to do next, whether the danger had passed, and if Harper had made it through the collapsing portal. She hadn't said goodbye.

"Emilio, you and your people may reside with us for as long as you wish while you decide what to do." Hieronymous inclined his head to the trio of former humans who clustered opposite Eileen and the Fianna. A few more of the newer Netherfae had escaped the tower, although most of them were still resting in their appointed rooms.

Emilio nodded. "We are grateful, but we can't stay here. We have to reverse what Badb did to us, and lab equip—"

"You'd best remain in the Lodge. None of the Courts will tolerate you any more than the dark Sidhe did, and the humans will accept you even less." Lord Ezrynhivar lifted his broad black hooves and propped them on the table in front of him. Beside him, Alphine rested her head on his shoulder.

Tamika flicked her colorful wings while Selina's unfocused eyes fixed on the floor. The half-strigoi had found a full, blood-red ruffled skirt and a white peasant shirt to replace her scrubs. The ensemble looked out of place with her pointed canine teeth and pale grey skin.

Selina's dark eyes met those of her ogre ex-husband. "We may have damaged the portal and escaped, but we don't know what remains of Badb's resources. Nuada would warn us not to be complacent. We have to return and see what is still there."

"Agreed. After a day's rest, we'll assemble a contingent for some reconnaissance. Badb's changed island is no longer a secret. If enough of her resources survived, and with the island intact, more will rally to her. And those who would oppose her will come to us. The battle lines have formed." Hieronymous steepled his clawed fingers. "But now is not the time for plans. We've accomplished all we can for now, and we survived. My staff will see you to your accommodations." Hieronymous shoved the thick carved chair back as he stood and beckoned to his Fae to cater to his guests.

Eileen remained seated as the others rose. Lost in thoughts of her daughter, she pulled the Lia Fail shard from her sweatshirt pocket and let its comforting glow wash over her. Harper lived, but Eileen still feared her lost.

"Come on, lass." Phelan had remained distant since the battle and her reunion with Ezrynhivar. He pointed to the stone. Behind him, Fintan, Aisling, and Michael waited. "See, she's fine. Our job now is to help her."

Eileen's eyes misted over. "How?"

"By joining the quest for the Spear of Lugh, of course. If Harper's going to win, she'll need the rest of the Four Treasures of the Tuatha." Fintan smiled like he was looking forward to an adventure vacation.

"Been a long time since I've seen Peru," Michael said.

Aisling nodded. "Or Scotland."

"But what am I supposed to do?" Eileen searched the faces of the Fianna.

Phelan shrugged. "Join us."

"Yeah, Eileen, you're pretty good in a fight." Aisling looped her arm around Eileen's waist while Phelan smiled and lowered his gaze. "Right, Fintan?"

"Aye." Fintan beamed. "And a half-decent shot."

Eileen smiled with a sense of relief. The thought of going back to her home in Gresham or meditating in a Fir Bolg village and being useless while anyone she cared about fought this strange war would send her back to the bottle. A small laugh escaped her lips. It was all ludicrous, this veering from suburban life to myth and madness. But it beat the alternatives.

"I'm in." The smile melted, replaced by a wistful longing. "I just wish I could have said goodbye. Told her I love her."

Phelan paused at the doorway. "She knows, lass. She knows."

Tamika sauntered around the room and approached Eileen. Emilio and Selina smiled behind her. "Mrs. O'Neill," she said.

"Eileen."

Paegrinn joined the circle and leaned on the thick table so his head rested at the same level as everyone else.

Tamika smiled. "Eileen. I think I can give you that chance to say goodbye." She explained what she could do to Eileen and the Fianna and her connection to Harper. "I don't know if it will work if she's in the Underworld. If the portal's still open a little, I think it might." She snapped a blue flower that resembled a forget-me-not from her hair and passed it to Eileen. "I need a piece of yours."

Eileen snapped off a couple strands of hair and mimicked Tamika tying them into her own hair.

"May I come too?" Paegrinn focused on his feet.

"Of course!" Tamika smiled at him and plucked a purple bellflower.

Aside from Hieronymous, they were the only ones remaining in the library. The group pulled some of the purple upholstered chairs into a circle and all eyes fell on Tamika.

"It may feel weird, but I can't read minds or anything. You'll hear the word *vanilla* in your mind, then you'll be in my childhood bedroom. If I can reach her, Harper will be there too."

The group nodded. Eileen wiped sweaty palms on her jeans and inhaled a deep breath.

*Vanilla.*

# CHAPTER 76

Harper jolted awake, wished she hadn't, and had a craving for vanilla ice cream. Everything ached. She had no recollection of falling asleep or hitting the ground, only endlessly falling after she leapt through the collapsing portal.

Cold from the dirt chilled her back and legs. Overhead, it was light out, but no sun hung in the sky. Just a hazy glow that emanated from every direction all at once. No clouds, just a monotone aqua sky. Definitely not in Kansas anymore.

She lay in the only patch of forest where the trees huddled close together and had any green. The broad leaves were a refreshing sight after the black, leafless ones on the island. Cool grass dappled with colorful wildflowers grew in a hundred-foot radius from her, and a thin stream meandered through the trunks.

Beyond the tiny oasis, things were very different. Black trunks like the trees overtaking Sauvie Island held up empty coiling branches, and each stood a hundred feet from the last. Very little grew between, and what did reminded Harper of the scrub brush of the desert half of her Oregon home.

"Phooka?" she whispered.

He wasn't in the green patch of woodland. She remembered his insistence they not let go of each other's hand lest they get separated. She swore she'd clung to him tight, but where was he?

*Vanilla.*

"Harper? Honey, can you hear me?" Harper's mother hovered at the edge of a brightly colored bed that materialized in the desolate woods beyond the oasis.

More of her friends rippled into the Underworld, though they were hazy and fuzzy, like an old television set with poor reception.

"Mom? Emilio?" Harper smiled and stretched a hand to them.

"Eileen, be quick. It's hard to keep this many of us in my mind. Or maybe it's that she's in another world." Tamika's back was pressed to her headboard and her chocolate brown hands cradled her head.

"You're all safe?" Harper said.

Emilio smiled. "Yeah, thanks to you."

"Hi Harper!" Paegrinn waved at her and waggled tiny Lego Batman's hand next to his face.

"Hi Paegrinn." Harper chuckled before stepping close to where Emilio leaned near a tree trunk. "No, Emilio, from what I saw, you did most of the saving."

Beside Emilio, Selina patted a spot on his arm not containing razor-sharp feathers. "Without him, we'd have gone insane before you arrived."

"Alan sacrificed himself to reopen our escape." Emilio's face pinched.

Harper felt a pang of guilt. If she'd not wasted so much time. Been faster.

"Love, there's nothing you could have done." Selina's necklaces jangled as she leaned for Harper. "Only what you can do now. Find the Tuatha. Bring back the Lia Fail so it can be repaired."

"And make it fast so we can hit up that new vegan restaurant on Burnside," Emilio said.

The tiny bedroom flickered and all but disappeared for a few seconds. Harper leapt to her feet and staggered forward a few steps, like she could stop it from fading.

"Can't hold it much longer," Tamika said. Her chest was heaving.

"Harper, honey, I saw Abraham. He's okay." Eileen's words rushed as fast as she could speak them.

Harper beamed. Abraham. Looking for him was what started this all.

"And Fintan says find Dagdha's Cauldron. No one knows where it is. It can resurrect Nuada," Eileen added. "And I'm going with the Fianna to search for the Spear of Lugh. Something about having all four of the Tuatha's Treasures can end this once and for all."

The image faded again.

"Mom! Emilio! Don't go."

"Honey, our time's almost up. I just needed you to know you did it. We're all safe." Tears poured down Eileen's face.

"Mom, I'm afraid. What if I can't make it to the Undying Lands?" Matching tears rolled down Harper's cheeks.

"You defeated Badb Catha. Yes, you can."

Selina clenched a fist. "I saw the strength in you at Mystic Island. You will be the High Queen."

Emilio was nodding. "You got this," he said.

"I've joined the solitary Fae." Paegrinn pulled himself up tall. "Hieronymous named me ambassador to the Fir Bolg so I can work on my dad to join you when you get back."

"Thank you, Paegrinn. Or now that you're Fae, can I not thank you anymore?"

The Fir Bolg teen crinkled his forehead. "I don't know? I'll ask Hieronymous."

"Mom, you sure you want to get any deeper into this?" Harper toyed with the edge of her shirt.

"Honey, I know it's a weird way to finally be a parent, but working with the Fianna makes sense. We share a pledge to protect you. Right now, looking for this Spear of Lugh is something I can do."

"Worst mother-daughter bonding activity. Ever." Harper hiccupped. There was so much she wanted to say. "Mom, Dad escaped. Gwyn helped Emilio smash the barrier, and Dad got away."

Eileen clamped a hand over her mouth, took a deep breath, and leaned toward her daughter. "Thank you, honey." She raised an eyebrow. "Gwyn helped the souls escape?"

"I was as surprised as you."

The room flickered out and back. Tamika groaned.

Harper's mother knitted her brows together. "I love you, Harper. All those years wasted because I—"

"I know, Mom. I love you, too. It's in the past." More than anything, Harper wanted to feel her arms embracing her mom. She might end up stuck in the Underworld forever. "If I don't return, the one thing you can do for me is be happy."

Eileen reached a hand for Harper's face. "I know you'll make—"

And the bedroom winked out.

"Mom! Emilio! Paegrinn!" Harper reached for the tiny flower twined in her hair. "Vanilla." She whirled around to see if the mindspace materialized behind her. "Vanilla!" she shouted.

"Vanilla," she whispered and slumped down the trunk of a tree. *I'm alone.* Harper curled onto her side, clasped her knees to her chest, and wept.

"You want every hobgoblin in the Underworld to find us?"

Harper rocketed upright. "Phooka! Where were you? I woke up and—"

"Have you been crying?" He scurried to her. "I said I'd not leave you. I just went to fill some waterskins."

"Tamika used her magic to let me see Mom, Emilio, and the others to say goodbye." Harper dragged the back of her hand across her eyes.

There were whispering voices behind her. She froze and tilted her head, straining to hear. Very faint. She thought she could make out the words 'Badb' and 'prevail.'

"Harper?" The Phooka's ears drooped as he scanned the area.

"Those enormous ears and you don't hear that?"

"Hear what?"

"Whispering. It says Badb. And mostly words I can't make out." Harper crept toward the sound and stopped at her own pack. Next to it, snug in its sheath, lay the Cliamh Solais. She slumped to a squat and picked up her blade.

"...return... must prevail..." echoed in her mind and she dropped the weapon, jaw slack.

"Phooka. The sword is speaking to me." She inched back several steps.

The Fae scampered over to the blade, pressed an ear close, and shook his head. "Do you hear it now?" Harper shook her head. "I was afraid of this."

"Of what?"

"Once the Sword of Light is drawn, it always completes its task. Victory over the target."

"I remember Nuada telling me that. So?"

He shrugged. "Well, Badb still lives."

"So what happens now?"

"No idea. Never happened before. But if I'd guess, I'd say the sword's going to be super chatty until the two of you complete that battle you began."

"What?!" Harper's hands slapped down on the outsides of her thighs.

"Well, I figured you knew what you were doing when you whipped it out."

"What has happened so far that would lead to the impression I know what I'm doing?"

"Fair point. But we may have a bigger problem. Gwyn."

Harper clutched her backpack and her heart pounded. "You saw him?"

"Well, no, but he was right on our heels and I'm pretty sure he made it through. He may be a day or two behind us, or ahead of us with the time dilation between worlds, but he will be or was here."

Harper squeezed her eyes shut. "You're giving me a headache. Time dilation?"

"I'll explain later, but we need to go."

"Please tell me you know a way to the Undying Lands."

"I do not. But I know someone who might, and if I'm correct about where we are, it's half a day's journey."

The Phooka started walking up a small hill. Harper shrugged, grabbed her pack and blade, and fell into step beside him. Movement caught her eye, and she ducked, face tilted to the cloudless sky.

A wispy, glimmering trail wove through the branches as it ascended.

The Phooka lifted his horned head up. "There's something no one's seen here in quite a while."

"What is it?"

"A human soul on its way to the hag's Cauldron. The gate must not have fully closed behind us."

Harper smiled up at the meandering soul. *We did it, Dad. We saved them.*

The Phooka scampered ahead. "We'll want to make it to my contact by nightfall."

"Do I need to be ready to fight when I meet this contact?"

He beamed over his shoulder. "I'm sure he's forgotten about all that, so he'll be delighted to see us!"

"Why do I think I'm going to regret this?"

# CHAPTER 77

Badb Catha collapsed next to the circular tree. Bark that once gleamed gold with silvery leaves now stretched dull and tan and paper thin. Only spidery veins of its former golden shine remained. She'd poured as much of herself into the tree as she dared, just to keep it clinging to life. The gateway between the Green World and the Underworld spanned barely five inches across.

"Badb, you cannot continue like this." Breas flicked his head to move a cascade of golden hair from his eye and reached a hand down to her.

She smacked it away with a snarl. "Then fix it. Get something into the cages."

"We lost many Sidhe and Underworlders to the battle. Let it close, it's lost."

"Never! Not until every loyal living thing escapes that decaying hell." Badb reached her arms overhead, clasped the railing, and hauled herself to unsteady feet.

Breas sighed. "You need to face—"

"Bring me the Dawn Court Fae." Badb clapped her hands, sending kelpies and goblins racing.

"You'd risk your alliance with Serotina—"

"She pledged her aid to me. This is how she can help until the doctor can make another batch of hybrids."

Visions of the insolent human girl with Macha's magic surged unbidden before Badb's eyes and she howled. Destroying the little whelp and taking the Tuatha magic should've been easy. It was rightfully hers and it would have made the portal everlasting.

With another bellow through clenched teeth, she lurched to the side and slammed a fist into a column. A long crack spread toward the ceiling.

She would find this Harper O'Neill and make her pay. That bumbling fool Gwyn dove in after her, but she didn't trust him to do the job. The girl had bested him before. She hated to admit it, but only a small army could subdue the Heir of Niall. An army she had on the other side, where the girl was. If she could get word to King Eveling, he could suspend his search for Underworld Fae to send to the Green World and hunt the girl instead. Bring her back.

Of course, all that hinged on repairing the gateway.

"Leander." A tall, thin Sidhe stepped forward and bowed.

"My Queen."

"Fetch me a dozen pixies."

The elf bowed and loped across the room, through the double doors and to the island outside.

Badb pulled her spine straight, swayed, and returned her palm to the raspy bark of the tree.

"The rest of you, bring whomever remains of the Dawn Court Fae and put them into the cages." Badb sighed and beckoned Breas. "Gather a hunting party. We need to be more aggressive in pursuing Fae who won't join us. They, too, can serve us in the cages."

"Using Fae this way is wasting a lot of resources and isn't gaining you allies."

Badb's eyes flared. "What else would you have me do? Our success saving the Green World and the magical races cannot fail. We need Underworld Fae to win."

"What if I have another way to bring about a decisive victory faster?"

"Impossible."

"Seemed that way until our ingenious birdman critiqued my little side project. Such a blow that one escaped. Aside from his powers, he had a brilliant scientific mind. Without him, I might never have seen my error."

Badb spoke through gritted teeth. "You've been keeping something from me."

"Only until I was sure it would work. Have you recovered enough to take a walk upstairs?" Breas held a hand to her.

Badb clasped it and pressed her lips into a line.

"I think you will be most excited." Breas let her rest her weight against him and led her to the central stairs.

Badb didn't like how much she relied on him to remain standing. Slowly, the pair ascended the stairs and stood before a blank patch of wall. Breas pressed a palm to the wall and an invisible door slid open. Inside, an enormous tank bubbled and frothed. Tendrils of mist poured over the side.

"Go on. Take a look. It's not mature enough yet to be dangerous, but it will be."

Badb took the last few steps toward the tank and leaned over the edge, fanning the thick white vapors aside. She gasped. "Is that—"

"Yes. That is a cloned Eye of Balor. When it completes its growth cycle, it will be no less deadly. And without the rest of Balor attached, fully under our control. At full strength it should be able to raze Portland to dust in mere hours."

A slow smile spread across Badb's face. "Do you know what this means?"

"Of course. Victory."

---

---

Before the Last Battle of Moytura, the boundary between the Fae and human world had closed. Discover how the Fae invasion of Portland began.

**A missing father. A mind-bending mist. An island where two worlds collide.**

Selina Leanabel survives by staying in the shadows, running a quiet apothecary far from the reach of the Fae. But when teen Charlotte Holloway arrives saying she can't go home...literally, with a story of a father lost behind a wall of unnatural fog, Selina's boundaries begin to crumble.

On Sauvie Island, the air is thick with a warding spell that breaks the mind and hungers for the soul. Entering the mist means risking the very stability Selina has fought so hard to reclaim.

**Click below and claim your copy.**

https://dl.bookfunnel.com/l4xleonwpi

You can also visit MollyJStanton.com/pages/badb.html to download your free book.

Shade and sweet water,

Molly

ACKNOWLEDGMENTS

Harper's continuing journey would not be possible without the support of my growing early reader team. This intrepid group of fantasy lovers provide a reader's perspective at various stages of the writing process to make this the best book possible for you.

So a huge thank you to Christine Lazor, Diane Gonzalez, Becca Bogin, and Heather Loveland Irons.

And special thanks to my Reader's Group. Writing can be a solitary endeavor, you fine souls are what keeps my fingers waggling over those keys.

# ABOUT THE AUTHOR

Molly J Stanton grew up in rural Idaho where cows outnumber humans fifty-to-one, and tipping them was an Olympic sport. Fed a steady diet of terrifying old Celtic fairy stories and the local firsthand tales of harrowing Sasquatch encounters, she cultivated a lifelong passion for unseen worlds.

While she loves rocks, trees, and water, she craved more excitement than Idaho could offer. So a couple short months after graduation, she up and left to attend Smith College in quaint Northampton, Massachusetts. After four years, she failed to develop a snazzy Massachusetts accent, not dropping even a single 'r'.

Graduate school in the Lehigh Valley of Pennsylvania shoved her into professional writing. Dull, pedantic scientific papers for academic journals that literally two people in the world read (thanks for enduring that Mom and Dad). During her subsequent career as an addictions therapist, Molly, for mysterious reasons, hoarded books on writing, yet never wrote a word other than snappy e-mails and clinical case notes.

Somewhere deep in her unconscious mind, Cerridwen stirred her great cauldron, brewing vicarious experiences as a counselor, Celtic myths, fairy abduction stories, and those Bigfoot tall tales into the inspiration and drive to finally write that Urban Fantasy series.

When she's not writing, Molly farms and sings off-key songs to her cat. To find out when her next book is released, or to watch the farm take shape and see pictures of her crazy cat, sign up for her newsletter at MollyJStanton-dot-com.

facebook.com/mollyjstantonauthor

instagram.com/mollyjstantonauthor

tiktok.com/@Tiktok.com.mollyjstantonwriter

www.ingramcontent.com/pod-product-compliance
Lightning Source LLC
Chambersburg PA
CBHW061202190726
48288CB00001B/32